CAUGHT IN THE BILLIONAIRE'S EMBRACE

BY
ELIZABETH BEVARLY

Elizabeth Bevarly is the RITA® award-nominated, nationally bestselling author of more than five dozen books. When she's not writing, she's watching *Project Runway* and *What Not to Wear*, but only for research purposes. She's also confident that she'll someday find a story in *House Hunters International*, so she watches that religiously, too. In the meantime, she makes do with her real life of ready-to-wear from Macy's and college exploratory trips around the Midwest with her husband and soon-to-be-a-senior son.

For everyone who's ever worked in women's fashion,
especially employees of the limited stores
in Cherry Hill and Echelon Malls,
where I got my start in writing by penning pages
in the stockroom during lunch.
I miss you guys. A lot.

One

There was only one thing that could make Della Hannan's thirtieth birthday better than she'd already planned for it to be, and it was a thing she hadn't even planned. That was saying something, since she'd been fine-tuning the details for the celebration since she was a little girl growing up in the kind of neighborhood where birthdays were pretty much unaffordable and therefore pretty much ignored. Where a lot of things were unaffordable and therefore ignored. Things like, well...Della, for instance. But that was why she had promised herself such a festive event. Because, even as a little girl, she'd known she had only herself to count on.

Of course, the past eleven months had rather thrown a wrench in that line of thinking, because since meeting Geoffrey, she'd had no choice but to count on him. Geoffrey wasn't here tonight, though, and she wasn't going to let herself think about him or anything else from that world. Tonight was special. Tonight was for her. And it would be everything an underprivileged kid from one of New York's roughest neighborhoods could have imagined.

Back then, Della had sworn that by the time she turned thirty, she would have escaped the mean streets of her borough and become a self-made millionaire living park-side uptown. And she'd vowed to mark the big three-oh in the style of the rich and famous, that she had imagined she'd become accustomed as this point in life. She wasn't about to renege on that promise, even if she was celebrating in Chicago instead of New York. She would begin with dinner at a five-star restaurant, follow that with a box seat at the opera and top it off with a nightcap at the sort of club that allowed entrée to only the crème de la crème of society. She was outfitted in thousands of dollars worth of haute couture, dripping in rubies and diamonds, and she had been coiffed and manicured at the city's finest salon.

She sighed with much contentment as she enjoyed the first part of her evening. Palumbo's on State Street was the sort of restaurant where prices rivaled the budgets of some sovereign nations. She had, it went without saying, ordered the most expensive items on the menu—four courses, all of which bore European names she'd had to practice all week to pronounce correctly. (Thank goodness the menu had been posted online so she could check in advance and not appear as some kind of philistine when she ordered. And how lovely to have the opportunity to use the word *philistine,* even if it was only in her head.) Because ordering the most expensive items on one's birthday was what anyone who was sophisticated and chic and rich would do, right?

The thought made her surreptitiously survey her surroundings, to make sure the other diners—sophisticated, chic and rich, every last one of them—were also enjoying the most expensive bounty. And, okay, okay, to also make sure Geoffrey hadn't somehow followed her, even though she'd done an excellent job sneaking out—she always did—and even though she wasn't scheduled to check in with him until her daily call tomorrow. He couldn't know where she was going, anyway, even if he did discover she'd slipped out when she wasn't supposed to. She'd planned tonight's escape even more meticulously than she'd planned her thirtieth birthday celebration.

For all anyone here knew, she was just as blue-blooded as they were and belonged in this society every bit as much. And, thankfully, there was no sign of Geoffrey anywhere. Check and check.

And Della did feel as if she belonged here, sipping champagne as she anticipated the arrival of her calamari appetizer. She'd been moving in environments like this for years, despite not having been born into a wealthy family. She'd clawed her way out of the slum and into the upper echelons of society—even if she'd only been a fringe member—and she'd studied and emulated everyone in this world until she'd had no trouble passing herself off as a pure-blooded member.

Tonight was no exception. She'd paid a not-so-small fortune to rent the crimson velvet Carolina Herrera gown and Dolce & Gabbana shoes, not to mention the Bulgari earrings and pendant and the black silk Valentino opera coat necessitated by the frigid December temperatures. The red hues, she knew, complemented her gray eyes and the dark blond hair that was long enough now to have been swept up into a French twist, held in place by a single hidden comb.

She lifted a hand to make sure every hair was in place, smiling at how much she enjoyed having it long. She'd worn it boyishly short all her life, until earlier this year, and hadn't sported her natural color since high school, when she'd dyed her hair black during her grunge phase and liked it enough to keep it that way. She hadn't even realized how it had deepened to such a beautiful honey-infused blond over the years. Between her natural color and the new length—not to mention her rented duds—no one from the old neighborhood would recognize her tonight.

But she wasn't thinking about any of that, either, she reminded herself. Tonight really was going to be perfect. It really was going to be everything she had planned all those years ago.

Except maybe for the handsome, elegantly attired man the hostess had seated at a table near hers a few moments ago, and whom she hadn't been able to resist sneaking peeks at during each of those moments. When Della was a kid, she'd never entertained the idea of having a companion for her special evening. She wasn't sure why not. Maybe because of the aforementioned knowing she would always have only herself to count on. Or maybe because, as a kid, she couldn't even imagine a guy like him. In her neighborhood, *elegantly attired* had meant one's shirt was buttoned. And *handsome* had meant a guy had all his teeth.

Without warning, the man glanced up, his gaze connecting with hers. Something between the two of them…clicked. Or something. The man dipped his dark head toward Della in silent acknowledgment, one corner of his mouth lifting in something vaguely resembling a smile. After only a moment's hesitation, she lifted her glass in a silent toast to him. Swathed in a tuxedo that had been tailored to emphasize every magnificent inch of him, he was framed by billows of amber silk that edged the window behind him. His dark eyes were warmed by the dreamy light of the candle flickering in a crystal holder in front of him, and his little half smile sent a shudder of something hot and electric skittering down Della's spine. Because it was the kind of smile that told a woman he was not just undressing her with his eyes, but he was also considering using a lot of his other body parts on her, too.

When she felt the heat of a blush creep into her cheeks, she hastily glanced away. Lifting her champagne to her mouth for a cooling sip, she did her best to focus on something else—the crisp white tablecloths, the sparkling china, the glittering crowd. Inescapably, however, her attention wandered back to the man at the table opposite hers.

Who was still gazing at her with much interest.

"So what do you think?" he asked her, raising his voice enough to be heard two small tables away from his own.

Della blinked at him, nonplussed. Understanding, for the first time in her life, what *nonplussed* actually meant: confusion mixed with a funny little buzz in the belly that wasn't altogether unpleasant. A million different possible replies to his question ricocheted around in her brain. *I think you're the most beautiful man I've ever seen,* for example. And, *what are you doing New Year's Eve?* Even a smooth, *hey, lover.* And of course—it went without saying—*oh,* bay-*bee!*

"For dinner," he added, holding up the menu. "What do you recommend?"

Ooooh, what did Della think about *that?* Well, that was a totally different question from the one she'd been thinking he asked, wasn't it? Good thing she'd been too nonplussed to answer.

"Um, I'm not sure," she said. "This is the first time I've dined here." Somehow, she didn't think a man like him would be too impressed if she told him to order whatever was most expensive, because it would make him appear chic, sophisticated and rich. He was all those things simply by existing on the planet.

Her answer seemed to surprise him. "But how can this be your first time? Palumbo's has been a Chicago institution for nearly a hundred years. Are you not from Chicago originally?"

There was no way Della was going to answer that question. Mostly because no one other than Geoffrey knew she was here, and he was keeping much too close an eye on her. Even if he didn't know exactly where she was at the moment, she wasn't about to risk his discovery of her little escape by breathing a word of it to anyone.

So she wouldn't—couldn't—tell this man that. Either she'd have to lie—which Della never did, even though her honesty had gotten her into trouble more than once, as evidenced by her having to rely on Geoffrey at the moment—or else her reply would lead to the kind of small talk that might make her talk about her past. Or, even worse, her present. And she wanted to be as far removed from both of those tonight as she could be, on account of nothing in her past or present lent itself to Carolina Herrera gowns or diamonds and rubies or box seats to *La Bohème*.

So she replied instead to the first question he'd asked. "I ordered the special. I adore seafood."

He said nothing for a moment, and Della wondered if it was because he was pondering her answer to his first question or trying to decide whether or not to press the fact that she hadn't replied to the second. Finally, he said, "I'll remember that."

For some reason, though, he made it sound as if it were the fact that she loved seafood that he would remember, and not that she had recommended it for dinner.

He opened his mouth to say something else, but his server arrived to place a short, amber-colored cocktail in front of him and a dewy pink cosmopolitan on the table at the place directly next to his.

He was expecting someone to join him, Della realized. A woman, judging by the color and daintiness of the drink. Couples didn't dine in places like Palumbo's unless their relationship went beyond casual—or one of them was looking to make it more than casual. This guy was throwing steamy glances her way, even flirting with her, despite the fact that there would be a woman joining him momentarily. That meant the guy was a complete jerk.

Okay, so maybe her thirtieth birthday celebration wasn't going to go *quite* as perfectly as she had planned, since she was going to have to be seated near a jerk. And—*oh, all right*—maybe it wasn't only because of the jerk that the celebration wouldn't be exactly what she'd had in mind. Maybe it wasn't even because her gown and accessories were rentals from a Michigan Avenue boutique instead of pulled casually from her own closet.

Maybe, just maybe, it was because, in addition to not being the life of a millionaire, Della's current life wasn't even her own. Everything about her life these days—every thing she did, every place she went, every word she spoke—had to be vetted and controlled by Geoffrey. Her life would never be normal again. Or, at least, it would never be the life she had made for herself or the one she had planned. It would be a life manufactured and orchestrated by someone else.

As soon as the thought formed, she pushed it to the furthest, darkest recesses of her brain. She wouldn't think about any of that tonight, she reminded herself again, wondering why she was finding it all so hard to forget. Because tonight, she didn't want to be Della anyway. Tonight, for one night, she wanted to be the woman she had envisioned herself to be two decades and two thousand miles ago: CinderDella, toast of the town and belle of the ball. Nothing was going to mar this evening. Not even Prince Less-Than-Charming over there who was still making bedroom eyes at her while waiting on a girlfriend who could do a helluva lot better.

As if cued by the thought, the hostess seated a boisterous party of four at the table between them, completely blocking the man from her view. For that Della was grateful and not disappointed, even if some twisted part of her made her think that was what she was feeling.

Well, even if he was a jerk, he was still the most beautiful man she'd ever seen.

And she saw him again an hour and a half later—at the Lyric Opera when she was trying to locate her seat. After realizing she was in the wrong part of the auditorium, Della asked an usher for directions, then found herself gazing at a box across the room that afforded an amazing view of the stage…and where sat the handsome stranger she'd seen at dinner. Just as he'd been at the restaurant, he was surrounded by gold, this time a cascade of engraved gilt that encrusted the walls and ensconced the stage. Likewise as he'd been at the restaurant, he was seated alone.

Okay, so maybe as she'd left Palumbo's, Della had happened to notice that his date still hadn't shown up. Not that she'd been *trying* to notice that. She just had, that was all. Though whether the woman had gotten waylaid somewhere and been unable to make their rendezvous, or she'd wised up about what kind of man he was, Della couldn't have said.

Not that she cared either way. Hey, she'd barely noticed. In case she hadn't mentioned that.

Now as she strode down the aisle to her seat, she similarly barely noticed that it was not only in the same box the man was occupying, but also in the same row, as well—a small one at the front that contained only three chairs. She also barely noticed that he had placed both a program and a long-stemmed rose on the seat beside his own, as if the chair would soon be occupied. So evidently his girlfriend had indeed been waylaid earlier and was intending to catch up to him here.

Butterflies head-butted Della's midsection at the prospect of having to sit in such close proximity to the man. Once she squeezed past him to get to her seat, there would be no escaping him—unless she wanted to pull a Groucho Marx maneuver from *A Night at the Opera* and swing across the auditorium on a cable.

She inhaled a single, fortifying breath and forced her feet to move forward until she stood at the edge of the row beside him. His head snapped up, and, when he recognized her, he grinned that shudders-down-the-spine grin again. Heat flared in her belly, her brain turned to mush, and the *excuse me* Della had been about to utter evaporated in her mouth.

He murmured a greeting as he stood, but she barely heard it, because she was too busy trying not to swoon. Not only did he smell delectable—a luscious mix of spice and wood smoke—but he was also much taller than she'd realized, forcing her to tip back her head to meet his gaze. It was an action to which she was unaccustomed, since she pushed the six-foot mark herself in the two-inch heels she was wearing. Even without heels, she was accustomed to being at eye level with virtually everyone. With this man, however, eye level meant gazing at shoulders that spanned a distance roughly the size of Montana.

But it was his face that drew her attention. His jawline was resolute, his nose was straight and refined, his cheekbones looked as if they'd been hewn from marble, and his eyes… Oh, his eyes. His eyes were the color of bittersweet chocolate, a brown so dark and so compelling that Della couldn't tear her gaze away. Then she realized it wasn't the depth or color of his eyes that so captivated her. It was her recognition of something in them that was at odds with his dazzling smile. A somberness, even sadness, that was unmistakable.

The moment she identified it, however, a shadow fell over his eyes, almost as if he was aware of her understanding and didn't want her to see too deeply into him.

"We've got to stop meeting like this," he said, his smile broadening.

The humor in his tone surprised her, coming as it did on the heels of the shadows in his eyes. Even so, she couldn't quite keep herself from smiling back. "It is a little odd, isn't it?"

"Actually, I'm thinking of a different word."

Not sure that she wanted to know what it was, she heard herself ask anyway, "Oh?"

"Lucky," he said immediately. "I was thinking it was *lucky*."

She wasn't sure what to say in response to that, so she held up her ticket and gestured toward her seat. She made sure to give the rose-laden chair between hers and his a meaningful inspection before saying, "If you don't mind? That's my seat."

For a minute, he only continued to gaze at her, his eyes revealing nothing now of what might be going through his head. Then, "Not at all," he replied, sidestepping into the aisle to give her room to pass.

When he did, she hastened to take her seat, immediately opening her program to read it before he had a chance to say anything that might start a conversation.

He didn't take the hint, however, and said as he returned to his seat, "How was your dinner?"

Not looking up from the program, Della replied, "Lovely."

Her one-word response did nothing to dissuade him, either. "I ended up ordering the pheasant. It was amazing."

When Della only nodded silently without looking up from her program, he added, "You should try it next time you're at Palumbo's. I highly recommend it."

He was fishing. Trying to find out if she lived here in town the same way he had when he'd asked her why she'd never been to Palumbo's. He was trying to gauge whether or not there was a chance the two of them might run into each other again, either by accident or by design. Even with a long-stemmed rose and mystery woman between them.

"I'll take it under advisement," she told him. And returned to reading her program.

But still, he didn't take the hint. "You know, I don't meet many people of my own generation who enjoy opera," he said, trying a new tack. "Especially not enough to see it performed live. Or spring for box seats. You must really love it."

Della sighed inwardly, silently cursing him for the change of subject. That was a low blow. There was no way she could resist a conversation about her most favorite thing in the world.

"I adore it, actually," she said helplessly, letting the program fall open onto her lap.

When she turned to look at him again, his expression made clear he was as delighted to be here as she was and that he felt every bit as passionately about opera. So passionately that his love for the medium had chased away the darkness that had clouded his eyes earlier. She realized now that they weren't entirely brown. Flecks of gold wreathed the irises, making his eyes appear more faceted somehow, drawing her in even more deeply.

"I've loved opera since I was a little girl," she told him. "Our next-door neighbor was a huge fan and introduced me to all the classics." She didn't add that that was only because she could hear Mrs. Klosterman's radio through the paper-thin walls of their tenement, or how Della had hung on every word of the announcer's analysis of each opera once it had concluded. "The first time I saw one performed live," she continued, not bothering to mention that it was live on PBS, not live on stage, "I was enchanted."

She actually would have loved to major in music and

make the study of opera her life's work. But college had been beyond the means of an average student from her economic stratum, so she'd gone directly to work after graduating from high school, as a gofer in the offices of one of Wall Street's most noted and respected brokerage houses. And even though she'd worked her way up the corporate ladder to become an executive assistant, Della had never made the time to go for the degree. She'd been supporting herself fairly well on her salary—certainly better than she'd ever imagined she would growing up in the sort of neighborhood she had—and she'd been happy with the way her life was going. At least until that life had shattered into a million pieces, and she'd been left with nothing but Geoffrey, who'd offered her a dubious sort of refuge—and not without a price.

Almost as if that thought had cued the orchestra, the music swelled, and the lights dimmed. Della couldn't resist one last look at her companion as the room grew dark, but when she saw him gazing at her—and noted the seat between them still empty—she quickly turned her attention to the stage.

After that, she fell into the world of Mimi and Rodolfo and their bohemian friends, leaving her own reality behind. So much so, that when the lights came up for intermission, it took Della a moment to return from nineteenth century Paris to twenty-first century Chicago. She blinked a few times and inhaled a deep breath and, before she could stop herself, looked over at her companion—who was looking at her in the same way he had been when the lights had dimmed, almost as if he'd spent the entire first half of the opera watching her instead.

That strange buzz erupted in her belly again, so she

quickly glanced at the crowd. The myriad splendor of the women's gowns made them look like brightly colored gems amid the gilt of the auditorium, the sparkle of their jewelry only enhancing the image. Della watched many of the ladies link arms with their companions as they left for intermission, and noted how the men bent their heads affectionately toward them as they laughed or chatted.

For a moment, she felt a keen regret that this night couldn't last forever. Wouldn't it be lovely to enjoy evenings like this whenever she wanted, without regard for their cost or the risk of being seen in a place where she shouldn't be? She couldn't remember the last time she'd had a night out at all, never mind one like this. Geoffrey kept her locked away like Rapunzel. She spent her time reading books, watching downloaded movies and staring at the walls that were, for all intents and purposes, her cell. Even if the place Geoffrey had provided lacked bars and held sufficient creature comforts, Della still felt like a prisoner. Hell, she was a prisoner. And she would be until Geoffrey told her she could go.

But even that thought brought little comfort, because she had no idea *where* she would go, or what she would do, once Geoffrey decided she was no longer necessary. She would have to start all over again with virtually nothing. The same way she had when she left the old neighborhood behind.

It was all the more reason to enjoy tonight to the fullest, Della told herself. Who knew what the future held beyond even the next few hours?

"So what do you think so far?"

She turned at the sound of the rich, velvety baritone, and her pulse rippled when she saw the smoky look he was giving her. Truly, she had to get a grip. Not only did the guy show evidence of being a class-A heel, flirting with one woman when he was supposed to be out with another, but he was also way out of Della's league.

"I have to confess that *La Bohème* isn't one of my favorites," she admitted. "I think Puccini was a bit reserved when he scored it, especially when you compare it to the exhilaration of something like *Manon Lescaut*. But I am enjoying it. Very much."

Of course, some of that might have had to do with the company seated in her box. Not that she had to tell him that. Not that she had to admit it to herself.

"How about you?" she asked. "What's your verdict?"

"I think I've seen it too many times to be objective anymore," he said. "But it's interesting you say that about Puccini's being too reserved with it. I've always kind of thought the same thing. I actually like Leoncavallo's interpretation of Murger's book much better."

She grinned. "I do, too."

He grinned back. "That puts us in the minority, you know."

"I know."

"In fact," he added, "I like Leoncavallo's *La Bohème* even better than his *Pagliacci,* an opinion that will get you tossed out of some opera houses."

She laughed at that. "I like it better than *Pagliacci,* too. Looks like we'll be kicked to the curb together."

He chuckled lightly, both of them quieting at the same time, neither seeming to know what to say next. After a couple of awkward seconds, Della ventured, "Well, if you've already seen *La Bohème* too many times, and you don't care for it as much as you do other operas, then why are you here tonight?"

He shrugged, but there was something in the gesture that was in no way careless, and the warmth that had eased his expression fled. "I have season tickets."

Tickets, she repeated to herself. Not *ticket.* Plural, not singular. Meaning he was indeed the owner of the empty seat beside his and had been expecting someone to occupy it tonight. Someone who might very well be with him all the other nights of the season. A wife, perhaps?

She hastily glanced at his left hand but saw no ring. Still, there were plenty of married people who eschewed the ring thing these days. Della wondered who normally joined him and why she wasn't here tonight. She waited to see if he would add something about the mysteriously empty chair. Something that might clarify the sudden drop in temperature that seemed to shimmer between them. Because she sensed that that vacant chair was what had generated the faint chill.

Instead, he shook off his odd, momentary funk and said, "That is how I know you don't normally attend Lyric Opera performances. At least not on opening night, and not in the seat you're sitting in tonight." He smiled again, and the chill abated some. "I would have noticed."

She did her best to ignore the butterflies doing the rumba in her stomach. "This is my first time coming here," she confessed.

His inspection of her grew ponderous. "Your first time at Palumbo's. Your first time at the Lyric. So you have just moved to Chicago recently, haven't you?"

She was saved from having to reply, because the opera gods and goddesses—Wagnerian, she'd bet, every one of them—smiled down on her. Her companion was beckoned from below by a couple who had recognized him and wanted to say hello—and who addressed him as Marcus, giving Della his first name, at least. Then they proceeded to say way more than hello to him, chatting until the lights flickered once, twice, three times, indicating that the performance was about to resume. At that, the couple scurried off, and he—Marcus—turned to look at Della again.

"Can you see all right from where you are?" he asked. He patted the chair next to him that still contained the unopened program and rose. "You might have a better vantage point from this seat. You want to have the best angle for 'Addio Dolce Svegliare Alla Mattina.'"

The Italian rolled off his tongue as if he spoke it fluently, and a ribbon of something warm and gooey unfurled in her. Even though the vantage point would be no different from the one she had now—which he must realize, too—Della was surprised by how much she wanted to accept his offer. Whoever usually sat there obviously wasn't coming. And he didn't seem to be as bothered by that as a man involved in a romantic relationship should be. So maybe his relationship with the usual occupant of the chair wasn't romantic, in spite of the red, red rose.

Or maybe he was just a big ol' hound dog with whom she'd be better off not sharing anything more than opera chitchat. Maybe he should only be another lovely, momentary memory to go along with all the other lovely, momentary memories she was storing from this evening.

"Thank you, but the view from here is fine," she said. And it was, she told herself. For now. For tonight. But not, unfortunately, forever.

Two

Marcus Fallon sat in his usual seat at his usual table drinking his usual nightcap in his usual club, thinking the most unusual thoughts. Or, at least, thoughts about a most unusual woman. A woman unlike any he'd ever met before. And not only because she shared his passion for, and opinions about, opera, either. Unfortunately, the moment the curtain had fallen on *La Bohème,* she'd hurried past him with a breathlessly uttered *good night,* scurried up the aisle ahead of everyone else in the box and he'd lost her in the crowd before he'd been able to say a word. He'd experienced a moment of whimsy as he'd scanned the stairs on his way out looking for a glass slipper, but even that small fairy-tale clue had eluded him. She was gone. Just like that. Almost as if she'd never been there at all. And he had no idea how to find her.

He lifted his Scotch to his lips again, filling his

mouth with the smooth, smoky liquor, scanning the crowd here as if he were looking for her again. Strangely, he realized he was. But all he saw was the usual crowd milling around the dark-paneled, richly appointed, sumptuously decorated room. Bernie Stegman was, as usual, sitting in an oxblood leather wingback near the fireplace, chatting up Lucas Whidmore, who sat in an identical chair on the other side. Delores and Marion Hagemann were having a late dinner with Edith and Lawrence Byck at their usual table in the corner, the quartet framed by heavy velvet drapes the color of old money. Cynthia Harrison was doing her usual flirting with Stu, the usual Saturday bartender, who was sidestepping her advances with his usual aplomb. He would lose his job if he were caught canoodling with the patrons.

Thoughts of canoodling brought Marcus's ruminations back to the mysterious lady in red. Not that that was entirely surprising, since the minute he'd seen her sitting opposite him at Palumbo's, canoodling had been at the forefront of his brain. She'd simply been that stunning. What was really strange, though, was that once he'd started talking to her at the Lyric, canoodling had fallen by the wayside, and what he'd really wanted to do with her was talk more about opera. And not only because she shared his unconventional opinions, either. But because of the way she'd lit up while talking about it. As beautiful as she'd been, seated alone at her table in the restaurant, she'd become radiant during their conversation.

Radiant, he repeated to himself, frowning. Now there was a word he'd never used to describe a woman before. Then again, that could be because he'd seldom moved past the stage with a woman where he found her beautiful. Meaning he'd seldom reached a stage where he actually talked to one. Once he bedded a woman—and that usually came pretty early after meeting one—he lost interest. But that was because few women were worth knowing beyond the biblical sense.

Unbidden, a reproving voice erupted in his brain, taking him to task for his less-than-stellar commentary, but it wasn't his own. It was Charlotte's sandpaper rasp, made that way by too many cigarettes over the course of her eighty-two years. More than once over the past two decades since making her acquaintance, he'd let slip some politically incorrect comment about the opposite sex, only to have her haul him up by his metaphorical collar—and sometimes by his not-so-metaphorical collar—to set him straight.

God, he missed her.

He glanced at the pink cosmopolitan sitting opposite his single malt on the table, the glass dewy with condensation since it had been sitting there for so long. The rose, too, had begun to wilt, its petals blackening at their edges. Even the opera program looked limp and tattered already. All of them were at the end of their lives. Just as Charlotte had been the last time he'd sat at this table looking in the same direction.

She'd died two days after closing night at the Lyric. It had been seven months since her funeral, and Marcus still felt her loss keenly. He wondered, not for the first time, what happened after a soul left this world to enter the next. Was Charlotte still able to enjoy her occasional cosmo? Did they have performances of Verdi and Bizet where she was now? And was she able to enjoy the rare prime rib she'd loved to order at Palumbo's?

Marcus hoped so. Charlotte deserved only the best,

wherever she was. Because the best was what she had always given him.

A flash of red caught his eye, and Marcus glanced up. But it was only Emma Stegman, heading from the bar toward her father. Marcus scanned the room again for good measure but saw only more of the usual suspects. He knew everyone here, he thought. So why was he sitting alone? Hell, Stu the bartender wasn't the only guy Cynthia Harrison had tried canoodling with. If Marcus wanted to, he could sidle up next to her and be headed to the Ambassador Hotel, which was adjacent to the club, in no time. And he sure wouldn't lose his job for it. All he'd lose would be the empty feeling inside that had been with him since Charlotte's death. Of course, the feeling would come back tomorrow, when he was alone again….

He lifted his glass and downed what was left of his Scotch, then, for good measure, downed Charlotte's cosmopolitan, too, in one long gulp. He squeezed his eyes shut for a moment as he waited for the taste to leave his mouth—how had she stood those things?—then opened them again…

…to see a vision in red seated at a table on the other side of the room. He could not believe his good fortune. Seeing her one time had been chance. Seeing her twice had been lucky. Seeing her a third time…

That could only be fate.

Forgetting, for now, that he didn't believe in such a thing, and before he risked losing her again, he immediately rose and crossed to where she was seated, signaling for Stu at the same time and gesturing toward her table. Without waiting to be invited, he pulled out the chair across from hers and seated himself.

She glanced up at his appearance, surprise etched

on her features. But her lips curled into the faintest of smiles, reassuring him. That was another new experience for him. He'd never had to be reassured of anything. On the contrary, he'd taken everything in life for granted. That was what happened when you were born into one of the Gold Coast's oldest and most illustrious families. You got everything you wanted, often without even having to ask for it. In fact, you even got the things you didn't ask for. Usually handed to you on a silver platter. Sometimes literally.

"We have got to stop meeting like this."

This time it was she, not Marcus, who spoke the words he had said to her at the Lyric.

"On the contrary," he replied. "I'm beginning to like meeting you like this."

A hint of pink bloomed on her cheeks at his remark, and delight wound through his belly at seeing her blush. He couldn't remember the last time he'd made a woman blush. Not shyly, anyway. Not becomingly. Usually, if he made a woman blush, it was because he'd suggested they do something in the bedroom that most of society considered shameful. It was all the more reason, in his opinion, why it should be enjoyed.

But he was getting way ahead of himself. Anything in the bedroom with this woman was still, oh…hours away.

"Mind if I join you?" he asked.

"I think you already have."

He feigned surprise. "So I have. Then you'll have to let me buy you a drink."

She opened her mouth to reply and, for a moment, he feared she would decline his offer. Another new experience for Marcus. Not only fearing a woman would turn him down—since that almost never happened—but also feeling a knot of disappointment in his chest at the possibility. On those rare occasions when a woman did turn him down, he simply shrugged it off and moved to the next one. Because, inevitably, there was always a next one. With this woman, however…

Well, he couldn't imagine a next one. Not even with Cynthia Harrison falling out of her dress less than ten feet away.

"All right," she finally said, as Stu arrived at their table. She looked at the bartender. "I'll have a glass of champagne, please."

"Bring a bottle," Marcus instructed before the bartender had a chance to get away. "The Perrier-Jouët Cuvée Belle Epoque. 2002."

"Really, that's not necessary…." she began, her voice trailing off on the last word.

Deciding it was because she didn't know how to address him—and because he wanted to give her his name so that he could get hers in return—he finished for her, "Marcus. Marcus—"

"Don't tell me your last name."

He halted before revealing it, less because she asked him not to than because he found her command curious.

"Why not?"

"Just don't, that's all."

He started to give it to her anyway—never let it be said that Marcus Fallon ever did as he was told—but for some reason decided to honor her request. That was even stranger, since never let it be said that Marcus Fallon did the honorable thing, either. "All right." He lifted his right hand for her to shake. "And you are…?"

She hesitated before taking his hand, then gingerly

placed her own lightly against his. Her fingers were slender and delicate against his large, blunt ones and, unable to help himself, he closed his hand possessively over hers. Her skin was soft and warm, as creamy as ivory, and he found himself wondering if that was true of the rest of her. The blush on her cheeks deepened as he covered her hand with his, but she didn't pull hers away.

His appeal for her name hung in the air between them without a response. "Della," she told him finally. "My name is Della."

No last name from her, either, then. Fine, he thought. He wouldn't push it. But before the night was over, he'd know not only her last name, but everything else about her, too. Especially where each and every one of her erogenous zones were and what kind of erotic sounds she uttered whenever he located a new one.

Neither of them said anything more, only studied each other's faces as their hands remained joined. She had amazing eyes. Pale, clear gray, the kind of eyes a man could lose himself in forever. The kind that hid nothing and said much. Honest eyes, he finally decided. Noble. The eyes of a person who would always do the right thing.

Damn.

Stu cleared his throat a little too obviously beside them, and she gave a soft tug to free her fingers. Reluctantly, he let them go. She lowered her hand to the table near his, however, resting it palm down on the white linen. So he did likewise, flattening his hand until his fingers almost—almost—touched hers.

"Will there be anything else, Mr.—?" Stu stopped before revealing Marcus's last name, obviously having overheard the exchange. Quickly, he amended, "Will there be anything else, sir?"

Marcus waved a hand airily in his direction, muttering that Stu should bring some kind of appetizer, too, but didn't specify what. He honestly didn't care about anything, other than the intriguing woman who sat across from him.

"Well," he began, trying to jump-start the conversation again. "If you're sitting here in the Windsor Club, you can't be too new to Chicago. They have a waiting list to get in, and last I heard, it was two years, at least, before anyone added to it could even expect an application. Unless you're here as a guest of another member?" That would be just his luck. That he'd meet a woman like this, and she'd be involved with someone else.

"I'm on my own," she told him. Then, after a small hesitation, she added, "Tonight."

Suggesting she wasn't on her own on other nights, Marcus thought. For the first time, it occurred to him to glance down at her left hand. Not that a wedding ring had ever stopped him from seducing a woman before. But she sported only one ring, and it was on her right hand. The left bore no sign of ever having had one. So she wasn't even engaged. At least not to a man who had the decency to buy her a ring.

"Or maybe," he continued thoughtfully, "you're a member of one of the Windsor's original charter families who earn and keep their membership by a simple accident of birth." He grinned. "Like me. As many times as they've tried to throw me out of this place, they can't."

She grinned back. "And why on earth would they

throw out a paragon of formality and decency like you?"

His eyebrows shot up at that. "You really are new in town if no one's warned you about me yet. That's usually the first thing they tell beautiful young socialites. In fact, ninety percent of the tourist brochures for the city say something like, 'Welcome to Chicago. While you're here, be sure to visit Navy Pier, the Hancock Tower, the Field Museum and the Shedd Aquarium. And whatever you do, stay away from Marcus—" Again he halted before saying his last name. "Well, stay away from Marcus-Whose-Last-Name-You-Don't-Want-To-Know. That guy's nothing but trouble.'"

She laughed at that. She had a really great laugh. Uninhibited, unrestrained, genuinely happy. "And what do the other ten percent of the travel brochures say?"

"Well, those would be the ones they give out to conventioneers looking for a good time while they're away from the ball and chain. Those are the ones that list all the, ah, less seemly places in town." He smiled again. "I'm actually featured very prominently in those. Not by name, mind you, but…" He shrugged. "Those damned photographers don't care who they take pictures of."

She laughed again, stirring something warm and fizzy inside Marcus unlike anything he'd ever felt before. "I don't believe you," she said. "I find it hard to jibe *The Bartered Bride* with bump and grind."

"There's more to me than opera, you know." He met her gaze levelly. "A lot more."

The blush blossomed in her cheeks again, making him chuckle more softly. She was saved from having to respond to his comment, however, when Stu arrived with their champagne and a tray of fruit and cheese. The bartender went a little overboard with the presentation and opening of the bottle, but it was probably because he, too, recognized that Della—yes, Marcus did like that name—wasn't a usual customer. In fact, there was nothing usual about her. She was, in a word, extraordinary.

After receiving approval for the champagne, Stu poured a glass for each of them. As he did, Marcus told Della, "I am notorious in this town. Ask anyone."

She turned to the bartender, who was nestling the champagne in a silver bucket of ice. "Is he really notorious?" she asked.

The bartender glanced first at Marcus, who nodded imperceptibly to let Stu know his tip wouldn't be compromised by his honesty, then at Della. "Oh, yes, ma'am. And not just in Chicago. He makes the society pages all over the country, wherever he goes, and he's a regular feature on a lot of those celebrity websites. If you're seen with him, it's a good bet you'll wind up there yourself. He's infamous."

Della turned to Marcus, her eyes no longer full of laughter, but now brimming with something akin to… fear? Oh, surely not. What would she have to be afraid of?

"Is that true?" she asked.

Still puzzled by her reaction, but not wanting to lie to her—especially since it would be easy enough for her to find out with a simple internet search—he told her, "I'm afraid so."

Her lips parted fractionally, and her expression became almost panicked. Deciding she must be feigning fear as a joke, he played along, telling her, "Don't worry. They never let riffraff like the paparazzi into the club.

You're perfectly safe with me here. No one will see you with me."

It occurred to him as he said it that that was exactly what she feared—being seen with him. Not just by the paparazzi, but by some individual in particular. An individual who might not like seeing her out with Marcus. Or anyone else, for that matter.

She did have that look about her, he decided as he considered her again. Pampered, well tended to, cared for—at least on the surface. The kind of woman who made her way in the world by making herself available to men who could afford her. There were still a surprising number of such women in society, even in this day and age when a woman shouldn't have to rely on her sexuality to make her way in the world. Beautiful, elegant, reserved, they tended to be. At least on the surface.

Not that he'd ever seen Della among such women in the level of society in which he traveled. That only fueled his suspicion that she was merely visiting the city. Dammit.

It took a moment for her expression to clear, but she finally emitted a single—albeit a tad humorless—chuckle. "Of course," she said. "I mean…I knew that. I was only kidding."

He nodded, but there was a part of him that wasn't quite convinced. Maybe she really was attached to someone else. Maybe she even *belonged* to that someone. Maybe that someone wouldn't be too happy about her being here tonight alone. Or anywhere alone. Maybe that someone would be even more unhappy to find her with another man. Maybe she really was afraid her photo would show up somewhere with Marcus at her side, and she'd be in big, big trouble with that someone.

Just who was she, this mysterious lady in red? And why did Marcus want so badly to find out?

In an effort to dispel the odd tension that had erupted between them, he lifted his glass of champagne and said, softly, "Cheers."

There was another small hesitation on her part before, she, too, lifted her glass. "Cheers," she echoed even more softly.

The toast didn't put an end to the frisson of uneasiness that still hovered over the table, but it did put a bit of the bloom back in her cheeks. It was enough, he decided. For now.

But certainly not forever.

Della gazed at the man seated across the table from her as she sipped her champagne, and she wondered exactly when the evening had jumped the track and started screeching headlong into a dark, scary tunnel. One minute, she'd been about to embark on the last leg of her evening by enjoying a final glass of champagne at Chicago's celebrated Windsor Club—which she'd gotten into only by bribing the doorman with another small fortune—and the next minute, she'd found herself gazing once again into the gold-flecked, chocolate-brown eyes that had so intrigued her at the opera.

Marcus. His name fit him. Stoic and classic, commanding and uncompromising. How strange that she should run into him at every destination she'd visited tonight. Then again, she'd gone out of her way to choose destinations that were magnets for the rich and powerful, and he certainly fit that bill. Of course, now she was learning he was part of that other adjective that went along with rich—*famous*—and that was a condition she most definitely had to avoid.

So what was she afraid of? He was right. There was no one in the club who didn't belong here. Other than herself, she meant. Nobody had even seemed to notice the two of them. Not to mention it was late and, even if it was Saturday, ninety percent of the city's population had gone home. There was snow in the forecast for later, even if it wasn't anything a city like Chicago couldn't handle. Most people were probably hunkered down in their living rooms and bedrooms, having stocked up on provisions earlier, and were looking forward to a Sunday being snowed in with nothing to do.

Della wished she could enjoy something like that, but she felt as though she'd been snowed in with nothing to do for the past eleven months. At least when she wasn't at Geoffrey's beck and call.

But tonight that wasn't the case. Tonight she was having fun. She should look at the opportunity to share the last couple of hours of her celebration with a man like Marcus as the icing on her birthday cake.

"So..." she began, trying to recapture the flirtatiousness of their earlier exchange. Still trying to figure out when, exactly, she'd decided to return his flirtations. "What kinds of things have you done to make yourself so notorious?"

He savored another sip of his champagne, then placed the glass on the table between them. But instead of releasing it, he dragged his fingers up over the stem and along the bowl of the flute, then up farther along the elegant line of its sides. Della found herself mesmerized by the voyage of those fingers, especially when he began to idly trace the rim with the pad of his middle finger. Around and around it went, slowly, slowly...oh, so slowly…until a coil of heat began to unwrap in her belly and purl into parts beyond.

She found herself wondering what it would be like to have him drawing idle circles like that elsewhere, someplace like, oh…she didn't know. Herself maybe. Along her shoulder, perhaps. Or down her thigh. Touching her in other places, too—places where such caresses might drive her to the brink of madness.

Her eyes fluttered closed as the thought formed in her brain, as if by not watching what he was doing, she might better dispel the visions dancing around in her head. But closing her eyes only made those images more vivid. More earthy. More erotic. More…*oh.* So much more *more.* She snapped her eyes open again in an effort to squash the visions completely. But that left her looking at Marcus, who was gazing at her with faint amusement, as if he'd seen where her attention had settled and knew exactly what she was thinking about.

As he studied her, he stilled his finger on the rim of the glass and settled his index finger beside it. Della watched helplessly as he scissored them along the rim, first opening, then closing, then opening again. With great deliberation, he curled them into the glass until they touched the top of the champagne, then he dampened each finger with the effervescent wine. Then he carefully pulled them out and lifted them to her lips, brushing lightly over her mouth with the dew of champagne.

Heat swamped her, making her stomach simmer, her breasts tingle and her heart rate quadruple, and dampening her between her legs. Without even thinking about what she was doing, she parted her lips enough to allow him to tuck one finger inside. She tasted the champagne then, along with the faint essence of Marcus. And Marcus was, by far, the most intoxicating.

Quickly, she drew her head back and licked the remnants of his touch from her lips. Not that that did anything to quell her arousal. What had come over her? How could she be this attracted to a man this quickly? She knew almost nothing about him, save his name and the fact that he loved opera and good champagne and had bought a rose for someone earlier in the evening who—

The rose. How could she have forgotten about that? She might very well be sitting here enjoying the advances of a married man! Or, at the very least, one who belonged to someone else. And the last thing she wanted to be was part of a triangle.

Where was the rose now? Had he thrown it resentfully into the trash or pressed it between the pages of the neglected opera program as a keepsake? Involuntarily, she scanned the other tables in the club until she saw an empty one not far away with a rose and opera program lying atop it. And another martini glass—though this time it was empty. Had the woman he was expecting finally caught up with him? Had he only moments ago been sharing a moment like this with someone else? Could he really be that big a heel?

"Who were you expecting tonight?"

The question was out of her mouth before Della even realized it had formed in her brain. It obviously surprised Marcus as much as it had her, because his dark eyebrows shot up again.

"No one," he told her. And then, almost as if he couldn't stop himself, he added, "Not even you. I could never have anticipated someone like you."

"But the rose… The pink drink…"

He turned to follow the track of her gaze, saw the table where he must have been sitting when she came in. His shoulders drooped a little, and his head dipped forward, as if in defeat. Or perhaps melancholy? When he looked at her, the shadows she'd noted before were back in his eyes. Definitely the latter.

"I did buy the rose and order the drink for someone else," he said. "And yes, she was someone special."

"Was?" Della echoed. "Then you and she aren't..."

"What?"

"Together?"

His expression revealed nothing of what he might be feeling or thinking. "No."

She wanted to ask more about the woman, but something in his demeanor told her not to. It was none of her business, she reminded herself. It was bad enough she'd brought up memories for him that clearly weren't happy. Whoever the woman was, it was obvious she wasn't a part of his life anymore. Even if it was likewise obvious that he still wanted her to be.

And why did that realization prick her insides so much? Della wouldn't even see Marcus again after tonight. It didn't matter if he cared deeply for someone else, and the less she knew about him, the better. That way, he would be easier to forget.

Even if he was the kind of man a woman never forgot.

In spite of her relinquishing the subject, he added, "I knew she wouldn't be coming tonight, but it felt strange not to buy the rose and order her a drink the way I always did before. She always ran late," he added parenthetically and, Della couldn't help but note, affectionately. "It felt almost as if I were betraying her somehow not ordering for her, when really she was the one who—" He halted abruptly and met Della's gaze again. But now he didn't look quite so grim. "An uncharacteristic bout of sentimentality on my part, I guess. But no, Della. I'm not with anyone." He hesitated a telling moment before asking, "Are you?"

Well, now, there was a loaded question if ever there was one. Della wasn't with anyone—not the way Marcus meant it, anyway. She hadn't been with anyone that way for nearly a year. And that one had been someone she never should have been with in the first place. Not just because of the sort of man Egan Collingwood turned out to be, either. But Della was indeed with someone—in a different way. She was with Geoffrey. For now, anyway. And as long as she was with Geoffrey, there was no way she could be with anyone else.

She didn't want to tell Marcus that, though, so she only lifted her champagne to her lips for another sip. When he continued to study her in that inquisitive way, she enjoyed another sip. And another. And another. Until—would you look at that?—the glass was completely empty. The moment she set it on the table, however, Marcus poured her a refill, allowing the champagne to almost reach to the brim before lowering the bottle.

She grinned at the ridiculously full glass. "Marcus, are you trying to get me drunk?"

"Yes," he replied immediately.

His frankness surprised her, and she laughed. Honestly, she couldn't remember the last time she'd laughed so much in one evening. Even before Egan, she hadn't been so prone to jollity. She'd never even used a word like *jollity* before.

"Well, it won't work," she said, even as she carefully

lifted the glass to her mouth. "I have a remarkable metabolism."

Now his smile turned faintly predatory. "I'm counting on that, actually."

Yikes.

Well, the joke was on him. Because Mr. Marcus Notorious might think he had the evening mapped out with the quickest route from chance dinner meeting to white-hot marathon of sex, but there was no way that was going to happen. Della had to have her rented clothes back tomorrow when Talk of the Town opened at noon or she'd lose her deposit. Even the promise of a white-hot marathon of sex with a maddeningly irresistible guy wasn't going to keep her from forgetting that.

She looked at Marcus, at his smoldering eyes and sizzling grin. At the brutally strong jaw and ruthless cheekbones. As if trying to counter the ruggedness of his features, an unruly lock of dark hair had tumbled carelessly over his forehead, begging for the gentling of a woman's fingers.

Well. Probably that wasn't going to keep her from getting her deposit. Hmm. Actually, that was kind of a tough call….

But then, Della couldn't spend the night doing anything anywhere, anyway. As it was, if Geoffrey called the house tonight and she didn't answer, he'd be hopping mad. Of course, he'd only have to call her on her cell phone to know she was okay, but he'd be furious that she wasn't cloistered where she was supposed to be. She'd been lucky enough so far that he hadn't ever called the house when she'd snuck out on those handful of occasions when she became bored to the point of lunacy. But she wasn't sure how much longer her luck would hold. If Geoffrey ever got wind of her excursions, he'd want to wring her neck. Then he'd become even more determined to keep her hidden.

Still looking at Marcus, but trying not to think about the way he was making her feel, she leaned back in her chair and said, "So you get women drunk and then take advantage of them. Now I know the kinds of things you've done to make yourself so notorious."

"Oh, I never have to get women drunk to take advantage, Della," he said with complete confidence and without an ounce of arrogance. "In fact, I never have to take advantage."

She had no doubt that was true. She'd just met the man, and she was already having thoughts about him and inclinations toward him she shouldn't be having. Too many thoughts. And *way* too many inclinations.

"Then what does make you so notorious?"

He leaned forward, bracing his elbows on the table as he invaded her space, effectively erasing what meager distance she'd put between them. "Where do I begin?" he asked. "And, more important, do you have all night?"

Double yikes.

Having no idea what to say to that, she lifted her champagne for another idle sip…only to enjoy a healthy quaff instead. Well, it was very good. And she was starting to feel a lovely little buzz that was buffing the rough edges off…oh, everything.

As if he realized the turn her thoughts had taken, Marcus pushed his hand across the table until his fingertips were touching hers. A spark shot through Della, even at that simple, innocent touch. And when his hand crept up over hers, that spark leaped into a flame.

"Because if you *do* have all night," he added, "I'd be more than happy to give you a *very* thorough illustration."

Triple yikes. And another quaff, for good measure.

Ah, that was better. Now, what was it she had been about to say? Something about needing to get home because it was approaching midnight and, any minute now, she was going to turn into a bumpkin. Um, she meant pumpkin. Not that that was much better.

She searched for something to say that would extricate her from her predicament, but no words came. Probably because no ideas came. And probably no ideas came because they were all being crowded out by the visions featuring her and Marcus that kept jumping to the forefront of her brain. He really was incredibly sexy. And it had been such a long time since she'd been with anyone who turned her on the way he did. And it would probably be even longer before she found someone she wanted to be with again. She had no idea what would happen once Geoffrey was done with her. All she had that was certain was right now. This place. This moment. This man. This sexy, notorious, willing man. This man she should in no way allow herself to succumb to. This man who would haunt her for the rest of her life.

This man who, for some reason, she couldn't bring herself to leave quite yet….

Three

Della tore her gaze from his, forcing herself to look at something—anything—other than Marcus. Gazing past him, she found herself looking at the windows of two French doors not far from their table. The snow the forecasters had promised earlier in the day had begun to fall—delicate, dazzling flecks of white shimmering in the lamplight outside. As a native New Yorker, Della was no stranger to snow. And Chicago had seen snow more than once already this season. But there was something as magical to her about snow today as there had been when she was a child. When it had snowed then, at least for a little while, her neighborhood ceased to be a broken landscape of grimy concrete and asphalt and would transform into an enchanted world of sparkling white. The rusty fire escape outside her bedroom window morphed into a diamond-covered staircase that led to the top of an imprisoned princess's turret. The piles of garbage at the curb turned into pillows of glittering fairy-dust. The corroded cars became pearly silver coaches. Snow drove the gangs and dealers inside, who preyed on the neighborhood like wicked witches and evil sorcerers, so that all Della could see for block after block were radiant castles of white.

At least for a little while.

How appropriate that it should snow tonight, when she was actually enjoying the sort of enchanted adventure she'd had to invent as a child. How strangely right it felt to see those fat, fantastic flakes falling behind the man who had been such a bewitching Prince Charming this evening.

"It's snowing," she said softly.

Marcus turned to follow her gaze, then looked at Della again. His expression indicated that snow didn't hold the same fascination or whimsical appeal for him that it did for her.

"They're predicting four or five inches," he said, sounding disappointed at the change of subject.

He looked down at their hands, at how his rested atop hers and how hers just lay there. With clear reluctance, he pulled his toward himself. It was what she wanted, Della told herself. A change in subject to change her feelings instead of changing her mind. So why did his withdrawal have the opposite effect? Why did she want him to take her hand again, only this time turn it so their palms were flat against each other and their fingers entwined?

Still, he didn't retreat completely. His fingertips still brushed hers, and she could feel the warmth of his skin clinging to her own. It was all she could do not to reach for him and arrange their hands the way they'd been before.

It was for the best, she told herself again. This was a momentary encounter. A momentary exchange. A momentary everything. Especially now that the snow had begun, she really should be leaving. She'd told the driver of her hired car that she would be at the club only until midnight. It was nearing that now. She definitely needed to wind down this…whatever it was…with Marcus. Then she needed to be on her way.

So why wasn't she?

"It will be just enough snow to turn everything into an ungodly mess," Marcus said distastefully, giving her the perfect segue she needed to say her farewells. Unfortunately, he added, "At least no one will have to battle rush hour to get to work," reminding her that tomorrow was Sunday, so it wasn't as though she had to get up *that* early. She could squeeze in another moment or two….

"By afternoon," he continued, "the city will be one big pile of black slush. Snow is nothing but a pain in the—"

"I love snow. I think it's beautiful."

Marcus smiled indulgently. "Spoken like someone who's never had to maneuver in it," he replied. Then he brightened. "But with that clue, I can add to my knowledge of you. I now know that, not only have you only arrived in Chicago recently, but you came here from some hot, sunny place that never has to worry about the hassle of snow."

She said nothing to contradict him. It wasn't lying when you didn't say anything. And the more misconceptions he had about her, the better.

At her silence, he grinned with much satisfaction.

"I'm right, aren't I? You came here from someplace where it's hot all the time, didn't you?"

Oh, if he only knew. It had certainly been "hot" for her in New York when she left. Just not the way he meant. So she only smiled and said, "Guilty."

And not only of being from a "hot" place. She was guilty of twisting the truth in an effort to stay honest with him. Guilty of letting him believe she was someone she wasn't. Guilty of leading him on…

But she wasn't doing that last, she tried to reassure herself. Neither of them was making any promises to the other. If anything, promises were exactly what the two of them were trying to avoid. And, truth be told, she still wasn't sure what her intentions were where Marcus was concerned. He was clearly interested in sharing more than champagne and an assortment of fruit and cheese with her. He was waiting for her to give him some sign that she was interested in more than that, too. And although there was a not-so-small part of her that was definitely interested, there was another part of her still clinging to rationality, to sanity, to fidelity.

Because even though succumbing to Marcus's seduction wouldn't make her unfaithful to another man, it would make her unfaithful to herself. She hadn't scrabbled her way out of the soul-swallowing slums and into one of Wall Street's most powerful, most dynamic investing firms by believing in fairy tales and capitulating to whimsy. She'd done it by being pragmatic, hardworking and focused.

Then again, being those things was also what had forced her to flee the very life she'd toiled in and fought so hard to build.

She sighed inwardly. There it was again. More thinking about things she wasn't supposed to be thinking about tonight. Recalling the dissolution of her old life and fretting over the irresolution of her new one didn't belong in the fantasy life she was living *now*. It was her birthday. The one day of the year where it was okay for a person to be selfish and self-indulgent. It was the perfect time for her to be thinking about the moment. The moment was all that mattered for now. The moment was all she had that was certain. The moment was all she had that she could control. With another glance at Marcus—whose place in this night, in this moment, she still hadn't determined—she rose from her chair and moved to the French doors to watch the snow.

There was a small terrace beyond them, dark because of the late hour and frigid season. Della could just discern the outline of a handful of tables and chairs—all covered for the winter—and some potted topiaries that lay dormant. A layer of white covered all of it, so it must have been snowing harder and for longer than either of them had realized. Then again, when a woman was preoccupied by a man such as Marcus, it was hard to recognize that there was anything else out in the world at all.

As if conjured by the thought, she felt him slip up behind her, close enough that his body was flush against her own. She told herself she was only imagining the way she could feel the heat from his body mingling with hers, but the scent of him… That was all too real. All too wonderful. All too exhilarating.

"It was barely flurrying when I came in," she said. "I'm surprised how much has already fallen."

He said nothing for a moment, only continued to exude warmth and his intoxicatingly spicy fragrance.

Finally, quietly, he said, "The snow isn't the only thing that's been surprising tonight."

She couldn't disagree. Yet as unexpected as Marcus had been, his presence somehow felt perfectly right. Prince Charming was the only thing that had been missing from Della's fairy-tale plan for the evening, even if he was a complete stranger. Then again, he wasn't a stranger, not really. They'd known each other for hours now. They'd shared, in a way, a lovely dinner, a spectacular opera, some quiet conversation and gentle touches. They'd made each other smile. They'd made each other laugh. They'd made each other…feel things.

Della liked Marcus. He liked her. That made them something more than strangers, surely. She just wasn't quite certain what.

Impulsively, she tested the handle of the door and found it unlocked. Another surprise. Or perhaps more magic. Unable to help herself, she pushed open the door and strode quickly out onto the terrace, turning around slowly in the falling snow.

"Della," Marcus objected from inside, "what are you doing? It's freezing out there."

Funny, but she didn't feel cold. On the contrary, being with him made her hot to her core.

"I can't help it," she said as she halted her rotation to face him. "It's so beautiful. And so quiet. Listen."

As happened with snow, the sounds of the city beyond the terrace were muffled and silent, but the snow itself seemed to make a soft, supple sound as it fell. Reluctantly, Marcus shoved his hands into his trouser pockets and walked onto the terrace, shaking his head at her.

"You're worse than a little kid," he said. But he was smiling that delicious smile again.

As he drew nearer, Della moved farther away, until she'd backed herself into the far corner of the terrace, away from the door. When her back bumped the wall, the motion unsettled a small bundle of snow from somewhere above her, sending it cascading down around over her. She laughed as she shook her head to scatter the flakes, then the comb that had been holding her hair came loose, making it fall around her shoulders. He came to her immediately, slipping a little on his way, grabbing the railing to steady himself as his laughter joined her own.

"Well, aren't we a mess?" she said.

Not that she cared. Her life had been a mess for a year now. At least this mess was a fun one. She extended her hand over the balcony to let the snowflakes collect in her palm one by one. As soon as they landed, they melted, but the moisture still sparkled against her skin. "Look at it, Marcus," she said. "How can you think it's not lovely?"

He tucked himself into the corner of the darkened terrace as snugly as she was. "It's cold," he corrected her. "And you left your coat inside."

As chivalrously as a paladin, he slipped off his tuxedo jacket and reached around her to drape it over her shoulders. The garment fairly swallowed her, but it was redolent with both his scent and his warmth, and she was helpless not to pull it more closely around herself.

"Now you'll get cold," she told him.

"I haven't been cold since the moment I laid eyes on you. A little thing like snow and subfreezing temperature isn't going to change that."

Della wasn't feeling cold, either. Not that that would make her return his jacket to him. It felt too nice being enveloped in it. Almost as if she were being enveloped by Marcus himself.

Almost.

As if reading her mind—again—he started to lean forward, dipping his head toward hers. Knowing he intended to kiss her, Della turned quickly away. Why, she had no idea. She wanted him to kiss her. She wanted to kiss him, too. But she still couldn't quite bring herself to allow it. She wasn't the woman he thought she was. She was beginning to wonder if she was even the woman *she* thought she was. Soon, she *would* be someone else—entirely and literally. And in a couple of hours, she and Marcus would be nothing but a fond memory lodged in each other's brains. What kind of memory did she want to be for him? What kind of memory did she want him to be for her?

Marcus didn't give her time to think about it, because the moment she had her back to him, he coiled both arms around her waist to pull her against himself. His broad chest more than spanned her shoulders, but his long torso aligned perfectly with hers. It was at the small of her back where she felt him most, however, because as he drew her closer, rubbing their bodies together, he stirred to life against her.

Della's heart rate quickened at the realization that he was becoming as aroused as she. Heat coursed through her when he dipped his head to hers, his mouth hovering just over her ear. His breath was warm and damp against her skin, at odds with the snow, clouding her senses until she was dizzy not knowing what was what.

"I can say the snow isn't lovely," he murmured, his

voice as hot and demanding as the rest of him, "because I've seen something much lovelier this evening. In fact, you, my intriguing Della, are absolutely electrifying."

Instead of replying to that—mostly because she was afraid of what she might say…and even more afraid of what she might do—Della leaned further over the railing and into the falling snow. She turned her face to the caress of cold air, hoping it would be the antidote she needed to quell the swirling, simmering sensations inside her. Instead, her new position pushed her backside even more intimately against Marcus, and she felt him swell to even greater life against her.

She swallowed hard at the recognition of his condition, curling her fingers tightly over the metal railing, afraid of where her hands might wander otherwise. She wasn't so lucky with her thoughts, though, because they wandered plenty, telling her things she didn't want to hear. Things about how she would never meet another man like Marcus, and how he could be out of her life in a matter of moments, and how there was nothing sadder in life than a missed opportunity. So she tipped her face upward, welcoming the soft cascade of snowflakes, hoping they would numb her brain and make her forget…

…everything. Every ugly memory of where she'd grown up. Every miserable feeling she'd had since discovering the truth about Egan Collingwood. Every anxious moment she'd experienced since discovering even worse truths at work. Every terrible shudder of loneliness that had plagued her over the past eleven months. Every reason why she shouldn't do exactly what she wanted to do with Marcus. He was the surprise birthday gift that fate had presented her, sporting a big, satin bow.

Again, as if he'd read her mind, he covered her hands with his and gently urged them apart, opening his jacket over the front of her dress so that he could slip his fingers between the two garments. They went immediately to her rib cage, strumming it as if fine-tuning a delicate instrument. Ripples of pleasure wound through Della as he touched her, and she sighed her delight, her breath a puff of fog in the frigid air. Unable to help herself, she leaned against him, reaching behind herself with both hands to curl her fingers into his hair. Marcus used her new position to plunder her at will, covering her breasts with sure fingers.

"Oh," she murmured at his touch. "Oh, Marcus."

He said nothing in response, only dipped his head to her neck to drag kisses along the column of her throat. One hand gently kneaded her breast, while the other began to venture lower, moving along the elegant curves of her waist and hip and thigh, where he bunched the fabric of her dress in his fist. Slowly, slowly, oh… so slowly, he drew the garment upward, until Della could feel the cold and snow on her stocking-clad legs. Because of the gown's length, and because of the cold, she'd worn tights that rolled just above the knee, leaving her thighs bare. When she felt the whip of cold on her naked skin, she gasped, not only because of the frosty air, but also because she realized how far, how fast, things had progressed between them.

"Marcus," she began to protest. But the words sounded halfhearted, even to her own ears.

"Shh," he told her. "I just want to touch you. I just want to feel your skin beneath my fingertips."

She told herself to tell him he'd done that by holding her hand, but the words stilled before emerging. It had been so long since she'd felt a man's touch. Too long.

She'd forgotten how delicious it felt to be this close to another human being. Had forgotten how essential it was to share physical intimacy with another person. Had forgotten how exquisite it could be, how alive it could make her feel. Had forgotten—

Marcus found the leg of her panties and pushed it aside, threading his fingers into the damp, molten core of her.

Oh…oh, Marcus… She'd forgotten how that could feel, too.

"You're so wet," he murmured against her ear, obviously surprised by her response to him. "Della… oh, sweetheart…it's like… It's like you're already ready for me to—"

He moved his fingers against her again, eliciting a groan from deep inside her. Her fingers fell to the railing again, convulsing on it, then relaxed, then gripped the fixture again. Hard. She turned her fists first one way, then the other, then began to move them up and down along the length of the railing, the way she would touch a man's—

Marcus stroked her again, and somehow, she knew he was watching the movement of her hands and thinking the same thing she was thinking. Feeling the same thing she felt. Wanting the same thing she wanted.

He nuzzled her neck again, this time nipping her lightly with his teeth, an action she found unbelievably erotic. In response, she moved a hand behind herself and fumbled for his belt, working both it and the fly of his trousers open with trembling fingers.

Well, why shouldn't she? It was her birthday. She was celebrating. She'd already given herself so many gifts tonight. Why not one more? Why not enjoy this man the way they both wanted to enjoy each other?

When Marcus realized what she was doing, he moved away from her long enough to help her complete the action. She started to turn around, but he placed both hands firmly on her waist and held her in place with her back to him. So she reached behind herself and thrust her hand into his trousers, finding him naked and hard and ready. He gasped at what must have been the coldness of her hand, but she quickly warmed them both. Cupping the heavy head of his shaft in one hand, she palmed him over the satiny balm of his anticipated release before moving her fingers lower along his length. And lower. And lower. Until she caught her breath at just how magnificent he was.

She honestly wasn't sure what she had been thinking she would do next, and in that moment, Marcus's thoughts seemed to mirror her own. Dropping one hand from her waist, he fisted the fabric of her skirt again. Only this time, it was in the back, and this time he hiked it over her waist. As Della clung to the damp railing, Marcus pulled down her panties, pushing them past her knees. Della did the rest, stepping completely out of them.

And then he was moving behind her again, deftly rolling on a condom he must have had at the ready. But then, he was notorious, wasn't he? She had only a scant second to marvel at how he was sexually indiscriminate enough to be so prepared for sex, yet responsible enough to take such a precaution. Then, as the snow cascaded around her, Marcus thrust himself into her from behind, burying himself deeply.

When she cried out at the depth of his penetration, he gently covered her mouth with his hand. Then he began to move inside her, pulling himself out almost completely before bucking against her again, going even deeper. She had to bite her lip to keep herself silent, but he rewarded her by moving his hand between her legs and fingering the damp folds of her flesh. Of course, that only made her want to cry out again…

But she didn't cry out. She only felt. Felt the tight coil of heat in her belly pull tighter still, until her entire body seemed ready to explode. She felt the man behind her fill her again and again and again, felt the dizzying sensations of hunger and desire and need mingling and twining until they all became one. And then she felt the white-hot release of her climax shaking her, followed immediately by his.

And then he was removing himself from inside her and wrapping up the spent condom, rearranging their clothes as best he could before he spun her around and covered her mouth with his. For a long time, he only kissed her and kissed her and kissed her. Then, finally, he pulled back enough so that he could frame her face with both hands. It was snowing harder now, swirls of powder blowing up onto the terrace, surrounding them in a virtual tornado of white. Marcus's breath was coming in gasps, puffs of white against the sparkle of snow that merged with her own hitched breathing.

He dipped his head until his forehead was pressed against hers. "Nothing like that has ever happened to me before," he said between breaths. "Della, my God. You're a narcotic."

She wasn't sure how to reply to that, so she said nothing. She only curled her fingers in the front of his shirt and clung to him. They stood that way for long moments, neither seeming to know what to say or do. Della was confident no one inside the club had seen what had happened. Not only was the place deserted by now, but the two of them had also been obscured by both the darkness and the blowing snow. She also noted with a smile that they'd managed to fog up the windows behind them to opacity.

Finally, Marcus pulled away from her. But only far enough that he could gaze into her face. She'd expected him to demand the return of his jacket and say something like, "Holy cow, would you look at the time? I gotta get outta here."

Instead, he threaded his fingers gently into her hair and, very softly, asked, "Do you know what my favorite thing is about the Windsor Club?"

Still not trusting her voice, Della only shook her head.

"My favorite thing is that it's connected to the Ambassador Hotel. On nights like this, when driving could be dangerous due to a mix of weather, darkness and extremely good champagne, you can just…spend the night there. You don't have to set foot outside to get there. You can walk down the hall and through a breezeway and be at the registration desk in a matter of minutes. And, thanks to your platinum club status, within minutes of that, you can be in a luxury suite ordering another bottle of champagne from their twenty-four-hour room service."

Finally finding her voice, Della told him, "But I don't have platinum club status at the Ambassador Hotel."

He feigned forgetfulness. "That's right. You just came to Chicago recently, didn't you? So I guess you'll have to be with someone else who has platinum club status."

She smiled. "And who could I possibly know who might have that?"

"So it wouldn't be a problem for you spending the

night at the Ambassador? With me? You don't have any…obligations waiting for you anywhere?"

Only the obligation of returning her clothes by noon and checking in with Geoffrey by nine, as she did every morning. And she always woke by five, even without an alarm, even after a sleepless night. It was ingrained in her because Mr. Nathanson, her boss, had always insisted she be at her desk the same time he was—at 7:00 a.m. sharp, before anyone else showed up for work. At the time, Della had thought it was because the man was a workaholic. Had she known it was actually because he was corrupt…

She turned her attention to Marcus again, where it belonged. He was a gift, she reminded herself. One night with him would be the most amazing birthday present she'd ever received—from herself to herself. It would be terrible not to accept a gift like him.

"No," she finally said. "I don't have any…obligations." She lifted a hand to thread her fingers through his hair, loving the way the snow had dampened it and their encounter had warmed it. "Not until tomorrow. One night, Marcus," she made herself say, because it was very, very important that he realize that was all it would be. It was even more important that she realize it. "One night is all I can promise you."

"One night is all I'm asking for, Della."

It was probably all he wanted from any woman, she thought. Because it was probably all a man like him could promise in return.

She told herself that made her feel better. They both wanted the same thing. They both needed the same thing. They were both willing to give and take equally. Tonight would be exactly what she had planned it to be all those years ago: One night. Of magic. Her gift to herself.

Marcus lifted his hand to trace a finger lightly over her cheek. “Well, then, my sweet, intriguing Della,” he said softly, “why don't you and I take a little walk and find out where it leads?”

Four

Marcus stood at the broad window of the hotel suite dressed in the plush royal blue robe the hotel so thoughtfully provided for all its guests and watched the snow fall. And fall. And fall. And fall. Fat, furious flakes coming down so thick and so fast, he could barely make out the buildings on the other side of Michigan Avenue.

Unbelievable. What was supposed to have been a manageable snowfall of three to five inches had turned into a blizzard during the night. The entire city was on hold until the snowplows could get out and do their thing, but since everyone had been caught by surprise, they couldn't do anything until the snow let up. A lot.

And the snow didn't show any sign of letting up. At all.

The situation was going to be untenable for a while. No one would be going anywhere until tomorrow at the earliest. Not that Marcus cared. Because it meant that the one night Della had promised was all she could give him would now, by necessity, become two.

That was something he should definitely care about. The last thing he looked for in a one-night stand was for it to last more than one night. Hell, half the time he was safely back at his place before the night was even over. Once he was sexually satisfied by a woman, there was never any reason to hang around. Even the prospect of being sexually satisfied a second time rarely kept him from leaving.

But with Della, even being satisfied a third time hadn't quelled his appetite for more. Once he'd regained enough strength to manage it. They'd both been insatiable last night, to the point where they'd slept only long enough to recover from their previous coupling, then come together even more fiercely than before. That third time, they'd had to rely on oral gratification alone to bring each other to climax, since the second time had been so rough. Not that either of them had seemed to mind. Della had been as demanding and wild as a tigress, and Marcus had mounted her the way a jungle cat would have claimed his mate.

And even that hadn't been enough to satisfy him. In fact, that had only made him want her more. When he'd awoken that morning beside her, their bodies had been so intricately entwined, he'd barely been able to tell where hers ended and his began. Marcus never slept with a woman after having sex with her. Never. And he'd certainly never gathered one close that way and held her with such possessiveness. For a long time after waking, he'd only lain silently beside her, holding her, listening to her soft respiration, inhaling her scent. It was different now. Last night she'd smelled soft and flowery. This morning she smelled musky and dark. And, God help him, Marcus had grown hard against her as he lay there, and it had been all he could do not to take her again in her sleep. Instead, he'd eased his way out of the bed without waking her, donned the robe and called for room service.

Even its arrival hadn't woken Della. But that might be because Marcus had intercepted the steward in the hallway when he'd heard the rattle of the approaching cart and brought it in himself. He hadn't wanted to wake her before she was ready. Strangely, however, that hadn't been because he wanted her rested up for another night like last night—and, hey, maybe a day like last night, too—but because he simply liked watching her sleep.

He turned away from the window and let go of the sheer curtains, throwing the room into an otherworldly dusk created by the thickly falling snow. He loved the understated luxury of the Ambassador, loved the taupe walls and buff-colored, cleanly tailored furnishings with the dashes of blues and greens in the form of throw pillows and abstract artwork. He'd wanted a suite, of course, but there hadn't been one available. At the time, it hadn't seemed a problem, since he'd known he and Della would only need the place for a few hours. Now that their stay was looking to be for most of the weekend, it would have been nice to have a little more room to spread out.

He looked over at the bed, where she still slept, and smiled. Then again, there was a lot to be said for close quarters. Even if those quarters were still five-star hotel roomy.

Della lay on her stomach, the ivory sheets tangled over her lower half, her creamy back and shoulders laid bare. Silently, he neared the bed, pausing beside it.

Her hair flowed like a honey river above her head and down the side of the pillow, and her hand was curled into a loose fist near her mouth. Her lips were swollen from the ferocity of their kisses, and her cheek was pink where his beard had abraded her. He remembered wrapping fistfuls of that hair around his fingers as he'd ridden her last night, then stroking it back into place as the two of them had gentled their movements in the afterglow. Even in the furiousness of their actions, he'd noted how thick and silky the strands were, and he'd loved the feel of her soft tresses tumbling through his fingers.

He was about to turn away to pour two cups of coffee—maybe the aroma of Jamaica Blue Mountain would rouse her—when she began to stir. Slowly, murmuring soft sounds of wakefulness, she inhaled a deep, satisfied breath and released it slowly. Her eyes still closed, she rolled over and arched her arms over her head for an idle stretch. The action displayed her full breasts to their best advantage, stiffening her rosy nipples. Then she straightened her legs to stretch them, too, the sheet falling away as she spread them open, making visible the dark blond nest between her legs.

Again, Marcus stirred to life simply looking at her. She was utter perfection, beauty so unflawed and pure that he almost wished he hadn't sullied her.

Almost.

Instead, unable to help himself, he leaned over and traced the pad of his middle finger along her calf.

She moaned softly in response to his touch, smiling a very tempting smile, but she still didn't open her eyes. So Marcus drew his finger higher, up over her knee and along her thigh. She gasped a little this time, then uttered a low, erotic sound that seemed to come from deep inside her. But she still didn't open her eyes.

So Marcus leaned over the bed, moving his finger to the inside of her thigh, closer to the juncture of her legs. Della, in turn, opened her legs wider. Now Marcus smiled, too, and drove his hand into the silky thatch of curls hiding the feminine core of her. For long seconds, he furrowed her with light, slow, measured movements, pushing his fingers through the hot, damp folds of flesh. Deliberately, he avoided the sweet little spot that would drive her over the edge, but he skirted close a time or two, just to hear her swift intake of breath and ensuing groan of pleasure. When he pulled away again, he slipped a finger inside her, gently, since he knew she must still be tender from the night before. When she lifted her hips from the mattress to pull him deeper, he withdrew his finger, then inserted it slowly again. And again. And again.

When he knew she was at the verge of coming apart, he brought his thumb into the action, this time settling it resolutely on her now-drenched skin. It was easy for him to rub the pad of his thumb over her sweet spot, even when she began bucking her hips wildly at the onslaught. His fingers were covered with her essence now, making his manipulations come more quickly, more insistently. With one final push, he brought her to climax, making her cry out at the sensations that rocked her. She arched one last time, then slowly came back down to the bed. Marcus drew his hand up along her naked torso, leaving a trail of her own satisfaction in his wake, circling first one nipple, then the other, before moving his hand to the delicate lines of her neck.

"Good morning," he said softly, as if the last few minutes hadn't happened.

She was still breathing raggedly and trembling from his touch, but she managed to whisper, "Oh, yes. It is a *very* good morning. I could wake up that way every morning."

The words should have had panic racing through Marcus. The last thing he wanted to hear was a woman including him in her everyday life. Instead, he found himself warming to the idea of waking her that way each day. Doubtless because any man who started his day knowing he'd brought a woman to climax took with him a sense of power and well-being. Not to mention smugness. It made a man feel as if he could do just about anything.

It had nothing to do with simply enjoying an intimate moment with an exceptional woman.

"There's coffee," he said. "And breakfast. I didn't know what you'd like, so I ordered some of everything."

"Coffee," she said, still a little breathless. "Black," she added as he was about to ask how she took it—almost as if she were reading his mind.

That, too, should have made him bristle. He didn't want women understanding the workings of his brain. Mostly because few of them would approve of his thoughts, since they generally consisted of: A) women other than the one he was with, B) work, C) women other than the one he was with, D) how well the Cubs, Bears or Blackhawks were performing, depending on the season or E) women other than the one he was with.

But he kind of liked the connection with Della and, strangely, didn't want to think of anyone or anything other than her. So he only said, "Coming right up."

By the time he finished pouring two cups and

removing the lids from the cold dishes the steward had brought up, Della was out of bed and wrapped in a robe identical to his own—except that hers swallowed her—and was standing at the window the same way he had been earlier. The snow was still coming down as opaquely as it had been then, and he thought he saw her shake her head.

"It's like a blizzard out there," she murmured incredulously.

"No, it *is* a blizzard out there," Marcus corrected as he came to a halt beside her and extended a cup of coffee, black like his own, toward her.

She took it automatically with one hand, still holding open the curtain with the other. "How are we going to get…home?"

He noted her hesitation on the last word, as if home for her were a somewhat tentative state. Another clue that she really was only visiting here. Nevertheless, she'd assured Marcus that no one would miss her—at least not until today. Both thoughts bothered him a lot more than they should. For one thing, it shouldn't matter if Della was tied to another man, since Marcus didn't want to stake a claim on her anyway. For another thing, they'd both only wanted and promised one night, that should have been more than enough to satisfy their desire to enjoy each other for a little while. The fact that she was only in Chicago temporarily or might be involved with someone else should be of no consequence. In fact, it should reassure him that there would indeed be no strings attached.

For some reason, though, Marcus didn't like the idea of her being only a visitor to Chicago. He liked even less that she might be involved with someone else.

Too much thinking, he told himself, and way too

early in the day for it. It was the weekend. He was snowbound with a gorgeous, incredibly sexy woman. Why was he thinking at all?

"No one is going anywhere today," he said before sipping his coffee. "Not even the snowplows will be able to get out until this lets up."

Della turned to look at him, and that strange, panicked look he'd seen for a few moments last night was back in her eyes. "But I can't stay here all day," she told him, the panic present in her voice now, too. "I have to get…home."

Again the hesitation before the final word, he noted. Again, he didn't like it.

"Is there someplace you absolutely have to be today?" When she didn't reply right away, only arrowed her eyebrows in even more concern, he amended, "Or should I ask, is there some*one* who's expecting you to be someplace today?"

She dropped her gaze at that. Pretty much the only reaction he needed. So there was indeed someone else in her life. Someone she'd have to answer to for any kind of prolonged absence.

"Is it a husband?" he asked, amazed at how casual the question sounded, when he was suddenly feeling anything but.

Her gaze snapped up to his, flashing with anger. Good. Anger was better than panic. Anger stemmed from passion, not fear. "I wouldn't be here with you if I had a husband waiting for me."

Marcus had no idea why he liked that answer so much.

"What about you?" she countered. "Is there a wife somewhere waiting for you? Or has she come to expect this kind of behavior from you?"

He chuckled at that. "The day I have a wife waiting for me somewhere is the day they put me in a padded cell." When she still didn't seem satisfied by the answer—he couldn't imagine why not—he told her bluntly, "I'm not married, Della." Not sure why he bothered to add it, he said, "There's no one waiting anywhere for me." Then, after only a small hesitation, he added, "But there is someone who will be worried about you if you don't come…home…today, isn't there?" He deliberately paused before the word *home,* too, to let her know he'd noticed her own hesitation.

She inhaled a deep breath and released it slowly, then dropped the curtain and curled both hands around the white china coffee cup. She gazed into its depths instead of at Marcus when she spoke. "Home is something of a fluid concept for me at the moment."

Fluid. Interesting word choice. "And by that you mean…?"

Still staring at her coffee, she said, "I can't really explain it to you."

"Can't or won't?"

Now she did meet his gaze. But her expression was void of anything. No panic, no anger, nothing. "Both."

"Why?"

She only shook her head. She brought the cup to her mouth, blew softly on its surface and enjoyed a careful sip. Then she strode to the breakfast cart to inspect its choices. But he couldn't help noting how she looked at the clock as she went, or how her eyes went wide in surprise when she saw the time. It wasn't even eight o'clock yet. On a Sunday, no less. It seemed too early for anyone to have missed her if she had been able to surrender an entire night.

"You really did order a little of everything," she said as she began lifting lids. "Pastries, bacon, sausage, eggs, fruit..."

He thought about saying something about how they both needed to regain their strength after last night, but for some reason, it felt crass to make a comment like that. Another strange turn of events, since Marcus had never worried about being crass before. Besides, what else was there for the two of them to talk about after the kind of night they'd had? Their response to each other had been sexual from the get-go. They'd barely exchanged a dozen words between the time they left the club and awoke this morning—save the earthy, arousing ones they'd uttered about what they wanted done and were going to do to each other. Ninety percent of their time together had been spent copulating. Nine percent had been spent flirting and making known the fact that they wanted to copulate. What were they supposed to say to each other that didn't involve sex? Other than, how do you take your coffee or what did you think of *La Bohème?* And they'd already covered both.

She plucked a sticky pastry from the pile and set it on one of the empty plates. Then, after a small pause, she added another. Then a third. Then she added some strawberries and a couple of slices of cantaloupe. Guess she, too, thought they needed to rebuild their strength after the night they'd had. But, like him, she didn't want to say it out loud.

"Sweet tooth, huh?" he asked as she licked a bit of frosting from the pad of her thumb.

"Just a little," she agreed. Balancing both the plate and cup, she moved to the bed and set them on the nightstand beside it. Then she climbed into bed.

Well, that was certainly promising.

Marcus filled the other plate with eggs, bacon and a bagel, then retrieved his coffee and joined her, placing his breakfast on the opposite nightstand. Where she had seated herself with her legs crossed pretzel-fashion facing him, he leaned against the headboard with his legs extended before him. Noting the way her robe gaped open enough to reveal the upper swells of her breasts, it occurred to him that neither of them had a stitch of clothing to wear except for last night's evening attire, that wasn't exactly the kind of thing a person wanted to wear during the day when a person was trying to make him- or herself comfortable.

Oh, well.

He watched her nibble a strawberry and wondered how he could find such an innocent action so arousing. Then he wondered why he was even asking himself that. Della could make changing a tire arousing.

"Well, since you won't tell me why home is so fluid," he said, "will you at least tell me where you're making it at the moment?"

"No," she replied immediately.

He thought about pressing her on the matter, then decided to try a different tack. "Then will you tell me what brings you to Chicago?"

"No," she responded as quickly.

He tried again. "Will you tell me where you're from originally?"

"No."

"How long you're going to be here?"

"No."

"Where you're going next?"

"No."

"How old you are?"

"Certainly not."

"Do you like piña coladas and getting caught in the rain?"

He wasn't sure, but he thought she may have smiled at that. "Not particularly."

"How about fuzzy gray kittens, volunteering for public television, long walks on the beach, cuddling by firelight and the novels of Philip Roth?"

At that, she only arrowed her eyebrows down in confusion.

"Oh, right. Sorry. That was Miss November. My bad."

Her expression cleared, but she said nothing.

"What's your sign?" Marcus tried again.

That, finally, did make her smile. It wasn't a big smile, but it wasn't bad. It was something they could work on.

"Sagittarius," she told him.

Now that said a lot about her, Marcus thought. Or, at least, it would. If he knew a damned thing about astrology. Still, it was something. Sagittariuses were born in June, weren't they? Or was it October? March?

All right, all right. So he knew as much about her now as he had when he started his interrogation. Which was nothing. Hell, he didn't even know if she was telling the truth about being a Sagittarius or not liking piña coladas and getting caught in the rain.

Immediately, however, he knew she was telling the truth about those things. He had no idea why, but he was confident Della wasn't a liar. She was just a woman who wouldn't reveal anything meaningful about herself and who was sneaking around on a lover. Had she been a liar, she would have had a phony answer for every question he asked, and she would have painted herself as someone she wasn't. Instead, he was left with a blank slate of a woman who could be anyone.

But that, too, wasn't right, he thought. There were a lot of things he knew about Della. He knew she loved an esoteric art form that most people her age had never even tried to expose themselves to. He knew she cried at all the sad parts of an opera, and that she was awed by the intricacies of the music. He'd seen all those reactions on her face when he'd watched her last night instead of *La Bohème*. He knew she liked champagne. He knew she was enchanted by a snowfall. He knew she laughed easily. He knew she was comfortable in red, red, red. All of those things spoke volumes about a person.

And he knew she came from a moneyed background, even if she was currently making her way by having someone else pay for it. It hadn't taken an inspection of her jewelry or a look at the labels in her clothing—even though he had as he'd picked up their things from the floor while she slept—to know that. She was smart, confident and articulate, and had clearly been educated at excellent schools. She carried herself with sophistication and elegance, obviously having been raised by parents for whom such things were important. She'd been perfectly at ease last night in every venue he'd encountered her. If she wasn't the product of wealth and refinement, Marcus was a bloated yak.

Not that wealth and refinement necessarily manufactured a product that was all the things Della was. He need only point to himself to prove that. He'd been kicked out of every tony private school his parents had enrolled him in, until his father finally bought off the director of the last one with a massive contribution for the construction of a new multimedia center. The same contribution had bought Marcus's diploma, since his grades hadn't come close to winning him that. Not because he hadn't been smart, but because he hadn't given a damn. As for sophistication and elegance, he had gone out of his way as a teenager to be neither and had embarrassed his family at every society function he'd attended. He'd raided liquor cabinets, ransacked cars and ruined debutantes—often in the same evening—and he'd earned an arrest record before he even turned sixteen. If it hadn't had been for Charlotte…

He pushed the memories away and instead focused on Della. If it hadn't had been for Charlotte, Marcus wouldn't be sitting here with her right now. And not only because Charlotte's absence last night had allowed him to strike up a conversation with Della, not once, but three times. But because if it hadn't had been for Charlotte, Marcus would now either be in a minimum security prison for wreaking havoc and general mischief past the age of eighteen, or he'd be lolling about on skid row, having been finally disowned by his family.

"What are you thinking about?"

Della's question brought him completely to the present. But it wasn't a question he wanted to answer. Hey, why should he, when she wouldn't answer any of his?

At his silence, she added, "You looked so far away there for a minute."

"I was far away."

"Where?"

He sipped his coffee and met her gaze levelly. "I'm not telling."

"Why not?"

"You won't tell me anything about you, so I'm not telling you anything about me."

For a minute, he thought maybe she'd backpedal and

offer up some answers to his questions in order to get answers to some of her own. Instead, she nodded and said, "It's for the best that way."

Damn. So much for reverse psychology.

"For you or for me?" he asked.

"For both of us."

The more she said, the more puzzled and curious Marcus grew. Just who the hell was she? Where had she come from? Where was she going? Why wouldn't she tell him anything about herself? And why, dammit, did he want so desperately to know everything there was to know about her?

"All right, if you really want to know, I was thinking about something at work," he lied.

She said nothing in response, only picked up one of the pastries and enjoyed a healthy bite.

"Don't you want to at least know what I do for a living?"

"No."

There was that word again. He was really beginning to hate it.

"I work for a brokerage house," he told her, deliberately being vague about his position there, since he still wasn't sure how much to say. Actually, that wasn't quite true. He wanted to say a lot about himself. But not for the usual reasons. Usually, he only opened up to a woman by saying things designed to impress her, in order to get her more quickly into bed. But he'd already gotten Della into bed and still wanted to impress her. That was strange enough in itself. Even stranger was how he suspected that the best way to impress her was to *not* brag about himself. Well, not just yet, anyway.

She was swallowing when he told her about his job,

but it must have gone down the wrong way, because she immediately began to cough. A lot. Marcus was about to reach over to pat her on the back—or administer the Heimlich if necessary—but she held up a hand to stop him and reached for her coffee instead. After a couple of sips, she was okay. Though her face still looked a little pale.

"I'm fine," she said before he could ask. "That swallow went down the wrong way."

He nodded. And once he knew she really was fine, he picked up the conversation where he'd left off. "I work at—"

"Stop," she said, holding up a hand as if trying to physically stop the information from coming. "Don't tell me what you do or where you work. Please, Marcus. We agreed. No background information. No last names. No strings. No past, no present, no future."

"We also agreed only one night, " he reminded her, "but that's obviously not going to be the case. We're stuck here for at least another twenty-four hours. There's no harm in getting to know each other a little better. Unless you can tell me one."

He could see by her expression she could think of at least one. Maybe two. Maybe ten. Never in his life had he met a woman whose face was such an open book. Forget mind reading. A man could discover a lot about Della just by looking at her face. And what Marcus discovered now was that there was no way she was going to open up about herself to him.

Still, that didn't mean he couldn't open himself up to her.

"I work at Fallon Brothers," he said before she could stop him. He didn't add that the Fallons in the name of the multibillion-dollar company that employed him were his great-great grandfather and great-great uncle or that he was the fourth generation of the Fallon empire that would someday be running the company, along with his cousin Jonathan. Except that Marcus was the one who would become CEO upon his father's retirement next year, that meant he would be doing even less work than he was now as a VP, and then the partying would *really* begin. If Marcus was a fixture of the tabloid rags and websites now, he intended to be a permanent, cemented, superglued fixture once he didn't have to answer to his father anymore.

"Marcus, please," Della said again, her voice laced with warning. "Don't say another—"

"My permanent residence is on Lakeshore Drive," he continued, ignoring her. He picked up the pad and pen labeled with the hotel's logo that lay on the nightstand near his breakfast. "Here. I'll write it down for you," he continued, and proceeded to do just that. "But I also have places in London, Hong Kong, Tokyo and Aruba. All the big financial capitals, in fact."

When he looked up after finishing the last digit of his cell number—he'd given her the numbers of the office and his penthouse, too—she was gazing at him with much consternation.

Damn, she was cute when she was consternated.

"Since when is Aruba a big financial capital?" she asked.

"Since I spent a fortune on a house there and spend another fortune on rum every time I go down there."

"I see."

"I'm thirty-eight years old and a Chicago native," he added as he dropped the pad with his address and phone numbers onto the mattress between them. Not that Della even glanced at them. "As an undergrad, I majored in business at Stanford, then got my MBA from Harvard. Yes, I am that clichéd businessman you always hear about, except that I didn't graduate anywhere near the top of my class either time. Doesn't mean I'm not good at what I do," he hastened to add, "it just means I'm not an overachiever—that's where the cliché ends—and that I make time for more than work." He threw her his most lascivious look, just in case she didn't get that part. Which he was pretty sure she did, because she blushed that becoming shade of pink she had last night.

"Marcus, I really wish you wouldn't—"

"Let's see, what else is worth mentioning?" he interrupted, ignoring her. "I broke my arm in a skiing accident when I was eight and broke my ankle in a riding accident when I was ten. I have two sisters—both older and married to men my parents chose for them… not that either of them would ever admit that—along with two nieces and three nephews. My favorite color is red." He hoped she got the significance of that, too, and was more than a little delighted when color bloomed on her cheeks again. "My favorite food is Mediterranean in general and Greek in particular. I usually drive a black Bentley, but I also have a vintage Jaguar roadster—it goes without saying that it's British racing green—and a red Maserati. You already know about the opera thing, but my second greatest passion is port wine. My sign is Leo. And," he finally concluded, "I don't like piña coladas or getting caught in the rain, either."

By the time he finished, Della's irritation at him was an almost palpable thing. He'd sensed it growing as he'd spoken, until he'd halfway expected her to cover her ears with her hands and start humming, then say something like, "La la la la la. I can't hear you. I have my fingers in my ears and I'm humming. La la la la la."

Instead, she'd spent the time nervously breaking her pastry into little pieces and dropping them onto her plate. Now that he was finished, she shifted her gaze from his to those little broken pieces and said, "I really wish you hadn't told me those things."

"Why not?"

"Because every time I discover something else about you, it makes you that much more difficult to forget."

Something stirred to life inside him at her words, but he couldn't say exactly what that something was. It wasn't an unpleasant sensation, but neither was it exactly agreeable. It was just…different. Something he'd never felt before. Something it would take some time to explore.

"That's interesting," he told her. "Because I don't know one tenth that much about you, and I know you're going to be impossible to forget."

Still studying the broken pastry, she made a face, as if she hadn't realized what a mess she'd made of it. She placed the plate on the mattress on top of the pad of paper with the information he'd written down, though he was pretty sure she'd given it a quick glance before covering it. With any luck, she had a photographic memory. With even more luck, he'd notice later that the slip of paper had moved from the bed into her purse.

Her purse, he thought. Women's purses were notorious for storing information—probably more than a computer's hard drive. Not that Marcus could vouch for such a thing. He'd never had the inclination to search a woman's purse before. It was actually a pretty despicable thing for a man to even consider doing.

He couldn't wait to get into Della's.

"All right," she said. "I'll tell you a few things about myself."

Finally, they were getting somewhere. Just where, exactly, he wasn't sure he could say. But it was farther down the road than they'd been a few minutes ago. He wished he could see farther still, to find out if the road was a long and winding one with hills and valleys and magnificent vistas, or if it ended abruptly in a dead end where a bridge had washed out, and where there were burning flares and warning sirens and pylons strung with yellow tape that read Caution!

Then again, did he really care? It wasn't as if anything as minor as cataclysmic disaster had ever stopped him from going after what he wanted before. And he did want Della. He wanted her a lot.

Five

Della tried not to notice how Marcus seemed to have moved closer to her during their exchange. She couldn't help noting other things, however. Such as how love-tousled his dark hair was and how the shadow of beard covered the lower half of his face, both qualities evoking an air of danger about him. Or maybe it was just that she realized now how very dangerous he was. How dangerous her behavior last night had been. How dangerous it was to still be with him this morning with no way to get home. Not only because she was at greater risk of Geoffrey discovering her absence, but also because she was beginning to feel things for Marcus that she had no business feeling. Things that would make it more difficult to leave him when the time came.

She never, ever, should have allowed herself to succumb to her desires last night. Hadn't she learned the hard way how doing that led to trouble? The last time she'd yielded so easily to a man, her life had been left in a shambles. And Egan had been nowhere near as compelling or unforgettable as Marcus.

"I'm originally from the East Coast," she said, hoping that small snippet of information—even if it was a hugely broad one that could mean anything—would appease him.

She should have known better.

"Where on the east coast?" he asked.

She frowned at him and repeated stubbornly, "The east coast."

"North or south?"

"That's all I'm giving you, Marcus. Don't push or that's the only thing you'll learn about me."

He opened his mouth to say more, then shut it again. He was probably recalling how she'd told him she came from someplace hot, and he was assuming it was the latter. But he was clearly not happy about having to acquiesce to her demand.

She wasn't sure whether or not to confess anything about her family, mostly because she hadn't seen any of them for years. Even when they'd all lived under one roof, they hadn't really been much of a family. It was a sad thing to admit, but Della really didn't have feelings for any of them one way or another. Still, if Marcus wanted information, maybe that would be the kind to give him because it wouldn't cost her anything emotionally. It would also potentially be misleading, since most people stayed in touch with their blood relations, so he might think she hadn't traveled too far from her own.

"I have an older brother," she admitted. "And a younger brother, as well." The first had taken off when he was sixteen and Della was fourteen, and she hadn't seen him since. The other, last time she'd heard—which had been about ten years ago—had joined a gang. At the tender age of fifteen. No telling where he was now, either.

On the few occasions when Della thought about her brothers, she tried to convince herself that they'd been motivated by the same things she had, and in the same way. She told herself they'd gotten out of the old neighborhood and found better lives, just as she had. Sometimes she even believed herself. But more often, she feared they had screwed up everything in their lives, too, the same way she had.

"Nieces and nephews?" Marcus asked.

She only shook her head in response to that. To her, the gesture meant *I don't know.* To Marcus, let it mean whatever he wanted it to.

"Any injuries sustained as a child?" he asked, referring to his own.

She supposed she could tell him about the time she cut her foot on a broken beer bottle in a vacant lot during a game of stickball and had to get stitches, but that didn't quite compare to skiing and riding accidents. So she only said, "None worth mentioning."

"Schooling?" he asked.

The School of Hard Knocks, she wanted to say. It was either that, or her infamously crime-ridden high school or disgracefully underachieving elementary school. But neither of those would be the answer he was looking for.

Della knew he was looking for specific answers. He wanted her to be a specific kind of woman. The kind of woman who came from the same society he did and who lived and moved there as easily as he. She wasn't sure if he was the sort of blue blood who would turn his nose up in disgust at her if he knew her true origins, but he would, without question, be disappointed. She was glamorous to him. He'd made that clear. She was intriguing. A woman of mystery and erotica. The last thing he wanted to hear her say was that she'd grown up in a slum, had no formal education, had clawed and fought to win every scrap she ever had, and had taught herself everything she knew by emulating others.

So she said, "Yes. I had schooling."

He smiled at that. "No. I meant where did you go to—"

"My favorite color is blue," she told him. "And my favorite food is *fruits de mer*." Her French, she was proud to say, sounded as good as his Italian had last night. Unfortunately, *fruits de mer* was about the only thing she could say in French, and only because she'd practiced it for her menu lesson.

"After opera," she continued, "my greatest passion is—"

She halted abruptly. Now here was a problem. Because other than opera, Della really had no passions. She'd never really had an opportunity to find any. After landing the job at Whitworth and Stone when she was eighteen, she'd focused entirely on it in order to stay employed there. She'd worked overtime whenever she could for the money, and she'd spent the rest of her time trying to better herself in whatever ways she could. Reading classic novels from the library. Emulating the speech of actors in movies. Swiping magazines she found in the apartment's recycling bin to educate herself about fashion and etiquette and how to act like a refined human being. Opera had been the only indulgence she'd allowed herself, both because she loved it and it contributed to the kind of person she wanted to be. Beyond that…

Beyond that, she'd never had much of anything else to love.

"After opera…" Marcus prodded her now.

She looked at him, biting back another surge of panic. Never had she felt like a greater impostor than she did in that moment. She really did have nothing. Not a thing in the world. For the first time since leaving her life—such as it was—in New York, she realized how utterly empty her life had been and how absolutely alone she was.

"After opera…" She felt the prickle of tears sting her eyes. No, please. Anything but that. Not here. Not now. Not in front of Marcus. She hadn't cried since she was a child. Not once. Not when things had fallen apart in New York. Not when Geoffrey had told her she had to leave with him. Not during the eleven months since, when she'd had to turn her entire life over to someone else. Why now? Why here? Why in front of the last person on earth she wanted to see her cry?

She lifted a hand to shield her face and jumped up from the bed. "Excuse me," she said hastily as she headed for the bathroom. "I think I have an eyelash in my eye." As she was closing the door, she said over her shoulder, "If you don't mind, I'll take the first shower." Without awaiting a reply, she pushed the door closed and locked it, then turned on the shower full blast. Then she grabbed a towel and dropped to the floor, shoving it hard against her mouth.

I will not cry. I will not cry. I will not cry. I will not cry.

Her eyes grew damp, so she squeezed them shut.

I will not cry. I will not cry. I will not cry. I will not cry.

And somehow, by some miracle, Della kept the tears at bay.

The moment Marcus heard the rattle of the shower curtain closing in the bathroom, he crossed to the dresser where Della had laid her purse the night before. Okay, so maybe this one couldn't hold as much as a computer's hard drive, since it was one of those tiny purses women carried to formal events that was roughly the size of a negative ion. But it was large enough to hold a driver's license, cash and a cell phone, all of which he found inside, along with a tube of lipstick, a collapsible hairbrush, a plain metal keychain from which dangled a single key—house key, not car key—and, curiously, a computer USB drive. But no credit card, he noted, thinking it odd. Meaning she'd paid for her dinner and whatever else last night—a not inconsiderable sum—with cash. Interesting. He just wasn't sure exactly how.

He looked at the driver's license first and saw that it was from New York State. So she had been honest with him about being from the East Coast, but hadn't dissuaded him of his assumption that she came from a hot climate. Also interesting. But again, he wasn't sure how. Looking closer at the license, he saw that her full name was Della Louise Hannan and that she was thirty years old. In fact, she'd turned thirty yesterday. So last night was her celebration of reaching that milestone. The fact that she'd celebrated it alone heartened him—more than it really should have.

He glanced at her address, but it was on one of the higher numbered streets, outside the part of Manhattan with which he was familiar. He knew the better parts of New York like the back of his hand and had expected he would be able to pinpoint Della's address with little effort—doubtless somewhere near or on Fifth Avenue or Central Park. But this was nowhere close to either of those. He memorized it for future investigation, stuck the license in her purse and withdrew her cell phone, flipping it open.

Unfortunately, it was one of those not-particularly-smart phones, a bare-bones model that didn't contain an easy-access menu. So he had to poke around a bit to find what he was looking for, namely her calls received and sent. After a moment, he found both and discovered that every single one had been to and from one person. A person identified simply as Geoffrey.

Any optimism Marcus had begun to feel dissolved at that. Geoffrey could be a first or last name, but somehow he knew that it was definitely a man's name. He fumbled through more screens until he found her contact list and began to scroll to *G*. It took a while to get there. She had dozens of contacts, most listed by last name, but a handful—mostly women—were identified by their first names and, when the names were duplicates, by a last initial. Finally, he came to Geoffrey and clicked on it. There were two numbers listed for him, one designated a work number, the other a cell. The work number was a three one two area code—the man worked in Chicago. The cell number, however, was eight four seven, that was in the suburbs. It was a revelation that revealed nothing to Marcus. A lot of people lived in the 'burbs and worked in the city. And eight four seven covered a lot of 'burbs.

He reminded himself that Geoffrey could be a brother or a cousin or some guy she knew from high school. There was no reason to think he was necessarily a love interest or the man who kept her. Except for the fact that he was clearly the only person she was in touch with, in spite of her knowing a lot more.

But that was what men like that did, didn't they? They isolated the woman they wanted to own from her friends and family until she had no one but the guy to rely on. Whoever this Geoffrey was, Marcus was liking him less and less. That was saying something, because Marcus had begun to really loathe the faceless, nameless man in Della's life without even knowing for sure one existed.

He scrolled through more screens until he found the one that contained her photographs and clicked on those. There weren't a lot, but there were enough to tell him more about her. Several of the photos were pictures of Della with a trio of other women, all about her age. But it took him a few moments to realize one of the women in the pictures *was* Della, since she looked different than she did now—her hair was short and black, not the shoulder-length deep gold it was now. But why would she cover up a color like that? Or wear it so short?

Women.

Judging by the length of her hair now, the photos on her phone must be at least a year old. In a few of them, Della and the other women were dressed in business attire and seated at a table with girly-looking drinks sitting in front of them, appearing as if they were blowing off steam at the end of a workday. Okay, so Della had a job and wasn't necessarily the idle socialite he'd thought her to be. It didn't mean she hadn't come from money. She might have even been a client of some kind of one or more of the other women.

Scrolling further down through the pictures, Marcus finally found what he was looking for. Photos of Della, still with short, dark hair, seated with a man on a beach somewhere. A man who looked old enough to be her father, but who was good-looking and fit. Obviously very rich. Obviously very powerful. Obviously very married.

Marcus knew those things about the guy because he knew the guy's type. Too well. He worked and dealt with men like him every day. A lot of them were his friends. This had to be Geoffrey. Who else would it be? No one else in Della's contact list was identified informally by first name except for her girlfriends.

He navigated to her call list and saw that the last time Geoffrey had called Della was three nights ago. The last time Della had called him was yesterday morning. And the morning before that. And the morning before that. He kept scrolling. She'd called Geoffrey every single morning, weekday or weekend, always either at nine o'clock or within minutes before or after that hour.

Whoever Geoffrey was, he was keeping tabs on her. And he was making sure she was the one who called him, not the other way around. Another way to exert his control over her. Della hadn't made or received phone calls from anyone else for more than three months, at least, that was how far back her call log went. Whoever this guy was, he'd had her disconnected from her friends and family for a long time.

Was that why she had come to Chicago? To escape an abusive lover? But she'd told Marcus last night that one night was all she could give him, and she'd phoned Geoffrey yesterday, so obviously this guy wasn't out of her life yet.

He glanced at the clock on the nightstand. It was

approaching 8:45 a.m. In fifteen minutes, Della would have to make her obligatory daily call. But it was a safe bet she wouldn't do it unless Marcus was out of the room—not if she didn't want him to overhear her. He'd been planning to take a shower after she was finished, but now he was thinking maybe he'd wait a bit. 'Til, say, well after nine o'clock. It would be interesting to see how Geoffrey—whoever the hell he was—would react to Della's lack of cooperation. Maybe he'd call her instead. And that, Marcus thought, was something he definitely wanted to be around for.

It wasn't so much that he wanted to confirm his suspicions that Della was attached to another man in some way—a thought that made the breakfast he'd consumed rebel on him. It was because if someone *was* mistreating her, whether emotionally or mentally or physically, Marcus wanted to know about it. Then he wanted to know the guy's full name. And address. So he could hop in his car the minute the roads were clear, and beat the holy hell out of the guy.

When the shower cut off, Marcus hastily closed the phone and returned it to Della's purse with her other belongings. Then he placed it on the dresser in exactly the same position it had been before. Quickly, he grabbed the newspaper that had been brought up with breakfast and returned to the bed, picked up his coffee and pretended to read.

By the time Della emerged from the shower wrapped in her blue robe again and scrubbing her damp hair with a towel, he'd managed to stow the rage he'd begun to feel for that son of a bitch Geoffrey—at least for the time being.

"The shower is all yours," she said as she drew nearer to the bed.

"Thanks," Marcus replied without looking up from the paper.

From the corner of his eye, he saw her glance at the clock. Mere minutes away from nine. He kept his gaze fixed blindly on the newspaper.

Della's agitation at his tepid response was an almost palpable thing. "You, ah, you might want to hurry. You wouldn't want them to run out of hot water." He looked up long enough to see her shift her weight nervously from one foot to the other. "Since it looks like no one will be checking out today. There are probably quite a few people using the shower."

He turned his attention back to the paper. "I don't think a hotel like the Ambassador got to be a hotel like the Ambassador by running out of hot water on its guests. It'll be fine."

"But still…"

"First I want to finish this article about—" Just what was he pretending to read, anyway? Damn. He'd picked up the Style section. "This article about the return of the, uh, the chunky metallic necklace," he said, somehow without losing a drop of testosterone. "Wow, did those ever go out of style in the first place? And then," he continued, "there were a couple of pieces in the Business section that looked even more interesting." He looked at Della again and saw that panicked look from last night creeping into her expression. "It's not like I have anywhere to go," he said. "And it's been a while since I've been able to take my time with the Sunday *Tribune*."

"But…" Her voice trailed off without her finishing. "Okay. Then I'll, ah, I'll dry my hair." She pointed halfheartedly over her shoulder. "I have a hairbrush in my purse."

Marcus nodded, pretending to be absorbed by the fashion icon that was the chunky metallic necklace.

The moment her back was turned, though, he looked up in time to see her withdraw both her brush and phone from the purse, then stash the cell in her robe pocket. When she started to spin around again, he quickly moved his gaze to the paper.

"You know what?" she said suddenly. "I love ice in my orange juice, so I'm going to run down the hall and see if there's an ice machine on this floor."

And then, Marcus thought, she would duck into a stairwell to check in with the man who was trying to control her life.

"Call room service to bring some up," he told her, still looking at the paper.

"I don't want to trouble them with something like that. They must be busy getting everyone's breakfast to them."

Now Marcus put down the paper. "Then I'll get some ice for you."

"No," she said, a little too quickly and a little too adamantly. She seemed to realize she'd overreacted, because she forced a smile and said, "I'm, ah, I'm starting to feel a bit of cabin fever. A little walk down the hall will be nice."

"In your robe and bare feet?" he asked, dipping his head toward her attire—or lack thereof.

"No one will see," she said as she began to sidestep toward the door. "Everyone else is probably sleeping in."

"Not if they're keeping room service hopping and using up all the hot water the way you say."

"You know what I mean."

"We're not sleeping in," he pointed out.

"Yes, but we—" She stopped abruptly, obviously not wanting to bring up the reason they'd woken early. Or maybe it was just that she wasn't any more certain about what the two of them were doing than Marcus was. "I mean…even if someone does see me," she said, trying a different tack, "what difference does it make? It's a hotel. It's Sunday morning. There must be plenty of people still in their robes and bare feet."

Not when there was a blizzard raging outside, Marcus wanted to say. The only reason he and Della weren't dressed was because they didn't have anything to change into. But he didn't point out any of those things. If he kept trying to prevent her from leaving the room, she would come up with more reasons why she needed to get out. And if he pressed her, she was only going to get suspicious of him.

"Fine," he said, looking at the paper again…and seeing nothing but red. "Don't forget to take the key."

"Of course," she said as she collected that from the dresser, too. "I won't be but a minute."

If she was able to make that promise, Marcus thought, then her conversations with Geoffrey must not involve much. Just enough for the guy to make sure she did what she was told.

He waited only until the door clicked shut behind her, then hurried over to silently open it, enough that he could see her making her way down the hall. She'd already withdrawn the phone from her pocket and was dialing one-handed, meaning she'd still be in sight when her conversation began, so Marcus was bound to miss some of it. Impatiently, he waited until she rounded a corner at the end of the hall, then he slipped the metal rod of the chain lock between it and the jamb and stole after her at twice her pace.

When he peered around the corner, he saw her duck through another door that led to the stairwell and heard her speaking into the phone. But she was speaking softly enough that he couldn't distinguish a word. So he raced after her and halted by the door through which she'd exited and cocked his head close. Unfortunately, he could still only hear incomprehensible murmuring. So, as quietly as he could, he turned the knob and pushed the door open a crack, to see that she had seated herself on the top step with her back to him. So he opened it a little bit more.

"Really, Geoffrey, I'm fine," he heard her say. "There's no reason for you to come over. You'd get stuck in the snow if you tried."

He tried to discern something in her voice that sounded fearful or cowering, but, really, she did sound fine.

"I mean, yeah, the snow is kind of a drag," she continued, "but it's not like you ever let me go anywhere anyway."

So she wasn't supposed to be out and about, Marcus thought. His suspicions were confirmed.

"I had groceries delivered this week," she said, "and I downloaded a couple of books. Thanks for the Kindle and the Netflix subscription, by the way. It's helped a lot."

It was the least the son of a bitch could do, since he wouldn't let her go anywhere.

"What?" he heard Della ask. Then she laughed lightly. "No, nothing like that. That's the last thing I need. Mostly romantic comedies. I need something light and escapist, all things considered."

She paused, though whether it was because Geoffrey was talking or because she was looking for something else to say, Marcus didn't know. Finally, though, she began to speak again. "Okay, if you must know, *Bridget Jones's Diary, Love, Actually* and *Pride and Prejudice.*" There was another pause, then she laughed again. "Yes. I love Colin Firth. So does your wife, if you'll recall."

It really wasn't the kind of conversation Marcus had expected to hear her having with a married man who was keeping her a virtual prisoner. But neither did it quite dispel his suspicions that Della was being controlled. What really bothered him, though, was that there was something different in her voice when she spoke to Geoffrey that wasn't there when she was talking to him. A casualness and easiness, a lack of formality, that she hadn't exhibited with Marcus. As if she were actually more comfortable with the other man than she was with him. As if she and Geoffrey shared a relationship that was based less on control and more on trust.

Just what the hell was this guy to her?

Then Marcus heard her say something that chilled him.

"Look, Geoffrey, how much longer am I going to have to live this way? You told me I'd only have to do this for six months. That was eleven months ago. You promised me that if I did everything you guys told me to—"

Guys? So Geoffrey wasn't the only one? She was being passed around among a group? Had he really heard that right?

"—that then I'd be free," she continued. "But I'm still—"

The other man must have cut her off before she could finish, because Della stopped talking and listened obediently without saying a word for several minutes.

He saw her lift a hand to her head and push back her hair with a jerky motion that suggested she was anxious. She murmured a few uh-huhs, then slumped forward with her free hand braced on her knee and her forehead pressed to her palm.

Finally, with clear dejection—and maybe a little fear?—she replied, "Two weeks? That's all the time I have left?"

Until what? Marcus wanted to yell. What the hell was she talking about? What the hell did the man expect her to do that made her sound so unwilling to do it?

"Then it's really going to happen," she said with clear resignation, sounding more reserved than ever. "I'm really going to have to do it."

Do what, for God's sake?

"No, I understand," she said. "I'll go through with it. I mean, it's not like I have much choice, do I?" There was another pause, then she continued, "I know I promised. And I'll hold up my end of the bargain. I just…I didn't think it would be like this, Geoffrey. I didn't think I'd feel like this about everything." More softly, she added, "I didn't think I'd feel like this about myself." Then, because Geoffrey must not have heard that last, she said with unmistakable melancholy. "It was nothing important. Never mind."

Nothing important. Marcus felt a little sick to his stomach. The way she felt about herself wasn't important. This guy had her so wound around his finger that Della didn't even realize how unbalanced and unhealthy the relationship was.

Relationship, hell. What she had with this guy was a bargain. She'd said so herself. And it was obviously a bad one. A least on her end.

"So two weeks then," she said again. "I have two

weeks to get myself ready and in the right frame of mind."

Marcus hated to think what that getting ready would involve. He hated more to think about what the *right frame of mind* for such a thing would be.

He heard her answer a few more yes-and-no questions—with little more than a yes or no, sounding more and more like a child with each one—then heard her promise she would call tomorrow morning at the usual time. Then he heard the sound of her phone flipping closed.

He was about to pull the door to and hurry to the room before she caught him eavesdropping, but he heard something else that stopped him short—the very soft sound of muffled crying.

Something twisted inside him. He wasn't accustomed to hearing a woman cry. Mostly because he made sure he got involved with women who were as shallow as he was. At least where things like emotional involvement were concerned. Obviously, Della wasn't shallow. Obviously, she cared a lot about things like involvement. Even if she was currently involved with the wrong man.

Putting aside, for now, the fact that that word probably applied to himself as much as it did Geoffrey, Marcus pushed open the door and silently moved through it. He didn't know why. It would have been best for him and Della both if he went back to the room and pretended he knew nothing of her conversation. It would have been best if they spent the rest of the weekend pretending there was nothing beyond that room until the two of them had to leave it.

But when he saw her sitting on the stair landing with her feet propped on the carpeted step below her, her arms crossed over her knees, her head rested on her arms, her shoulders shaking lightly, he knew he could never go back to pretending anything. She still had the cell phone clasped in one hand, but it fell, landing with a dull thud when she began to cry harder, and she didn't bother to retrieve it. Instead, she surrendered to her sobs, muffling them by pressing her mouth to the sleeve of her robe. She was so lost in her despair that she had no idea Marcus stood behind her.

He didn't know what to do or say, could only stand there feeling helpless. It was an alien concept, this helplessness, and he didn't like it at all. His instincts told him to flee before she saw him, but his conscience—and he was surprised to discover he actually had one—dictated he do something to make her feel better. He let the two war with each other, to see who would win, but when instinct and conscience kept bickering, he stepped in and made the decision himself. He took a tentative step forward, then another.

As he was reaching down to curl his fingers over her shoulder, she whirled her head quickly around. When she saw him there, her eyes went wide with panic, and she stood so quickly, she almost pitched backward down the stairs. He wrapped his fingers around her wrist as she managed to right herself, but neither seemed to know what to say or do after that. For a long moment, they only stood silently looking at each other. Then, finally, Della stepped onto the landing with Marcus. He released her wrist, but brushed away a tear from her cheek with the pad of his thumb.

He had no idea what to say. He, Marcus Fallon, who had never been at a loss for words in his life. The man who could find a quip—whether appropriate or not—to alleviate any tense situation, who could make light of even the most difficult circumstances, couldn't scrape up one word that would ease the tension in this one. Some knight in shining armor he was turning out to be. But then, he'd never wanted to be a knight in shining armor.

Not until now.

"Are you okay?" he asked softly, threading his fingers into her damp hair.

Her eyes were huge, seeming larger thanks to the presence of her tears, making her look vulnerable and fragile. He knew she was neither of those things, and realizing that one conversation with Geoffrey could make her feel that way made him despise the man even more.

She nodded, but said nothing, only swiped at her wet eyes with both hands before shoving them into the pockets of her robe.

"You don't look okay," Marcus said. He lifted his other hand and wove those fingers through her hair, too, until he found the nape of her neck and cradled it in his palm.

"I'm fine," she assured him quietly, sounding anything but.

Knowing it would be pointless to pretend he hadn't heard her on the phone, he asked, "Who were you talking to?"

She looked at the phone on the floor, then up at Marcus. "How much of that did you hear?"

He thought about telling her he'd heard enough to know she was mixed up with someone she shouldn't be who was obliging her to do something she obviously didn't want to do, but that was kind of like the pot calling the kettle black. She shouldn't be mixed up with Marcus, either. Not being the kind of woman she was.

Namely, the kind whose emotions ran deeper than a sheaf of paper.

"Not very much," he lied. "I got worried when you didn't come back, so I came looking for you."

"Was I gone that long?"

He smiled, unable to help himself. "A few seconds was too long to be away from you."

When she didn't smile back, his own fell. "So who were you talking to, Della?"

"No one," she said. "No one important."

"He's the one you were worried about missing you today, isn't he?"

She hesitated for a moment, then nodded. "But not the way—" She expelled an irritated sound.

"Not the way what?" Marcus asked.

"Nothing." She pulled away from him, then bent down to scoop up her phone and the still-empty ice bucket. She looked at his face, but her gaze immediately ricocheted to the door. "Look, Marcus, can we go back to the room and forget this happened?"

When he said nothing, she looked at him again, her eyebrows arrowed downward. "Can we? Please?"

He crossed his arms over his chest, telling himself the gesture was *not* defensive. Marcus Fallon didn't get defensive. Marcus Fallon was the most offensive human being on the planet. "I don't know, Della. Can we?"

She glanced away again. "I can if you can."

Somehow, he doubted that. Because in addition to being the man who currently claimed Della as his own, Geoffrey seemed like the kind of man who wouldn't let her forget about anything.

In spite of that, Marcus nodded. Once. "Fine. Let's just forget it happened."

Still not looking at him, she replied, "You promise?"

"I do."

When she looked at him again, all traces of her former sadness were gone. She looked matter-of-fact and a little blank. She sounded that way, too, when she said, "Thank you. I appreciate it."

It was only then, when she sounded so formal, that Marcus realized she had, for a few moments, been as familiar with him as she had been with the man on the phone. But now the reserve was in her voice again. When he looked at her, he realized it was in her posture, too. They were indeed back to pretending. He should be relieved about that.

Instead, for some reason, now Marcus kind of wanted to cry.

Six

The mood in the room was considerably darker when they returned, Della couldn't help noticing. As was the room itself. She strode directly to the window and pulled back the curtains to find her worst fears confirmed. She wouldn't have thought it possible, but the snow was coming down even thicker and faster now than it had been when she'd first awoken.

She was never going to get out of here.

But then, what did she care? It wasn't as though she had anything waiting for her out there. Nothing but a nondescript house full of nondescript furnishings in a nondescript Chicago suburb populated by nondescript families. Middle-class, middle-income, middle America. The area had been chosen specifically because it was so unremarkable and unmemorable. Della had been living there for eleven months now, and even she would have been hard-pressed to describe from memory what any of her neighbors or their houses looked like. It was the last place she wanted to be, the last place she should be living, the last place anyone would think to look for her.

That, of course, was the whole point.

What made it worse was that she'd been expressly forbidden to interact with anyone or set foot outside unless absolutely unavoidable, and never without asking Geoffrey for permission first. So far, he hadn't considered a single one of her reasons to be absolutely unavoidable. Hence the sneaking around on those occasions when staying in the house would have driven her unavoidably insane.

As disconcerting as it was to be stuck here with Marcus until tomorrow—at least—a part of her thrilled at the prospect. She'd never felt as free or unencumbered—or uninhibited—as she did with him. She scarcely recognized herself this morning. Never in her life had she behaved with a man the way she had behaved with him. Not only the part about having sex with someone she'd just met, but also the sheer volume of sex they'd had. And the earthiness of it. The carnality of it. She'd *never* done things with other men that she'd done with Marcus last night. But with him, she'd felt no reticence or self-consciousness at all. Probably because he hadn't had any himself. On the contrary—he'd been demanding and exacting when it came to what he wanted. But he'd been every bit as generous when giving himself to her.

Something warm and fizzy bubbled inside, an unfamiliar percolation of both desire and contentment, of want and satisfaction. She'd felt it on and off throughout the night, usually between bouts of lovemaking when their bodies had been damp and entwined. But Marcus was on the other side of the room now, and their exchange in the stairwell had been a less than satisfying one. Even so, she could still feel this way, simply by being in the same room with him, knowing he wasn't leaving her. Not yet.

So really, why was she so eager to leave?

Maybe, she answered herself, it was because a part of her still knew this couldn't last forever and saw no point in prolonging it. The longer it went on, the harder it would be when it came time for the two of them to part. And they would have to part. Soon. The fantasy she and Marcus had carved out last night should have been over already. They should have separated before dawn, before the harsh light of day cast shadows over what they had created together.

They both had obligations that didn't involve the other—Della to Geoffrey and Marcus to the faceless woman for whom he obviously still had deep feelings. Even if he was no longer "with" her, as he claimed, it was clear he still cared very much for her. Too much for the possibility of including someone new in his life. Even if Della was in a position to become that someone new, which she definitely was not. Not here. Not now. Not ever.

How much *had* he heard of her conversation with Geoffrey? she wondered as she turned from the window and saw Marcus pouring himself another cup of coffee. She tried to remember if she'd said anything that might have offered a hint of what her life had become, but she was confident he would never suspect the truth. Because the truth was like something straight out of fiction.

He glanced up suddenly, and when he saw her looking at him, lifted the coffee carafe and asked, "Would you like some?"

It was a mundane question from a man who looked as if this was just another typical morning in his life. But Della could practically feel a vibe emanating from him that reached all the way across the room, and it was neither mundane nor typical. It was cool and distant, and it was, she was certain, a remnant of their exchange in the stairwell.

Was this how it would be for the rest of their time together? Strained and difficult? Please, no, she immediately answered herself. Somehow, they had to recapture their earlier magic. If only for a little while.

"Yes," she said, even though her stomach was roiling too much for her to consume anything. She only wanted some kind of conversation with him that wasn't anxious. "Please."

She strode to the breakfast cart, standing as close to Marcus as she dared, watching him pour. He had magnificent hands, strong with sturdy fingers and no adornments. Looking at his hands, she would never have guessed he worked for a brokerage house. He had the hands of someone who used them for something other than pushing the keys of a computer or cell phone all day.

"Do you play any sports?" she asked impulsively.

His expression was surprised as he handed her her coffee. "I thought you didn't want to know anything about me."

Oh, yeah. She didn't. She already knew more than she wanted to. So maybe it wouldn't hurt to know a little bit more. Ignoring the convoluted logic in that, she said, "I changed my mind."

He handed her her coffee with a resigned sigh. "Squash," he told her. "Three times a week. With another one of the—" He halted, as if he'd been about to reveal something else about himself, but this time it was something he *didn't* want her to know. "With a coworker," he finally finished. He sipped his coffee, then met her gaze levelly. "Why do you ask?"

"Your hands," she said before she could stop herself. "You have good hands, Marcus. They're not the hands of an office worker."

His eyes seemed to go a little darker at that, and she remembered that there were other ways his hands were good, too. Lots and lots of other ways. She spun around, striding away on slightly shaky legs. But when she realized she was walking straight toward the bed, she quickly sidetracked toward two chairs arranged on each side of a table near the window.

"It's still snowing," she said as she sat. "Maybe even harder than before."

Marcus strode to the window, lifted one curtain for a scant moment, then let it drop. "I guess we could turn on the TV to see what the weather guys are saying about how much longer this will last."

"I suppose we could."

But neither of them did. They only looked at each other expectantly, almost as if they were daring the other to do it. Della knew why she didn't. She wondered if Marcus's reason mirrored her own.

Finally, he folded himself into the other chair, setting his cup on the table beside hers. He crossed his legs with deceptive casualness, propped an elbow on the chair arm to rest his chin in his hand and, looking her right in the eye, asked, "Who's Geoffrey?"

Della felt as if someone punched her right in the stomach. Obviously he'd heard more of the phone conversation than he'd let on. She wondered how much. She wondered even harder about how she was supposed to explain her relationship with Geoffrey to Marcus. It wasn't as though she could be vague about something like that.

She reminded herself she didn't have to tell Marcus anything. Not the truth, not a fabrication, nothing. She could say it was none of his business, repeat their agreement not to disclose any personal details about each other—which he'd already breached a number of times, one of which had been at her own encouragement—and change the subject.

But she was surprised to discover there was a part of herself that wanted to tell him about Geoffrey. And not just Geoffrey, but about everything that had led to her meeting him. She wanted to tell Marcus everything about the mess that had started on New Year's Day to herald the beginning of the worst year of her life, about the months of fear and uncertainty that had followed, right up until her encounter with him at Palumbo's. She wanted to tell him about how she hadn't felt safe or contented for eleven months. About how lonely she'd been. About how hopeless and scared she'd felt.

At least until her encounter with him at Palumbo's. It was only now that Della realized she hadn't experienced any of those feelings since meeting Marcus. For the first time in eleven months—maybe for the first time in her life—she'd been free of anxiety and pleasantly at ease. She'd spent the past twelve hours ensconced in a perfect bubble of completeness, where nothing intruded that could cause her harm or pain. All because of a man whose last name she didn't even know.

But she couldn't tell him any of that, either.

She couldn't say a word. She'd taken a virtual vow of silence about what had happened in New York, and she'd been told that if she revealed anything to anyone, it could compromise everything. And then the last eleven months of living in hiding and being so relentlessly alone would have been for nothing.

Two weeks, she reminded herself. That was how long Geoffrey had told her she had to wait. Only two more weeks. In sixteen days, everything would be revealed, everything would come to light, and Della would be free of all of them. Of Geoffrey, of Egan Collingwood, of her boss Mr. Nathanson and everyone else at Whitworth and Stone. And even if that freedom meant losing everything she had now and starting all over somewhere else, even if it meant becoming an entirely new person, at least she would be done with all of it. She would be safe. She would be free. She would be *done*. She just had to hold on for two more weeks.

She opened her mouth to tell Marcus that Geoffrey was none of his business and then change the subject, but instead she hedged, "Well. So much for forgetting about the episode in the stairwell. And you promised."

"I've made a lot of promises since meeting you," he reminded her. "And I haven't kept many of them. You should probably know that about me. I'm great at making promises. Terrible at keeping them."

She nodded. "Good to know."

"Doesn't make me a terrible person," he told her. "It just makes me more human."

It also made him an excellent reminder, Della thought. His assertion that he couldn't keep promises illustrated more clearly why she couldn't tell him anything more about herself. She might very well become the topic of his next cocktail party anecdote or an inadvertently shared story with a colleague who had some connection to the very life she was trying to escape. Not because he was a bad person, as he had said. But because he was human. And humanity was something Della had learned not to trust.

"So who is he, Della?"

She hesitated, trying to remind herself again of all the reasons why she couldn't tell Marcus the truth—or anything else. Then, very softly, she heard herself say, "Geoffrey is a man who…who kind of…" She sighed again. "He kind of takes care of me."

Marcus said nothing for a moment, then nodded slowly. His expression cleared some, and he looked as if he completely understood. That was impossible, because there was still a lot of it that even Della didn't understand.

"You're his mistress, you mean," Marcus said in a remarkably matter-of-fact way. "It's all right, Della. I'm a big boy. You can spell it out for me."

It took a moment for what he was saying to sink in. And not only because the word *mistress* was so old-fashioned, either. Marcus thought she and Geoffrey had a sexual relationship. That he was a wealthy benefactor who was giving her money and gifts in exchange for sexual favors. That she, Della Hannan, the only girl in her neighborhood who had been determined to claw her way out of the slum *not* using sex as the means to get there, was now making her way in the world by renting herself out sexually to the highest bidder.

She should have been insulted. Instead, she wanted to laugh. Because compared to the reality of her situation, his assumption, as tawdry as it sounded, was just so… so… So adorably innocent.

Wow. If she *were* Geoffrey's mistress, that would make her life a million times easier. But number one, the guy was married. Number two, he was old enough to be her father. Number three, he looked like a sixty-something version of Dwight Schrute. And number four, there was no way he could afford a mistress when he had two kids in college and a daughter getting married in six months. After all, federal marshals weren't exactly the highest paid people on the government payroll.

Marcus must have mistaken her lack of response as being offended instead of off guard, because he hastily continued, "Look, Della, it doesn't matter to me. I'm the last person who should, or would, judge the way another person lives their life. I don't consider your situation to be appalling or bad or cheap or dirty or embarrassing or—" He seemed to realize how badly he was belaboring his objections—and he'd barely made a dent if he was going to be all alphabetical about it—something that made them sound even less convincing than they already did. He gave his head a single shake, as if he were trying to clear it. "Besides, it's not like I haven't, ah, kept a woman myself in the past."

Della wasn't sure, but he almost sounded as if he were about to offer her such a job now.

He tried again, holding out one hand as if he were literally groping for the right words. "What I'm trying to say is that I don't think any less of you for it. Sometimes, in order to survive in this world, people have to resort to unconventional methods. It doesn't make them any less a human being than anyone else. In a lot of ways, it makes them better than the people who don't have to struggle to make their way. Because they're…they're survivors, Della. That's what they do. They…they survive. That's what you are, too. You're a survivor. You're unconventional and you're… you're making your way in the world, and you're… You're surviving. You're—"

"No man's mistress," she finished for him, interrupting him before he broke into song. Or broke a blood vessel in his brain trying to cope. Whatever. "That's not how Geoffrey takes care of me, Marcus. We don't have a sexual relationship *at all*. I mean, Geoffrey is his last name. I don't even call him by his first name." It was Winston, and probably why he asked everyone to call him by his last name.

Marcus's relief was almost palpable. So much for not thinking less of anyone who survived in the world through unconventional methods. She might have laughed if he hadn't been right about one thing: She was surviving. And she did depend on Geoffrey's presence in her life to accomplish that.

Della couldn't give Marcus any details about what had happened in New York or the fact that she was a material witness in a federal case that involved her former Wall Street employer, Whitworth and Stone, and her former boss, Donald Nathanson. Especially knowing as she did now that Marcus worked for the equally illustrious Fallon Brothers. It wasn't unlikely that he knew people at Whitworth and Stone and moved in the same circles. Not that she feared he would report her to anyone, since no one there even knew—yet—about the case the feds were building. As far as anyone at Whitworth and Stone was concerned, the reason Della had stopped showing up for work without giving notice was because of personal reasons that would make performing her job intolerable. After all, Egan had been one of Whitworth and Stone's up-and-coming executives.

She had no way of knowing how Marcus would react to the revelation that Della had, in her position as executive assistant to one of the company's vice presidents, discovered a trail of illegal money laundering for unsavory overseas groups and the gross misuse of government bailout funds. She couldn't tell him about how she'd smuggled out files over a period of two weeks, or about going to the FBI with what she'd uncovered, or about how they'd immediately put her into protective custody with the U.S. Marshals and moved her out of New York to keep her under wraps until she could appear before the grand jury. She couldn't tell him how she'd been in hiding for the past eleven months while the feds built their case.

And she for sure couldn't tell him about how, once the trial was over—and Geoffrey had just told her the grand jury was convening in two weeks—she was probably going to be placed in the Witness Security Program, for safe measure. Even though her life hadn't been threatened, and even though none of the crimes committed had been violent ones, being a whistleblower wasn't exactly the most celebrated gig in the world. There was no way she'd ever find work in the financial world again.

And, well, even though it was unlikely, there was no guarantee there wouldn't be some other kind of retaliation against her. Some of the groups to which Whitworth and Stone had diverted funds had done some pretty terrible things in other parts of the world. It would be best for her to start over somewhere as a new person, with a new identity and a new life. A place where nobody knew her real name and where there was no chance she would ever be discovered.

A place completely removed from the spotlight Marcus so joyfully embraced in his own life. The last thing Della could afford was to have someone see her with him and recognize her from her former position. It would be even worse for her to be recognized after she'd given her testimony and put a lot of powerful people behind bars. At best, she would be a social pariah. At worst… Well, she didn't want to think about things like that.

Bottom line, there was no way this thing with Marcus could last beyond a weekend. He would never give up the big, showy lifestyle he loved. And she was a woman who had to avoid a big, showy life at all costs.

"Well, if Geoffrey isn't your…benefactor," Marcus said now, "then who is he? A relative?"

Stalling, she asked, "Why do you want to know? What difference does it make? Once the snow lets up, you and I are never going to—"

"I just want to know, Della."

"But why?"

"Maybe because you burst into tears after talking to the guy?"

Oh, right. That. That had kind of startled Della, too. But for some reason, during this morning's talk with Geoffrey, she had begun to feel keenly how truly alone she was. Geoffrey had been her only tie to the outside world for eleven months—at least until she met Marcus—and the conversations she had with him never lasted any longer than it took for her to check in every day and let him know she was okay. She always wanted to talk longer, since she never got to talk to anyone. Just to hear a human voice that wasn't coming from an electronic device. Every time, Geoffrey cut short the conversation because there was no reason to prolong it. Especially on weekends, he wanted to be with his family. Geoffrey always had things to do, places to go, people to see after he hung up. And Della always had to go back to the vast nothingness of waiting, all alone.

But this morning, after hanging up, she'd realized she *didn't* have to go back to being alone. This morning, she'd known Marcus was waiting for her. Someone who would talk to her. Someone who would share breakfast with her. Someone who would care for her. Be with her. Touch her. If only for a little while. And the thought that she would have such intimacy—even if it was only temporary and superficial—only made it worse to think about leaving it, leaving him, behind. Something about that was so intolerable. So bleak. So heartbreaking. Della simply hadn't been able to stop the tears from coming.

She felt the sting of tears threatening again and shoved the thought to the furthest, darkest corner of her brain. "He's not a relative, either," she said wearily.

When she didn't elaborate, Marcus asked, "Then how and why is he taking care of you?"

She expelled an impatient sound. "I don't guess you'd settle for 'It's complicated,' would you?"

He shook his head. "The directions for assembling a nuclear warhead are complicated," he told her. "Life? Not so much."

She managed a smile. "Trust me, Marcus. My life is currently *very* complicated."

"In what way?"

She couldn't tell him. She couldn't even hint. Maybe if he didn't have the job he had. Maybe if he wasn't a rich guy who didn't keep his finger on the pulse of the financial world. Maybe if he was just some average guy with an average job who didn't for a minute understand the workings of Wall Street…

She still couldn't tell him, she knew. So she stalled. "The place where I come from on the East Coast I had to leave a while back, because I—I got into some trouble there."

His expression wavered not at all. "You did something illegal?"

"No," she was quick to assure him. "Nothing like that. But I—I got caught up in something…not good… without intending to. So Geoffrey found me a place to live until things blow over. And I call him every day so he knows I'm okay."

"That doesn't sound complicated," Marcus said. "That sounds dangerous."

Della opened her mouth to contradict him, then realized she couldn't do that without lying. The chances of her being in danger were very small. The main reason the feds wanted to keep her under wraps was so no one at Whitworth and Stone would catch on to the fact that they were being investigated. And, too, to make sure Della didn't skip out on them after promising to give testimony.

"Not dangerous," she said. "They just want to be sure."

"And by *they,* you would mean…who?" Marcus asked. "The police?"

She shook her head, but didn't elaborate. It wasn't the police keeping an eye on her. Not technically. She was much further up the law enforcement ladder than that.

"Then who?"

"I can't tell you any more than that," she said. "I only said that much because I wanted you to know the truth about Geoffrey. I'm not…tied to him. Not that way."

Marcus hesitated a moment. "Are you…tied to anyone…that way?"

She should tell him yes. Make him think she was

involved with someone who meant a great deal to her. Maybe that would make it easier when the time came for them to part. If Marcus thought she was going home to another man, and if he thought she was shallow enough to have sex with him when she was involved with someone else, then it would be easier for him to put her in his past and keep her there.

If only she could do the same with him.

But instead of lying, her damnable honesty surfaced again. "There's no one," she said. "There hasn't been for a long time."

That, she supposed, was why she capitulated to Marcus so quickly and easily the night before. Because he was the first person she'd had face-to-face contact with for months. The first person who'd conversed with her. Who'd smiled at her. Who'd laughed with her. Who'd touched her. She'd gone too long without the most basic human need—the need to bond with someone else. Even if it was only over an article in a tabloid while waiting in line at the supermarket or sharing a few words while making change for another person at the Laundromat. People needed to be with other people in order to feel whole. Della hadn't had that for too long.

Marcus eyed her thoughtfully for another moment, then said, "So if it wasn't legal trouble, then what kind of trouble was it?"

"I can't tell you any more than I have, Marcus."

"Why not?"

"Because…it's complicated."

He dragged his chair around the table until it was directly facing hers, then sat close enough that their knees were touching. He took both of her hands in his.

"Look, there's a good chance I can help you out. I know a lot of people on the East Coast. Good friends. People I trust and who can pull strings. Some owe me favors. Others I know things about they'd rather not see made public so they'd be happy to grant me favors."

"I'm not sure those sound like friends to me."

"Maybe not. But I can still trust them to do what I tell them to. A lot of them are people with clout. They know people who know people who know people who can get things done."

And it was precisely that network of people who knew other people that was what Della was afraid of. Marcus might inadvertently tip her hand to the very people who were under investigation. His friends might be their friends, too. They were people like him—rich, powerful, enjoying an elevated social standing they didn't want to have compromised. They worked in the same industry. They were of the same tribe. Hell, he might not even want to help her if he found out what was at stake.

"You can't help," she said. "I appreciate the offer, Marcus, but you can't."

"How do you know?"

"I just do."

He studied her for another moment. "It's because you don't trust me. Because you just met me and don't know anything about me. But that doesn't have to be the case, Della. I—"

"It isn't that." And she was surprised to realize that was the truth. She did trust Marcus. In spite of having just met him. And she knew more about him after one night than she did about a lot of people she'd known in New York for years. But money made people do funny things. Lots of money made people do bad things. And billions of dollars… That made people do desperate things.

"There must be something I can do, Della," he insisted, his voice laced with something akin to pleading. "The thought of you being in trouble somehow…it isn't right."

Unable to help herself, she leaned forward and cupped his strong jaw in her hand. "You're a good guy, Marcus. And it's nice of you, wanting to help. But this is on me. Eventually, things will be better, but for now…"

She didn't finish. Mostly because, for now, she wanted to forget. She had another day and night to spend with Marcus, here in this hotel room where nothing from the outside could get to them. For now, she only wanted to think about that.

He covered her hand with his, then turned his face to place a soft kiss at the center of her palm. Warmth ebbed through her at the gesture. It was so sweet. So tender. So unlike their couplings of the night before.

"There must be something I can do to help," he said again. "Please, Della. Just tell me what to do."

She reached out with her other hand and threaded it through his hair, letting the silky tresses sift through her fingers before moving them to his forehead, his jaw, his mouth. "You can make love to me, again," she said softly. "You can hold me and touch me and say meaningless things that both of us know aren't true anywhere but here in this room. You can make me feel safe and warm and cherished. You can make me forget that there's anything in the world except the two of us. Do that for me and I'll—"

She stopped herself before saying *I'll love you forever.* Even though she was confident he would know it was hyperbole, it didn't feel like something she should put out there in the world.

He smiled, but there was something in the gesture that was a little hollow. His eyes were dark with wanting, however, when he reached for her and murmured, "Well, if you insist…"

Seven

Without hesitation, Marcus leaned forward and covered Della's mouth with his, dipping his hands into the deep V of her robe to curl his fingers over her bare shoulders as he deepened the kiss. Her skin was warm and fragrant from her recent shower, and the soft scent grew both stronger and more delicate as he slowly spread open the fabric of the garment. He traced the delicate line of her collarbone to the divot at the base of her throat, then his fingers stole around to her nape, spreading into the silk of her hair. It was still damp, and tangled around his fingers as if trying to trap his hand there forever. He wished they could stay embraced this way forever. He would never grow tired of touching her.

Della seemed to sense his thoughts, because her hands fell to the knot in her robe and untied it before she cupped his face in her palms. Spurred by her silent invitation, Marcus moved his hand lower, skimming the backs of his knuckles over the sensitive skin above her breasts before dragging his middle finger down the delicate valley between them. She gasped as he curved his fingers under one heavy breast and lifted it, then opened her mouth wider to invite him deep inside.

His last coherent thought was that he was responding to her the same way he had the night before, losing himself to her with a velocity and intensity that surpassed every other reaction, every other emotion, he had. The moment he touched her, everything else in the world ceased to exist. There was only heat and hunger, demand and desire, all of it commanding satisfaction.

Della seemed to understand that, too—or maybe she was feeling the same thing herself—because she was suddenly working feverishly at the sash of his robe, jerking it free so that she could dip her hands inside and explore him. Her fingers fumbled a bit as he gently began to knead her breast, but she recovered quickly, pushing his robe backward, over his shoulders and arms, spreading the fabric wider still. The next thing Marcus knew, she was on her knees in front of him, one hand curving over his taut thigh, the other moving on his hard shaft.

He nearly exploded at the contact, closing his eyes and sucking in a desperate breath as she gently palmed him. For long moments, she pleasured him that way, making his heart pound and his blood race until the rhythm of his passion roared in his ears. And when he felt her mouth close over him…

Oh, Della… Oh, baby…

When his fingers convulsed in her hair, she must have sensed how close he was to coming apart, because she stood and she took his hand in hers, then led him to the bed. When she pushed his robe completely from his shoulders and nudged him down to the mattress, he went willingly, watching with great interest as she shrugged out of her robe, too. She joined him in bed, but when she tried to face him, he cupped his hands over her shoulders, gently turned her around and positioned her on her hands and knees. Then he moved his hands to her hips and knelt behind her. He splayed his palms open on her back, skimming them up and down as he slowly entered her, then leaned forward until his chest was flush with her back. He caught her breasts in his hands and held them for a moment, thumbing her stiff nipples and eliciting a wild little sound from deep inside her. Then he withdrew himself slowly and thrust forward again. Hard.

She cried out at the depth of his penetration, curling her fingers into the fabric of the sheet. Marcus filled her again, even harder this time, eliciting a response from her that was hot, erotic and demanding. So what could Marcus do but obey her? He had never been with a woman who was so uninhibited about sex. Della both commanded and surrendered in ways no other woman ever had. She rode astride him, wrapped her legs around his waist when she was beneath him, demanded he take her kneeling and sitting and standing. When they finally surrendered to the climaxes that shook them simultaneously, she was bent over the chair where they had started as Marcus pummeled her from behind again. They came together, cried out their satisfaction together, rode out the waves of their orgasms together. Then, together, they relaxed and reined themselves in, and collapsed into the chair.

For long moments, they sat entwined, Marcus on the chair and Della in his lap, neither willing—or perhaps able—to say a word. Della opened her hand over the center of Marcus's chest, and he mimicked the gesture with her, noting how the rapid-fire beating of her heart kept time with his own. Gradually, it slowed along with his, too, until both of them were thumping along in happy, contented rhythm. At least, for now. Marcus suspected it wouldn't be long before their desires overtook them again.

But there had been something different in this coupling that hadn't been there before. He wasn't sure what it was or how it mattered, but it was there all the same. Yes, the sex had been hot, intense and carnal. Yes, they had both been consumed by an almost uncontrollable passion. Yes, they had said and done things they might not have said and done with other partners.

But there had been something else there that Marcus hadn't had with other partners, too. Not just a lack of inhibition, but a lack of fear. As if coming together with Della was simply a natural reaction to feelings he'd had for a very long time. He didn't know any other way to describe it, even though they'd known each other only a matter of hours. Sex with Della felt…right somehow. As if everything up until now had merely been a warm-up. *Della* felt right somehow. As if every woman before her had been practice. It meant something, he was sure of it. If he could only figure out what…

Marcus knew the moment he awoke that Della was gone. Even though it was still dark in the hotel room. Even though her fragrance still lingered on the pillow beside his own. Even though the sheets were still warm where she had lain. Maybe it had been the snick of the hotel room door closing behind her that woke him, he thought with surprising clarity for having just woken. Maybe if he hurried, he could still catch her before she made it to the elevator. Or if she had already disappeared into it, maybe he could hurry faster and catch her in the lobby before she made it out of the building.

But even as the thoughts raced through his head, he knew, too, that none of them were true. Because, somehow, he knew what had woken him wasn't a sound at all. What had woken him was the simple awareness, on some subconscious level, that Della was irretrievably gone and that he was irrevocably alone.

Alone, he marveled as he jackknifed up in the bed and palmed his eyes. It was a familiar condition, but it had never felt quite like this. It had never bothered Marcus to live alone or eat alone or work alone or do anything else alone. On the contrary, he'd always preferred his own company to that of others. Well, except for Charlotte, but that was because she had been a solitary creature herself. Marcus had never really felt as if he had that much in common with others, anyway. If he wanted companionship, it was easy to find it. There was always someone he could call or someplace he could go where, in a matter of minutes, he would be surrounded. Sometimes by friends, more often by acquaintances he pretended were friends, but the point was, he liked being alone.

He didn't like it this morning. Della's absence surrounded him like a rank, fetid carcass.

He rose and shrugged on his robe, knotting it around his waist as he moved to the window. In the sliver of moonlight that spilled through a slit in the curtains, he glimpsed a piece of paper lying on the table between the two chairs where he and Della had sat only hours ago.

Something hitched tight in his chest as he reached for it, because he thought it was a note from her. But it was the paper on which he'd written his numbers for her the day before. She'd left it behind. Because she'd wanted to make clear to him that she wouldn't be contacting him in the future.

She'd said she'd found trouble in New York. He couldn't imagine what kind of trouble a woman like her could be in. But if Della said she was in trouble, then she was in trouble. And if she'd said he couldn't help her…

Well, there she could be wrong.

Marcus crumpled the paper in his palm and tossed it onto the table, then pulled back the drape. The sky was black and crystal clear beyond, dotted with stars that winked like gemstones under theater lights. Uncaring of the bitter cold, he unlatched the window and shoved it open as far as it would go—which was barely wide enough for him to stick his head through—then gazed down onto Michigan Avenue. He'd never seen the street deserted before, regardless of the hour, but it was now, even though the snowplows had been through. People had yet to brave their way out into the remnants of the blizzard and probably wouldn't until after the sun rose.

For some reason, Marcus looked to his right and saw the red lights of a retreating car disappear around a corner some blocks up. Another light atop it indicated it was a taxi. Della's taxi. He knew that as well as he knew his own name.

As well as he knew her name, too.

Never had he been more grateful for his lack of decorum than he was in that moment. Had he not rifled through her purse, he would have nothing of her now save her first name. Well, that and the memory of the most unforgettable weekend he'd ever spent with anyone. Now there was another reason he wouldn't forget it. Because he knew where to find Della Hannan. Maybe not in Chicago, but he did in New York. And that alone was worth its weight in gold. Provided one knew the right people.

And Marcus definitely knew the right people.

His cheeks began to burn in the freezing temperature, so he closed the window and retreated into the room. He scooped up his jacket from the back of the chair as he passed it, then sat on the side of the bed and dug his phone out of the inside pocket. He and Della had switched off their phones shortly after entering the room and had promised to keep them off, and he had kept that promise—at least where his own phone was concerned. Now that their brief interlude was over, he switched it back on. A dozen voice mails awaited him. He ignored them all and went right to his contacts, scrolling through to the one he wanted. A private detective he'd used a number of times, but always only with regard to business. Nevertheless the man had an excellent reputation when it came to investigations of a personal nature, too. Just how excellent, Marcus was about to discover.

He punched the talk button, and after three rings, a voice on the other end answered. Answered with a filthy epithet, but then, that wasn't unexpected considering the source. Or the time of night.

"Damien, it's Marcus Fallon." He gave the other man a few seconds for the synapses in his brain to connect the dots.

"Right," Damien finally said. "Whattaya need?"

"I need your services for something a little different from what I normally hire you for."

"No problem."

"I have a name, a physical description and a former address in New York City. Can you find a person who's now living in Chicago with that?"

"Sure."

"Can you do it soon?"

"Depends."

"On what?" Marcus asked.

"On how bad the person wants to be found."

"How about on how bad *I* want the person found?"

It took another few seconds for more synapses to find their way to the meaning. "How much?" Damien asked.

Marcus relaxed. This was the thing he did best in the world. Well, other than the thing he and Della had spent the weekend doing. He started to turn on the bedside lamp, then remembered he would only see an empty room and changed his mind. "Tell you what," he said, "let's you and I negotiate a deal."

Della had been forced to part with a lot of things in her life. Her family, her friends and her home—such as they were—when she left the old neighborhood at eighteen. Jobs, offices and acquaintances as she'd climbed the professional ladder, moving from one part of Whitworth and Stone to another. An entire new life she'd built for herself in Manhattan. Soon she'd be parting with everything that had become familiar to her in Chicago.

But she didn't think any of those things had been as painful to part with as the crimson velvet Carolina Herrera gown and Dolce & Gabbana shoes, not to mention the Bulgari earrings and pendant and the black silk Valentino opera coat. Not because they were so beautiful and rich and expensive. But because they were the only mementos she had of the time she'd spent with Marcus.

The only physical mementos, at any rate, since she'd left behind the paper on which he'd recorded all of his phone numbers—something for which she was kicking herself now, even if she had memorized all of them. It would have been nice to have something he'd touched, something personal in his own handwriting.

And when had she turned into such a raging sentimentalist? Never in her life had she wanted a personal memento from anyone. Not even Egan Collingwood. That was probably significant, but she refused to think about how.

Besides, it wasn't as though she didn't have plenty of other reminders of Marcus, she thought as she watched Ava Brenner, the proprietress of Talk of the Town, write out a receipt for the return of the rentals. Della had her memories. Memories that would haunt her for the rest of her life. The way Marcus had traced his fingertips so seductively over the rim of his champagne glass when they were in the club. How his brown eyes had seemed to flash gold when he laughed. The way his jacket had felt and smelled as he draped it over her shoulders. How the snow had sparkled as it had fluttered around him on the terrace and came to rest against his dark hair. The way his voice had rumbled against her ear when he murmured such erotic promises during their lovemaking

But mostly, she would remember the way he looked lying asleep in their bed before she left him.

He'd been lying on his side facing the place where she

had been sleeping, his arm thrown across the mattress where she had lain—she'd awoken to find it draped over her. He'd been bathed in a slash of moonlight that tumbled through the window from the clear sky outside. His hair had been tousled from their final coupling, and his expression, for the first time since she met him, had been utterly, absolutely clear. He'd looked… happy. Content. Fulfilled. As if he'd learned the answer to some ancient question that no one else understood.

She'd tried to write him a note, had tried to capture in writing what she so desperately wanted to say to him. But when she'd realized what it was she wanted to say, she'd torn the paper into tiny pieces and let them fall like snowflakes into the tiny handbag that now lay on the counter between her and Ava. They had been silly, anyway, the feelings she'd begun to think she had for him. Impossible, too. Not only because she'd known him less than forty-eight hours. And not only because he was still carrying a torch for someone else. But also because Della wasn't the sort of woman to fall in love. Love was for dreamers and the deluded. And God knew she'd never been either of those.

"There," Ava said as she finished tallying everything. "If you'll sign here that we agree to agree that you returned everything safe and sound, I'll return the full amount of your damage deposit."

"But I'm late getting everything back," Della said. "I was supposed to be here at opening on Sunday. Not Monday."

Ava made a careless gesture with her hand. "I was supposed to be here Sunday, too. But Mother Nature had other ideas for all of us, didn't she?"

Boy, did she ever.

"So Monday morning is the next best thing," Ava continued. "I appreciate you being here so promptly."

Yeah, that was Della. Always perfect timing. Especially when it came to anything that would thoroughly disrupt her life. Had she been five minutes later meeting Egan on New Year's Eve, she would have missed seeing him with the woman she would learn was his wife. Had she been ten minutes later to the office on New Year's Day, she would have missed the memo to her boss that had set everything into motion. She would still be living her life blissfully unaware in New York. Even if she'd ultimately realized Egan was married, and even if she'd quit her job because of him, she would have found another position elsewhere on Wall Street in no time. She would still be picking up her morning coffee at Vijay's kiosk, would still be enjoying Saturdays in Central Park, would still have the occasional night at the Met when she could afford it.

And she never, ever, would have met Marcus.

She couldn't decide if that was a good thing or not. Traditional thinking said it was better to have loved and lost than never to have loved at all, but Della wondered. Maybe it was better to never know what you were missing. Not that she *loved* Marcus. But still…

"Did you enjoy *La Bohème,* Miss Hannan?" Ava asked, bringing Della's thoughts back to the present.

She smiled, only having to fake part of it. "It was wonderful," she said. "I can't remember the last time I enjoyed an evening so much." Or a night afterward, she added to herself. Or a day after that. Or a night after that.

"I've never been to the opera," Ava told her. "Never mind a red-carpet event like opening night. It must have been very exciting, rubbing shoulders with such refined company in a gorgeous setting like the Lyric with everyone dressed in their finest attire."

The announcement surprised Della, though she wasn't sure why. Certainly there were a lot of people out there, especially her age, which Ava seemed to be, who didn't care for opera enough to see it performed live. It was the red-carpet comment and the breathless quality of her voice when she talked about the refined company that didn't gibe. There was an unmistakable air of refinement and wealth about Ava that indicated she must move in the sort of social circle that would promote opera attendance and red-carpet events, never mind gorgeous settings and fine attire.

Both times Della had encountered Ava, the other woman had exuded elegance and good breeding, and had been extremely well put together in the sort of understated attire that only reinforced it. Today, she wore a perfectly tailored taupe suit with pearly buttons, her only jewelry glittering diamond studs in her ears—large enough and sparkly enough for Della to guess they alone cost a fortune. Her dark auburn hair was arranged in a flawless chignon at her nape, and her green eyes reflected both intelligence and sophistication.

Standing across the counter from her, Della was more aware than ever of her impoverished roots. Although she was dressed nicely enough in brown tweed trousers and an ivory cashmere sweater under her dark chocolate trench coat, she felt like more of an impostor than ever. Ava Brenner obviously came from the sort of old money background that Della had had to insinuate herself into—and still never really belonged in. She recognized all the signs, having been surrounded by people like Ava in her job.

Not for the first time, she wondered why the other

woman ran a shop like this. She was probably rich enough on her own to do nothing but be idly rich, but she'd been at the boutique late Saturday afternoon when Della picked up her clothes, and she was here bright and early Monday morning, too. For some reason, that made Della glance down at Ava's left hand—no wedding ring. No engagement ring, for that matter. She wondered if Ava had ever loved and lost and how she felt about it.

Della pushed the thought away. Women like Ava could pick and choose whomever they wanted for a mate. She was beautiful, smart, successful and chic. Once she set her sights on a man, he wouldn't stand a chance. He would love her forever and make her the center of his universe. No way would she settle for a one-night stand with a guy she'd never see again.

"Well," Ava said now as she counted out the last of Della's refund, "I hope you'll keep Talk of the Town in mind the next time you need to look your best."

Right. The next time Della would need to look her best would be when she appeared before the grand jury in two weeks. Somehow, though, she was pretty sure one of her suits from her old life would work just fine for that. But maybe in her new life…

She pushed that thought away, too. Her new life would be miles away from Chicago. And there was little chance she'd need to don haute couture for anything in it. It would be nothing but business attire, since she'd be doing little other than establishing herself in a new job, starting all over again from square one. It was going to be a long time before she was earning enough to recapture the sort of life she'd had in New York.

It would be even longer before she trusted any man enough to let him get close to her again.

That hadn't been the case with Marcus, a little voice

inside her head piped up. *You got close to him pretty fast. And you trusted him enough to have sex with him.*

But Marcus was different, Della assured the little voice. Marcus had been a one-night stand. It was easy to trust someone you knew you were never going to see again.

Seriously? the voice asked. *Is that the reason you want to go with?*

Um, yeah, Della told the voice.

Fine. But you're only kidding yourself, you know.

Shut up, voice.

"Be careful out there," Ava said, bringing Della's attention back around. "The snow may have stopped, but there are still some slick spots on the sidewalk and slush in the gutters and all kinds of things that could harm you."

Oh, Ava didn't need to tell Della that.

"Don't worry," she said. "I can take care of myself."

And she could, Della knew. She'd been doing it her entire life. That wasn't going to change simply because she had a new life to get under way. Especially since there wouldn't be any Marcuses in her future. Men like him only came along once in a lifetime—if even that often. No way would a man like that show up twice.

In two weeks, Della would be embarking on a second life. A life in which she'd be alone again. Alone still, really, since Egan had never actually been with her the way he could have—should have—been.

Only once in her life had Della really felt as if she was sharing that life—sharing herself—with someone else. And it was someone she would never—could never—see again.

Eight

Nine days after returning the red dress to Talk of the Town, Della was still struggling to go back to her usual routine. It felt like anything but routine now that she had memories of Marcus shouldering their way into her thoughts all the time. The safe house where the feds had placed her was what one would expect to find in middle-class, middle-income, Middle America: sturdy early American furnishings in neutral colors and synthetic fabrics, with white walls and artwork that might have been purchased at any yard sale in suburbia. The lack of personality on the house's part had only contributed to Della's feelings of entrapment during her time here, but that feeling was compounded in the wake of her separation from Marcus. The handful of days she had left here stretched before her like an oceanful of centuries.

And she was even more fearful now than she'd been

before about the uncertainty of her future. Before, she'd been prepared to face life on her own and had felt reasonably certain she would be able to manage. But now she knew what might have been under other, better circumstances. Wonderful. Life with Marcus would have been wonderful. Because he was wonderful. No other man would ever be able to hold a candle to him.

She sighed fitfully. There he was again, at the front of her thoughts. She told herself the only reason she thought him so wonderful was because she knew so little about him. Anyone could be wonderful for thirty-six hours in a small room with no one watching. The time she'd spent with him had been a fantasy. *He'd* been a fantasy. They'd both been playing the role of the phantom, perfect lover. Once free of the hotel room, he might be the same kind of man Egan had turned out to be.

How could she be so certain that Marcus hadn't lied about everything that weekend anyway? He'd said the woman he was waiting for was out of his life, but what if he'd only said that to further his seduction of Della? How could she expect him to have been completely open and honest about himself when she hadn't been open and honest about herself? Once she learned more about him, once she'd discovered what kind of person he really was…

But then, how could she do that when she would never see him again? When she didn't even know his last name? At this rate, he would always be a fantasy to her, and as time went on, he'd grow into an even more legendary lover and all-around great guy, and then she'd really never have a chance to fall in lo—ah, she meant—never have a chance to appreciate someone else she might be compatible with.

A way to counter that possibility came to her immediately, and it wasn't the first time the idea had crept into her brain. This time, it wasn't creeping, though. This time, it was stampeding like a herd of wild, trumpeting wildebeest. And those wildebeest were running right to the laptop in the bedroom.

Maybe she didn't know Marcus's last name. But she knew where he worked. Fallon Brothers. The company must employ thousands of people nationwide, but Marcus wasn't the most common name in the world, and she could narrow the search to Chicago. He'd said himself he was a fixture on a number of websites, so by doing an internet search of his first name and Fallon Brothers and the city of Chicago, she'd probably get a lot of hits. A lot of *notorious* hits. Maybe if she could see him on notorious sites, surrounded by notoriously beautiful women in notoriously compromising situations, she'd realize he wasn't the kind of man she needed in her life anyway. Maybe if she could see him in his natural state of debauchery, it would be easier to forget him.

What could it hurt? She would never see him again. He would never be able to find her, if he was even trying. In a matter of days, she would be swallowed up even deeper into the system with a new name, address and social security number. And then there would *really* be no way for him to find her.

As she folded herself onto the bed and fired up the laptop, Della's heart began to race, and her stomach erupted with nerves. She wasn't sure what was more exciting—the prospect of learning more about Marcus or the prospect of seeing his face again, even if it was just in an online photo.

She brought up the Google page and clicked on the

image option, then typed in the name *Marcus* and the word *Chicago,* along with the words *Fallon Brothers* in quotation marks. And in the blink of an eye—literally—she was staring at the first three rows of what the site told her was hundreds of images. Marcus was in every one of the first batch. And the second, third and fourth batches, too. As she scrolled down the page, she saw him in even more, sometimes alone, but more often with women. Lots of women. Lots of different women. All of them smiling. All of them clinging. All of them beautiful.

Only when Della moved her hand to run her finger over the mouse pad did she realize it was trembling. In fact, all of her was trembling. She had no idea why. Maybe because seeing Marcus online only reaffirmed that the weekend had really happened. That he really existed. That she had some link, however tenuous, to him. From now on, no matter where she was, or what she was doing, or who she was, she would still be able to find him. She would have physical photographs of him to go along with the insubstantial pictures in her mind. He wouldn't be ephemeral, as she had feared. He could still be with her forever.

Even if he wouldn't be with her forever.

She flexed her fingers to calm them and chose a photo of Marcus alone to move the mouse over. It wasn't one of the candid shots, but rather a posed, formal portrait that must have been one he'd had taken for professional reasons. It was probably from the Fallon Brothers website. When the cursor moved over it, the picture grew larger and added information, starting with a url, then the fact that it was a jpg—sized seventy-something by eighty-seven-something else—then, finally, a description that read Marcus Fallon, Chief Investment Officer, Fallon Brothers Chicago.

Della's hand began to tremble again, and her stomach pitched with nausea.

Marcus Fallon. He was a member of the Fallon family and one of the highest ranking executives in the company. She'd known he must be well-connected to the business. It didn't take seeing him in a place like the Windsor Club to know how well-paid he was or how many perks he must have enjoyed. But this… This went beyond well-connected. And it went way beyond well-paid with excellent perks. He was a descendent of some of the very people who had designed the way the country did business. His ancestors had been the equivalent to royalty in this capitalist society. As such, he was, for all intents and purposes, a prince.

So CinderDella's Prince Charming really was a prince. And she… Well, that would put her in the role of pauper, wouldn't it?

She recalled his assurances that he had friends with clout on the East Coast who might be able to help her out, and her stomach pitched again. Those friends were probably of equal rank to him in New York's financial district. Some of them might very well be officers of Whitworth and Stone. She wouldn't be surprised if some of his friends ended up behind bars because of her. Oh, yeah. He would have loved to help her once he learned what the nature of her "trouble" was. He would have been on the phone in no time flat, tipping off everyone he knew that might be at risk.

Any small hope that Della might have been harboring that she and Marcus still had a chance—and she was surprised to discover she had indeed been entertaining hope, and not such a small amount at that—was well and truly squashed at the realization. Once she gave her testimony to the grand jury, she would be an exile in the financial world. It didn't matter that she was bringing to light illegal activity that should be stopped and punished. No one on Wall Street was going to applaud her, and every door would slam in her face. People like Marcus—and Marcus himself—would want nothing to do with her. She would be bringing down some very powerful people. And other very powerful people didn't like it when that happened. Especially when it was a peasant doing the tearing down.

Unable to help herself, Della clicked on the link and found herself looking at a larger version of Marcus's photo, and it was indeed on the Fallon Brothers website. She read that he was the eldest great-grandson of one of Fallon Brothers' founding members who would be moving into his father's position as CEO in the not-too-distant future. She read about his hobbies and favorite pastimes—she already knew about opera, squash and port, but the sailing and polo came as something of a surprise—and about his education at the country's finest schools. All in all, it was a sanitized version of the Marcus she knew and wasn't particularly helpful. Once she got past the part about him being the crown prince of the Chicago financial kingdom, she meant.

So she went back to Google and began clicking on some of the other pictures she'd found. There was one of Marcus with a former Miss Illinois taken at a New Year's Eve party last year. That would have been right around the time Della's world was beginning to fall apart, but Marcus looked as if he didn't have a care in the world. Another photo showed him and a *very* generously endowed redhead at a fundraiser for a children's hospital. Yet another had him sitting on the deck of a high-rise with Lake Michigan in the background and a *very* generously endowed blonde in his lap. The next was a picture of him at some red-carpet event with a woman who looked very much like a certain Hollywood starlet who was known for appearing in public without underwear.

This was how she needed to remember him, Della told herself. In photos taken within months of each other in which he was with a different woman every time. She had to stop thinking of him as Prince Charming and start recognizing the fact that he was just another rich guy with a sense of entitlement who took advantage of everyone who crossed his path. His emotions ran as deep as a strand of hair, and he thought of little other than how to make his own life more enjoyable. He had probably stopped thinking about Della the moment he woke up and found her gone.

He wasn't Prince Charming from a fantastic castle in an enchanted land, she told herself again. He was a big, nasty toad from the toxic swamp of entitlement. The sooner she forgot about him, the better.

She told herself the same thing in a dozen different ways, every time she clicked on a new photograph. But her memories of him crowded out her admonitions. She remembered his smile and his tender touches, and the genuine sadness in his eyes when he had talked about the woman who hadn't been with him that night. That was the real Marcus Fallon, she knew. Maybe not Prince Charming. But not a toad, either.

She just hoped that, wherever he was, he was remembering her fondly, too.

Marcus sat in the study of his Lakeshore Drive penthouse, his black silk robe open over a pair of matching pajama bottoms, nursing a glass of port and sifting through a thin file of information that had been couriered to him that afternoon. Beyond the expansive picture window to his right, Lake Michigan was as inky black as the sky above it, dotted here and there with lights from commercial vessels in the usual shipping lanes that twinkled the same way the stars above them did.

He didn't much notice the vista, however, settled as he was in a boxy, overstuffed club chair that was bathed in the pale amber glow of a floor lamp beside it. Much of the room was amber, in fact, from the coppery fabric of the chair to the golds and browns of the area rug, to the bird's-eye maple paneling to the small, sculpted bronze originals displayed on the built-in shelves. Marcus liked the warm colors. They made him feel calm.

Usually.

Tonight, he felt anything but. Because the file he had thought would be stuffed with information about Della Louise Hannan of New York City contained little he couldn't have discovered by himself. That didn't, however, make what information was here any less interesting. Especially the part about her having worked at Whitworth and Stone, one of Wall Street's biggest—if not *the* biggest—powerhouses. Marcus knew more than a few people who worked there. And since Della's position as executive assistant to one of its executives would have had her moving in the upper echelon of the business, there was a small chance someone he knew there had at least made her acquaintance. Tomorrow, as soon as the business day started on the East Coast, he would make some phone calls.

Not that having any information about Della's time at

Whitworth and Stone would help him much now, since she hadn't worked at the brokerage house for nearly a year. In fact, Della Hannan had pretty much dropped off the face of the map in mid-January of this year and hadn't been seen or heard from since. The apartment where she had lived was now being rented by a married couple who had moved into it in March—and it had been advertised as being a "furnished apartment," because Della had left virtually all of her belongings behind, and her landlord had claimed them on the grounds she hadn't fulfilled the terms of her lease. She'd left her job as abruptly, had simply not come to work one day…or any day afterward.

What was even more troubling was that, in spite of her sudden disappearance, no one had reported her missing. Not a family member, not a friend, not a neighbor, not a lover, not her employer. There was no police report on file, no formal complaint from her landlord, nothing in her personnel file at Whitworth and Stone about why she may have stopped coming to work after more than a decade of not missing a single day.

There was, however, office chatter about why that may have happened. Word in her department was that Della had been dating an executive in another part of the business who had turned out to be married. Whether or not Della had known about his marital status was a bit murky. Either she had known and then been angry that the man refused to leave his wife, or she hadn't known and had left once she discovered the truth. In either event, her office affair seemed to be the reason everyone cited as to why she no longer worked at the company.

It was a reasonable enough explanation. It might even

offer a reason for why she had left New York. Except that she was a native New Yorker without family or friends in any other part of the country to whom she might turn for help. Except for the fact that she hadn't started working somewhere else. Except for the fact that there was no record of her having done *any*thing, *any*where, after January 16th. She hadn't applied for any jobs. Hadn't applied for a new driver's license in any state. Hadn't accessed her bank accounts or used her credit cards. Her cell phone service had been canceled due to her failure to pay, in spite of her having had a tidy sum in both a checking and a savings account, neither of which had been touched.

His thoughts halted there for a moment. Her cell phone. He recalled scrolling through her information at the hotel, all the photos and numbers she still had, even though she hadn't called any of them. Obviously she was using a different number now than the one that had been cut off, but why wasn't there a record of her having applied for a new number? Even if she'd requested it be unlisted, his man Damien should have been able to find out what it was. Why hadn't he?

And why had she had all her contacts from the old phone transferred to a new one, clearly wanting to hang on to them even if she wasn't using any of them? He spared a moment to give himself a good mental smack for not bringing up her number on her phone when he'd had it in his hand. Then he cut himself a little slack because he'd been in such a hurry and so preoccupied by the photos he'd discovered. Still, had he remembered to get her number, it really would have made things a lot easier.

He returned his attention to the P.I.'s report. Marcus might have begun to wonder whether or not the woman he'd met even *was* Della Hannan if it hadn't been for the photographs contained in the file along with the information. He had the picture from her ID badge at Whitworth and Stone, along with copies of photos from her high school yearbook and early driver's licenses. The woman he had met was definitely the same woman in those photos, but, as had been the case with the pictures on her phone, her hair was shorter and darker in all of them.

She'd changed her appearance after she disappeared, but not her name, and his contact hadn't found any evidence that she had any aliases. So there was little chance she was some con artist and a very good chance that everything she had told him about being in trouble was true. The file also had information about Della's early life, which also corroborated what she had told him. There was information about the two brothers she had said she had—one older, one younger. What she hadn't mentioned—probably because she hadn't wanted to dissuade him of his completely wrong ideas—was that she had come from a notoriously bad neighborhood and wasn't the product of wealthy society at all.

At the end of the file was a handwritten note from Damien. It was short and to the point:

> *The only time someone drops off the face of the planet like this, it's because they're in the hands of the feds. Or else they're trying to avoid the feds and are tapped into a network that makes that happen. I have a friend on the government payroll who owes me a favor. I'll let you know what he finds out.*

Marcus lifted his glass to his mouth. But the warm, mellow port did little to soothe the tumultuous thoughts tumbling in his head. So the trouble Della had found herself in in New York was criminal, after all. But which was it with her? Was she helping the authorities or hiding from them?

Who the hell was she? In a lot of ways, she seemed like a stranger to him now. But in another way, she felt even closer than she had been before.

But why and how had she disappeared so completely, not once but twice now? Because she had disappeared again. Damien hadn't been able to find a single clue that might indicate where she was living in Chicago, how long she had been here or when she was planning to leave. Another reason why the man had made the assumption he had in the note, Marcus was certain. Della herself had said she was in trouble. Whether she was helping or hiding, it must be something pretty bad for her to have made herself so invisible.

He closed the file and tipped his glass to his lips again but the glass was empty. He grimaced as he set both the file and the glass on the end table, then rose. He started to walk away, then stopped and went back. For the glass, he told himself. To put it in the dishwasher before he went to bed.

But he picked up the file, too, and opened it again. He took out the photo of Della that had been on her ID badge at Whitworth and Stone. She was the picture of businesslike gravity, unsmiling, wearing no makeup, her short, mannish hair combed back from her face. She looked nothing like she had during the time he'd spent with her. Even after she had washed off her makeup, she had still been beautiful. Even after the inconvenience of the snow, she had still been happy.

And so had he.

That was when Marcus began to understand his

obsession with finding her. Not because she was a mysterious woman in red he couldn't get out of his mind. But because the time he'd spent with her had marked the first time in his life he'd been truly happy. He wasn't sure of the why or when or how of it. He only knew that, with Della, he'd felt different. The same way Charlotte had entered his life when he was a teenager and guided him toward finding contentment with himself, Della had entered his life when he was an adult and guided him toward finding contentment with someone else.

That was what had always been missing before—the sharing. He had shared his life with Charlotte while she was alive, and that had made living it so much better. With Della, he had shared himself. And that made himself so much better. He had been grieving since Charlotte's death, not just for her, but for the emptiness in his life her absence had brought with it. Over the weekend he'd spent with Della, that emptiness had begun to fill again. The hole Charlotte's vacancy had left in his life had begun to close. The wound had begun to heal. With Della, Marcus had begun to feel again. And the feelings he had…

He started to tuck the photograph into the file, but halted. Instead, after taking his glass to the kitchen, he carried everything into his bedroom. He placed the picture of Della on his dresser, propping it up in front of a lamp there. Even if the woman in the photo didn't look much like the one he remembered, Marcus liked having her in his home. He liked that a lot.

Nine

Two nights after finding Marcus on the internet, Della was still feeling at loose ends about everything that had happened and everything left to come. The media frenzy she had feared would follow the announcement of the arrests at Whitworth and Stone had actually been fairly mild. Geoffrey had told her that wasn't surprising at this point, that when people were that rich and that powerful, it was easy for their attorneys to keep a tight rein on how much information was made available to the press. It would only be after the grand jury arraignment, when evidence was presented to support the charges, thereby making any arguments on the defense's part moot, that the media storm would break. Probably with the fury of a category five hurricane. Geoffrey had also assured her, though, that by the time that happened, Della would be safely ensconced in her new life elsewhere, hidden away from any repercussions.

Hidden away from everything.

But she was doing her best not to think about any of that yet. It was Friday night, the eve of her last weekend in Chicago. On Monday, she would be returning to New York. On Tuesday, she would make her first appearance before the grand jury. In a week, give or take, she would be ushered out of this life and into a new one.

One week. That was all Della Hannan had left. After that…

Oh, boy. She really needed a glass of wine.

She changed into her pajamas, poured herself a glass of pinot noir and grabbed a book that had arrived in that morning's mail. She was settling into a chair in the den when the doorbell of the safe house rang. To say the sound startled her was a bit of an understatement, since she jumped so hard, she knocked over her wine, spilling it over both the book and the snowflake print of her pajama shirt, leaving a ruby-red stain at the center of her chest in its wake.

No one had ever rung the doorbell of the safe house. Not even Geoffrey on those few occasions when he had been here. He always called first to tell her he was coming and at what time, and he gave a couple of quick raps and called out his name once he arrived.

She had no idea who was on the other side of the door now. Not Geoffrey, that was certain. It could be another marshal, or someone from the FBI or SEC who needed to brief her about her grand jury appearance next week. But Geoffrey would have let her know about something like that before he sent anyone over. And no such meeting would ever take place after 10:00 p.m. on a Friday night.

She wasn't sure whether she should sit tight and pretend no one was home, or go to the bedroom for her cell phone to call Geoffrey. Any movement she made might tip-off whoever was outside. Of course, it could just be someone who'd mistaken her address for another on the street. It could be someone delivering a pizza to the wrong house. It could be neighbor kids who thought it would be funny to play a joke on the weird neighbor lady who never left her house. It could be any of those things. It could.

But Della doubted it.

As silently as possible, she closed the book and set it and her half-empty wineglass on the side table, then rose carefully from the chair. The doorbell rang again as she was taking her first step toward the bedroom, setting off explosions of heat in her belly. She went as quickly as she could to the bedroom and grabbed her phone, punching the numbers to Geoffrey's home phone into it but not pushing the send button yet. If it *was* the pizza guy making a mistaken delivery, she didn't want to bother Geoffrey for nothing.

The doorbell rang a third time as she approached the living room, but this time, it was followed by a series of quick, rapid knocks. The front drapes were drawn, as they were every evening, and there were no lights turned on in that room. Della clasped her cell phone tightly in one hand as she came to a halt at the front door, then placed the other hand over the trio of light switches to the left of it. The one closest to her turned on an overly bright bug light on the porch, something that would temporarily blind whoever was out there if she flipped it on. For the moment, however, she only pressed her eye to the peephole to see who was on the other side

Oh, great. A dark, shadowy figure who could be almost anyone. That helped ever so much.

The dark, shadowy figure must have sensed her nearness or heard her approach, however, because as she was drawing back from the peephole, a voice called from the other side, "Della? Are you home? Let me in. We need to talk."

The sound of Marcus's deep voice startled her even more than the doorbell had. Her phone slipped from her fingers and clattered to the floor, her heart began to pound like a marathon runner's and her mind raced in a million different directions. How had he found her? Why was he here? If he'd found her, did someone else know she was here, too? Would his being here compromise the case? Would the feds go so far as to arrest Marcus to keep him under wraps, too?

What should she do?

"Della?" he called out again. "Are you there?"

How *had* he found her? *Why* had he found her? And if he knew her whereabouts, did he know about everything else that had happened, too?

What should she do?

Instead of panicking, however, a strange sort of calm suddenly settled over her, in spite of all the questions, in spite of her confusion, in spite of her fears and misgivings. Even though Della didn't know *what* to do, she knew, very well, what she *wanted* to do….

The chain was latched, as it always was, so, ignoring the phone on the floor, Della turned the three dead bolts on the door and opened it. It was still too dark on the other side for her to make out Marcus clearly, but the absence of light made her feel better. If she couldn't see him, he couldn't see her, either. But it wasn't because of vanity about being in wine-stained pajamas and no makeup or having her hair pulled back in a lopsided ponytail. It was because she knew Marcus couldn't see the real Della Hannan this way. She could still be the fantasy she hoped he remembered her as.

"Della?" he said again, evidently still not certain he'd found her.

All she could manage in response was, "Hi, Marcus."

His entire body seemed to relax at her greeting. "It's really you," he said softly.

The remark didn't invite a response, so Della said nothing. Truly, she had no idea what to say. If Marcus knew she was here, he must know why she was here, too. The marshals had kept her hidden for eleven months without any problems. Yet in less than two weeks, Marcus had managed to find her, without having anything more than her first name. He must know everything about what had happened at this point.

For a long moment, neither of them said a word, and neither moved a muscle. The cold winter wind whipped up behind him, sending his overcoat fluttering about his legs and his hair shuffling around his face. Even though she couldn't make out his features in the darkness, she remembered every elegant contour of his face—the rugged jawline, the patrician nose, the carved cheekbones. As the wind blew past him and against her, it brought his scent, too, the spicy, smoky one she recalled too well. Smelling him again, even one fleeting impression, filled her with desire and hunger and need. It was all she could do not to pull back the chain and throw the door open wide and welcome him into the house, into her life, into her.

But she couldn't do that. She wasn't the woman he thought she was. He might not be the man she'd thought him to be. And even if they could both be what the other wanted, in a matter of days, Della would be disappearing into another life Marcus couldn't be a part of. Her new life would be one into which she was retreating, one that would necessitate living quietly and unobtrusively. His life was one into which he would always go boldly and always live lavishly. And neither the twain could meet.

"Can I come in?" he asked.

"No," she said quickly.

"Della, please. We need to talk."

"We are talking."

"No, we're not. We're greeting each other."

"Then start talking."

He growled out an epithet. "It's cold. Let me in."

Well, he did have a point there, she conceded. Her sock-clad toes were already screaming that they were about to get frostbite. Not to mention her robe was in the other room.

Not to mention she really wanted to see him again. Up close and in good light. She wanted to stand near enough to feel his warmth. Near enough to inhale his scent. And she wanted to pretend again, just for a little while, as she had during their weekend together, that nothing in her life would ever be wrong again.

Unable to help herself, she pushed the door closed enough to unhook the chain, then pulled it open again. Strangely, Marcus didn't barrel immediately through and close it behind himself. Instead, he remained at the threshold, waiting for some cue from her.

Striving to lighten the mood, she said, "Unless you're a vampire, you don't need a formal invitation."

He hesitated a moment, then said, "I'd like to be invited anyway."

She remembered the night at the club, how he had joined her without asking first, and how he had taken the lead for everything after that. There had been no uncertainty in him that night two weeks ago. But tonight, it was as if he were as uncertain about everything as she was. For some reason, that made her feel a little less uncertain.

"Would you like to come in?" she asked quietly.

He nodded, then took a few steps forward. When she stepped out of the way to let him enter, her foot hit the cell phone on the floor and skittered it to the other side of the foyer. As Della stooped to pick it up, Marcus closed the door behind himself. In the dark room, she could still sense nothing of what he might be feeling or thinking, so she led him into the den. As she walked, she restlessly tugged the rubber band from her ponytail and did her best to fluff and tame her hair at the same time. There was nothing she could do about the wine-spattered pajamas, however, so she only crossed her arms over the stain as best she could and told herself the posture wasn't defensive.

Even if she was feeling a little defensive.

She gestured toward the sofa. "Have a seat," she said as she tucked herself into the chair.

But Marcus didn't sit. Instead, he stood with his hands shoved into his coat pockets, gazing at her.

He looked magnificent, different from the last time she had seen him, but somehow completely unchanged. In person, she'd seen him dressed only in the tuxedo and the bathrobe—one extreme to another—and this incarnation of him was somewhere in between. His trousers were casual and charcoal in color and paired with a bulky black sweater. Coupled with the dark coat and his dark hair, and having come in from the darkness the way he had, he still seemed as overwhelming as he had been the first time she saw him. But his eyes were anxious and smudged with faint purple crescents.

His hair was a bit shaggy, and his face wasn't closely shaved. His posture was both too tense and too fatigued, as if he were trapped in some state between the two. Or maybe both conditions had just overwhelmed him. All in all, he looked like a man who had been worrying about something—or perhaps someone—a lot.

When he didn't sit, Della automatically stood again. "Wine?" she asked. Her words were rushed and unsteady as she prattled on. "I just opened a bottle of pinot noir. It's good on a night like this. I'll get you a glass."

Without awaiting a reply, she grabbed her glass and headed into the kitchen to retrieve one for him, her mind racing once again with all the repercussions his arrival into her reality brought with it. Why, oh, why, had she let him in? Why hadn't she called Geoffrey the minute she heard a knock at the door? What if it hadn't been Marcus standing there?

When she turned to go back into the den, she saw him standing framed by the kitchen doorway. He'd removed his coat and ran a hand through his wind-tossed hair, but he didn't look any more settled than she felt. Crumbling under his scrutiny, Della looked away, then, leaving both glasses neglected on the counter, went to the table to fold herself into one of the chairs. Marcus pulled out the chair immediately next to hers and, after sitting down, scooted it in close enough so that his thigh was aligned with her own. For another long moment, neither of them spoke. Neither looked at the other. Neither moved. Finally, unable to stand the silence, Della took the initiative.

"How did you find me?"

He didn't say anything for a minute, only looked down at the table and began to restlessly trace the wood grain with his finger. All he said, though, was, “I’m well-connected.”

“No one is that well-connected, Marcus. I’ve been here for eleven months without anyone knowing. All you had was my first name, and you managed to find me less than two weeks after we—”

She halted when she saw the stain of a blush darkening his cheek. It hadn’t been there when he came in, so it couldn’t be a result of the cold. That meant something she’d said had made him uncomfortable. He looked up at her when she stopped talking, then, when he saw her staring at him, his gaze ricocheted away again.

“Marcus, how *did* you find me knowing only my first name?”

Still, he avoided her gaze. “Yeah, about that. I, uh, I actually had more than your first name. I kind of took the liberty of going through your purse while you were in the shower, and I got your last name and your address in New York from your driver’s license.”

Della closed her eyes at that. How could she have been so careless? She never left the safe house without her driver’s license, on the outside chance that if there was an accident of some kind, she could still be returned to the proper authorities. The thought of dying nameless bothered her almost as much as dying friendless. But Della had never expected anyone other than an emergency medical worker or law enforcement officer to see it. She knew enough to use cash instead of her credit cards to keep from being identified, and her phone was one Geoffrey had given her that couldn’t be traced. But the personal ID thing…

The fact that she hadn’t given it a thought while she was with Marcus was another indication of how much of her trust she had placed in him. Or perhaps misplaced, as the case may be.

"So I had more than your first name to give to…my contact," Marcus confessed.

"The address on my license isn't my address anymore," she told him. "I haven't lived in New York for almost a year."

"I know. But having even your most recent known address along with your full name gave my guy all the information he needed to track you down."

Della let that sink in for a minute. It had been that easy for someone to find her. But no one had. Geoffrey had told Della, too, that all of the defendants had been made aware during questioning and as charges were filed that there was a federal witness in custody who was willing to testify against all of them. And that there were documents this witness had smuggled out that corroborated every charge.

She hadn't slept or eaten much after hearing that, so anxious had she been about whether someone from Whitworth and Stone was trying to track down who the witness was and what information they had, putting together her disappearance with the timing of the investigation.

But no one had. Or, if they did, none had tried to locate her. Or, at least succeeded. Not until Marcus. Who, one would think, didn't have nearly as much at stake. Then she remembered that Marcus was a part of the world she had just punched a big hole in. Who said he wasn't here for the very reason she feared?

No, she immediately told herself. No way. In spite of everything, she still trusted him. In spite of everything, she still…cared for him.

When she trusted her voice again, she asked, "You hired someone to find me?"

"Yes," he acknowledged without hesitation.

"Why?"

This time, his response came less quickly. Finally, he told her, "Because I couldn't stand the thought of never seeing you again."

Something that had been knotted tight inside Della began to loosen and flow free at his words. Until she remembered how impossible it would be for them to be together.

He started to say something else, but she held up a hand to stop him. "How much do you know about my situation? I mean, if the person you hired to find me found me, he must have uncovered a lot of other information about me, too."

Marcus looked disappointed that she had changed the subject, but he replied, "I know you're in the custody of the U.S. Marshals. I know you're slated to be a material witness for a federal case. Beyond that, I didn't ask for details, except about where you were living now."

She shook her head. "I still can't believe you found me as easily as you did," she said, stalling. "Just what kind of system are the feds running, anyway?"

"It wasn't easy to find you," Marcus countered. "The P.I. I always use to get the information I need can usually get it for me within forty-eight hours."

"Even when it's federally protected?"

"Nothing is foolproof, Della. My guy used to be a highly placed operative on the government payroll before he went into business for himself. He can find things out others can't because he still has a lot of contacts in high places. In federal, state and city governments."

"He must cost a fortune," she muttered.

"He does."

She spared a moment to find enormous pleasure in the fact that Marcus would spend an exorbitant amount of money to find her, then sobered again when the impact of his discovery settled over her again.

"But even he couldn't work as fast as he usually does," he continued. "And I still didn't get everything I wanted."

She wasn't sure if Marcus was talking only about information in that statement, so she diverted to their original subject. But she did her best to be as vague as possible. She didn't want to say anything that might compromise the hearing next week. She couldn't stand the thought that everything she'd gone through over the last eleven months might end up being for nothing.

But then, without the last eleven months, she never would have had her weekend with Marcus, would she? So regardless of what did or didn't happen in the future, those tedious, anxious, interminable months could never have been for nothing.

"Look, Marcus, I can't give you any particulars about the case I'm involved in," she said. "I'm not even sure if your mere presence here right now is going to mess everything up or not. Suffice it to say that one day, I was doing my job and living my life and everything was as normal as it could be. The next day, I discovered something my employer was doing that was illegal, and I turned all the information I had over to the proper authorities. The next thing I knew, I was being told I couldn't go back to work, and that I was going to be placed into protective custody while the government took over the investigation. I was told it would only be for a couple of months. That was eleven months ago."

"And to explain your disappearance," Marcus said, "they concocted a story about you having an affair with a married man in another department."

Now it was Della's turn to blush and look away. "That wasn't concocted," she said softly. "And if you know that, then you *do* know something about my situation."

His expression changed then, turning contemplative, and he said nothing for a moment. Then his expression changed once more, this time to one of understanding. "Whitworth and Stone," he said. "That was your employer."

"Yes."

His lips parted fractionally, as if he were going to say something else, then closed again. For another moment, he studied her in silence, then he opened his mouth again. But, again, it took a moment before he spoke. "I read in the trades and the *Wall Street Journal* about the arrests. It was because of you, wasn't it?"

Her stomach knotted again, and she shook her head vehemently. "I can't say anything about it."

"You don't have to," he told her. "It didn't occur to me until now to put it all together. There just hasn't been that much in the news about what's really going on there. There was so little fanfare, in fact, that most of us figured the charges were bogus, just the government flexing its muscle to keep Wall Street in its place, or that it would turn out with one or two guys getting a slap on the wrist for some minor infractions. It never occurred to me that they'd actually make a federal case out of it."

Della said nothing, but couldn't pull her gaze away from his. The wheels were clearly spinning in his brain now, and he was obviously able to put way more than two and two together. A man like him, as highly placed as he was in the financial community, could fully appreciate how much was at stake here, and how much trouble a company like Whitworth and Stone could be in. A man like him would know exactly how important Della's role was in what was happening, and he would understand completely how devastating her impact would be.

He nodded slowly. "But the reason there hasn't been much media coverage is precisely because of how massive a case this is going to be. Executives that high up, with that much money and that many resources at their disposal—not to mention that much to lose—can afford the kind of lawyers who can keep things quiet, at least for a while."

Still, Della said nothing. Still, she couldn't look away.

"It never occurred to me to put those arrests together with your disappearance," Marcus said. "The married lover story made a lot more sense."

"I didn't know he was married," she said, finally relieved to be able to talk about something that wouldn't compromise the case. "I was supposed to meet him on New Year's Eve. Though after midnight because he said he had a professional dinner to attend. I arrived a little early and saw him kissing another woman good night before putting her into a cab. When I asked who she was, he informed me she was his wife, who he had no intention of leaving because, by the way, he also had three kids and his wife's family was so well-connected socially and financially, and he couldn't afford to lose those connections."

Marcus's expression then indicated the wheels were still turning in his head, though they might be going in a different direction now. "You disappeared in mid-January, meaning you must have uncovered the wrongdoing at Whitworth and Stone right before that."

"On New Year's Day," she said without thinking. But that wasn't compromising information, was it? Surely not.

Marcus nodded slowly, as if making more connections. "So you found out on New Year's Eve that the man you were seeing was married, and then, hours later, discovered that your employer was involved in matters that threatened national security."

"That's it in a nutshell, yeah."

"Sucky way to start the new year."

She wished she could laugh, then wondered if she would ever be able to find humor in anything again. "Yeah."

"You know, anyone else would have been devastated by either one of those things, but even after suffering both, you still had the presence of mind, and the courage, to do the right thing."

Della had never really looked at it like that. "I just did what anyone else in that position would do."

"No, you didn't," he said. "A lot of people would have walked away from both and wallowed in self-pity. Or they would have kept their mouths shut and not risked losing their job or their benefits or anything else that might mess up their life."

"Maybe..."

"Instead, you risked everything to make sure the people who were putting other people—strangers you didn't even know—in danger didn't get away with what they were doing."

"Yes."

He lifted a hand and started to reach for her, then hesitated, as if fearing how she would react. Reluctantly, without touching her, he dropped his hand to the table. "And you have to ask why I came looking for you."

Whatever was left of the knot inside her unraveled. In spite of that, she told him, "You shouldn't have come, Marcus."

"Why not?"

"Because I'm leaving Chicago in three days, and I'm not coming back."

"I know that was your plan before, but now—"

"Now, it's still the plan," she told him. "I can't stay here, Marcus."

"Why not?"

How did she say this without having it sound melodramatic and paranoid? Probably, she should simply spell it out. "Because after I give my testimony to the grand jury, I'm going to be one of the most hated people on Wall Street. No one's going to give me a job. The people I'm going to help put away have contacts everywhere. Not only in other brokerage houses, but in banks and all kinds of businesses. They have corporate America eating out of their hands. No one will hire me. Whistle-blowers might make for great movies and documentaries, but in the real world, their lives are shattered. They can't find work. They can't support their families. They lose everything."

He was still looking at her in a way that made clear he didn't understand what she was saying. So Della spelled it out further. "After this thing is over, the government is giving me a new ID. New name, new social security number, new history, new everything. They're going to move me someplace where I have a chance to start over again where no one will know me, and where there's no chance I'll be recognized. I'll be able to find a job doing something I love, something I'm good at. I won't be Della Hannan anymore."

Marcus sat back in his chair and inspected her openly now. "Then who will you be? Where will you go?"

"I don't know yet," she said. "But it won't be here."

"Why not here? It's as easy to start over in Chicago as anywhere else. Better. There's a vital financial community here. Where else are you going to go and find that? Go ahead and change your name and history. You'll still be Della. You'll still be the woman I met at Palumbo's. You'll still be the woman I spent the most amazing weekend of my life with. You'll still be the woman I—"

He halted before finishing, probably because Della had started shaking her head as soon as he finished his first sentence. "If I stay here, Marcus, I'll want to be with you."

He gaped at her. "And that's a problem?"

"Yes!" she cried. "Because you're so..." She recalled the adjective he'd used himself. "Notorious. You're all over the society pages and a regular fixture on a lot of celebrity websites. You said so yourself."

Now he closed his mouth. She was pretty sure he was starting to understand. But since she was still in spell-it-out mode, Della continued, "You live a big life, Marcus. It's what makes you happy. It's who you are. You like your notoriety. And I don't blame you," she hastened to add. "Big life suits you. You were born for the spotlight. But me..." She shrugged lightly. "I wasn't born for a big life. And now, more than ever, I need to be invisible. It's the only way I'll be able to rebuild my life. It's the only way I'll be able to get back everything I've lost."

"In other words, you don't want to be seen with me."

"I *can't* be seen with you," she corrected him. "What if someone recognizes me? What if, as I'm starting to get my groove back, someone in your world realizes who I really am? They could destroy everything I have." She swallowed hard against the anguish she felt threatening. "And they could hurt you, too. Doing what you do for a living, if you were seen consorting with the woman who brought down Whitworth and Stone, no one would ever trust you again. Then your life would be shattered, too. I can't let that happen to you. I can't be responsible for it."

"I'd never worry about something like that," he told her.

"I would always worry about it," she said. "It would never work out for us, Marcus," she said. "It would be a mistake for me to stay. That is just as well, because after Monday, I'll be gone."

He leaned forward in his chair, taking both of her hands in his. "No, Della, you can't. We need to talk more about—"

This time, when Marcus stopped speaking, it wasn't because he cut himself off. This time, it was because of a loud crash in the living room—which Della was pretty sure was the sound of the front door being broken in—followed by a wildly shouted, "Della, it's Geoffrey! Are you okay?"

And then, just like in the movies, everything turned to chaos.

Ten

Marcus sat on the sofa in Della's house—even though both obviously really belonged to Uncle Sam—and wondered when his life had morphed into a Quentin Tarantino film. One minute, he'd been sitting at the kitchen table trying to tell her how he felt about her, and the next, he had been face down on the linoleum with some guy's knee in the small of his back yelling that he should keep his hands where the guy could see them at all times.

At least the guy, whom Della had eventually been able to introduce as the federal marshal assigned to keep an eye on her, had taken off the handcuffs after shoving Marcus onto the sofa. Now, as he rubbed at his wrists and tried to crane his head around the man to see how Della was faring, the guy—who Marcus couldn't help thinking looked like an older version of Dwight Schrute, only not as well-dressed—leaned the same way he was trying to look, cutting off his view of Della. Again.

"Geoffrey, it's okay," Della said. Again.

Marcus had gathered from the frantic exchange between Della and the marshal only moments ago that before answering her front door, she had dialed Geoffrey's number without pressing the call button, and that when she dropped the phone on the floor, it had somehow performed that function anyway. Geoffrey had answered his phone after seeing Della's name attached to the caller ID and heard her talking to someone in the distance. Even though the conversation hadn't sounded threatening and she hadn't sound frightened, she wasn't supposed to be talking to *anyone,* so he had leaped into action and driven to the safe house to check on her. Then, when he mistook the wine stain on her shirt for blood…

Well, that was when the knee in Marcus's back had nearly broken his spine.

Now, however, all was well. The marshal was only looking at him as if he planned to cap him in both kneecaps with the sidearm he hadn't even had the decency to reholster. At least he wasn't pointing the weapon at Marcus anymore.

"Tell me one more time," Geoffrey said, "what the hell you think you're doing here."

Marcus had already told him that twice—as had Della—but Geoffrey didn't seem satisfied. This, okay, maybe Marcus could understand, since he hadn't been completely honest with the guy. But there was no way he was going to tell a total stranger he was here because he was in love with Della Hannan when he hadn't even told Della that yet.

"He's a friend," Della said. Again.

Marcus looked at Geoffrey to see if that would satisfy him. It clearly did not.

"I thought you didn't have any friends in Chicago," Geoffrey told Della. Still looking at Marcus.

When Della didn't reply right away, the marshal glanced over his shoulder in silent inquiry, then quickly returned his attention to Marcus. As if realizing his dilemma in not being able to see them both at the same time, Della moved to sit on the sofa, too. Marcus tried not to read too much into the fact that she crowded herself into the corner as far from him as she could get. But—call him an alarmist—the gesture wasn't exactly encouraging.

Della glanced at Geoffrey, then back at the floor, looking like a twelve-year-old who'd been caught with her first cigarette. "I met him two weeks ago," she said.

Geoffrey narrowed his eyes at her. "How could you have met him two weeks ago when you never leave the house?"

Della nibbled her lip nervously but said nothing.

"Della?" Geoffrey prodded.

"Yeah, about that," she said. She then launched into a long, winding, somewhat convoluted explanation about sneaking out of the safe house from time to time due to extreme cabin fever, then about some promise she'd made to herself as a child, then she spoke at length about opera in general and *La Bohème* in particular, then she backtracked to something about a little shop off Michigan Avenue and haute couture, then she moved on to dinner, then Marcus, and then—

And then she stopped abruptly. Probably, Marcus thought, because she'd gotten to the part about where the two of them checked into the Ambassador Hotel.

At that point, had Geoffrey been a character in an old-time novel, he was what would have been referred to as *apoplectic*. But his voice was level when he told Della, "I cannot believe you've been sneaking out of the house on a regular basis without letting me know where you were going."

"Only a few times," she said defensively. When she looked up and saw how sternly her caretaker was eyeing her, she amended, "Okay, six. But that's all. And if I'd told you, you wouldn't have let me go. I was always careful."

Geoffrey spent a few more minutes admonishing her like a child and making her look even guiltier, but there was little he said that Della—or Marcus—could take exception to.

That didn't, however, stop Marcus from taking exception. "Give it a rest, Geoffrey," he interrupted the man midsentence. "It's the feds' fault for keeping her cooped up here for eleven months."

Both Geoffrey and Della glared at him for that. Geoffrey's irritation Marcus could understand, but Della's?

"Don't make this worse than it already is," she told him. "Geoffrey's right. I shouldn't have left the safe house. Ever."

Something in the way she said it made Marcus think her reasoning had less to do with the fact that she'd broken the rules and more to do with the repercussions of her actions. He just hoped one of the repercussions in question wasn't having met—and spending a weekend with—him.

He opened his mouth to try and reassure her that the weekend the two of them had spent together had been anything but wrong, but Geoffrey jingled the handcuffs he was still holding and said, "Keep it up, Fallon, and you're going to find yourself in federal custody, too. Only it won't be a safe house you'll be going to."

Yeah, yeah, yeah, Marcus wanted to say. He knew his rights when it came to law enforcement. He watched network television.

"I only meant—"

"I don't care what you meant," Geoffrey admonished. "I really ought to take you into custody, at least until Della leaves town."

"But—"

"But since she'll vouch for you, and since, like she said, you're such a paragon of professionalism and a scion of the community—" there was no mistaking the sarcasm in his voice when he said that last part "—I'm going to let you go."

Marcus bit back the indignation he felt and forced himself to mutter a reasonably tempered, "Thank you."

"But you'll have to leave the premises now and not come back."

Okay, so much for the reasonable temper. "What? But you just said yourself that Della vouched for me, so what's the harm in—"

"I don't have to explain the harm again," Geoffrey stated emphatically. Then, to hammer it home, he added, "To either of you. Now maybe the physical threat to Della is minimal, but she's got a big job to do next week, and we can't have it messed up because she gets a little stir-crazy being cooped up."

Both Marcus and Della started to speak at once, but Geoffrey lifted a hand to stop them. When neither of them stopped, the marshal raised his voice louder than theirs and talked right over them.

"Here's what's going to happen," he said. "Fallon, you're going to go home and forget you ever saw Della Hannan here in Chicago."

"Oh, no I'm not," Marcus said. He didn't care how loud the other guy was talking.

"Yes. You are," Geoffrey countered. "And, Della." He turned his attention to her before Marcus had a chance to object again. "You're going to pack everything you brought with you to Chicago while I wait."

"What? But why?" Della sounded as annoyed as Marcus was.

"Because you're checking out of Chez Uncle Sam tonight," Geoffrey told her. "The safe house has been compromised. You can't stay here."

"But Marcus is the only one who knows—"

"The safe house has been compromised," Geoffrey repeated. "You can't stay here. Now go pack your bags. We'll find you somewhere else to stay for the next couple of nights—not that you're going to be let out of my sight, meaning I'll be missing my favorite nephew's bar mitzvah on Sunday, thank you very much—and then, Monday, you'll fly back to New York as scheduled."

For a moment, Marcus thought Della was going to fight the other man's edict. Her back went ramrod-straight, her eyes flashed with anger and her hands doubled into fists. Then, as quickly, her entire posture changed. Her shoulders rolled forward, her gaze dropped to the floor, her fingers uncurled.

"All right," she conceded softly. "I guess it's inevitable."

"And, Della," Geoffrey said, bringing her attention to him. "I want the cell phone that we gave you. You're not to have any contact with the outside world until after the grand jury hearing. And you're going to be assigned a twenty-four-hour escort in New York—no, *two* twenty-four-hour escorts in New York," he hastily corrected himself, "until the powers that be say it's okay to cut you loose into the program."

"The program?" Marcus asked.

Now Geoffrey turned to look at him. "WITSEC," he said. "The Witness Security Program. You might know it better as witness protection, thanks to our good buddies in Hollywood," he added with more sarcasm.

Marcus looked at Della. "Is that true?" he said.

She continued to study the floor as she replied. "Yes."

"You're going into the witness protection program?"

"I told you I had to start over somewhere new, Marcus, where no one would know me. Where I had a whole new identity."

"I know, but I thought..."

Now she did look at him. "You thought what?"

He struggled over his words. "I thought...I mean, I just figured... After everything that happened between you and me..." He halted, took a deep breath and released it slowly. "Witness protection means you'll never be able to contact anyone from your old life," he finally said. "It means I won't have any way to find you. Not even my guy with the contacts could find you there."

"What guy with the contacts?" Geoffrey asked, turning suspicious again.

Marcus ignored him. Della still looked at the floor.

"Della," he pleaded. "Don't do it."

"What guy with the contacts?" Geoffrey repeated. "If he knows how to get past government smoke-screens, we need to know about him."

"Then you can question me at home later." Marcus ground out the words without sparing the marshal a glance.

"Oh, we will, Mr. Fallon. We will."

Della remained silent.

Marcus knew there was no way he would be able to find her once she disappeared. It was obvious that Geoffrey's concern for her went beyond what a federal marshal would undertake. From the moment he'd crashed into the kitchen, there had been an unmistakable air of paternity about the guy. He was protecting Della the way he would protect a daughter. Marcus might as well be doing battle with a mama polar bear.

"Della," he said again, "please. You and I need to talk."

"Not tonight, you won't," Geoffrey assured him. Then, to Della, in a much gentler voice, he said, "Go pack your stuff. I'll call around and find another place for you. A place that's *safe,*" he said, looking back at Marcus, still obviously not trusting him.

Della lifted her head and looked at Marcus, her eyes brimming with tears. "I'm sorry," she told him. "I—I just...I can't—" She shook her head. "Goodbye, Marcus."

And then she was off the sofa and disappearing into the hallway. Unthinkingly, Marcus stood to follow her, but a heavy hand on his shoulder stopped him.

"Front door's that way," Geoffrey told him. "Use it."

Marcus didn't have much choice but to obey. He took two broad steps in that direction, but stopped to look down the hall. There was a light on in one of the bedrooms at the end, and he could see Della's shadow moving around in front of the lamplight. That was all she was to him now—a shadow. Just as he'd been before she came into his life, Marcus was back to being alone.

No, wait, he realized as the thought formed in his head. It wasn't like before at all. Because before, Marcus hadn't realized what he was missing. Before, he hadn't recognized the emptiness, because he'd been able to fill it with mind-numbing carousing and willing, if faceless, women. Before, Marcus had been able to delude himself that he had everything he could possibly ever want and that his life lacked absolutely nothing. Before, he had been able to pretend that he was happy and contented. But now…

Now he really did know what happiness and contentment were. Because those were the things he'd felt when he was with Della. Now he knew how full, how fun, how fantastic his life could be. Now he understood how much more enjoyable it was to share life with someone else. He realized that loving someone wasn't just something a person *did,* but how being in love was something a person *was.* Marcus was in love with Della, and that completed him as a human being. It was something that brought him greater joy, greater peace, than he ever could have imagined. With Della gone…

Well. He would still be in love with her. He would always be in love with her. But with her gone, so went a part of himself. A part she would always keep with her, but a part he would never have back. Not unless he had Della.

And Della would be someplace where the feds would make sure she was never found again.

Although the grand jury hearings lasted less than a week, they seemed even more interminable and emotionally draining than the eleven months Della had spent cooped up in Chicago. Because she was the only witness the federal prosecutors had, her testimony took up the majority of the time, and she spoke for hours every day, until she thought she would run out of voice and words and nerve. By the end of the proceedings, all she wanted was to escape into her new life where she would be left alone.

Until she remembered that being alone would mean, well, being alone. If only she could take Marcus with her…

But she couldn't do that. What made things more difficult was that, even after the grand jury hearing concluded, she still wouldn't be left alone—not yet. At some point, she would have to return to New York to repeat everything she'd said. Because the grand jury had been given an overwhelming amount of evidence against Whitworth and Stone and a number of its highest-placed executives. They would, without question, rule that the case go to trial. A trial that would involve the same star witness—her. Only then would she be able to slip back into her new anonymity. Only that time, it *would* be forever.

For some reason, the word *forever* made her think about Marcus. But then, nearly everything made her think about Marcus. Every time someone brought her a cup of coffee, she thought about him pouring one for her in the hotel. Whenever room service showed up with her dinner at the hotel where she was staying in New York, she thought of how Marcus had ordered such a breakfast feast for her. When she looked out over all the power suits in the courtroom, she thought of him. When she saw men in long overcoats on the streets of New York, she thought of him.

But worst of all, Friday evening, as she left the federal courthouse in New York City, dressed for the weather in a camel-hair coat and red scarf, mittens and hat, with an equally bundled-up marshal on each side of her, it started to snow. Maybe not as furiously as it had the night she met Marcus in Chicago, but seeing the sparkling white snowflakes tumbling out of the inky sky, Della was overwhelmed by memories of what had happened on the terrace of the Windsor Club, when she'd had the most incredible sexual experience of her life with a mysterious lover named Marcus.

Though he hadn't been a mystery for long. Della had gotten to know him pretty well during their time together, even better than she had realized. Over the time that had passed since their weekend together—and even more since they'd parted ways in Chicago—she had come to understand exactly how very well she did know Marcus, and how very deeply she'd come to feel for him. She couldn't pinpoint the moment when it had happened during their weekend together—maybe when he was wiping away her tears or pouring her a cup of coffee or tracing a finger lovingly over her naked shoulder—but she had fallen in love with Marcus. What had started as a sexual response had grown in mere hours to an emotional bond. She only wished she had admitted that to herself when she still had the chance to tell him.

She loved Marcus. Maybe she hadn't admitted it to herself at the time because the feeling was so new and unfamiliar to her. But it was that newness and unfamiliarity that finally made her realize she was in love. Being with Marcus had made her feel complete for the first time in her life. When she was with him, she'd felt as if she could handle anything. Everything that had been wrong in her life had suddenly seemed less likely to overtake her. She'd been less fearful when she was with Marcus. Less anxious. Less troubled. But most of all, with Marcus, she'd been happy. Since leaving him…

Since leaving him, nothing felt right. Even the snow falling down around her now didn't have the magic for her it would have had—that it did have—only a few weeks ago.

"Stop," she said to the two marshals as she paused halfway down the courthouse steps.

The man on her right, whose name was Willoughby, halted in his tracks, but the woman on her left, Carson, continued down two more steps, glancing right, then left, before turning to face Della.

"What's wrong?" Carson asked.

"Nothing. I just… It's snowing," she finally said, as if that should explain everything.

"So?"

"So I want to stand here for a minute and enjoy it." *Or at least try to.*

She heard Willoughby expel an irritated sigh, saw Carson roll her eyes. Della didn't care. She'd done a lot for her country this week. She'd sacrificed the past year of her life. The least her country could do was let her enjoy a minute in the snow.

She closed her eyes and tipped her head back, letting the icy flakes collect on her bare cheeks, nose and mouth. She sighed as she felt them melt one by one, only to be replaced by others. She heard the sound of a honking taxi, felt the bustle of people around her, inhaled the aroma of a passing bus. And she smiled. She loved the city. She didn't care what anyone said about noise and crowds and traffic. All those things only proved how alive the city was. She had grown up in this place. It was a part of her. No matter how badly it had treated her—as a child or as an adult—she couldn't imagine living anywhere else. She hoped, wherever her new life was, she would live in a big city again. Because maybe, just maybe, being surrounded by people—even if they were strangers—would help keep the loneliness at bay.

"Della."

Her eyes flew open at the sound of the familiar voice. The first thing she saw was Carson's back, because the woman had stepped in front of her. The second thing she saw was how Willoughby was reaching inside his open overcoat for what she knew would be a weapon. The third thing she saw was Marcus.

At first, she thought she was imagining him, because he looked so much as he had that night at the Windsor Club, dark and handsome and mysterious, surrounded by swirls of snow. The only difference was that he'd exchanged the tuxedo for a dark suit. That and the fact that he looked so very lost and alone.

"Marcus," she said softly. She covered Carson's shoulder with one hand as she curled the fingers of the other over Willoughby's arm. "It's okay," she told them both. "He's…a friend."

Carson didn't even turn around as she said, "Our orders, Ms. Hannan, are to—"

"I'll take full responsibility for anything that happens," Della said.

"That's not the problem," Carson told her. "The problem is—"

But Della didn't wait for her to finish. She strode away from the two marshals, down the steps of the courthouse, until she stood on the one above Marcus, facing him. It was only then that she realized he was holding a suitcase. He must have come here straight from the airport. He must have been following the court proceedings and knew that by today, they'd come to an end.

"Hi," she said softly.

"Hi," he replied just as quietly.

Neither of them said anything more for a moment. Marcus set his suitcase on the ground beside him and shoved his hands deep into his overcoat pockets. So Della took the initiative, raised her mittened hands to his shoulders, leaned forward and covered his mouth with hers. She told herself it was because she hadn't had a chance to kiss him goodbye. Not at the hotel, and not at the safe house. So this was what that would be. A chance to tell him goodbye properly.

Funny, though, how the moment her lips met his, it didn't feel like goodbye at all. Because the next thing she knew, Marcus was roping his arms around her waist and crushing her body against his, pulling her completely off the concrete. What had been frigid air surrounding her suddenly turned blistering, and heat exploded at her center, igniting every extremity. The memories of him that had tortured her all week evaporated, replaced by the impressions of his reality. She felt his arms around her waist again, the scruff of his beard against her cheek again, the solid strength of his shoulders beneath her hands again. She couldn't believe he was actually here.

Wait a minute. What was he doing here?

The thought made her pull away from him, but Marcus followed and captured her mouth with his again. Although he set her down on the step, he curved his hands over her hips to keep her there and kissed her more deeply still. She allowed herself to get lost in blissful sensations for another long moment. But when she heard the sound of not one, but two throats clearing not so indiscreetly behind her, she found the wherewithal to pull away from him again.

Marcus must have heard the marshals' reactions, too, because he didn't try to reclaim Della this time. He did, however, move to the same step she was on and loop an arm around her shoulders, then he pulled her close, as if he were afraid her guardians would try to take her from him again.

But neither marshal seemed eager to come between them. In fact, they were both smiling.

"He looks like more than…a friend," Carson said.

"Yeah, I don't have any…friends…like that," Willoughby agreed. "I don't think my wife would like it too much if I did."

Della felt Marcus relax beside her. But he still didn't loosen his hold on her. Not that she cared.

"Do you mind?" Della said to the two marshals. "Can I have a few minutes to talk to my…friend?"

Carson and Willoughby exchanged a wary look, then turned back to Della.

"I'm sorry, Ms. Hannan," Carson said, "but privacy is one thing a federal witness doesn't get much of. And you're not out of protective custody yet. If you want to talk to your…friend…it's going to have to be in front of me and Willoughby."

"It's okay, Della," Marcus said.

With one more pleading look aimed at her escorts—who both regretfully shook their heads in response—she turned to Marcus. He lifted a hand to her face to trace the line of her cheekbone, her nose, her jaw and her mouth. He didn't seem to be bothered by their audience. Then again, Della was so happy to see him, she didn't really care who saw them, either.

"I'm going to have to get used to this witness security thing sooner or later, anyway," Marcus said. "It might as well be now."

The remark puzzled her. "Why do you have to get used to it?"

He inhaled a deep breath and released it slowly, then dropped his hand from her face so that he could take her hand in his. When her mittens hindered his efforts, he gently tugged one off. Then he wove their fingers together and squeezed tight.

"I have to get used to it," he said, "because I'm going with you."

Her mouth fell open a bit at that. "What are you talking about?"

"I'm going with you."

She shook her head. "Marcus, that's crazy talk. You don't know what you're saying."

"I know exactly what I'm saying." He lifted her hand to his mouth and pressed a small kiss in the center of her palm. Then he said a third time, "I'm going with you."

"But you can't," she insisted. "You have a life in Chicago. A big life. A larger-than-life life. There are lots of people who will miss you if you disappear."

"None that matters as much as you," he told her.

"But your friends—"

"—are not particularly close ones," he finished for her. "They don't matter as much as you."

"Your family—"

"—is more of a corporate entity than a family," he assured her. "I've spent ninety percent of my life rebelling against them and the other ten percent taking advantage of them. We're not that close, either. They definitely don't matter as much as you."

"But your business. Your job is—"

"—mostly as a figurehead," he told her. "It especially doesn't matter as much as you." He gave her hand another gentle squeeze. "I don't do that much for Fallon Brothers as it is now, Della. Once I'm in charge, I'll do even less. I'll just make a lot more money for that lack of performance. Corporate America is kind of funny that way."

She latched on to the money thing. "Your money. You can't walk away from all that. It's—"

"—money," he concluded easily. "That's all. Just money. It doesn't even come close to mattering as much as you."

"That's all?" she echoed incredulously. "Marcus, that's a lot of money you're talking about. Millions of dollars."

He only smiled, tugged off her other mitten and took that hand in his, too, giving it a kiss identical to the other one. "Billions, actually," he said matter-of-factly.

All Della could manage in response to that was a soft squeak.

That only made Marcus laugh. "Della. I would think you, of all people, would understand how that much money can bring *a lot* of trouble into a person's life. It's not that hard to walk away from it."

"Oh, right," she sputtered. "Spoken like someone who's never had to go without money in his life."

"Della, there's more to life than money," he stated unequivocally. "The best things in life are free. Simple pleasures are the best. Money is the root of all evil."

She shook her head at him, but couldn't help smiling.

Probably because of the warm, gooey sensations meandering through her. "When did you open an unlimited account at Platitudes 'R' Us?" she asked.

"Actually," he said lightly, "the account is at words-to-live-by-dot-com. But you're right—it is an unlimited one." He leaned in close, moving his mouth to her ear. Very quietly, he whispered, "Besides, the woman I intend to spend the rest of my life with is adamant about rebuilding her career. She can take care of me. She loves me to distraction, after all."

The warm gooeyness inside her swirled into a river of sweet, sticky goodness. Unable to help herself, Della leaned forward to press her forehead against Marcus's shoulder. He looped his arms around her waist and settled his chin on the crown of her head.

"See there?" he said softly. "You do love me, don't you?"

She was amazed to hear an unmistakable uncertainty in his voice. "Yes," she whispered against the fabric of his coat.

Now he pressed a kiss to the crown of her head. "Good. Because I love you, too."

He loved her, too, Della thought. He loved her, too. He loved her, too. It was like a magic incantation in her brain, breaking all the evil spells of her old life and bestowing new ones in their wake. He loved her, too. He loved her, too.

"But, Marcus," she said softly, "there's so much more you should consider besides—"

"Della, there's *nothing* more to consider than you. I've had weeks to think about you and me, and you know what I figured out that was most significant?"

With her head still pressed against his chest—it felt so good to have it there—she asked, "What?"

"What was significant was that I didn't need weeks to think about it. I didn't even need days to think about it. I didn't need to think at all. I only needed to feel. And what I feel for you, Della..."

When he didn't finish, she tilted her head back to look at him. He was still smiling, but there was something in this one she hadn't seen in any of the others before. Peace. Contentment. Happiness. She recognized it, because with him here beside her, she felt all those things, too.

"What I feel for you is like nothing I've felt before in my life. And I like it, Della. I like it a lot. I want to feel this way forever." He dipped his head to hers and kissed her again. When he pulled back, he repeated resolutely, "So I'm coming with you."

Della didn't know why she kept wanting to object, but she couldn't quite keep herself from giving it one more shot. "But what if—"

Marcus lifted his hand to press his fingers lightly against her mouth. "It doesn't matter what if," he said. "Whatever happens, Della, we'll face it together. We'll *be* together. That's all that matters."

"But—"

"Shh," he said.

And then he dropped his fingers from her mouth to place a chaste kiss there instead. It was enough to quiet her voice if not quell her reservations. He was right, she told herself. It didn't matter what the future brought, as long as the two of them were together. She'd brought herself up from very humble beginnings and made a decent life for herself before everything went wrong at Whitworth and Stone. And she'd managed to make the best of a bad situation for eleven months in Chicago. The place from which she would be starting over again now was infinitely better than the places where she'd started off before. And this time, she wouldn't be embarking on the journey alone. This time, she would be with Marcus. And that made even the bleakest prospects tolerable.

He tucked a strand of dark blond hair behind her ear and leaned down until his mouth hovered just next to it. His warm breath on her cold skin sent a delicious shiver down her spine. Or maybe it was his simple nearness that did that. As he had with her mouth, he placed a small, soft kiss on her ear lobe. Then he pulled back far enough to murmur in a voice too soft for anyone but her to hear, "Besides. Thirty percent of my wealth is liquid and highly accessible. It's in conveniently numbered Swiss bank accounts, and I'll be able to get to it whenever I want. We won't starve, sweetheart. Trust me."

Meaning, she thought with a grin, that she would never have to settle for rented clothing again. A single, genuinely happy chuckle escaped her. But even this information didn't matter. It was as Marcus said, all that mattered was that the two of them would be together. Forever.

She looked at the suitcase by his feet. It was the size of one that could be carried onto a plane. There wasn't much that would fit in a bag that size.

"That's all you're bringing with you into our new life?" she asked.

He glanced down at the bag, then back at Della. "It's more than I need, really. Because everything I need is right here."

And then he kissed her again. And kissed her. And kissed her. And kissed her. In fact, he kissed her so long, and so many times, that only the appearance of

Carson and Willoughby on each side of them made him stop. Even at that, it took a moment for Della to remember her surroundings. But when she saw the two marshals smiling at her, she remembered all too well.

She'd completed what she'd come to New York to do. Now it was time to head into a new chapter of her life.

"Carson, Willoughby," she said to the two marshals. "Tell your boss there's been a slight change in my plan." She turned to Marcus and looped her arm through his. "Tell her I'm going to have one more piece of baggage than I'd planned."

And as baggage went, she thought, Marcus was the kind she would happily carry with her forever.

* * * * *

BILLIONAIRE, M.D.

BY
OLIVIA GATES

Olivia Gates has always pursued creative passions—singing and many handicrafts. She still does, but only one of her passions grew gratifying enough, consuming enough, to become an ongoing career. Writing.

She is most fulfilled when she is creating worlds and conflicts for her characters, then exploring and untangling them bit by bit, sharing her protagonists' every heart-wrenching heartache and hope, their every heart-pounding doubt and trial, until she leads them to an indisputably earned and gloriously satisfying happy ending.

When she's not writing, she is a doctor, a wife to her own alpha male and a mother to one brilliant girl and one demanding angora cat. Visit Olivia at www.oliviagates. com.

To Natashya and Shane.
This one is definitely for you both.

One

She opened her eyes to another world.

A world filled with grainy grayness, like a TV channel with no transmission. But she didn't care.

This world had an angel watching over her.

And not just any angel. An archangel. If archangels were the personification of beauty and power, were hewn out of living rock and bronze and unadulterated maleness.

His image floated in the jumble of light and shadow, making her wonder if this was a dream. Or a hallucination. Or worse.

Probably worse. In spite of the angel's presence. Or because of it. Angels didn't watch over anyone who wasn't in some serious trouble, did they?

Would be a shame if he turned out to be the angel of death. Why make him so breathtaking if he was just a life-force extractor? He was way overqualified. Such overkill was uncalled for, if you asked her. Or maybe his extreme attractiveness was designed to make his targets willing to go where he led?

She'd be more than willing. *If* she could move.

She couldn't. Gravity overwhelmed her, squashed her back onto something that suddenly felt like a bed of thorns. Every cell in her body started to squirm, every nerve firing impulses. But the cells had no connection to each other and the nerves were unable to muster one spark of voluntary movement. Distress bombarded her, noise rose in her ears, pounding, nauseating her….

His face came closer, stilled the vertigo, swept over the cacophony, stifling it.

Her turmoil subsided. She didn't have to fight the pull of gravity, didn't have to fear the paralysis.

He was here. And he'd take care of everything.

She had no idea how she knew that. But she knew it.

She knew *him.*

Not that she had any idea who he was.

But everything inside her told her that she was safe, that everything would be okay. Because he was here.

Now if only she could get any part of her to work.

She shouldn't feel so inert upon waking up. But was she waking up? Or was she dreaming? That would explain the detachment between brain and body. That would explain *him.* He was too much to be real.

But she knew he was real. She just knew she wasn't imaginative enough to have made him up.

She knew something else, too. This man was important. In general. And to her, he was more than important. Vital.

"Cybele?"

Was that his voice? That dark, fathomless caress?

It so suited the sheer magnificence of his face….

"Can you hear me?"

Boy, could she. She more than heard him. His voice spread across her skin, her pores soaking it up as if they were starved for nourishment. It permeated her with its richness, its every inflection sparking an inert nerve, restarting a vital process, reviving her.

"Cybele, if you can hear me, if you're awake this time, *por favor,* answer me."

Por favor? Spanish? Figured. So that's where the tinge of an accent came from—English intertwining with the sensuous music of the Latin tongue. She wanted to answer him. She wanted him to keep talking. Each syllable out of those works of art he had for lips, crooned in that intoxicating voice, was lulling her back to oblivion, this time a blissful one.

His face filled her field of vision. She could see every shard of gold among the emerald, moss and caramel that swirled into a luminous color she was certain she'd never seen except in his eyes.

She wanted to stab her fingers into the lushness of his raven mane, cup that leonine head, bring him even closer so she could pore over every strand's hue and radiance. She wanted to trace each groove and slash and plane that painted his face in complexity, wanted to touch each radiation of character.

This was a face mapped with anxiety and responsibility and distinction. She wanted to absorb the first, ease the second and marvel at the third. She wanted those lips against her own, mastering, filling her with the tongue that wrapped around those words and created such magic with them.

She knew she shouldn't be feeling anything like that now, that her body wasn't up to her desires. Her *body* knew that, but didn't acknowledge its incapacitation. It just needed him, close, all that maleness and bulk and power, all that tenderness and protection.

She craved this man. She'd always craved him.

"Cybele, *por Dios*, say something."

It was the raggedness, tearing at the power of his voice, that stirred her out of her hypnosis, forced her vocal cords to tauten, propelled air out of her lungs through them to produce the sound he demanded so anxiously.

"I c-can hear you…."

That came out an almost soundless rasp. From the way he tilted his ear toward her mouth, it was clear he wasn't sure whether she *had* produced sound or if he'd imagined it, whether it had been words or just a groan.

She tried again. "I'm a-awake…I think…I hope, a-and I h-hope you're r-real…."

She couldn't say anything more. Fire lanced in her throat, sealing it with a molten agony. She tried to cough up what felt like red-hot steel splinters before they burned through her larynx. Her sand-filled eyes gushed tears, ameliorating their burning dryness.

"Cybele!"

And he was all around her. He raised her, cradled her in the curve of a barricade of heat and support, seeping warmth into her frozen, quivering bones. She sank in his power, surrendered in relief as he cupped her head.

"Don't try to talk anymore. You were intubated for long hours during your surgery and your larynx must be sore."

Something cool touched her lips, then something warm and spicily fragrant lapped at their parched seam. Not his lips or his tongue. A glass and a liquid. She instinctively parted her lips and the contents rushed in a gentle flow, filling her mouth.

When she didn't swallow, he angled her head more securely. "It's a brew of anise and sage. It will soothe your throat."

He'd anticipated her discomfort, had been ready with a remedy. But why was he explaining? She would swallow anything he gave her. If she could without feeling as if nails were being driven into her throat. But he wanted her to. She had to do what he wanted.

She squeezed her eyes against the pain, swallowed. The liquid slid through the rawness, its peppery tinge bringing more tears to her eyes. That lasted only seconds. The soreness subsided under the balmy taste and temperature.

She moaned with relief, feeling rejuvenated with every encouraging sweep of tenderness that his thumb brushed over her cheek as she finished the rest of the glass's contents.

"Better now?"

The solicitude in his voice, in his eyes, thundered through her. She shuddered under the impact of her gratitude, her need to hide inside him, dissolve in his care. She tried to answer him, but this time it was emotion that clogged her throat.

But she *had* to express her thankfulness.

His face was so close, clenched with concern, more magnificent in proximity, a study of perfection in slashes of strength and carvings of character. But haggardness had sunk redness into his eyes, iron into his jaw, and the unkemptness of a few days' growth of rough silk over that jaw and above those lips caused her heart to twist. The need to absorb his discomforts and worries as he had hers mushroomed inside her.

She turned her face, buried her lips into his hewn cheek. The bristle of his beard, the texture of his skin, the taste and scent of him tingled on her flesh, soaked into her senses. A gust of freshness and virility coursed through her, filled her lungs. His breath, rushing out on a ragged exhalation.

She opened her lips for more just as he jerked around to face her. It brought his lips brushing hers. And she knew.

This was the one thing she'd needed. This intimacy. With him.

Something she'd always had before and had missed?

Something she'd had before and had lost? Something she'd never had and had long craved?

It didn't matter. She had it now.

She glided her lips against his, the flood of sensuality and sweetness of her flesh sweeping against his sizzling through her.

Then her lips were cold and bereft, the enclosure of muscle and maleness around her gone.

She slumped against what she now realized was a bed.

Where had he gone? Had it all been a hallucination? A side effect of emerging from a coma?

Her eyes teared up again with the loss. She turned her swimming head, searching for him, terrified she'd find only emptiness.

Far from emptiness, she registered her surroundings for the first time, the most luxurious and spacious hospital suite she'd ever seen. But if he wasn't there…

Her darting gaze and hurtling thoughts came to an abrupt halt.

He *was* there. Standing where he'd been when she'd first opened her eyes. But his image was distorted this time, turning him from an angel into a wrathful, inapproachable god who glowered down at her with disapproval.

She blinked once, then again, her heart shedding its sluggish rhythm for frantic pounding.

It was no use. His face remained cast in coldness. Instead of the angel she'd thought would do anything to protect her, this was the face of a man who'd stand aside and brood down at her as she drowned.

She stared up at him, something that felt as familiar as a second skin settling about her. Despondence.

It had been an illusion. Whatever she'd thought she'd seen

on his face, whatever she'd felt flooding her in waves, had been her disorientation inventing what she wanted to see, to feel.

"It's clear you can move your head. Can you move everything else? Are you in any pain? Blink if it's too uncomfortable to talk. Once for yes, twice for no."

Tears surged into her eyes again. She blinked erratically. A low rumble unfurled from his depths. Must be frustration with her inability to follow such a simple direction.

But she couldn't help it. She now recognized his questions for what they were. Those asked of anyone whose consciousness had been compromised, as she was now certain hers had been. Ascertaining level of awareness, then sensory and motor functions, then pain level and site. But there was no personal worry behind the questions anymore, just clinical detachment.

She could barely breathe with missing his tenderness and anxiety for her well-being. Even if she'd imagined them.

"Cybele! Keep your eyes open, stay with me."

The urgency in his voice snapped through her, made her struggle to obey him. "I c-can't…."

He seemed to grow bigger, his hewn face etched with fierceness, frustration rippling off him. Then he exhaled. "Then just answer my questions, and I'll leave you to rest."

"I f-feel numb but…" She concentrated, sent signals to her toes. They wiggled. That meant everything in between them and her brain was in working order. "Seems…motor functions are…intact. Pain—not certain. I feel sore…like I've been flattened under a—a brick wall. B-but i-it's not pain indicating damage…"

Just as the last word was out, all aches seemed to seep from every inch of her body to coalesce in one area. Her left arm.

In seconds she shot beyond the threshold of containable pain into brain-shredding agony.

It spilled from her lips on a butchered keen. “M-my arm…”

She could swear he didn’t move. But she found him beside her again, as if by magic, and cool relief splashed over the hot skewers of pain, putting them out.

She whimpered, realized what he’d done. She had an intravenous line in her right arm. He’d injected a drug—a narcotic analgesic from the instantaneous action—into the saline, flicked the drip to maximum.

“Are you still in pain?” She shook her head. He exhaled heavily. “That’s good enough for now. I’ll come back later….” He started to move away.

“No.” Her good hand shot out without conscious volition, fueled by the dread that he’d disappear and she’d never see him again. This felt instinctive, engrained, the desperation that she could lose him. Or was it the resignation that he was already lost to her?

Her hand tightened around his, as if stronger contact would let her read his mind, reanimate hers, remind her what he’d been to her.

He relinquished her gaze, his incandescent one sweeping downward to where her hand was gripping his. “Your reflexes, motor power and coordination seem to be back to normal. All very good signs you’re recovering better than my expectations.”

From the way he said that, she guessed his expectations had ranged from pessimistic to dismal. “That…should be…a relief.”

“Should be? You’re not glad you’re okay?”

“I am. I guess. Seems…I’m not…all there yet.” The one thing that made her feel anything definite was him. And he could have been a mile away with the distance he’d placed between them. “So…what happened…to me?”

The hand beneath hers lurched. "You don't remember?"

"It's all a…a blank."

His own gaze went blank for an endless moment. Then it gradually focused on her face, until she felt it was penetrating her, like an X-ray that would let him scan her, decipher her condition.

"You're probably suffering from post-traumatic amnesia. It's common to forget the traumatic episode."

Spoken like a doctor. Everything he'd said and done so far had pointed to him being one.

Was that all he was to her? Her doctor? Was that how he knew her? He'd been her doctor before the "traumatic episode" and she'd had a crush on him? Or had he just read the vital statistics on her admission papers? Had she formed dependence on and fascination for him when she'd been drifting in and out of consciousness as he'd managed her condition? Had she kissed a man who was here only in his professional capacity? A man who could be in a relationship, maybe married with children?

The pain of her suppositions grew unbearable. And she just had to know. "Wh-who are you?"

The hand beneath hers went still. All of him seemed to become rock, as if her question had a Medusa effect.

When he finally spoke, his voice had dipped an octave lower, a bass, slowed-down rasp, "You don't know me?"

"Sh-should I?" She squeezed her eyes shut as soon as the words were out. She'd just kissed him. And she was telling him that she had no idea who he was. "I know I should…b-but I can't r-remember."

Another protracted moment. Then he muttered, "You've forgotten me?"

She gaped up at him, shook her head, as if the movement would slot some comprehension into her mind. "Uh…I may have forgotten…how to speak, too. I had this…distinct belief language skills…are the last to go…e-even in total…memory loss. I thought…saying I can't remember you…was the same as saying…I forgot who y-you are."

His gaze lengthened until she thought he wouldn't speak again. Ever. Then he let out a lung-deflating exhalation, raked his fingers through his gleaming wealth of hair. "I'm the one who's finding it hard to articulate. Your language skills are in perfect condition. In fact, I've never heard you speak that much in one breath."

"M-many fractured…breaths…you mean."

He nodded, noting her difficulty, then shook his head, in wonder it seemed. "One word to one short sentence at a time was your norm."

"So you…*do* know me. E-extensively, it seems."

The wings of his thick eyebrows drew closer together. "I wouldn't label my knowledge of you extensive."

"I'd label it…en-encyclopedic."

Another interminable silence. Then another darkest-bass murmur poured from him, thrumming every neuron in her hypersensitive nervous system. "It seems your memory deficit is the only thing that's extensive here, Cybele."

She knew she should be alarmed at this verdict. She wasn't.

She sighed. "I love…the way…you say…my name."

And if she'd thought he'd frozen before, it was nothing compared to the stillness that snared him now. It was as if time and space had hit a pause button and caught him in their stasis field.

Then, in such a controlled move, as if he were afraid she was made of soap bubbles and she'd burst if he as much as rattled the air around her, he sat down beside her on her pristine white bed.

His weight dipped the mattress, rolling her slightly toward

him. The side of her thigh touched his through the thickness of his denim pants, through her own layers of covering. Something slid through the mass of aches that constituted her body, originating from somewhere deep within her, uncoiling through her gut to pool into her loins.

She was barely functioning, and he could wrench that kind of response from her every depleted cell? What would he do to her if she were in top condition? What *had* he done? Because she was certain this response to him wasn't new.

"You really don't remember who I am at all."

"You really…are finding it hard…to get my words, aren't you?" Her lips tugged. She was sure there was no humor in this situation, that when it all sank in she'd be horrified about her memory loss and what it might signify of neurological damage.

But for now, she just found it so endearing that this man, who she didn't need memory to know was a powerhouse, was so shaken by the realization.

It also said he cared what happened to her, right? She could enjoy that belief now, even if it proved to be a delusion later.

She sighed again. "I thought it was clear…what I meant. At least it sounded…clear to me. But what would I know? When I called your…knowledge of me…encyclopedic, I should have added…compared to mine. I haven't only…forgotten who you are, I have no idea…who *I* am."

Two

Rodrigo adjusted the drip, looking anywhere but at Cybele.

Cybele. His forbidden fruit. His ultimate temptation.

The woman whose very existence had been like corrosive acid coursing through his arteries. The woman the memory of whom he would have given anything to wake up free of one day.

And it was she who'd woken up free of the memory of him.

It had been two days since she'd dropped this bomb on him.

He was still reverberating with the shock.

She'd told him she didn't remember the existence that was the bane of his. She'd forgotten the very identity that had been behind the destruction of one life. And the poisoning of his own.

And he shouldn't care. Shouldn't *have* cared. Not beyond

the care he offered his other patients. By all testimonies, he went above and beyond the demands of duty and the dictates of compassion for each one. He shouldn't have neglected everyone and everything to remain by her side, to do everything for her when he could have delegated her care to the highly qualified professionals he'd painstakingly picked and trained, those he paid far more than money to keep doing the stellar job they did.

He hadn't. During the three interminable days after her surgery until she woke up, whenever he'd told himself to tend to his other duties, he couldn't. She'd been in danger, and it had been beyond him to leave her.

Her inert form, her closed eyes, had been what had ruled him. The drive to get her to move, to open her eyes and look at him with those endless inky skies that had been as inescapable as a black hole since they'd first had him in their focus, had been what motivated him.

Periodically she had opened them, but there had been no sight or comprehension in them, no trace of the woman who'd invaded and occupied his thoughts ever since he'd laid eyes on her.

Yet he'd prayed that, if she never came back, her body would keep on functioning, that she'd keep opening her eyes, even if it was just a mechanical movement with no sentience behind it.

Two days ago, she'd opened those eyes and the blankness had been replaced by the fog of confusion. His heart had nearly torn a hole in his ribs when coherence had dawned in her gaze. Then she'd looked at him and there had been more.

He should have known then that she was suffering from something he hadn't factored in. Finding her distance and disdain replaced by warmth that had escalated to heat should have given him his first clue. Having her nuzzle him like a feline delighted at finding her owner, then that kiss that had rocked him to his foundations, should have clenched the diagnosis.

The Cybele Wilkinson he knew—his nemesis—would never have looked at or touched him that way if she were in her right mind. If she knew who he was.

It had still taken her saying that she wasn't and didn't to explain it all. And he'd thought *that* had explained it all.

But it was even worse. She didn't remember herself.

There was still something far worse. The temptation not to fill in the spaces that had consumed her memories, left her mind a blank slate. A slate that could be inscribed with anything that didn't mean they had to stay enemies.

But they had to. Now more than ever.

"I see you're still not talking to me."

Her voice, no longer raspy, but a smooth, rich, molten caress sweeping him from the inside out, forced him to turn his eyes to her against his will. "I've talked to you every time I came in."

"Yeah, two sentences every two hours for the past two days." She huffed something that bordered on amusement. "Feels like part of your medication regimen. Though the sparseness really contrasts with the intensiveness of your periodic checkups."

He could have relegated *those*, which hadn't needed to be so frequent, or so thorough, to nurses under his residents' supervision. But he hadn't let anyone come near her.

He turned his eyes away again, pretended to study her chart. "I've been giving you time to rest, for your throat to heal and for you to process the discovery of your amnesia."

She fidgeted, dragging his gaze back to her. "My throat has been perfectly fine since yesterday. It's a miracle what some soothing foods and drinks and talking to oneself can do. And I haven't given my amnesia any thought. I know I should be alarmed, but I'm not. Maybe it's a side effect of the trauma, and it will crash on me later as I get better. *Or*...I'm subconsciously relieved not to remember."

His voice sounded alien as he pushed an answer past the brutal temptation, the guilt, the rage, at her, at himself, at the whole damned universe. "Why wouldn't you want to remember?"

Her lips crooked. "If I knew, it wouldn't be a subconscious wish, would it? Am I still making sense only in my own ears?"

He tore his gaze away from her lips, focused on her eyes, cleared thorns from his throat. "No. I am not having an easy time processing the fact that you have total memory loss."

"And without memories, my imagination is having a field day thinking of outlandish explanations for why I'm not in a hurry to have my memories back. At least they seem outlandish. They might turn out to be the truth."

"And what are those theories?"

"That I was a notorious criminal or a spy, someone with a dark and dangerous past and who's in desperate need of a second chance, a clean slate. And now that it's been given to me, I'd rather not remember the past—my own identity most of all."

She struggled to sit up, groaning at the aches he knew her body had amassed. He tried to stop himself.

He failed. He lunged to help her, tried not to feel the supple heat of her flesh fill his hands as he pulled her up, adjusted her bed to a gentle slope. He struggled to ignore the gratitude filling her eyes, the softness of trust and willingness exhibited by every inch of her flesh. He roared inwardly at his senses as the feel and scent of her turned his insides to molten lava, his loins to rock. He gritted his teeth, made sure her intravenous line and the other leads monitoring her vital signs were secure.

Her hands joined his in checking her line and leads, an

unconscious action born of engrained knowledge and ongoing application. He stepped away as if from a fiery pit.

She looked up at him, those royal blue eyes filling with a combo of confusion and hurt at his recoil. He took one more step back before he succumbed to the need to erase that crestfallen expression.

She lowered her eyes. “So—you’re a doctor. A surgeon?”

He was, for once, grateful for her questions. “Neurosurgeon.”

She raised her eyes again. “And from the medical terms filling my mind and the knowledge of what the machines here are and what the values they’re displaying mean—I’m some kind of medical professional, too?”

“You were a senior trauma/reconstructive surgery resident.”

“Hmm, that blows my criminal or spy theories out of the water. But maybe I was in another form of trouble before I ended up here? A ruinous malpractice suit? Some catastrophic mistake that killed someone? Was I about to have my medical license revoked?”

“I never suspected you had this fertile an imagination.”

“Just trying to figure out why I’m almost relieved I don’t remember a thing. Was I perhaps running away to start again where no one knows me? Came here and…hey, where *is* here?”

He almost kept expecting her to say *gotcha*. But the notion of Cybele playing a trick on him was more inconceivable than her total memory loss. “This is my private medical center. It’s on the outskirts of Barcelona.”

“We’re in Spain?” Her eyes widened. His heart kicked. Even with her lids still swollen and her face bruised and pallid, she was the most beautiful thing he’d ever seen. “Okay, scratch that question. As far as my general knowledge can tell—and I feel it remains unaffected—there is no Barcelona anywhere else."

"Not that I know of, no."

"So—I sound American."

"You are American."

"And you're Spanish?"

"Maybe to the world, which considers all of Spain one community and everyone who hails from there as Spanish. But I am Catalan. And though in Catalonia we have the same king, and a constitution that declares 'the indissoluble unity of the Spanish nation,' we were the first to be recognized as a *Nacionalidad* and a *Comunidad Autónoma* or a distinct historical nationality and an autonomous community, along with the Basque Country and Galicia. There are now seventeen such communities that make up Spain, with our rights to self-government recognized by the constitution."

"Fascinating. Sort of a federation, like the United States."

"There are similarities, but it's a different system. The regional governments are responsible for education, health, social services, culture, urban and rural development and, in some places, policing. But contrary to the States, Spain is described as a decentralized country, with central government spending estimated at less than twenty percent." And he was damned if he knew why he was telling her all that, now of all times.

She chewed her lower lip that was once again the color of deep pink rose petals. His lips tingled with the memory of those lips, plucking at them, bathing them with intoxicating heat and moistness. "I knew some of that, but not as clearly as you've put it."

He exhaled his aggravation at the disintegration of his sense and self-control. "Pardon the lesson. My fascination with the differences between the two systems comes from having both citizenships."

"So you acquired the American citizenship?"

"Actually, I was born in the States, and acquired my Spanish citizenship after I earned my medical degree. Long story."

"But you have an accent."

He blinked his surprise at the implication of her words, something he'd never suspected. "I spent my first eight years in an exclusively Spanish-speaking community in the States and learned English only from then on. But I was under the impression I'd totally lost the accent."

"Oh, no, you haven't. And I hope you never lose it. It's *gorgeous*."

Everything inside him surged. This was something else he'd never considered. What she'd do to him if, instead of hostility, admiration and invitation spread on her face, invaded her body, if instead of bristling at the sight of him, she looked at him as if she'd like nothing more than to feast on him. As she was now.

What was going on here? How had memory loss changed her character and attitude so diametrically? Did that point to more neurological damage than he'd feared? Or was this what she was really like, what her reaction to him would have been if not for the events that had messed up their whole situation?

"So…what's your name? What's mine, too, apart from Cybele?"

"You're Cybele Wilkinson. I'm Rodrigo."

"Just…Rodrigo?"

She used to call him Dr. Valderrama, and in situations requiring informality she'd avoided calling him anything at all. But now she pressed back into her pillows, let his name melt on her tongue as if it were the darkest, richest chocolate.

He felt her contented purr cascade down his body, caress his aching hardness….

This was unbelievable. That she could do this to him *now*. Or at all. It was worse than unbelievable. It was unacceptable.

He shredded his response. "Rodrigo Edmundo Arrellano i Bazán Valderrama i de Urquiza."

Her eyes widened a fraction more with each surname. Then a huff that bordered on a giggle escaped her. "I did ask."

His lips twisted. "That's an excerpt of my names, actually. I can rattle off over forty more surnames."

She giggled for real this time. "That's a family tree going back to the Spanish Inquisition."

"The Catalan, and the Spanish in general, take family trees very seriously. Because both maternal and paternal ancestors are mentioned, each name makes such a list. The Catalan also put *i* or *and* between surnames."

"And do I have more than the measly Wilkinson?"

"All I know is that your father's name was Cedric."

"Was? H-he's dead?"

"Since you were six or seven, I believe."

She seemed to have trouble swallowing again. He had to fist his hands against the need to rush to her side again.

His heart still hammered in protest against his restraint when she finally whispered, "Do I have a mother? A family?"

"Your mother remarried and you have four half siblings. Three brothers and one sister. They all live in New York City."

"D-do they know what happened to me?"

"I did inform them. Yesterday." He hadn't even thought of doing so until his head nurse had stressed the necessity of alerting her next of kin. For the seventh time. He hadn't even registered the six previous times she had mentioned it.

He waited for her next logical question. If they were on their way here to claim responsibility for her.

His gut tightened. Even with all he had against her, not the least of which was the reaction she wrenched from him, he hated to have to answer that question. To do so, he'd have to tell her that her family's response to her danger had been so offhand, he'd ended the phone call with her mother on a barked, "Don't bother explaining your situation to me, Mrs. Doherty. I'm sure you'd be of more use at your husband's business dinner than you would be at Cybele's bedside."

But her next question did not follow a logical progression. Just as this whole conversation, which she'd steered, hadn't. "So…what happened to me?"

And this was a question he wanted to avoid as fiercely.

No way to do that now that she'd asked so directly. He exhaled. "You were in a plane crash."

A gasp tore out of her. "I just knew I was in an accident, that I wasn't attacked or anything, but I thought it was an MVA or something. But…a plane crash?" She seemed to struggle with air that had gone thick, lodging in her lungs. He rocked on his heels with the effort not to rush to her with an oxygen mask and soothing hands. "Were there many injured o-or worse?"

Dios. She really remembered nothing. And he was the one who had to tell her. Everything. "It was a small plane. Seated four. There were only…two onboard this time."

"Me and the pilot? I might not remember anything, but I just know I can't fly a plane, small or otherwise."

This was getting worse and worse. He didn't want to answer her. He didn't want to relive the three days before she'd woken up, that had gouged their scars in his psyche and soul.

He could pretend he had a surgery, escape her interrogation.

He couldn't. Escape. Stop himself from answering her. "He was flying the plane, yes."

"Is—is he okay, too?"

Rodrigo gritted his teeth against the blast of pain that detonated behind his sternum. "He's dead."

"Oh, God…." Her tears brimmed again and he couldn't help himself anymore. He closed the distance he'd put between them, stilled the tremors of her hand with both of his. "D-did he die on impact?"

He debated telling her that he had. He could see survivor's guilt mushrooming in her eyes. What purpose did it serve to tell her the truth but make her more miserable?

But then he always told his patients the truth. Sooner or later that always proved the best course of action.

He inhaled. "He died on the table after a six-hour surgery."

During those hours, he'd wrestled with death, gaining an inch to lose two to its macabre pull, knowing that it would win the tug-of-war. But what had wrecked his sanity had been knowing that while he fought this losing battle, Cybele had been lying in his ER tended to by others.

Guilt had eaten through him. Triage had dictated he take care of her first, the one likely to survive. But he couldn't have let Mel go without a fight. It had been an impossible choice. Emotionally, professionally, morally. He'd gone mad thinking she'd die or suffer irreversible damage because he'd made the wrong one.

Then he'd lost the fight for Mel's life among colleagues' proclamations that it had been a miracle he'd even kept him alive for hours when everyone had given up on him at the accident scene.

He'd rushed to her, knowing that while he'd exercised the ultimate futility on Mel, her condition had worsened. Terror of losing her, too, had been the one thing giving him continued access to what everyone extolled as his vast medical knowledge and surgical expertise.

"Tell me, please. The details of his injuries."

He didn't want to tell her how terrible it had all been.

But he had to. He inhaled a stream of what felt like aerosolized acid, then told her.

Her tears flowed steadily over a face gone numb with horror throughout his chilling report.

She finally whispered, "How did the accident happen?"

He needed this conversation to be over. He gritted his teeth. "That is one thing only you can know for sure. And it'll probably be the last memory to return. The crash site and plane were analyzed for possible whys and hows. The plane shows no signs of malfunction and there were no distress transmissions prior to the crash."

"So the pilot just lost control of the plane?"

"It would appear so."

She digested this for a moment. "What about my injuries?"

"You should only concern yourself now with recuperating."

"But I need to know a history of my injuries, their progression and management, to chart my recuperation."

He grudgingly conceded her logic. "On site, you were unconscious. You had a severely bleeding scalp wound and bruising all over your body. But your severest injury was comminuted fractures of your left ulna and radius."

She winced as she looked down on her splinted arm. "What was my Glasgow Coma Scale scoring?"

"Eleven. Best eye response was three, with your eyes opening only in response to speech. Best verbal response was four, with your speech ranging from random words to confused responses.

Best motor function was four with flexion withdrawal response to pain. By the time I operated on you, your GCS had plunged to five."

"Ouch. I was heading for decorticate coma. Did I have intracranial hemorrhage?"

He gave a difficult nod. "It must have been a slow leak. Your initial CTs and MRIs revealed nothing but slight brain edema, accounting for your depressed consciousness. But during the other surgery, I was informed of your deteriorating neurological status, and new tests showed a steadily accumulating subdural hematoma."

"You didn't shave my hair evacuating it."

"No need. I operated via a new minimally invasive technique I've developed."

She gaped at him. "You've developed a new surgical technique? Excuse me while my mind, tattered as it is, barrels in awe."

He grunted something dismissive. She eyed him with a wonder that seemed only to rise at his discomfort. Just as he almost growled *stop it*, she raised one beautifully dense and dark eyebrow at him. "I trust I wasn't the guinea pig for said technique?"

Cybele gazed up at Rodrigo, a smile hovering on her lips.

His own lips tightened. "You're fine, aren't you?"

"If you consider having to get my life story from you as *fine*."

The spectacular wings of his eyebrows snapped together. That wasn't annoyance or affront. That was mortification. Pain, even.

Words couldn't spill fast enough from her battered brain to her lips. "God, that was such a lame joke. Just shows I'm in no condition to know how or when to make one. I owe you my life."

"You owe me nothing. I was doing my job. And I didn't even do it well. I'm responsible for your current condition. It's my failure to manage you first that led to the deepening of the insult to your brai—"

"The pilot's worst injuries were neurological." She cut him short. It physically hurt to see the self-blame eating at him.

"Yes, but that had nothing to do with my decision—"

"And I bet you're the best neurosurgeon on the continent."

"I don't know about that, but being the most qualified one on hand didn't mea—"

"It *did* mean you had to take care of him yourself. And my initial condition misled you into believing my case wasn't urgent. You did the right thing. You fought for this man as he deserved to be fought for. And then you fought for me. And you saved me. And then, I'm certain my condition is temporary."

"We have no way of knowing that. Having total memory loss with the retention of all faculties of language and logic and knowledge and no problem in accumulating new memories is a very atypical form of amnesia. It might never resolve fully."

"Would that be a bad thing, in your opinion? If the idea of regaining my memories is almost…distressing, maybe my life was so bad, I'm better off not remembering it?"

He seemed at a loss for words. Then he finally found some. "I am not in a position to know the answer to that. But I am in a position to know that memory loss is a neurological deficit, and it's my calling to fix those. I can't under any circumstances wish that this wouldn't resolve. Now, if you'll excuse me, I need to tend to my other patients. I'll be back every three hours to check on you."

With a curt nod, he turned and left her, exiting the huge, opulent suite in strides loaded with tense grace.

She wanted to run after him, beg him to come back.

What could possibly explain all this turmoil and her severe attraction to him? Had they been lovers, married even, and they'd separated, or maybe divorced…?

She suddenly lurched as if from the blow of an ax as a memory lodged in her brain. No…a knowledge.

She *was* married.

And it was certainly not to Rodrigo.

Three

Rodrigo did come back in three hours. And stayed for three minutes. Long enough to check on her and adjust her medical management. Then he repeated that pattern for the next three days. She even felt him come in during her fitful sleep.

She hadn't had the chance to tell him what she'd remembered.

No. She hadn't *wanted* to tell him. Discovering she was married, even if she didn't know to whom, wasn't on her list of things to share with him of all people.

And he probably already knew.

She *could* have told him that she'd also remembered who she was. But then, she hadn't remembered much beyond the basics he'd told her.

This boded well for her memory deficit, if it was receding so early.

She didn't want it to recede, wanted to cling to the blankness with all her strength.

But it was no use. A few hours ago, a name had trickled into the parting darkness of her mind. Mel Braddock.

She was certain that was her husband's name. But she couldn't put a face to the name. The only memory she could attach to said name was a profession. General surgeon.

Beyond that, she remembered nothing of the marriage. She knew only that something dark pressed down on her every time the knowledge of it whispered in her mind.

She couldn't possibly feel this way if they'd been on good terms. And if he wasn't here, days after his wife had been involved in a serious accident, were they separated, getting divorced even? She was certain she was still married. Technically, at least. But the marriage was over. That would explain her overriding emotions for Rodrigo, that she innately knew it was okay to feel them.

On the strike of three hours, Rodrigo returned. And she'd progressed from not wanting to bring up any of it to wanting to scream it all at the top of her lungs.

He made no eye contact with her as he strode in flanked by two doctors and a nurse. He never came unescorted anymore. It was as if he didn't want to be alone with her again.

He checked her chart, informed his companions of his adjustment of her medications as if she wasn't in the room much less a medical professional who could understand everything they were saying. Frustration frothed inside her. Then it boiled over.

"I remembered a few things."

Rodrigo went still at her outburst. The other people in the room fidgeted, eyed her uncomfortably before turning uncertain gazes to their boss. Still without looking at her, he hung her chart back at the foot of the bed, murmured something clearly meant for the others' ears alone. They rushed out in a line.

The door had closed behind the last departing figure for over two minutes before he turned his eyes toward her.

She shuddered with the force of his elemental impact.

Oh, please. Let me have the right to feel this way about him.

The intensity of his being buzzed in her bones—of his focus, of his…wariness?

Was he anxious to know what she remembered? Worried about it? Because he suspected what it was—the husband she remembered only in name? He'd told her of her long-dead father, her existing family, but not about that husband. Would he have told her if she hadn't remembered?

But there was something more in his vibe. Something she'd felt before. After she'd kissed him. Disapproval? Antipathy?

Had they been on bad terms before the accident? How could they have been, if she felt this vast attraction to him, untainted by any negativity? Had the falling out been her fault? Was he bitter? Was he now taking care of her to honor his calling, his duty, giving her extra special care for old times' sake, yet unable to resume their intimacy? *Had* they been intimate? Was he her lover?

No. He wasn't.

She might not remember much about herself, but the thought of being in a relationship, no matter how unhealthy, and seeking involvement with another felt abhorrent to her, no matter how inexorable the temptation. And then, there was him. He radiated nobility. She just knew Rodrigo Valderrama would never poach on another man's grounds, never cross the lines of honor, no matter how much he wanted her or how dishonorable the other man was.

But there was one paramount proof that told her they'd never been intimate. Her body. It burned for him but knew it had never had him. It would have borne his mark on its every cell if it had.

So what did it all mean? He had to tell her, before something beside memories short-circuited inside her brain.

He finally spoke. “What did you remember?”

“Who I am. That I’m married.” He showed no outward reaction. So he *had* known. “Why didn’t you tell me?”

“You didn’t ask.”

“I asked about family.”

“I thought you were asking about flesh-and-blood relatives.”

“You’re being evasive.”

“Am I?” He held her gaze, making her feel he was giving her a psyche and soul scan. Maybe trying to steer her thoughts, too. “So you remember everything?”

She exhaled. “I said I remembered ‘a few things.’ Seems I’m a stickler for saying exactly what I mean.”

“You said you remembered who you were, and your marriage. That’s just about everything, isn’t it?”

“Not when I remember only the basics about myself, the name you told me, that I went to Harvard Medical School, that I worked at St. Giles Hospital and that I’m twenty-nine. I know far less than the basics about my marriage. I remembered only that I have a husband, and his name and profession.”

“That’s all?”

“The rest is speculation.”

“What kind of speculation?”

“About the absence of both my family and husband more than a week after I’ve been involved in a major accident. I can only come up with very unfavorable explanations.”

“What would those be?”

“That I’m a monster of such megaproportions that no one

felt the need to rush to my bedside." Something flared in his eyes, that harshness. So she was right? He thought so, too? Her heart compressed as she waited for him to confirm or negate her suspicions. When he didn't, she dejectedly had to consider his silence as corroboration, condemnation. She still looked for a way out for herself, for her family. "Unless it is beyond them financially to make the trip here?"

"As far as I know, finances are no issue to your family."

"So you told them I was at death's door, and no one bothered to come."

"I told them no such thing. You weren't at death's door."

"It *could* have gone either way for a while."

Silence. Heavy. Oppressive. Then he simply said, "Yes."

"So I'm on the worst terms with them."

It seemed he'd let this go uncommented on, too. Then he gave a noncommittal shrug. "I don't know about the worst terms. But it's my understanding you're not close."

"Not even with my mother?"

"Especially with your mother."

"Great. See? I was right when I thought I was better off not remembering. Not knowing."

"It isn't as bad as you're painting it. By the time I called your family, you were stable, and there really was nothing for any of them to do but wait like the rest of us. Your mother did call twice for updates, and I told her you were doing very well. Physically. Psychologically, I suggested it might not be a good thing in this early phase for you to be jogged by their presence or contact, any more than you already are."

He was making excuses for her family, her mother. If they'd cared, they wouldn't have been satisfied with long-distance assurances. Or maybe he had discouraged them from coming, so he wouldn't introduce an unpredictable emotional element into her neurological recovery?

The truth was, she didn't care right now how things really stood with her family. What she was barely able to breathe from needing to know was her status with her husband.

"And that's my not-so-bad situation with my family. But from my husband's pointed absence, I can only assume the worst. That maybe we're separated or getting divorced."

She wanted him to say, *Yes, you are.*

Please, say it.

His jaw muscles bunched, his gaze chilled. When he finally spoke it felt like an arctic wind blasting her, freezing her insides with this antipathy that kept spiking out of nowhere.

"Far from being separated, you and your husband have been planning a second honeymoon."

Cybele doubted the plane crashing into the ground had a harder impact than Rodrigo's revelation.

Her mind emptied. Her heart spilled all of its beats at once.

For a long, horrified moment she stared at him, speech skills and thought processes gone, only blind instincts left. They all screamed *run, hide, deny.*

She'd been so certain…so…certain…

"A second honeymoon?" She heard her voice croaking. "Does that mean we…we've been married long?"

He waited an eternity before answering. At least it felt that way. By the time he did, she felt she'd aged ten years. "You were married six months ago."

"Six *months?* And already planning a second honey-moon?"

"Maybe I should have said honeymoon, period. Circumstances stopped you from having one when you first got married."

"And yet my adoring husband isn't here. Our plans probably were an attempt to salvage a marriage that was malfunctioning beyond repair, and we shouldn't have bothered going through the motions…."

She stopped, drenched in mortification. She instinctively knew she wasn't one to spew vindictiveness like that. Her words had been acidic enough to eat through the gleaming marble floor.

Their corrosiveness had evidently splashed Rodrigo. From the way his face slammed shut, he clearly disapproved of her sentiments and the way she'd expressed them. Of her.

"I don't know much about your relationship. But his reason for not being at your bedside *is* uncontestable. He's dead."

She lurched as if he'd backhanded her.

"He was flying the plane," she choked.

"You remember?"

"No. Oh, God." A geyser of nausea shot from her depths. She pitched to the side of the bed. Somehow she found Rodrigo around her, holding her head and a pan. She retched emptily, shook like a bell that had been struck by a giant mallet.

And it wasn't from a blow of grief. It was from one of horror, at the anger and relief that were her instinctive reactions.

What kind of monster was she to feel like that about somebody's death, let alone that of her husband? Even if she'd fiercely wanted out of the relationship. Was it because of what she felt for Rodrigo? She'd wished her husband dead to be with him?

No. *No.* She just knew it hadn't been like that. It had to have been something else. Could her husband have been abusing her? Was she the kind of woman who would have suffered humiliation and damage, too terrified to block the blows or run away?

She consulted her nature, what transcended memory, what couldn't be lost or forgotten, what was inborn and unchangeable.

It said, no way. If that man had abused her, emotionally or physically, she would have carved his brains out with forceps and sued him into his next few reincarnations.

So what did this mess mean?

"Are you okay?"

She shuddered miserably. "If feeling mad when I should be sad is okay. There must be more wrong with me than I realized."

After the surprise her words induced, contemplation settled on his face. "Anger *is* a normal reaction in your situation."

"What?" He knew why it was okay to feel so mad at a dead man?

"It's a common reaction for bereaved people to feel anger at their loved ones who die and leave them behind. It's worse when someone dies in an accident that that someone had a hand in or caused. The first reaction after shock and disbelief is rage, and it's all initially directed toward the victim. That also explains your earlier attack of bitterness. Your subconscious must have known that he was the one flying the plane. It might have recorded all the reports that flew around you at the crash site."

"You're saying I speak Spanish?"

He frowned. "Not to my knowledge. But maybe you approximated enough medical terminology to realize the extent of his injuries…."

"Ya lo sé hablar español."

She didn't know which of them was more flabbergasted.

The Spanish words had flowed from a corner in her mind to her tongue without conscious volition. And she certainly knew what they meant. *I know how to speak Spanish.*

"I…had no idea you spoke Spanish."

"Neither did I, obviously. But I get the feeling that the knowledge is partial…fresh."

"Fresh? How so?"

"It's just a feeling, since I remember no facts. It's like I've only started learning it recently."

He fixed her with a gaze that seeped into her skin, mingled into the rapids of her blood. Her temperature inched higher.

Was he thinking what she was thinking? That she'd started learning Spanish because of him? To understand his mother tongue, understand *him* better, to get closer to him?

At last he said, "Whatever the case may be, you evidently know enough Spanish to validate my theory."

He was assigning her reactions a perfectly human and natural source. Wonder what he'd say if she set him straight?

She bet he'd think her a monster. And she wouldn't blame him. She was beginning to think it herself.

Next second she was no longer thinking it. She knew it.

The memory that perforated her brain like a bullet was a visual. An image that corkscrewed into her marrow. The image of Mel, the husband she remembered with nothing but anger, whose death aroused only a mixture of resentment and liberation.

In a wheelchair.

Other facts dominoed like collapsing pillars, crushing everything beneath their impact. Not memories, just knowledge.

Mel had been paralyzed from the waist down. In a car accident. *During* their relationship. She didn't know if it had been before or after they'd gotten married. She didn't think it mattered.

She'd been right when she'd hypothesized why no one had rushed to her bedside. She was heartless.

What else could explain harboring such harshness toward someone who'd been so afflicted? The man she'd promised to love in sickness and in health? The one she'd basically felt "good riddance" toward when death *did* them part?

In the next moment, the air was sucked out of her lungs from a bigger blow.

"Cybele? *¿Te duele?*"

Her ears reverberated with the concern in Rodrigo's voice, her vision rippled over the anxiety warping his face.

No. She wasn't okay.

She was a monster. She was amnesic.

And she was pregnant.

Four

Excruciating minutes of dry retching later, Cybele lay surrounded by Rodrigo, alternating between episodes of inertness and bone-rattling shudders.

He soothed her with the steady pressure of his containment, wiping her eyelids and lips in fragrant coolness, his stroking persistent, hypnotic. His stability finally earthed her misery.

He tilted the face she felt had swollen to twice its original size to his. "You remembered something else?"

"A few things," she hiccupped, struggled to sit up. The temptation to lie in his arms was overwhelming. The urge only submerged her under another breaker of guilt and confusion.

He helped her sit up, then severed all contact, no doubt not wanting to continue it a second beyond necessary.

Needing to put more distance between them, she swung her numb legs to the floor, slipped into the downy slippers that were among the dozens of things he'd supplied for her comfort, things that felt tailored to her size and needs and desires.

She wobbled with her IV drip pole to the panoramic window overlooking the most amazing verdant hills she'd ever seen. Yet she saw nothing but Rodrigo's face, seared into her retinas, along with the vague but nausea-inducing images of Mel in his wheelchair, his rugged good looks pinched and pale, his eyes accusing.

She swung around, almost keeled over. She gasped, saw Rodrigo's body bunch like a panther about to uncoil in a flying leap. He was across the room, but he'd catch her if she collapsed.

She wouldn't. Her skin was crackling where he'd touched her. She couldn't get enough of his touch but couldn't let him touch her again. She held out a detaining hand, steadied herself.

He still rose but kept his distance, his eyes catching the afternoon sun, which poured in ropes of warm gold through the wall-to-wall glass. Their amalgamated color glowed as he brooded across the space at her, his eyebrows lowered, his gaze immobilizing.

She hugged her tender left shoulder, her wretchedness thickening, hardening, settling into concrete deadness. "The things I just remembered…I wouldn't call them real memories. At least, not when I compare them to the memories I've been accumulating since I regained consciousness. I remember those in Technicolor, frame by frame, each accompanied by sounds and scents and sensations. But the things I just recalled came in colorless, soundless and shapeless, like skeletons of data and knowledge. Like headings without articles. If that makes any sense."

He lowered his eyes to his feet, before raising them again, the surgeon in him assessing. "It makes plenty of sense. I've dealt with a lot of post-traumatic amnesia cases, studied endless records, and no one described returning memories with more economy and efficiency than you just did. But it's still early. Those skeletal memories will be fleshed out eventually...."

"I don't want them fleshed out. I want them to stop coming, I want what came back to disappear." She squeezed her shoulder, inducing more pain, to counteract the skewer turning in her gut. "They'll keep exploding in my mind until they blow it apart."

"What did you remember this time?"

Her shoulders sagged. "That Mel was a paraplegic."

He didn't nod or blink or breathe. He just held her gaze. It was the most profound and austere acknowledgment.

And she moaned the rest, "And I'm pregnant."

He blinked, slowly, the motion steeped in significance. He knew. And it wasn't a happy knowledge. Why?

One explanation was that she'd been leaving Mel, but he'd become paralyzed and she'd discovered her pregnancy and it had shattered their plans. Was that the origin of the antipathy she had felt radiating from him from time to time? Was he angry at her for leading him on then telling him that she couldn't leave her husband now that he was disabled and she was expecting his child?

She wouldn't know unless he told her. It didn't seem he was volunteering any information.

She exhaled. "Judging from my concave abdomen, I'm in the first trimester."

"Yes." Then as if against his better judgment, he added, "You're three weeks pregnant."

"Three *weeks*...? How on earth do you know that? Even if you had a pregnancy test done among others before my surgery, you can't pinpoint the stage of my pregnancy that accurate—" Her words dissipated under another gust of realization. "I'm pregnant through IVF. That's how you know how far along I am."

"Actually, you had artificial insemination. Twenty days ago."

"Don't tell me. You know the exact hour I had it, too."

"It was performed at 1:00 p.m."

She gaped at him, finding nothing to explain that too-specific knowledge. And the whole scenario of her pregnancy.

If it had been unplanned and she'd discovered it after she'd decided to leave Mel, that would still make her a cold-blooded two-timer. But it hadn't been unplanned. Pregnancies didn't come more planned than *that.* Evidently, she'd *wanted* to have a baby with Mel. So much that she'd made one through a procedure, when he could no longer make one with her the normal way. The intimate way.

So their marriage *had* been healthy. Until then. Which gave credence to Rodrigo's claim that they'd been planning a honeymoon. Maybe to celebrate her pregnancy.

So how come her first reaction to his death was bitter relief, and to her pregnancy such searing dismay?

What kind of twisted psyche did she have?

There was only one way to know. Rodrigo. He kept filling in the nothingness that had consumed most of what seemed to have been a maze of a life. But he was doing so reluctantly, cautiously, probably being of the school that thought providing another person's memories would make reclaiming hers more difficult, or would taint or distort them as they returned.

She didn't care. Nothing could be more tainted or distorted than her own interpretations. Whatever he told her would provide context, put it all in a better light. Make her someone she could live with. She had to pressure him into telling her what he knew....

Her streaking thoughts shrieked to a halt.

She couldn't *believe* she hadn't wondered. About *how* he knew what he knew. She'd let his care sweep her up, found his knowledge of her an anchoring comfort she hadn't thought to question.

She blurted out the questions under pressure. "Just how do you know all this? How do you know me? And Mel?"

The answer detonated in her mind.

It was that look in his eyes. Barely curbed fierceness leashed behind the steel control of the surgeon and the suave refinement of the man. She remembered *that* look. *Really* remembered it. Not after she'd kissed him. Long before that. In that life she didn't remember.

In that life, Rodrigo had despised her.

And it hadn't been because she'd led him on, then wouldn't leave Mel. It was worse. Far worse.

He'd been Mel's best friend.

The implications of this knowledge were horrifying.

However things had been before, or worse, *after* Mel had been disabled, if she'd exhibited her attraction to Rodrigo, then he had good reason to detest her. The best.

"You remembered."

She raised hesitant eyes at his rasp. "Sort of."

"Sort of? Now that's eloquent. More skeletal headlines?"

There was that barely contained fury again. She blinked back distress. "I remember that you were his closest friend, and that's how you know so much about us, down to the hour we had a procedure to conceive a baby. Sorry I can't do better." And she was damned if she'd ask him what the situation between *them* had been. She dreaded he'd verify her speculations. "I'm sure the rest will come back. In a flood or bit by bit. No need to hang around here waiting for either event. I want to be discharged."

He looked at her as if she'd sprouted two more sets of eyes. "Get back in bed, now, Cybele. Your lucidity is disintegrating with every moment on your feet, every word out of your mouth."

"Don't give me the patronizing medical tone, Dr. Valderrama. I'm a license-holding insider, if you remember."

"You mean if *you* remember, don't you?"

"I remember enough. I can recuperate outside this hospital."

"You can only under meticulous medical supervision."

"I can provide that for myself."

"You mean you don't 'remember' the age-proven adage that doctors make the worst patients?"

"It has nothing to do with remembering it, just not subscribing to it. I can take care of myself."

"No, you can't. But I will discharge you. Into my custody. I will take you to my estate to continue your recuperation."

His declaration took the remaining air from her lungs.

His custody. His estate. She almost swayed under the impact of the images that crowded her mind, of what both would be like, the temptation to jump into his arms and say *Yes, please.*

She had to say no. Get away from him. And fast. "Listen, I was in a terrible accident, but I got off pretty lightly. I would have died if you and your ultra-efficient medical machine hadn't intervened, but you did, and you fixed me. I'm fine."

"You're so far from fine, you could be in another galaxy."

It was just *wrong*. That he'd have a sense of humor, too. That it would surface now. And would pluck at her own humor strings.

She sighed at her untimely, inappropriate reaction. "Don't exaggerate. All I have wrong with me is a few missing memories."

"A few? Shall we make a list of what you do remember, those headlines with the vanished articles, and another of the volumes you've had erased and might never be able to retrieve, then revisit your definition of 'a few'?"

"Cute." And he was. In an unbearably virile and overruling way. "But at the rate I'm retrieving headlines, I'll soon have enough to fill said volumes."

"Even if you do, that isn't your only problem. You had a severe concussion with brain edema and subdural hematoma. I operated on you for ten hours. Half of those were with orthopedic and vascular surgeons as we put your arm back together. Ramón said it was the most intricate open reduction and internal fixation of his career, while Bianca and I had a hell of a time repairing your blood vessels and nerves. Afterward, you were comatose for three days and woke up with a total memory deficit. Right now your neurological status is suspect, your arm is useless, you have bruises and contusions from head to toe and you're in your first trimester. Your body will need double the time and effort to heal during this most physiologically demanding time. It amazes me you're talking, and that much, moving at all and not lying in bed disoriented and sobbing for more painkillers."

"Thanks for the rundown of my condition, but seems I'm more amazing than you think. I'm pretty lucid and I can talk as endlessly as *you* evidently can. And the pain is nowhere as bad as before."

"You're pumped full of painkillers."

"No, I'm not. I stopped the drip."

"What?" He strode toward her in steps loaded with rising tension. He inspected her drip, scowled down on her. "When?"

"The moment you walked out after your last inspection."

"That means you have no more painkillers in your system."

"I don't need any. The pain in my arm is tolerable now. I

think it was coming out of the anesthesia of unconsciousness that made it intolerable by comparison."

He shook his head. "I think we also need to examine your definition of 'pretty lucid.' You're not making sense to me. Why feel pain at all, when you can have it dealt with?"

"Some discomfort keeps me sharp, rebooting my system instead of lying in drug-induced comfort, which might mask some deterioration in progress. What about *that* doesn't make sense to you?"

He scowled. "I *was* wondering what kept you up and running."

"Now you know. *And* I vividly recall my medical training. I may be amnesic but I'm not reckless. I'll take every precaution, do things by the post-operative, post-trauma book...."

"I'm keeping you by my side until I'm satisfied that you're back to your old capable-of-taking-on-the-world self."

That silenced whatever argument she would have fired back.

She'd had the conviction that he didn't think much of her.

So he believed she was strong, but despised her because she'd come on stronger to him? Could she have done something so out-of-character? She abhorred infidelity, found no excuse for it. At least the woman who'd awakened from the coma did not.

Then he surprised her more. "I'm not talking about how you were when you were with Mel, but before that."

She didn't think to ask how he knew what she'd been like before Mel. She was busy dealing with the suspicion that he was right, that her relationship with Mel *had* derailed her.

More broad lines resurfaced. How she'd wanted to be nothing like her mother, who'd left a thriving career to serve the whims of Cybele's stepfather, how she'd thought she'd never marry, would have a child on her own when her career had become unshakable.

Though she didn't have a time line, she sensed that until months ago, she'd held the same convictions.

So how had she found herself married, at such a crucial time as her senior residency year, and pregnant, too? Had she loved Mel so much that she'd been so blinded? Had she had setbacks in her job in consequence, known things would keep going downhill and that was why she remembered him with all this resentment? Was that why she'd found an excuse to let her feelings for Rodrigo blossom?

Not that there could be an excuse for that.

But strangely, she wasn't sorry she was pregnant. In fact, that was what ameliorated this mess, the one thing she was looking forward to. That…and, to her mortification, being with Rodrigo.

Which was exactly why she couldn't accept his carte blanche proposal.

"Thank you for the kind offer, Rodrigo—"

He cut her off. "It's neither kind nor an offer. It's imperative and it's a decision."

Now *that* was a premium slice of unadulterated autocracy.

She sent up a fervent thank-you for the boost to her seconds-ago-nonexistent resistance. "Imperative or imperious? Decision or dictate?"

"Great language recall and usage. And take your pick."

"I think it's clear I already did. And whatever you choose to call your *offer*, I can't accept it."

"You mean you won't."

"Fine. If you insist on dissecting my refusal. I won't."

"It seems you *have* forgotten all about me, Cybele. If you remembered even the most basic things, you'd know that when I make a decision, saying no to me is not an option."

Cybele stared at him. Life was grossly, horribly unfair. How did one being end up endowed with all that?

And she'd thought he had it all before she'd seen him crook his lips in that I-click-my-fingers-and-all-sentient-beings-obey quasi smile.

Now there was one thought left in her mind. An urge. To get as far away from him as possible. Against all logic. And desire.

Her lips twisted, too. "I didn't get that memo. Or I 'forgot' I did. So *I* can say no to you. Consider it a one-off anomaly."

That tiger-like smirk deepened. "You can say what you want. I'm your surgeon and what *I* say goes."

The way he'd said *your surgeon*. Everything clamored inside her, wishing he was her anything-and-everything, for real.

She shook her head to disperse the idiotic yearnings. "I'll sign any waiver you need me to. I'm taking full responsibility."

"I'm the one taking full responsibility for you. If you do remember being a surgeon, you know that my being yours makes me second only to God in this situation. You have no say in God's will, do you?"

"You're taking the God complex too literally, aren't you?"

"My status in your case is an uncontestable fact. You're in my care and will remain there until I'm satisfied you no longer need it. The one choice I leave up to you is whether I follow you up in my home as my guest, or in my hospital as my patient."

Cybele looked away from his hypnotic gaze, his logic. But there was no escaping either. It *had* been desperation, wanting to get away from him. She *wasn't* in a condition to be without medical supervision. And who best to follow her up but her own surgeon? The surgeon who happened to be the best there was?

She knew he was. He was beyond the best. A genius. With billions and named-after-him revolutionary procedures and equipment to prove it.

But even had she been fit, she wouldn't have wanted to be

discharged. For where could she go but home? A home she recalled with nothing but dreariness?

And she didn't want to be with anyone else. Certainly not with her mother and family. She remembered them as if they were someone else's unwanted acquaintances. Disappointing and distant. Their own actions reinforced that impression. The sum total of their concern over her accident and Mel's death had been a couple of phone calls. When told she was fine, didn't need anything, it seemed they'd considered it an excuse to stop worrying—if they *had* been worried—dismiss her and return to their real interests. She didn't remember specifics from her life with them, but this felt like the final straw in a string of lifelong letdowns.

She turned her face to him. He was watching her as if he'd been manipulating her thoughts, steering her toward the decision he wanted her to make. She wouldn't put mental powers beyond him. What was one more covert power among the glaringly obvious ones?

She nodded her capitulation.

He tilted his awesome head at her. "You concede your need for my supervision?" He wanted a concession in words? Good luck with that. She nodded again. "And which will it be? Guest or patient?"

He wanted her to pick, now? She'd hoped to let things float for a couple of days, until she factored in the implications of being either, the best course of action....

Just great. A scrambled memory surely hadn't touched her self-deception ability. Seemed she had that in spades.

She knew what the best course of action was. She *should* say patient. Should stay in the hospital where the insanities he provoked in her would be curbed, where she wouldn't be able to act on them. She *would* say patient.

Then she opened her mouth. "As if you don't already know."

She barely held back a curse, almost took the sullen words back.

She didn't. She was mesmerized by his watchfulness, by seeing it evaporate in a flare of…something. Triumph?

She had no idea. It was exhausting enough trying to read her own thoughts and reactions. She wasn't up to fathoming his. She only hoped he'd say something superior and smirking. It might trip a fuse that would make her retreat from the abyss of stupidity and self-destructiveness, do what sense and survival were yelling for her to do. Remain here, remain a patient to him, nothing more.

"It'll be an honor to have you as my guest, Cybele." Distress brimmed as the intensity in his eyes drained, leaving them as gentle as his voice. It was almost spilling over when that arrogance she'd prayed for coated his face. "It's a good thing you didn't say 'patient,' though. I would have overruled you again."

She bristled. "Now look here—"

He smoothly cut across her offense. "I would have, because I built this center to be a teaching hospital, and if you stay, there is no way I can fairly stop the doctors and students from having constant access to you, to study your intriguing neurological condition."

Seemed not only did no one say no to him, no one ever won an argument with him, either. He'd given her the one reason that would send her rocketing out of this hospital like a cartoon character with a thick trail of white exhaust clouds in her wake.

No way would she be poked and prodded by med students and doctors-in-training. In the life that felt like a half-remembered documentary of someone else's, she'd been both, then the boss of a bunch of the latter. She knew how nothing—starting with patients' comfort, privacy, even basic human rights—stood in the way of acquiring their coveted-above-all experience.

She sighed. "You always get what you want, don't you?"

"No. Not always."

The tormented look that seized his face arrested her in midbreath. Was this about…her? Was *she* something he wanted and couldn't get?

No. She just knew what she felt for him had always been only on her side. On his, there'd been nothing inappropriate. He'd never given her reason to believe the feelings were mutual.

This…despondency was probably about failing to save Mel. That had to be the one thing he'd wanted most. And he hadn't gotten it.

She swallowed the ground glass that seemed to fill her throat. "I—I think I'll take a nap now."

He inhaled, nodded. "Yes, you do that."

He started to turn away, stopped, his eyes focusing far in the distance. He seemed to be thinking terrible things.

A heart-thudding moment later, without looking back again, he muttered, "Mel's funeral is this afternoon." She gasped. She'd somehow never thought of that part. He looked back at her then, face gripped with urgency, eyes storming with entreaty. "You should know."

She gave a difficult nod. "Thanks for telling me."

"Don't thank me. I'm not sure I should have."

"Why? You don't think I can handle it?"

"You seem to be handling everything so well, I'm wondering if this isn't the calm before the storm."

"You think I'll collapse into a jibbering mess somewhere down the road?"

"You've been through so much. I wouldn't be surprised."

"I can't predict the future. But I'm as stable as can be now. I—I want to go. I have to."

"You don't have to do anything, Cybele. Mel wouldn't have wanted you to go through the added trauma."

So Mel had cared for her? Wanted the best for her?

She inhaled, shook her head. "I'm coming. You're not going to play the not-neurologically-stable-enough card, are you?"

His eyes almost drilled a crater of conflicted emotions between her own. "You should be okay. If you do everything I say."

"And what is that?"

"Rest now. Attend the funeral in a wheelchair. And leave when I say. No arguments."

She hadn't the energy to do more than close her eyelids in consent. He hesitated, then walked back to her, took her elbow, guided her back to the bed. She sagged down on it.

He, too, dropped down, to his haunches. Heartbeats shook her frame as he took one numb foot after the other, slid off slippers that felt as if they were made of hot iron. He rose, touched her shoulder, didn't need to apply force. She collapsed like water in a fountain with its pressure lost. He scooped up her legs, swung them over the bed, swept the cotton cover over her, stood back and murmured, "Rest."

Without another look, he turned and crossed the room as if he'd been hit with a fast-forward button.

The moment the door clicked shut, shudders overtook her.

Rest? He really thought she could? After what he'd just done? Before she had to attend her dead husband's funeral?

She ached. For him, because of him, because she breathed, with guilt, with lack of guilt.

She could only hope that the funeral, the closure ritual, might open up the locked, pitch-black cells in her mind.

Maybe then she'd get answers. And absolution.

Five

She didn't rest.

Four hours of tossing in bed later, at the entry of a genial brunette bearing a black skirt suit and its accessories, Cybele staggered up feeling worse than when she'd woken from her coma.

She winced a smile of thanks at the woman and insisted she didn't need help dressing. Her fiberglass arm cast was quite light and she could move her shoulder and elbow joints well enough to get into the front-fastening jacket and blouse.

After the woman left, she stood staring at the clothes Rodrigo had provided for her. To attend the funeral of the husband she didn't remember. Didn't want to remember.

She didn't need help dressing. She needed help de-stressing.

No chance of that. Only thing to do was dress the part, walk in and out of this. Or rather, get wheeled in and out.

In minutes she was staring at her reflection in the full-wall mirror in the state-of-the-art, white and gray bathroom.

Black wool suit, white silk blouse, two-inch black leather shoes. All designer items. All made as if for her.

A knock on the door ripped her out of morbid musings over the origin of such accuracy in judging her size.

She wanted to dart to the door, snatch it open and yell, *Let's get it over with.*

She walked slowly instead, opened the door like an automaton. Rodrigo was there. With a wheelchair. She sat down without a word.

In silence, he wheeled her through his space-age center to a gigantic elevator that could accommodate ten gurneys and their attending personnel. This was obviously a place equipped and staffed to deal with mass casualty situations. She stared ahead as they reached the vast entrance, feeling every eye on her, the woman their collective boss was tending to personally.

Once outside the controlled climate of the center, she shivered as the late February coolness settled on her face and legs. He stopped before a gleaming black Mercedes 600, slipped the warmth of the cashmere coat she realized had been draped over his arm all along around her shoulders as he handed her into the back of the car.

In moments he'd slid in beside her on the cream leather couch, signaled the chauffeur and the sleek beast of a vehicle shot forward soundlessly, the racing-by vistas of the Spanish countryside the only proof that it was streaking through the nearly empty streets.

None of the beauty zooming by made it past the surface of her awareness. All deeper levels converged on him. On the turmoil in the rigidity of his profile, the coiled tension of his body.

And she couldn't bear it anymore. "I'm…so sorry."

He turned to her. "What are you talking about?"

The harshness that flickered in his eyes, around his lips made her hesitate. It didn't stop her. "I'm talking about Mel." His eyes seemed to lash out an emerald flare. She almost backed down, singed and silenced. She forged on. "About your loss." His jaw muscles convulsed then his face turned to rock, as if he'd sucked in all emotion, buried it where it would never resurface for anyone to see. "I don't remember him or our relationship, but you don't have that mercy. You've lost your best friend. He died on your table, as you struggled to save him…."

"As I *failed* to save him, you mean."

His hiss hit her like the swipe of a sword across the neck.

She nearly suffocated on his anguish. Only the need to drain it made her choke out, "You didn't fail. There was nothing you could have done." His eyes flared again, zapping her with the force of his frustration. "Don't bother contradicting me or looking for ways to shoulder a nonexistent blame. Everyone knew he was beyond help."

"And that's supposed to make me feel better? What if I don't want to feel better?"

"Unfounded guilt never did anyone any good. Certainly not the ones we feel guilty over."

"How logical you can be, when logic serves no purpose."

"I thought you advocated logic as what serves every purpose."

"Not in this instance. And what I feel certainly isn't hurting me any. I'm as fit as an ox."

"So you're dismissing emotional and psychological pain as irrelevant? I know that as surgeons we're mainly concerned with physical disorders, things we can fix with our scalpels, but—"

"But nothing. I'm whole and hearty. Mel is dead."

"Through no fault of yours!" She couldn't bear to see him

bludgeoning himself with pain and guilt that way. "That's the only point I'm making, the only one to *be* made here. I know it doesn't make his loss any less traumatic or profound. And I am deeply sorry for—everyone. You, Mel, his parents, our baby."

"But not yourself?"

"No."

The brittle syllable hung between them, loaded with too much for mere words to express, and the better for it, she thought.

Twenty minutes of silence later her heart hiccupped in her chest. They were entering a private airport.

With every yard deeper into the lush, grassy expanses, tentacles of panic slid around her throat, slithered into her mind until the car came to a halt a few dozen feet from the stairs of a gleaming silver Boeing 737.

She blindly reached out to steady herself with the one thing that was unshakeable in her world. Rodrigo.

His arm came around her at the same moment she sought his support, memories billowing inside her head like the sooty smoke of an oil-spill fire. "This is where we boarded the plane."

He stared down at her for a suspended moment before closing his eyes. "*Dios, lo siento,* Cybele—I'm so sorry. I didn't factor in what it would do to you, being here, where your ordeal began."

She snatched air into her constricted lungs, shook her head. "It's probably the right thing to do, bringing me here. Maybe it'll get the rest of my memories to explode back at once. I'd welcome that over the periodic detonations."

"I can't take credit for attempting shock therapy. We're here for Mel's funeral." She gaped at him. He elaborated. "It's not a traditional funeral. I had Mel's parents flown over from the States so they can take his body home."

She struggled to take it all in. Mel's body. Here. In that hearse over there. His parents. She didn't remember them. At all. They must be in the Boeing. Which had to be Rodrigo's. They'd come down, and she'd see them. And instead of a stricken widow they could comfort and draw solace from, they'd find a numb stranger unable to share their grief.

"Rodrigo..." The plea to take her back now, that she'd been wrong, couldn't handle this, congealed in her throat.

He'd turned his head away. A man and a woman in their early sixties had appeared at the jet's open door.

He reached for his door handle, turned to her. "Stay here."

Mortification filled her. She was such a wimp. He'd felt her reluctance to face her in-laws, was sparing her.

She couldn't let him. She owed them better than that. She'd owe any grieving parents anything she could do to lessen their loss. "No, I'm coming with you. And no wheelchair, please. I don't want them to think I'm worse than I am." He pursed his lips, then nodded, exited the car. In seconds he was on her side, handing her out. She crushed his formal suit's lapel. "What are their names?"

His eyes widened, as if shocked all over again at the total gaps in her memory. "Agnes and Steven Braddock."

The names rang distant bells. She hadn't known them long, or well. She was sure of that.

The pair descended as she and Rodrigo headed on an intercept course. Their faces became clearer with every step, setting off more memories. Of how Mel had looked in detail. And in color.

Her father-in-law had the same rangy physique and wealth of hair, only it was gray where Mel's had been shades of bronze. Mel had had the startlingly turquoise eyes of her mother-in-law.

She stopped when they were a few steps way. Rodrigo didn't.

He kept going, opened his arms, and the man and woman rushed right into them. The three of them merged into an embrace that squeezed her heart dry of its last cell of blood.

Everything hurt. Burned. She felt like strips were being torn out of her flesh. Acid filled her eyes, burned her cheeks.

The way he held them, the way they sought his comfort and consolation as if it was their very next breath, the way they all clung together… The way he looked, wide open and giving everything inside him for the couple to take their fill of, to draw strength from…

Just when she would have cried out *Enough—please*, the trio dissolved their merger of solace, turned, focused on her. Then Agnes closed the steps between them.

She tugged Cybele into a trembling hug, careful not to brush against her cast. "I can't tell you how worried we were for you. It's a prayer answered to see you so well." So well? She'd looked like a convincing postmortem rehearsal last time she'd consulted a mirror. But then, compared to Mel, she was looking great. "It's why we were so late coming here. Rodrigo couldn't deal with this, with anything, until you were out of danger."

"He shouldn't have. I can't imagine how you felt, having to put th-this off."

Agnes shook her head, the sadness in her eyes deepening. "Mel was already beyond our reach, and coming sooner would have served no purpose. You were the one who needed Rodrigo's full attention so he could pull you through."

"He did. And while everyone says he's phenomenal with all his patients, I'm sure he's gone above and beyond even by his standards. I'm as sure it's because I was Mel's wife. It's clear what a close friend of the whole family he is."

The woman looked at her as if she'd said Rodrigo was in reality a reptile. "But Rodrigo isn't just a friend of the family. He's our son. He's Mel's brother."

* * *

Cybele felt she'd stared at Agnes for ages, feeling her words reverberating in her mind in shock waves.

Rodrigo. Wasn't Mel's best friend. Was his brother. *How?*

"You didn't know?" Agnes stopped, tutted to herself. "What am I asking. Rodrigo told us of your memory loss. You've forgotten."

She hadn't. She was positive. This was a brand-new revelation.

Questions heaved and pitched in her mind, splashed against the confines of her skull until she felt they'd shatter it.

Before she could relieve the pressure, launch the first few dozen, Rodrigo and Steven closed in on them. Rodrigo stood back as Steven mirrored his wife's actions and sentiments.

"We've kept Cybele on her feet long enough," Rodrigo addressed the couple who claimed to be his parents. "Why don't you go back to the car with her, Agnes, while Steven and I arrange everything."

Agnes? Steven? He didn't call them mother and father?

She would have asked to be involved if she wasn't burning for the chance to be alone with Agnes, to get to the bottom of this.

As soon as they settled into the car, Cybele turned to Agnes. And all the questions jammed in her mind.

What would she ask? How? This woman was here to claim her son's body. What would she think, feel, if said son's widow showed no interest in talking about him and was instead panting to know all about the man who'd turned out to be his brother?

She sat there, feeling at a deeper loss than she had since she'd woken up in this new life. Rodrigo's chauffeur offered them refreshments. She parroted what Agnes settled on, mechanically sipped her mint tea every time Agnes did hers.

Suddenly Agnes started to talk, the sorrow that coated her face mingling with other things. Love. Pride.

"Rodrigo was six, living in an exclusively Hispanic community in Southern California, when his mother died in a factory accident and he was taken into the system. Two years later, when Mel was six, we decided that he needed a sibling, one we'd realized we'd never be able to give him."

So that was it. Rodrigo was adopted.

Agnes went on. "We took Mel with us while we searched, since our one criteria for the child we'd adopt was that he get along with Mel. But Mel antagonized every child we thought was suited to our situation, got them to turn nasty. Then Rodrigo was suggested to us. We were told he was everything Mel wasn't—responsible, resourceful, respectful, with a steady temperament and a brilliant mind. But we'd been told so many good things about other children and we'd given up hope that any child would pass the test of interaction with Mel. Then Rodrigo walked in.

"After he introduced himself in the little English he knew, enquired politely why we were looking for another child, he asked to be left alone with Mel. Unknown to both boys, we were taken to where children's meetings with prospective parents were monitored. Mel was at his nastiest, calling Rodrigo names, making fun of his accent, insulting his parentage and situation. We were mortified that he even knew those…words, and would use them so viciously. Steven thought he felt threatened by Rodrigo, as he had by any child we sought. I told him whatever the reason, I couldn't let Mel abuse the poor boy, that we'd been wrong and Mel didn't need a sibling but firmer treatment until he outgrew his sullenness and nastiness. He hushed me, asked me to watch. And I watched.

"Rodrigo had so far shown no reaction. By then, other boys had lashed out, verbally and physically, at Mel's bullying. But

Rodrigo sat there, watching him in what appeared to be deep contemplation. Then he stood up and calmly motioned him closer. Mel rained more abuse on him, but when he still didn't get the usual reaction, he seemed to be intrigued. I was certain Rodrigo would deck him and sneer *gotcha* or something. I bet Mel thought the same.

"We all held our breath as Rodrigo put a hand in his pocket. My mind streaked with worst-case scenarios. Steven surged up, too. But the director of the boys' home detained us. Then Rodrigo took out a butterfly. It was made of cardboard and elastic and metal springs and beautifully hand-painted. He wound it up and let it fly. And suddenly Mel was a child again, giggling and jumping after the butterfly as if it were real.

"We knew then that Rodrigo had won him over, that our search for a new son was over. I was shaking as we walked in to ask Rodrigo if he'd like to come live with us. He was stunned. He said no one wanted older children. We assured him that we did want him, but that he could try us out first. He insisted it was he who would prove himself to us. He turned and shook Mel's hand, told him he'd made other toys and promised to teach him how to make his own."

The images Agnes had weaved were overwhelming. The vision of Rodrigo as a child was painfully vivid. Self-possessed in the face of humiliation and adversity, stoic in a world where he had no one, determined as he proved himself worthy of respect.

"And did he teach him?" she asked.

Agnes sighed. "He tried. But Mel was short-fused, impatient, never staying with anything long enough for it to bear fruit. Rodrigo never stopped trying to involve him, get him to experience the pleasures of achievement. We loved him with all our hearts from the first day, but loved him more for how hard he tried."

"So your plan that a sibling would help Mel didn't work?"

"Oh, no, it did. Rodrigo did absorb a great deal of Mel's angst and instability. He became the older brother Mel emulated in everything. It was how Mel ended up in medicine."

"Then he must have grown out of his impatience. It takes a lot of perseverance to become a doctor."

"You really don't remember a thing about him, do you?" Now what did that mean? Before she pressed for an elaboration, Agnes sighed again. "Mel was brilliant, could do anything if only he set his mind to it. But only Rodrigo knew how to motivate him, to keep him in line. And when Rodrigo turned eighteen, he moved out."

"Why? Wasn't he happy with you?"

"He assured us that his need for independence had nothing to do with not loving us or not wanting to be with us. He confessed that he'd always felt the need to find his roots."

"And you feared he was only placating you?"

Agnes's soft features, which showed a once-great beauty lined by a life of emotional upheavals, spasmed with recalled anxiety. "We tried to help as he searched for his biological family, but his methods were far more effective, his instincts of where to look far sharper. He found his maternal relatives three years later and his grandparents were beside themselves with joy. Their whole extended family welcomed him with open arms."

Cybele couldn't think how anyone wouldn't. "Did he learn the identity of his father?"

"His grandparents didn't know. They had had a huge quarrel with his mother when she got pregnant and she wouldn't reveal the father's identity. She left home, saying she'd never return to their narrow-minded world. Once they had calmed down, they searched for her everywhere, kept hoping she'd come home. But they never heard from her again. They were devastated to learn their daughter was long dead, but ecstatic that Rodrigo had found them."

"And he changed his name from yours to theirs then?"

"He never took our name, just kept the name his mother had used. There were too many obstacles to our adopting him, and when he realized our struggles, he asked us to stop trying, said he knew we considered him our son and we didn't need to prove it to him. He was content to be our foster son to the world. He was eleven at the time. When he found his family, he still insisted *we* were his real family, since it was choice and love that bound us and not blood. He didn't legally take their names until he made sure we knew that it just suited his identity more to have his Catalan names."

"And you still thought he'd walk out of your life."

Agnes exhaled her agreement. "It was the worst day of my life when he told us that he was moving to Spain as soon as his medical training was over. I thought my worst fears of losing him had come true."

It struck Cybele as weird that Agnes didn't consider the day Mel had died the worst day of her life. But she was too intent on the story for the thought to take hold. "But you didn't lose him."

"I shouldn't have worried. Not with Rodrigo. I should have known he'd never abandon us, or even neglect us. He never stopped paying us the closest attention, was a constant presence in our lives—more so even than Mel, who lived under the same roof. Mel always had a problem expressing his emotions, and showed them with material, not moral, things. That's probably why he…he…" She stopped, looked away.

"He what?" Cybele tried not to sound rabid with curiosity. They were getting to some real explanation here. She knew it.

She almost shrieked with frustration when Agnes ignored her question, returned to her original topic. "Rodrigo continued to rise to greater successes but made sure we were there to share the joy of every step with him. Even when he moved here, he never let us or Mel feel that he was far away. He was constantly after us to move here, too, to start projects we've long dreamed of, offered us everything we'd need to establish them. But Mel said Spain was okay for vacations but he was a New Yorker and could never live anywhere else. Though it was a difficult decision, we decided to stay in the States with him. We thought he was the one who…needed our presence more. But we do spend chunks of every winter with Rodrigo, and he comes to the States as frequently as possible."

And she'd met him during those frequent trips. Over and over. She just knew it. But she was just as sure, no matter how spotty her memory was, that *this* story hadn't been volunteered by anyone before. She was certain she hadn't been told Rodrigo was Mel's foster brother. Not by Mel, not by Rodrigo.

Why had neither man owned up to this fact?

Agnes touched her good hand. "I'm so sorry, my dear. I shouldn't have gone on and on down memory lane."

And the weirdest thing was, Agnes's musings hadn't been about the son she'd lost, but the son she'd acquired thirty years ago. "I'm glad you did. I need to know anything that will help me remember."

"And did you? Remember anything?"

It wasn't a simple question to ascertain her neurological state. Agnes wanted to know something. Something to do with what she'd started to say about Mel then dropped, as if ashamed, as if too distressed to broach it.

"Sporadic things," Cybele said cautiously, wondering how to lead back to the thread of conversation she just knew would explain why she'd felt this way about Mel, and about Rodrigo.

Agnes turned away from her. "They're back."

Cybele jerked, followed Agnes's gaze, frustration backing

up in her throat. Then she saw Rodrigo prowling in those powerful, control-laden strides and the sight of him drowned out everything else.

Suddenly a collage of images became superimposed over his. Of her and Mel going out with Rodrigo and a different sexpot each time, women who'd fawned over him and whom he'd treated with scathing disinterest, playing true to his reputation as a ruthless playboy.

Something else dislodged in her mind, felt as if an image had moved from the obscurity of her peripheral vision into the clarity of her focus. How Mel had become exasperating around Rodrigo.

If these were true memories, they contradicted everything Agnes had said, everything she'd sensed about Rodrigo. They showed him as the one who was erratic and inconstant, who'd had a disruptive, not a stabilizing, effect on Mel. Could she have overlooked all that, and her revulsion toward promiscuous men, under the spell of his charisma? Or could that have been his attraction? The challenge of his unavailability? The ambition of being the one to tame the big bad wolf? Could she have been that perverse and stupid…?

"Are you ready, Agnes?"

Cybele lurched at the sound of Rodrigo's fathomless baritone.

Stomach churning with the sickening conjectures, she dazedly watched him hand Agnes out of the car. Then he bent to her.

"Stay here." She opened her mouth. A gentle hand beneath her jaw closed it for her. "No arguments, remember?"

"I want to do what you're all going to do," she mumbled.

"You've had enough. I shouldn't have let you come at all."

"I'm fine. Please."

That fierceness welled in his eyes again. Then he gave a curt nod, helped her out of the car.

She didn't only want to be there for these people to whom she felt such a powerful connection. She also hoped she'd get more answers from Agnes before she and Steven flew back home.

Cybele watched Rodrigo stride with Steven to the hearse, where another four men waited. One was Ramón Velázquez, her orthopedic surgeon and Rodrigo's best friend—for real—and partner.

Rodrigo and Ramón shared a solemn nod then opened the hearse's back door and slid the coffin out. Steven and the three other men joined in carrying it to the cargo bay of the Boeing.

Cybele stood transfixed beside Agnes, watching the grim procession, her eyes flitting between Rodrigo's face and Steven's. The same expression gripped both. It was the same one on Agnes's face. Something seemed…off about that expression.

Conjectures ping-ponged inside her head as everything seemed to fast-forward until the ritual was over, and Steven walked back with Rodrigo to join Agnes in hugging Cybele farewell. Then the Braddocks boarded the Boeing and Rodrigo led Cybele back to the Mercedes.

The car had just swung out of the airfield when she heard the roar of the jet's takeoff. She twisted around to watch it sail overhead before it hurtled away, its noise receding, its size diminishing.

And it came to her, why she knew that off expression. It was the exhausted resignation exhibited by families of patients who died after long, agonizing terminal illnesses. It didn't add up when Mel's death had been swift and shocking.

Something else became glaringly obvious. She turned to Rodrigo. He was looking outside his window.

She hated to intrude on the sanctity of his heartache. But she had to make sense of it all. “Rodrigo, I’m sorry, but—”

He rounded on her, his eyes simmering in the rays penetrating the mirrored window. “Don’t say you’re sorry again, Cybele.”

“I’m sor—” She swallowed the apology he seemed unable to hear from her. “I was going to apologize for interrupting your thoughts. But I need to ask. *They* didn’t ask. About my pregnancy.”

He seemed taken aback. Then his face slammed shut. “Mel didn’t tell them.”

This was one answer she hadn’t considered. Yet another twist. “Why? I can understand not telling them of our intention to have a baby this way, in case it didn’t work. But after it did, why didn’t he run to them with the news?”

His shrug was eloquent with his inability to guess Mel’s motivations. With his intention to drop the subject.

She couldn’t accommodate him. “Why didn’t *you* tell them?”

“Because it’s up to you whether or not to tell them.”

“They’re my baby’s grandparents. Of course I want to tell them. If I’d realized they didn’t know, I would have. It would have given them solace, knowing that a part of their son remains.”

His jaw worked for a moment. Then he exhaled. “I’m glad you *didn’t* bring it up. You’re not in any shape to deal with the emotional fallout of a disclosure of this caliber. And instead of providing the solace you think it would have, at this stage, the news would have probably only aggravated their repressed grief.”

But it *hadn’t* been repressed grief she’d sensed from them.

Then again, what did she know? Her perceptions might be as scrambled as her memories. “You’re probably right.” *As usual,* she added inwardly. "I'll tell them when I'm back to normal and I'm certain the pregnancy is stable."

He lowered his eyes, his voice, and simply said, "Yes."

Feeling drained on all counts, she gazed up at him—the mystery that kept unraveling only to become more tangled. The anchor of this shifting, treacherous new existence of hers.

And she implored, "Can we go home now, please?"

Six

He took her home. His home.

They'd driven back from the airport to Barcelona city center. From there it had taken over an hour to reach his estate.

By the time they approached it at sunset, she felt saturated with the sheer beauty of the Catalan countryside.

Then they passed through the electronic, twenty-foot wrought iron gates, wound through the driveway, and with each yard deeper into his domain, she realized. There was no such thing as a limit to the capacity to appreciate beauty, to be stunned by it.

She turned her eyes to him. He'd been silent save for necessary words. She'd kept silent, too, struggling with the contradictions of what her heart told her and what her memories insisted on, with wanting to ask him to dispel her doubts.

But the more she remembered everything he'd said and done, everything everyone had said about him in the past days, the more only one conclusion made sense. Her memories had to be false.

He turned to her. After a long moment, he said, deep, quiet, “Welcome to Villa Candelaria, Cybele.”

She swallowed past the emotions, yet her “Thank you” came out a tremulous gasp. She tried again. “When did you buy this place?”

“Actually, I built it. I named it after my mother.”

The lump grew as images took shape and form. Of him as an orphan who’d never forgotten his mother until he one day was affluent enough to build such a place and name it after her, so her memory would continue somewhere outside of his mind and…

Okay, she’d start weeping any second now. Better steer this away from personal stuff. “This place looks…massive. Not just the building, but the land, too.”

“It’s thirty thousand square feet over twenty acres with a mile-long waterfront. Before you think I’m crazy to build all this for myself, I built it hoping it would become the home of many families, affording each privacy and land for whatever projects and pursuits they wished for. Not that it worked out that way.”

The darkness that stained his face and voice seared her. He’d wished to surround himself with family. And he’d been thwarted at every turn, it seemed. Was he suffering from the loneliness and isolation she felt were such an integral part of her own psyche?

“I picked this land completely by chance. I was driving once, aimlessly, when I saw that crest of a hill overlooking this sea channel.” She looked where he was pointing. “The vision slammed into my mind fully formed. A villa built into those rock formations as if it was a part of them.”

She reversed the process, imagining those elements without

the magnificent villa they now hugged as if it *were* an intrinsic part of their structure. "I always thought of the Mediterranean as all sandy beaches."

"Not this area of the northern Iberian coastline. Rugged rock is indigenous here."

The car drew to a smooth halt in front of thirty-foot wide stone steps among landscaped, terraced plateaus that surrounded the villa from all sides.

In seconds Rodrigo was handing her out and insisting she sit in the wheelchair she hadn't used much today. She acquiesced, wondered as he wheeled her up the gentle slope beside the steps if it had always been there, for older family members' convenience, or if it had been installed to accommodate Mel's condition.

Turning away from futile musings, she surrendered to the splendor all around her as they reached a gigantic patio that surrounded the villa. On one side it overlooked the magnificent property that was part vineyards and orchards and part landscaped gardens, with the valley and mountains in the distance, and on the other side, the breathtaking sea and shoreline.

The patio led to the highest area overlooking the sea, a massive terrace garden that was illuminated by golden lights planted everywhere like luminescent flowers.

He took her inside and she got rapid impressions of the interior as he swept her to the quarters he'd designated for her.

She felt everything had been chosen with an eye for uniqueness and comfort, simplicity and grandeur, blending sweeping lines and spaces with bold wall colors, honey-colored ceilings and furniture that complemented both. French doors and colonial pillars merged seamlessly with the natural beauty of hardwood floors accentuated by marble and granite. She knew she could spend weeks poring over every detail, but in its whole, she felt this was a place this formidable man had wanted his family to love, to feel at home in from the moment they set foot in it. She knew *she* did. And she hadn't technically set foot in it yet.

Then she did. He opened a door, wheeled her in then helped her out of the chair. She stood as he wheeled the chair to one side, walked out to haul in two huge suitcases that had evidently been transported right behind them.

He placed one on the floor and the other on a luggage stand at the far side of the room, which opened into a full-fledged dressing room.

She stood mesmerized as he walked back to her.

He was overwhelming. A few levels beyond that.

He stopped before her, took her hand. She felt as though it burst in flames. "I promise you a detailed tour of the place. Later. In stages. Now you have to rest. Doctor's orders."

With that he gave her hand a gentle press, turned and left.

The moment the door clicked closed behind him, she staggered to lean on it, exhaled a choppy breath.

Doctor's orders. *Her* doctor…

She bit her lip. Hours ago, she'd consigned her husband's body to his parents. And all she could think of was Rodrigo. There wasn't even a twinge of guilt toward Mel. There *was* sadness, but it was the sadness she knew she'd feel for any human being's disability and death. For his loved ones' mourning. Nothing more.

What was wrong with her? What had been wrong with her and Mel? Or was there more wrong with her mind than she believed?

Her lungs deflated on a dejected exhalation.

All she could do now was never let any of those who'd loved and lost Mel know how unaffected by his loss she was. What did it matter what she felt in the secrecy of her heart and mind if she never let the knowledge out to hurt others? She couldn't change the way she felt, should stop feeling bad about it. It served no purpose, did no one any good.

With that rationalization reached, she felt as if a ten-pound rock had been lifted off her heart. Air flowed into her lungs all of a sudden, just as the lovely surroundings registered in her appreciation centers.

The room—if a thirty-something- by forty-something-foot space with a twelve-foot ceiling could be called that—was a manifestation of the ultimate in personal space.

With walls painted sea-blue and green, furniture of dark mahogany and ivory ceilings and accents, it was soothingly lit by golden lamps of the side and standing variety. French doors were draped in gauzy powder-blue curtains that undulated in the twilight sea breeze, wafting scents of salt and freshness with each billow. She sighed away her draining tension and pushed from the wood-paneled door.

She crossed the gleaming hardwood floor to the suitcases. They were more evidence of Rodrigo's all-inclusive care. She was certain she'd never owned anything so exquisite. She wondered what he'd filled them with. If the outfit she had on was any indication, no doubt an array of haute couture and designer items, molding to her exact shape and appealing to her specific tastes.

She tried to move the one on the floor, just to set it on its wheels. Frantic pounding boomed in her head.

Man—what *had* he gotten her to wear? Steel armor in every shade? And he'd made the cases look weightless when he'd hauled them both in, simultaneously. She tugged again.

"*¡Parada!*"

She swung around at the booming order, the pounding in her head crashing down her spine to settle behind her ribs.

A robust, unmistakably Spanish woman in her late thirties was plowing her way across the room, alarm and displeasure furrowing the openness of her olive-skinned beauty.

"Rodrigo warned me that you'd give me a hard time."

Cybele blinked at the woman as she slapped her hand away from the suitcase's handle and hauled it onto the king-sized, draped-in-ivory-silk bed. She, too, made it look so light. Those Spaniards—uh, Catalans—must have something potent in their water.

The woman rounded on her, vitality and ire radiating from every line. Even her shoulder-length, glossy dark brown hair seemed pissed off. "He told me that you'd be a troublesome charge, and from the way you were trying to bust your surgery scar open, he was right. As he always is."

So it wasn't only she who thought he was always practically infallible. Her lips tugged as she tried to placate the force of nature before her. "I don't have a surgery scar to bust, thanks to Rodrigo's revolutionary minimally invasive approach."

"You have things in there—" the woman stabbed a finger in the air pointing at Cybele's head "—you can bust, no? What you busted before, necessitating such an approach."

From the throb of pain that was only now abating, she had to concede that. She'd probably raised her intracranial pressure tenfold trying to drag that behemoth of a bag. As she shrugged, she remembered Rodrigo telling her something.

She'd been too busy watching his lips wrap around each syllable to translate the words into an actual meaning. She now replayed them, made sense of them.

Rodrigo had said Consuelo, his cousin who lived here with her husband and three children and managed the place for him, would be with her shortly to see to her every need and to the correct and timely discharge of his instructions. She'd only nodded then, lost in his eyes. She now realized what he'd meant.

He didn't trust her to follow his instructions, was assigning a deputy to enforce their execution. And he certainly knew how to pick his wardens.

She stuck out her hand with a smile tugging at her lips. "You must be Consuelo. Rodrigo told me to expect you."

Consuelo took her hand, only to drag her forward and kiss her full on both cheeks.

Cybele didn't know what stunned her more, the affectionate salute, or Consuelo resuming her disapproval afterward.

Consuelo folded her arms over an ample bosom artfully contained and displayed by her floral dress with the lime background. "Seems Rodrigo didn't *really* tell you what to expect. So let *me* make it clear. I received you battered and bruised. I'm handing you back in tip-top shape. *I* won't put up with you not following Rodrigo's orders. I'm not soft and lenient like him."

"Soft and lenient?" Cybele squeaked her incredulity. Then she coughed it out on a laugh. "I wasn't aware there were two Rodrigos. I met the intractable and inexorable one."

Consuelo tutted. "If you think Rodrigo intractable and inexorable, wait till you've been around me twenty-four hours."

"Oh, the first twenty-four seconds were a sufficient demo."

Consuelo gave her an assessing look, shrewdness simmering in her dark chocolate eyes. "I know your type. A woman who wants to do everything for herself, says she can handle it when she can't, keeps going when she shouldn't, caring nothing about what it costs her, and it's all because she dreads being an imposition, because she hates accepting help even when she dearly needs it."

"Whoa. Spoken like an expert."

"*¡Maldita sea, es cierto!*—that's right. It takes one mule-headed, aggravatingly independent woman to know another."

Another laugh overpowered Cybele. "Busted."

"*Sí,* you are. And I'm reporting your reckless behavior to Rodrigo. He'll probably have you chained to my wrist by your good arm until he gives you a clean bill of health."

"Not that I wouldn't be honored to have you as my…uh, keeper, but can I bribe you into keeping silent?"

"You can. And you know how."

"I don't try to lift rock-filled suitcases again?"

"And do everything I say. *When* I say it."

"Uh…on second thought, I'll take my chances with Rodrigo."

"Ha. Try another one. Now hop to it. Rodrigo told me what kind of day—what kind of *week* you've had. You're doing absolutely nothing but sleeping and resting for the next one. And eating. You look like you're about to vanish."

Cybele laughed as she whimsically peered down at her much lesser endowments. She could see how they were next to insubstantial by the super-lush Consuelo's standards.

This woman would be good for her. As she was sure Rodrigo had known she would be. Every word out of her mouth tickled funny bones Cybele hadn't known existed.

Consuelo hooked her arm through Cybele's good one, walked her to bed then headed alone to the en suite bathroom. She talked all the time while she ran a bubble bath, emptied the suitcases, sorted everything in the dressing room, and laid out what Cybele would wear to bed. Cybele loved listening to her husky, vibrant voice delivering perfect English dipped in the molasses of her all-out Catalan accent. By the time she led Cybele to the all-marble-and-gold-fixtures, salonlike bathroom, she'd told her her life story. At least, everything that had happened since she and her husband had become Rodrigo's house- and groundskeepers.

Cybele insisted she could take it from there. Consuelo insisted on leaving the door open. Cybele insisted she'd call out to prove she was still awake. Consuelo threatened to barge in after a minute's silence. Cybele countered she could sing to prove her wakefulness then everyone within hearing distance would suffer the consequences of Consuelo's overprotection.

Guffawing and belting out a string of amused Catalan, Consuelo finally exited the bathroom.

Grinning, Cybele undressed. The grin dissolved as she stared at herself in the mirror above the double sinks' marble platform.

She had a feeling there'd once been more of her. Had she lost weight? A lot of it? Recently? Because she'd been unhappy? If she had been, why had she planned a pregnancy and a second honeymoon with Mel? What did Rodrigo think of the way she looked? Not now, since she looked like crap, but before? Was she his type? Did he have a type? Did he have a woman now? More than one…?

Oh, God…she couldn't finish a thought without it settling back on him, could she?

She clamped down on the spasm that twisted through her at the idea, the images of him with a woman…any other woman.

How insane was it to be jealous, when up to eight days ago she'd been married to his brother?

She exhaled a shuddering breath and stepped into the warm, jasmine-and-lilac-scented water. She moaned as she submerged her whole body, felt as if every deep-seated ache surged to her surface, bled through her pores to mingle with the bubbles and fluid silk that enveloped her.

She raised her eyes, realized the widescreen window was

right across from her, showcasing a masterpiece of heavenly proportions. Magnificent cloud formations in every gradation of silver morphing across a darkening royal blue sky and an incandescent half moon.

Rodrigo's face superimposed itself on the splendor, his voice over the lapping of water around her, the swishing of blood in her ears. She shut her eyes, tried to sever the spell.

"Enough."

Consuelo's yelled *"¿Qué?"* jerked Cybele's eyes open.

Mortification threatened to boil her bathwater.

God—she'd cried that out loud.

She called out the first thing that came to her, to explain away her outburst. "Uh…I said I'm coming out. I've had enough."

And she had. In so many ways. But there was one more thing that she prayed she would soon have enough of. Rodrigo.

Any bets she never would?

It was good to face her weakness. Without self-deception, she'd be careful to plan her actions and control her responses, accept and expect no more than the medical supervision she was here for during her stay. Until it came to an end.

As it inevitably would.

Rodrigo stood outside Cybele's quarters, all his senses converged on every sound, every movement transmitted from within.

He'd tried to walk away. He couldn't. He'd leaned on her door, feeling her through it, tried to contain the urge to walk back in, remain close, see and hear and feel for himself that she was alive and aware.

The days during which she'd lain inert had gouged a fault line in his psyche. The past days since she'd come back, he hadn't been able to contemplate putting more than a few minutes' distance between them. It had been all he could do not to camp out in her room as he had during her coma. He had constantly curbed himself so he wouldn't suffocate her with worry, counted down every second of the three hours he'd imposed on himself between visits.

After he'd controlled the urge, he'd summoned Consuelo, had dragged himself away. Then he'd heard Consuelo's shout.

He hadn't barged into the room only because he'd frozen with horror for the seconds it took him to realize Consuelo had exclaimed *Stop,* and Consuelo's gregarious tones and Cybele's gentler, melodic ones had carried through the door, explaining the whole situation.

Now he heard Cybele's raised voice as she chattered with Consuelo from the bathroom. In a few minutes, Consuelo would make sure Cybele was tucked in bed and would walk out. He had to be gone before that. Just not yet.

He knew he was being obsessive, ridiculous, but he couldn't help it. The scare was too fresh, the trauma too deep.

He hadn't been there for Mel, and he'd died.

He had to be there for Cybele.

But to be there for her, he had to get ahold of himself. And to do that, he had to put today behind him.

It had felt like spiraling down through hell. Taking her to that airfield, realizing too late what he'd done, seeing his foster parents after months of barely speaking to them, only to give them the proof of his biggest failure. Mel's body.

The one thing mitigating this disaster was Cybele's memory loss. It *was* merciful. For her. For him, too. He didn't know if he could have handled her grief, too, had she remembered Mel.

But—was it better to have reprieve now, than to have it all come back with a vengeance later? Wouldn't it have been better if her grief coincided with his? Would he be able to bear it, to be of any help if she fell apart when he'd begun healing?

But then he had to factor in the changes in her.

The woman who'd woken up from the coma was not the Cybele Wilkinson he'd known the past year. Or the one Mel had said had become so volatile, she'd accused him of wanting her around only as the convenient help rolled into one with a medical supervisor—and who'd demanded a baby as proof that he valued her as his wife.

Rodrigo had at first found that impossible to believe. She'd never struck him as insecure or clingy. Just the opposite. But then her actions had proved Mel right.

So which persona was really her? The stable, guileless woman she'd been the past five days? The irritable introvert she'd been before Mel's accident? Or the neurotic wreck who'd made untenable emotional demands of him when he'd been wrecked himself?

And if this new persona was a by-product of the accident, of her injuries, once she healed, once she regained all her memories, would she revert? Would the woman who was bantering so naturally with Consuelo, who'd consoled him and wrestled verbally with him and made him forget everything but her, disappear?

He forced himself away from the door. Consuelo was asking what Cybele would like for breakfast. In a moment she'd walk out.

He strode away, speculations swarming inside his head.

He was staring at the haggard stranger in mourning clothes in his bathroom mirror when he realized something.

It made no difference. Whatever the answers were, no matter what she was, or what would happen from now on, it didn't matter.

She was in his life now. To stay.

Seven

"You don't have post-traumatic amnesia."

Cybele's eyes rounded at Rodrigo's proclamation.

Her incredulity at his statement was only rivaled by the one she still couldn't get over; that he'd transferred a miniature hospital to his estate so he could test and chart her progress daily.

Apart from wards and ORs, he had about everything else on site. A whole imaging facility with X-ray, MRI, CT machines and even a PET scan machine, which seemed like overkill just to follow up her arm's and head's healing progress. A comprehensive lab for every known test to check up on her overall condition and that of her pregnancy. Then there were the dozen neurological tests he subjected her to daily, plus the physiotherapy sessions for her fingers.

They'd just ended such a session and were heading out to the barbecue house at the seafront terrace garden to have lunch, after which he'd said they'd explore more of the estate.

He was walking beside her, his brows drawn together, his eyes plastered to the latest batch of results from another dozen tests. So what did he mean, she didn't have…?

Terrible suspicion mushroomed, clouding the perfection of the day.

Could he think she'd capitalized on a transient memory loss and had been stringing him along for the past four weeks? Or worse, that she'd never had memory loss, that she was cunning enough, with a convoluted enough agenda, to have faked it from the start?

And she blurted it out, "You think I'm pretending?"

"What?" He raised his eyes sluggishly, stared ahead into nothingness as if the meaning of her words was oozing through his mind, searching for comprehension. Then it hit him. Hard. His head jerked toward her, his frown spectacular. *"No."*

She waited for him to elaborate. He didn't, buried his head back into the tests.

So she prodded. "So what do you mean I don't have PTA? I woke up post-trauma with amnesia. Granted, it's not a classic case, but what else could it be?"

Instead of answering, he held the door of the terrace pergola open for her. She stepped out into the late March midday, barely stopped herself from moaning as the sweet saltiness of the sea breeze splashed her face, weaved insistent fingers through her hair.

He looked down at her as they walked, as if he hadn't heard her question. She shivered, not from the delicious coolness of the wind, but from the caress of his gaze, which followed the wind's every movement over her face and through her hair.

At least, that was how it felt to her. It was probably all in her mind, and he was lost in thought and not seeing her at all.

He suddenly turned his eyes again to the tests, validating her interpretation. "Let's review your condition, shall we? You started out having total retrograde amnesia, with all the memories formed before the accident lost. Then you started retrieving 'islands of memory,' when you recalled those 'skeletal' events. But you didn't suffer from any degree of anterograde amnesia, since you had no problems creating new memories after the injury. Taking all that into account, and that it has been over four weeks and the 'islands' have not coalesced into a uniform landmass..."

"As uniform as could be, you mean," she interrupted. "Even so-called healthy people don't remember everything in their lives—most things not in reliable detail and some things not at all."

"Granted. But PTA that lasts that long indicates severe brain injury, and it's clear from your clinical condition and all of your tests that you are not suffering from any cognitive, sensory, motor or coordination deficits. An isolated PTA of this magnitude is unheard of. That is why I'm leaning toward diagnosing you with a hybrid case of amnesia. The trauma might have triggered it, but the major part of your memory deficit is psychogenic, not organic."

She chewed her lip thoughtfully. "So we're back to what I said minutes after I regained consciousness. I *wanted* to forget."

"Yes. You diagnosed yourself fresh out of a coma."

"It wasn't really a diagnosis. I was trying to figure out why I had no other symptoms. When I didn't find an explanation, I thought either my medical knowledge had taken a hit, or that neurology was never my strong point in my parallel existence. I thought you would know that cases like mine exist. But they don't. Turns out I don't really have amnesia, I'm just hysterical."

His gaze whipped to hers, fierce, indignant. "Psychogenic

amnesia is no less real than organic. It's a self-preservation mechanism. I also wouldn't label the psychogenic ingredient of your memory loss as hysterical, but rather functional or dissociative. In fact, I don't support the hysterical nomenclature and what it's come to be associated with—willful and weak-willed frenzy."

Hot sweetness unfurled inside her. He was defending her to herself. Pleasure surged to her lips, making them tingle. "So you think I have a repressed-memory type functional amnesia."

He nodded, ultraserious. "Yes. Here, take a look at this. This is your last MRI." She looked. "It's called functional imaging. After structural imaging revealed no physical changes in your brain, I looked at the function. You see this?" She did. "This abnormal brain activity in the limbic system led to your inability to recall stressful and traumatic events. The memories are stored in your long-term memory, but access to them has been impaired through a mixture of trauma and psychological defense mechanisms. The abnormal activity explains your partial memory recovery. But now that I'm certain there's nothing to worry about organically, I'm relaxed about when total recovery occurs."

"*If* it ever does." If he was right, and she couldn't think how he wasn't, she might be better off if it never did.

Psychogenic amnesia sufferers included soldiers and childhood abuse, rape, domestic violence, natural disaster and terrorist attack victims. Sufferers of severe enough psychological stress, internal conflict or intolerable life situations. And if her mind had latched on to the injury as a trigger to purge her memories of Mel and her life with him, she'd probably suffered all three.

But that still didn't explain her pregnancy or the honeymoon they were heading to when they'd had the accident.

Rodrigo stemmed the tide of confusion that always overcame her when she came up against those points.

"Anyway," he said. "While explanations have been proposed to explain psychogenic amnesia, none of them have been verified as the mechanism that fits all types. I prefer to set aside the Freudian, personal semantic belief systems and betrayal trauma theories to explain the condition. I lean toward the theory that explains the biochemical imbalance that triggers it."

"That's why you're a neurosurgeon and not a neurologist or psychiatrist. Where others are content to deal with insults to the psyche, you dig down to the building blocks of the nervous system, cell by cell, neurotransmitter by neurotransmitter."

"I admit, I like to track any sign or symptom, physical or psychological, back to its causative mechanism, to find the '*exactly* how' after others explain the 'why.'"

"And that's why you're a researcher and inventor."

He focused on her eyes for a second before he turned his own back to the tests, his skin's golden-bronze color deepening.

He was embarrassed!

She'd noticed on many occasions that, although he was certain of his abilities, he wasn't full of himself and didn't expect or abide adulation, despite having every reason to feel superior and to demand and expect being treated as such.

But this—to actually blush at her admiration! Oh, Lord, but he was delicious, scrumptious. Edible. And adorable.

And he ignored her praise pointedly. "So—I favor the theory that postulates that normal autobiographical memory processing is blocked by altered release of stress hormones in the brain during chronic stress conditions. With the regions of expanded limbic system in the right hemisphere more vulnerable to stress and trauma, affecting the body's opioids, hormones and neurotransmitters, increased levels of glucocorticoid and mineralocorticoid receptor density affect the anterior temporal, orbitofrontal cortex, hippocampal and amygdalar regions."

She couldn't help it. Her lips spread so wide they hurt. "I bet you're having a ball talking to a doctor/patient. Imagine all the translation into layman's terms you'd have to do if you wanted to say *that* to someone who didn't get the lingo."

He blinked, surprise tingeing his incredible eyes. Then that incendiary smile of his flowed over his face, crooked his divine-work-of-art lips. "It has been a very freeing experience, spoiling even, not to keep looking for ways to explain what I'm doing or what's happening and fearing I won't be clear enough or that you'll misinterpret it no matter what I say and develop false expectations, positive or negative." He shook his head in self-deprecation, switching back to solemn in a blink. "But that was far too involved, anyway. My point is, you might have appeared or thought you were coping with your situation before the accident, but according to your current condition, you weren't."

She pursed her lips in an effort to stop herself from grinning uncontrollably and giving in to the urge to lunge at him, tickle him out of his seriousness. "So you're saying I was headed for psychogenic amnesia, anyway?"

"No, I'm saying the unimaginable stress of experiencing a plane crash, plus the temporary brain insult you suffered, disrupted the balance that would have kept your memory intact in the face of whatever psychological pressure you were suffering."

She raised an eyebrow, mock-indignant. "You're trying very hard to find neurologically feasible explanations backed by complex theories and medical expressions to dress up the fact that you've diagnosed me as a basket case, aren't you?"

"No! I certainly haven't. You're in no way..." He stopped abruptly when she couldn't hold back anymore, let the smile split her face. Incredulity spread over his face. "You're playing me!"

She burst out laughing. "Yep. For quite some time now. But you were so involved in your explanations, so careful not to give me any reason to feel silly or undeserving of concern or follow-up since my condition is 'only in my mind,' you didn't notice."

One formidable eyebrow rose, a calculating gleam entering his eyes, an unbearably sexy curl twisting his lips. "Hmm, seems I have underestimated the stage of your progress."

"Been telling you so for—"

"Quite some time now. Yes, I get it. But now that I'm certain your brain is in fine working order, nuts-and-bolts-wise, being the guy who cares about nothing but the hardware, I think I can safely stop treating you like you're made of fresh paint."

A laugh cracked out of her at his metaphor. He kept surprising her. She'd be thinking he was this ultra-cerebral, all-work genius of a man, then out of the blue, he'd let this side of him show. The most witty and wickedly fun person she'd ever known. And she did know that for a fact. She remembered all of her life before Mel now.

She pretended to wipe imaginary sweat off her brow. "Phew, I thought I'd never get you to stop."

"Don't be so happy. Until minutes ago, I would have let you trampoline-jump all over me. Now I think you don't warrant the walking-on-eggshells preferential treatment anymore. You deserve some punishment for making fun of my efforts to appear all-knowing."

"Making fun of them, or debunking them?"

"Payback is getting steeper by the word."

She made a cartoonish face. "What can you do to a poor patient who has expanded limbic system issues and increased levels of glucocorticoid and mineralocorticoid receptor density messing with her anterior temporal, orbitofrontal cortex, hippocampal and amygdalar regions?"

"That's it. I'm exacting retribution."

"What will you do? Make me go to my room?"

"I'll make you eat what I cook. And that's for starters. I'll devise something heinous while phase one is underway."

"You mean *more* heinous than your cooking?"

He rumbled something from his gut, devilry igniting in his eyes. She giggled and rushed ahead, felt like she was flying there, borne on the giddy pleasure of his pursuing chuckles.

When she reached the steps, his voice boomed behind her, concern gripping its rich power. "Slow down."

She did, waited for him to catch up with her in those strides that ate up ten of her running steps in five.

She grinned up into his no-longer-carefree, admonishing eyes. "I thought I wasn't getting the fresh-paint treatment any longer."

"You've hereby moved to getting the uninsured, last-known-piece-of-Ming-dynasty-China treatment."

He slipped a steadying hand around her waist as they scaled the steps. She felt she'd be secure if the whole country fell into the sea. Or he'd clasp her to his body and take off into the sky.

She leashed her desire to press into him. "Aha! I should have known you'd default on your declaration of my independence."

He grinned down at her as they reached the barbecue house. "Tales of your independence *have* been wildly exaggerated."

She made a face, ducked under the shade of the canvas canopy.

He gave her a smug look as he seated her, then went to the kitchen area and began preparing her "punishment."

She watched his every graceful move as putting out cooking

utensils and food items and chopping and slicing were turned into a precision performance like his surgeries. When he ducked inside to get more articles, she exhaled at the interruption of her viewing pleasure, swept her gaze to the sparkling azure-emerald waters of the magnificent, channellike part of the sea, the mile-long breathtaking sandy beach ensconced in a rocky hug.

The living, breathing tranquility imbued her. Most of the time she couldn't remember how she'd come to be here, or that she'd ever been anywhere else, that a world existed outside.

This place wasn't just a place. It was an…experience. A sense of completion, of arrival. A realm in time and space she'd never seen approximated, let alone replicated. An amalgam of nature's pristine grandeur and man's quest for the utmost in beauty and comfort. But all this would have been nothing without him.

It was being with him that made it embody heaven.

During the past weeks they'd made real fires, collected ripe fruits and vegetables, eaten their meals in the apartment-sized kitchen or in the cool barbecue house and held their after-dinner gatherings and entertainment in its lounge or in the huge pergola terrace.

She'd watched him play tennis on the floodlit court with the tireless Gustavo, swim endless laps in the half-Olympic-sized pool, drooled over his every move, longed to tear off her cast and shed her aches and throw herself into that pool after him….

"Ready for your punishment?"

She twinkled up at him. "Is it too heinous?"

He looked down at the salad bowls in his hands. "Atrocious."

"Gimme." She took her bowl, set it in front of her. And gaped. Then she crooked a challenging smile up at him. "It's colorful, I'll give you that. And…odorous." She tried not to wince as she picked up her fork. "*And* I didn't know these food items could go together."

He sat down across from her. "I didn't hear any objections as I tossed them into each other's company."

She chuckled. "I don't even know what said food items are."

His glance said her delaying tactics weren't working. "Eat."

She took a mouthful, trying not to inhale the stench, trying not to have what produced it hit her taste buds, to slide directly into her throat. Then it did hit, everywhere. And…wow.

She raised incredulous eyes to him. "You better get this patented. It's a-maaazing!"

He raised both eyebrows in disbelief. "You're just trying to prove nothing can gross you out, that I didn't and wouldn't succeed in punishing you, 'cause you can take anything."

"What am I, twelve?" She wolfed down another huge forkful.

He crooked his head to one side, considering. "So you like it."

"I love it," she exclaimed, mumbling around the food she'd stuffed into her mouth. "I *can* do without the smell, but it actually lessens as you eat, or your senses forgive it for being coupled with the delicious taste. At first I thought it was rotten fish."

"It *is* rotten fish."

She almost choked. "Now you're pulling my leg."

"Nope." The wattage of the wickedness in his eyes reached electrocuting levels. "But if you like it, does the label matter?"

She thought about that for a second, then said "Nah" and stuffed another forkful into her mouth.

He laughed as he began to eat his own serving. "It's actually only *semi*-rotten. It's called *feseekh*—sun dried then salted gray mullet. It's considered an acquired taste—which you must be the quickest to ever acquire—and a delicacy around here. It came to Catalonia with the Berbers, and they brought it all the way from Egypt. But I bet I'm the first one to mix it with a dozen unnamed leafy greens and the wild berries Gustavo grows and collects and gives to me to consume, assuring me they're the secret to my never needing any of our esteemed colleagues' services."

"So you can give me rotten and unidentified food to consume, but you balk at my walking faster than a turtle."

"The rotten ingredient has proved through centuries of folk experience to have potent antibacterial and digestive-regulating properties. It and the rest of the unidentified food have been repeatedly tested on yours truly, and I'm living proof to their efficacy. I haven't been sick a day in the last twenty years."

Her eyes rounded in alarm. "Okay, jinx much?"

He threw his head back on a guffaw. "You're superstitious? You think I'll get deathly sick now that I've dared tempt fate?"

"Who knows? Maybe fate doesn't like braggarts."

"Actually, I think fate doesn't like gamblers." Something dark flitted across his face. Before she analyzed it, he lowered his gaze, hid it. "Since I'm anything but, I'm a good candidate for staying on its good side. For as long as possible. That brings us back to your hare tactics. Maybe you don't have loose components inside your brain to be shaken and stirred, but running like one, if you stumble, you have only one hand to ward off a fall, and you might injure it, too, or end up reinjuring your arm. And though your first trimester has been the smoothest I've ever heard about, probably as a compensation for what you're already dealing with, you *are* pregnant."

She *did* forget sometimes that she was. Not that she wanted to forget. When she did remember, it was with a burst of joy, imagining that she had a life growing inside her, that she'd have a baby to love and cherish, who'd be her flesh and blood, the family she'd never had. If there had been one thing to thank Mel for, it was that he'd somehow talked her into conceiving that baby. But because she had no symptoms whatsoever, sometimes it *did* slip her mind.

"Okay, no hare tactics." Her smile widened as she repeated his term for her jog. "But since I have no loose components, you must tell Consuelo to stop chasing me around as if I'll scatter them."

He turned his head to both sides, looked behind him. Then he turned back to her, palm over chest with an expression of mock horror. "You're talking to *me?*"

Her lips twitched. "You're the one who sicced her on me."

"A man can start a nuclear reaction, but he surely has no way of stopping it once it becomes self-perpetuating."

"You gotta call her off. She'll brush my teeth for me next!"

"You really expect me to come between her and her hurt chick? I may be lord of all I survey back at the center, but here I'm just another in the line that marches to Consuelo's tune."

"Yeah, I noticed." She chuckled, loving how he could be so alpha and capable and overriding and yet be totally comfortable letting another, and a woman, have the upper hand where she was best suited to take it. She cocked her head at him. "Families are very matriarchal here, aren't they?"

He tossed her a piece of breath-freshening gum then piled their bowls in one hand and raised the other, ring and middle fingers folded by his thumb, fore and little fingers pointing up. "Women rule."

She spluttered at the sight of him, so virile and formidable and poised, making that goofy expression and pop culture gesture.

He headed into the barbecue house and she melted back in her chair, replete and blissful. She'd never laughed like that before him. Before being here with him in his paradise of a home.

He'd only left her side to fly to work—literally, via helicopter—and had cut down on his working hours, to be there for her. She'd insisted he shouldn't, that she was perfectly all right on her own or with Consuelo, Gustavo and their children.

But she'd stopped objecting, certain he wasn't neglecting his work, had everything under control. And she couldn't get enough of being with him. Against all resolutions, she reveled in his pampering, wished with all she had in her that she could repay him in kind. But he had everything. Needed nothing. Nothing but to heal emotionally.

So she contented herself with being there for him, hoping to see him heal. And he was healing. His moroseness had dissipated and his distance had vanished, had become a closeness like she'd never known, as they discovered each other, shared so many things she'd never thought she'd share with another.

She kept waiting for him to do something to annoy her, to disappoint her, as all human beings inevitably did. But the impossible man just wouldn't. Then he went further into the realm of impossibility, kept doing things that shocked her by how much they appealed to her, delighted her.

He was everything his foster parents had said they'd picked him for and far more. Everything she admired in a human being and a man, and the most effective power for good she'd ever had the fortune to meet. And that was what he was to the world.

To her, he was all that resonated with her preferences and peculiarities. They agreed on most everything, and what they disagreed on, they discussed, came out conceding a respect for the other's viewpoint and thrilled to have gained a new awareness.

And when she added up everything he'd done for her, had been to her—her savior, protector and support—he was, yes, just incredible.

Which was why every now and then the question popped into her head—where had this man been before the accident?

From the tatters she remembered, besides his reported promiscuity, he'd treated Mel with fed-up annoyance and everyone else with abrasive impatience. His treatment of her had been the worst. He'd barely spoken to her, had watched her with something almost vicious in his eyes, as if he'd thought her beneath his friend—his brother.

And every time there was one answer. The conclusion she'd made the first day she'd come here. Her memories had to be faulty.

This, *he,* must be the truth. The magnificent truth.

"Ready to go back to your keeper?"

Everything became more beautiful with his return. She surrendered to his effortless strength, let him draw her to feet that barely touched the ground because he existed, was near.

She ended up ensconced in his protective embrace. His face clenched with the intensity she now adored, his freshness and potency filling her lungs. And it was as necessary as her next breath that she show him what he was to her.

She moved against his solid heat and power, raised her face to him, the invocation that filled her with life and hope and the will to heal, to be, trembling on her lips. "Rodrigo…"

Eight

Cybele's whisper skewered through Rodrigo, wrenching at all the emotions and responses he'd been repressing.

From every point where her body touched his, torrents of what felt like molten metal zapped through his nerves, converging to roar through his spine, jamming into his iron-hard erection.

Nothing was left in his raging depths but the need to crush her to his aching flesh, claim her, assimilate her into his being.

And he couldn't.

But how could he not—and remain sane?

Not that he was sane anymore. He hadn't been since the first time he'd laid eyes on her. And with every moment in her company, he'd been surrendering any desire to cling to sanity.

He'd plunged into the wonder of experiencing her, discovering her, sharing with her everything from his daily routines and professional pressures to his deepest beliefs and slightest whims.

And she was far more than anything he'd ever dreamed of. She was the best thing that had ever happened to him.

But whenever he was away from her, he kept dredging up the past, the suspicions and antipathies that had at once poisoned his existence and fueled his resistance. He'd *wanted* to hate and despise her, to believe the worst of her then. Because she'd been the only woman he'd ever truly wanted—and she'd been forever off-limits.

She was no longer off-limits. Not on account of Mel, nor on that of his objections to her character.

He'd moved from condemning her for tormenting Mel with her volatility to suspecting that the instability had been created in Mel's twisted psyche. Now that he was no longer jumping on anything to paint her as black as possible, and had seen all the evidence to the contrary, it made sense that a man in Mel's condition could have interpreted her acts of love—which he couldn't reciprocate in any healthy fashion—as emotional pressure and blackmail.

Later on, after their relationship had deteriorated further under the harsh realities of Mel's disability, it stood to reason that the money Mel had asked Rodrigo for to buy her things hadn't been things she'd hinted that she'd wanted. Mel had said he'd understood her demands, that she deserved some compensation to cheer her up in their endlessly trying situation.

But it could have been Mel who'd tried to satisfy any material desire of hers to placate her, to express his love in the only way he'd ever known how, and then to keep her from walking out on him in a fit of despair. And when that, too, had failed, he'd been down to the last thing he could do to prove to her that he didn't consider her his live-in nurse—give her a baby.

Rodrigo now thought her memory loss was probably her

mind's way of protecting itself from being pulverized by grief if she remembered Mel and the desperate, traumatic love she'd felt for him.

After he'd reached that conviction, he'd fluctuated between thinking she was being so wonderful to *him* because she subconsciously saw him as all she had left of Mel, to thinking she treated him as she did *because* she didn't remember loving Mel, and that when she did she'd become cold and distant again. He'd thought her coolness had been a reaction to his own barely leashed antipathy. But maybe she'd really disliked him, for reasons that were now gone with her memory. Or maybe the injury *had* caused some radical changes in her personality.

Too many maybes, too many questions the answers to which only she knew and no longer remembered. And it was driving him mad.

What if her dislike came back in full force, and this persona he adored vanished when her mind and psyche did heal completely?

The temptation to claim her now, bind her to him, negate the possibility, was too much.

He looked down in her eyes. They were fathomless with need. He could reach out and take her, and she'd be his. Ecstatically. She seemed to want him as much as he wanted her.

But did she? Or did she only think she did, because of some need to reassert her own life after surviving the accident that had claimed Mel's? Was he merely convenient, close? Or was she responding to him out of gratitude?

Whatever the reason, he didn't believe she was responsible for her desires, or capable of making a decision with so much missing from her memory.

And then there was *his* side of the story.

He had no doubt he wouldn't be betraying Mel's memory. Mel was dead, and even while he'd lived, his relationship with

Cybele had been anything but healthy or happy. If *he* could be the one to offer her that relationship, he would do anything for that chance.

But how could he live with himself if he betrayed *her* trust? And she did trust him. Implicitly. With her life. Was now showing him that she trusted him with her body, maybe her heart and future.

Yet how could he resist? Need was gnawing him hollow. And feeling her answering yearning was sending him out of his mind.

He had to plan a distraction, an intervention.

He stopped himself from cupping her face, running his fingers down her elegant nose, her sculpted cheekbones, teasing those dainty lips open, plunging his thumb inside their moistness and dampening their rose-petal softness, bending to taste her then absorbing her gasps, thrusting inside her….

He staggered away from temptation, rasped, "I have to get back to work."

She gasped at the loss of his support, bit her lip, nodded.

Coward. Work was a few hours' excuse to stay away.

He *had* to do whatever would keep him away from her until she healed and came to him with her full, unclouded, unpressured choice.

He exerted what remained of his will. "And before I forget, I wanted to tell you that I'm inviting my family for a visit."

Cybele stared up at Rodrigo.

For a moment there, as he'd held her against him, she'd thought he felt what she did, wanted what she did. She'd thought he'd take her in his arms, and she'd never be homeless again.

But it had all been in her mind. He'd torn himself away, the fierceness and the bleakness that had evaporated during the past four weeks settling back over him. She'd read him all wrong.

But he'd read her all right. There was no way he hadn't seen her desire, understood her plea for him.

And he'd recoiled from her offer, from her need, as if they'd injured him, or worse, tainted him.

But though he was too kind to castigate her for testing the limits of their situation when he'd never encouraged her to, he'd still found a way to draw the line again and keep her behind it.

He was inviting his family over. Now that she'd been so stupid as to come on to him, to offer him what he hadn't asked for and didn't want, he was making sure she'd no longer have unsupervised access to him to repeat the mistake. He was inviting them as chaperones.

That had to be his reason for suddenly thinking of inviting them. Just yesterday, they'd been talking about their families and he hadn't brought up his intention. He'd even said it would be the first year that no one came to stay at his estate at all. And she'd gotten the distinct feeling he'd been…relieved about that fact. Probably because he'd had all the distractions he could afford in the form of Mel's death and her recuperation.

But her irresponsible behavior was forcing him to put up with even more distractions than she'd caused him, through his extensive family's presence, probably until he decreed she was well enough to be let back into the wild. Which could mean weeks, maybe months.

It felt like a wake-up slap. One she'd needed. Not only couldn't she let him swamp himself with family just to keep her at arm's length, she couldn't burden him with more responsibility toward her, this time over her emotions and desires—which in his terminal nobility he was probably taking full blame for inciting. She'd burdened him enough, when she had no right to burden him at all. She had to stop leaning on him, stop taking advantage of his kindness and support. And she had to do it now, before her emotions got any deeper.

Not that she thought they could. What she felt for him filled her, overflowed.

Only one bright side to this mess. Though she'd betrayed herself and imposed on him, she was now certain she hadn't done that when Mel had been in the picture. She'd repressed her feelings before, and they must have broken free after the accident.

All she could do now was fade from his life, let him continue it free from the liability of her. She had to pick up the pieces of her life, plan how to return to a demanding job with a baby on the way, without counting on the help of a mother she was now sure wouldn't come through for her as Cybele had remembered she'd promised.

Cybele didn't need her mother. She'd long ago learned not to. And it wasn't Rodrigo's fault that she needed him emotionally. Any other kind of need had to end. Right now.

She had to leave immediately, so he wouldn't have to call his whole family to his rescue. She had to stop wasting his time, cutting into his focus and setting back his achievements.

The moment they reentered the house, she opened her mouth to say what she had to, but he talked over her.

"When I relocated here, it seemed to me that Catalans search for reasons to gather and celebrate. It was explained to me that because they've fought so fiercely to preserve their language and identity, they take extra pride in preparing and executing their celebrations. My family is thoroughly Catalan, and they're big on family unity and cultural traditions. And since I built this place over five years ago, it has replaced my grandparents' home as the place to gather. It would be a shame to interrupt the new tradition."

He was trying to make his sudden decision look as though it

had nothing to do with her snuggling up against him like a cat in heat. She wanted to cry out for him to shut up and quit being so thoughtful. She had to say her piece and he was making it so much harder. Comparing those festivities and family gatherings with the barrenness of her own life was another knife that would twist in her heart once she was away from here.

She couldn't say anything. Her throat sealed over a molten pain that filled it as he escorted her like always to her quarters, continuing her education in Catalan traditions and his family's close-knit pursuits—all the things she'd never had and would never have. "Spring and summer are rife with *fiestas i carnaval*...that means—"

"Feasts and carnivals. I know," she mumbled. "But I—"

A smile invaded his eyes and lips again, cutting her off more effectively than if he'd shouted. "I sometimes forget how good your Spanish is, and I'm blown away by how colloquial your Catalan has become in this short period."

She nearly choked on the surge of emotion and pleasure his praise provoked, only for it to be followed by an even deeper dejection.

That deepened further when he swept his gaze ahead, animation draining from his voice, the newscaster-like delivery coming back. "The closest upcoming festival is *La Diada De Sant Jordi,* or St. George's Day, celebrating the patron saint of Catalonia, on the 23rd of April. There are many variations of the legend of St. George, but the Catalan version says there was a lake that was home to a dragon to which a maiden had to be sacrificed every day. One day, St. George killed the dragon and rescued that day's maiden. A red rose tree is supposed to have grown where the dragon's blood was spilled. Now on the day, the streets of Catalonia are filled with stands selling *rosas i libros*—roses and books. The rose is a symbol of love, while the book is a symbol of culture."

"I'm sure it would be a great time to be in Catalonia—"

He bulldozed over her attempt to interrupt him. "It certainly is. The celebrations are very lively and very participatory. Anyone walking down the streets anywhere in Catalonia is invited to join. Another similar celebration is Mother of God of Montserrat, on the 27th of April. In addition to these dates, each village and town has its own designated patron saint to pay homage to. Those celebrations are much like the larger celebrations, with parades of giants made of papier-mâché, fireworks, music from live bands and more. My family may stay until the 23rd of June, which is the shortest day of the year and coincides with the summer solstice celebration and the festival honoring St. John. Here in Catalonia, we light bonfires when the sun is at its most northern point. Catalans believe this wards off disease, bad luck and assorted other demons."

She tried again. "Sounds like a fun time ahead for you and your family—"

"And for you, too. You'll love the energy and sheer fun of this time of year."

"I'm sure I would. But I won't be here for all that, so maybe another time?"

She felt his eyes turn to her then, felt their gaze as if it were his powerful arms hauling her back to him.

"What are you talking about?"

She kept walking, struggled not to give in to the need to look at him and catch his uncensored reaction to her announcement before the barrier of his surgical composure descended, obscured it. Stupid. Still wishing she mattered beyond being a duty.

"Based on your latest tests and diagnosis of my condition, and since you obviously won't do it, I'm giving myself a clean bill of health. Time to return to my life and job."

"And how do you propose to do that?" He stopped her midway in the huge sunlit corridor leading to her quarters.

"You're left-handed and can barely move your fingers. It's going to be weeks before you can do a lot of basic things for yourself, months before you can go back to work."

"Countless people with more severe and permanent disabilities are forced to fend for themselves, and they manage—"

"But you won't only be fending for yourself now. You're having a baby. And you're *not* forced to do anything—you don't have to manage on your own. I won't allow you to, and I sure as hell am not allowing you to leave. And this is the last time we have this conversation, Cybele Wilkinson."

Her heart flapped faster with each adamant word until it felt blurred like the wings of a hummingbird.

She tried to tell herself it was moronic to feel that way. That even if she had to concede that he was correct, she should listen to the voice telling her to be indignant at his overruling tactics, to rebel against his cornering her at every turn into doing what he thought was right for her. That voice also insisted there was nothing to be so giddy about, that he wasn't doing it out of concern for *her*, but for his patient.

She couldn't listen. And if another voice said she was criminally weak to be forgetting her minutes-ago resolution and clinging to whatever time she could get with him, she could only admit it. She wasn't strong enough to throw away one second she could have in his company, extensive family and all.

As for walking away for his peace of mind, she believed his acute feelings of duty wouldn't leave him any if he let her go before he judged she could handle being on her own. She also had to believe *he* could handle her being here, or he would have been relieved at her offer to leave. And since he wasn't, she shouldn't feel bad about staying. She'd offered to go, and he'd said no. Such an incredibly alpha, protective and overriding *no*.

Still, some imp inside her, which she was certain had come to life during this past month, wouldn't let her grab at his lifeline without contention. Or without trying to do what it could to erase the damage her blunder had caused to their newfound ease and rapport.

"Okay, it's clear you believe you're right—"

"I *am* right."

She went on as if he hadn't growled over her challenging opening "—but that doesn't automatically mean I agree. I came here as an alternative to staying in your center as a teaching pincushion. *But,* if I'd been there, you would have discharged me long ago. No one stays in hospital until their fractures heal."

His eyebrows descended a fraction more. "Do you enjoy futility, Cybele? We've established that when I make a decision—"

"—saying no to you isn't an option," she finished for him, a smile trembling on her lips, inviting him to smile back at her, light up the world again, tell her that he'd look past her foolish moment of weakness. "But that was a decision based on a clinical picture from a month ago. Now that I'm diagnosed as having no rattling components, I should be left to fend for myself."

She waited for him to smile back at her, decimate her argument, embroil her in another verbal tournament that neither of them wanted to win, just to prolong the match and the enjoyment.

He did neither. No smile. No decimation. He brooded down at her, seemed to be struggling with something. A decision.

Then he voiced it. "*Muy bien,* Cybele. You win. If you insist on leaving, go ahead. Leave."

Her heart plummeted down a never-ending spiral.

And he was turning around, walking away.

He'd taken no for an answer.

But he never did. He'd told her so. She'd believed him. That was why she'd said what she had.

He *couldn't* take no for an answer. That meant she'd lose him now, not later. And she couldn't lose him now. She wasn't ready to be without him for the rest of her life.

She wanted to scream that she took it all back. That she'd only been trying to do what she thought she should, assert an independence she still couldn't handle, to relieve him of the burden of her.

She didn't make a sound. She couldn't. Because her heart had splintered. Because she had no right to ask for more from him, of him. He'd given her far more than she'd thought anyone could ever give. He'd given her back her life. And it was time to give him back his, after she'd inadvertently hijacked it.

She turned away, feeling as though ice had skewered from her gut to her heart, only the freezing felt now, the pain and damage still unregistered.

Her numb hand was on her doorknob when she heard him say, "By the way, Cybele, good luck getting past Consuelo."

She staggered around. He was looking at her over his shoulder from the end of the corridor, the light from the just-below-the-ceiling windows pouring over him like a spotlight. He looked like that archangel she'd thought him before. His lips were crooked.

He was teasing her!

He didn't want her to leave, hadn't accepted that she could.

Before she could do something colossally stupid, like run and throw herself into his arms and sob her heart out, Consuelo, in a flaming red dress with a flaring skirt, swept by Rodrigo and down the corridor like a missile set on her coordinates.

She pounced on her. "You trying to undo all my work? *Seven* hours running around?" Consuelo turned and impaled Rodrigo with her displeasure. "And *you!* Letting your patient call the shots."

Rodrigo glared at her in mock-indignation before he gave Cybele a get-past-this wink. Then he turned and walked away, his bass chuckles resonating in the corridor, in her every cell.

Consuelo dragged her inside the room.

Feeling boneless with the reprieve, Cybele gave herself up to Consuelo's care, grinned as she lambasted her for her haggardness, ordered her on the scales and lamented her disappointing gains.

She'd missed out on having someone mother her. And for the time being, she'd enjoy Consuelo's mothering all she could. Along with Rodrigo's pampering and protection.

It would come to an end all too soon.

But not yet. *Not yet.*

Nine

Rodrigo stood looking down at the approaching car procession.

His family was here.

He hadn't even thought of them since the accident. He hadn't for a while before that, either. He'd had nothing on his mind but Cybele and Mel and his turmoil over them both for over a year.

He'd remembered them only when he needed their presence to keep him away from Cybele. And he'd gotten what he deserved for neglecting them for so long. They'd all had other plans.

He'd ended up begging them to come. He'd evaded explaining the reason behind his desperation. They'd probably figure it out the moment they saw him with her.

In the end, he'd gotten them to come. And made them

promise to stay. Long. He'd always wished they'd stay as long as possible.

This time he wondered if he'd survive it.

And here began his torment.

His grandparents stepped out of the limo he'd sent them, followed by three of his aunts. Out of the vans poured the aunts' adult children and their families plus a few cousins and their offspring.

Cybele stepped out of the French doors. He gritted his teeth against the violence of his response. He'd been wrestling with it for the past three days since that confrontation. He'd still almost ended up storming her bedroom every night. Her efforts to offer him sexually neutral friendliness were inflaming him far worse than if she'd been coming on to him hot and heavy.

Now she walked toward him with those energetic steps of hers, rod-straight, no wiggle anywhere, dressed in dark blue jeans and a crisp azure blouse that covered her from throat to elbows.

The way his hormones thundered, she could have been undulating toward him in stilettos, a push-up bra and a thong.

Dios. The…containment he now lived in had better be obscuring his condition.

He needed help. He needed the invasion of his family to keep him away from her door, from carrying her off to his bed.

Before she could say anything, since anything she said blinded him with an urge to plunder those mind-destroying lips, he said, "Come, let me introduce you to my tribe."

Tribe is right, Cybele thought.

She fell in step with Rodrigo as she counted thirty-eight men, women and children. More still poured from the vans. Four generations of Valderramas.

It was amazing what one marriage could end up producing.

Rodrigo had told her that his mother had been Esteban and Imelda's first child, had been only nineteen when she had him, that his grandparents had been in their early twenties when they got married. With him at thirty-eight, his grandparents must be in their late seventies or early eighties. They looked like a very good sixty. Must be the clean living Rodrigo had told her about.

She focused on his grandfather. It was uncanny, his resemblance to Rodrigo. This was what Rodrigo would look like in forty-something years' time. And it was amazingly good.

Her heart clenched on the foolish but burning wish to be around Rodrigo through all that time, to know him at that age.

She now watched as he met his family three-quarters of the way, smile and arms wide. Another wish seared her—to be the one he received with such pleasure, the one he missed that much. She envied each of those who had the right to rush to fill his arms, to be blessed by the knowledge of his vast and unconditional love. Her heart broke against the hopelessness of it all as his family took turns being clasped to his heart.

Then he turned to her, covered in kids from age two to mid-teens, his smile blazing as he beckoned to her to come be included in the boisterous affection of his family reunion.

She rushed to answer his invitation and found herself being received by his family with the same enthusiasm.

For the next eight hours, she talked and laughed nonstop, ate and drank more than she had in the last three days put together, put a name and a detailed history to each of the unpretentious, vital beings who swept her along the wave of their rowdy interaction and infectious joie de vivre.

All along she felt Rodrigo watching her even as he paid

attention to every member of his family, clearly on the best possible terms with them all. She managed not to miss one of his actions either, even as she kept up her side of the conversations. Her pleasure mounted at seeing him at such ease, surrounded by all these people who loved him as he deserved to be loved. She kept smiling at him, showing him how happy she was for him, yet trying her best not to let her longing show.

She was deep in conversation with Consuelo and two of Rodrigo's aunts, Felicidad and Benita, when he stood up, exited her field of vision. She barely stopped herself from swinging around to follow his movement. Then she felt him. At her back. His approach was like a wave of electromagnetism, sending every hair on her body standing on end, crackling along her nerves. She hoped she didn't look the way she felt, a woman in the grip of emotional and physical tumult.

His hands descended on her shoulders. Somehow she didn't lurch. "Who's letting her patient call the shots, now?"

She looked up, caught his eyebrow wiggle at Consuelo. The urge to drag him down and devour that teasing smile right off his luscious lips drilled a hole in her midsection.

The three vociferous women launched into a repartee match with him. He volleyed each of their taunts with a witticism that was more funny and inventive than the last, until they were all howling with laughter. She laughed, too, if not as heartily. She was busy having mini-heart attacks as one of his hands kept smoothing her hair and sweeping it off her shoulders absently.

By the time he bent and said, "Bed," she almost begged, *Yes, please.*

He pulled her to her feet as everyone bid her a cheerful good-night. She insisted he didn't need to escort her to her room, that he remain with his family. She didn't think she had the strength tonight not to make a fool of herself. Again.

* * *

On *La Diada De Sant Jordi*, St. George's Day, Rodrigo's family had been there for four weeks. After the first four weeks with him, they were the second-best days of her life.

For the first time, she realized what a family was like, what being an accepted member of such a largely harmonious one could mean.

And they had more than accepted her. They'd reached out and assimilated her into their passionate-for-life, close-knit collective. The older members treated her with the same indulgence as Rodrigo, the younger ones with excitement and curiosity, loving to have someone new and interesting enter their lives. She almost couldn't remember her life before she'd met these people, before they'd made her one of their own. She didn't want to remember any time when Rodrigo hadn't filled her heart.

And he, being the magnificent human being that he was, had felt the melancholy that blunted her joy, had once again asked if her problems with her own family couldn't be healed, if he could intervene, as a neutral mediator, to bring about a reconciliation.

After she'd controlled her impulse to drown him in tears and kisses, she'd told him there hadn't exactly been a rift, no single, overwhelming episode or grievance that could be resolved. It was a lifetime of estrangement.

But the good news was—and that might be a side effect of her injuries—she was at last past the hurt of growing up the unwanted child. She'd finally come to terms with it, could finally see her mother's side of things. Though Cybele had been only six when her father had died, she'd been the difficult child of a disappointment of a husband, a constant reminder of her mother's worst years and biggest mistake. A daddy's girl who'd cried for him for years and told her mother she'd wished she'd been the one who'd died.

She could also see her stepfather's side, a man who'd found himself saddled with a dead man's hostile child as a price for having the woman he wanted, but who couldn't extend his support to tolerance or interest. They were only human, she'd finally admitted to herself, not just the grown-ups who'd neglected her. And that made it possible for her to put the past behind her.

As more good news, her mother had contacted her again, and though what she'd offered Cybele was nowhere near the unreserved allegiance Rodrigo's family shared, she wanted to be on better terms.

The relationship would never be what she wished for, but she'd decided to do her share, meet her mother halfway, take what was on offer, what was possible with her family.

Rodrigo hadn't let the subject go until he'd pressed and persisted and made sure she was really at peace with that.

She now stood looking down the beach where the children were flying kites and building sand castles. She pressed the sight between the pages of her mind, for when she was back to her monotone and animation-free life.

No. She'd never go back to that. Even when she exited Rodrigo's orbit, her baby would fill her life with—

"Do you have your book?"

She swung around to Imelda, her smile ready and wholehearted. She'd come to love the woman in that short time.

She admired Imelda's bottle-green outfit, which matched the eyes she'd passed on to Rodrigo, and was again struck by her beauty. She could barely imagine how Imelda might have looked in her prime.

Her eyes fell on the heavy volume in Imelda's hand. "What book?"

"*La Diada De Sant Jordi* is *rosas i libros* day."

"Oh, yes, Rodrigo told me."

"Men give women a red rose, and women give men a book."

Her heart skipped a beat. "Oh. I didn't know that."

"So now you know. Come on, *muchacha*, go pick a book. The men will be coming back any time now."

"Pick a book from where?"

"From Rodrigo's library, of course."

"I can't just take a book from his library."

"He'll be more than happy for you to. And then, it's what you choose that will have significance when you give it to him."

Okay. Why would Imelda suggest she give Rodrigo a book? Had she realized how Cybele felt about him and was trying to matchmake? Rodrigo hadn't been the one to betray any special emotions. He'd been no more affectionate to her than he'd been to his cousins.

Better gloss over this. "So a woman picks any man she knows, and gives him a book?"

"She can. But usually she picks the most important man in her life."

Imelda knew what Rodrigo was to her. There was certainty in her shrewd eyes, along with a don't-bother-denying-it footnote.

Cybele couldn't corroborate her belief. It would be imposing on Rodrigo. He probably knew how she felt, but it was one thing to know, another to have it declared. And then, *he* wouldn't give her a rose. Even if he did, it would be because all the women had their husbands with them for the fiesta, or because she was alone, or any other reason. She wasn't the most important woman in his life.

But after she walked back into the house with Imelda and they parted ways, she found herself rushing to the library.

She came out with the book of her choice, feeling agonizingly exposed each time one of the women passed her and commented on her having a book like them.

Then the men came back from the next town, bearing copious amounts of prepared and mouthwatering food. And each man had a red rose for his woman. Rodrigo didn't have one.

Her heart thudded with a force that almost made her sick.

She had no right to be crushed by disappointment. And no right to embarrass him. She'd give the book to Esteban.

Then she moved, and her feet took her to Rodrigo. Even if she had no claim on him, and there'd never be anything between them, he *was* the most important man in her life, and everyone knew it.

As she approached him, he watched her with that stillness and intensity that always made her almost howl with tension.

She stopped one step away, held out the book.

"Happy *La Diada De Sant Jordi*, Rodrigo."

He took the book, his eyes fixing on it, obscuring his reaction from her. She'd chosen a book about all the people who'd advanced modern medicine in the last century. He raised his eyes to her, clearly uncertain of the significance of her choice.

"Just a reminder," she whispered, "that in a collation of this century's medical giants, you'll be among them."

His eyes flared with such fierceness, it almost knocked her off her feet. Then he reached for her hand, pulled her to him. One hand clasped her back, the other traveled over her hair to cup her head. Then he enfolded her into him briefly, pressed a searing kiss on her forehead. *"Gracias mucho, querida.* It's enough for me to have your good opinion."

Next second, he let her go, turned to deliver a few festive words, starting the celebrations.

She didn't know how she functioned after that embrace. That kiss. Those words. That *querida*.

She evidently did function, even if she didn't remember anything she said or did during the next hours. Then Rodrigo was pulling her to her feet.

"Come. We're starting the Sardana, our national dance."

She flowed behind him, almost hovered as she smiled up at him, her heart jiggling at seeing him at his most carefree.

The band consisted of eleven players. They'd already taken their place at an improvised stage in the terrace garden that had been cleared for the dancers, evidently all of Rodrigo's family.

"I had the nearest town's *cobla*, our Catalan music ensemble, come over to play for us. The Sardana is never the same without live music. It's always made of four Catalan shawm players…" He pointed toward four men holding double-reed woodwinds. "Two trumpets, two horns, one trombone and a double bass."

"And what's with that guy with the flutelike instrument and the small drum attached to his left arm?"

"He plays the *flabiol*, that three-holed flute, with his left hand and plays that *tamborí* with the right. He keeps the rhythm."

"Why not just have twelve players, instead of saddling one with this convoluted setup?"

He grinned. "It's a tradition some say goes back two thousand years. But wait till you see him play. He'll make it look like the easiest thing in the world."

She grimaced down at her casted arm. "One thing's for sure, I'm not a candidate for a *flabiol/tamborí* player right now."

He put a finger below her chin, raised her face to him. "You soon will be." Before she gave in and dragged his head down to her to take that kiss she was disintegrating for, he turned his head away. “Now watch closely. They’re going to dance the first *tirada,* and we’ll join in the second one. The steps are very simple.”

Letting out a steaming exhalation, she forced her attention to the circle of dancers that was forming.

“It’s usually one man, one woman and so on, but we have more women than men here, so excuse the nontraditional configuration.”

She mimicked his earlier hand gesture, drawled, “Women rule.”

He threw his head back on a peal of laughter at her reminder, kept chuckling as he watched his womenfolk herding and organizing their men and children. “They do indeed.”

The dance began, heated, then Rodrigo tugged her to join the *rotllanes obertes,* the open circles. They danced the steps he’d rehearsed with her on the sidelines, laughed together until their sides hurt. Everything was like a dream. A dream where she felt more alert and alive than she ever had. A dream where she was one with Rodrigo, a part of him, and in tune with the music, his family and the whole world.

Then, like every dream, the festivities drew to an end.

After calling good-night to everyone, Rodrigo walked her as usual to her quarters, left her a few steps from her door.

Two steps into the room, she froze. Her mouth fell open. Her breath left her lungs under pressure, wouldn’t be retrieved.

All around. On every surface. *Everywhere.*

Red roses.

Bunches and bunches and *bunches* of perfect, bloodred roses.

Oh. God. Oh…*God*…

She darted back outside, called out to him. But he’d gone.

She stood there vibrating with the need to rush after him, find him wherever he was and smother him in kisses.

But…since he hadn't waited around for her reaction, maybe he hadn't anticipated it would be this fierce. Maybe he'd only meant to give her a nice surprise. Maybe he'd had every other woman's room filled with flowers, too. Which she wouldn't put past him. She'd never known anyone with his capacity for giving.

She staggered back into her room. The explosion of beauty and color and fragrance yanked her into its embrace again.

The need expanded, compressing her heart, her lungs.

It was no use. She had to do it. She had to go to him.

She grabbed a jacket, streaked outside.

His scent, his vibe led her to the roof.

He was standing at the waist-high stone balustrade overlooking a turbulent, after-midnight sea, a lone knight silvered by the moon, carved from the night.

She stopped a dozen steps away. He didn't turn, stood like a statue of a Titan, the only animate things his satin mane rioting around his leonine head and his clothes rustling around his steel-fleshed frame. There was no way he could have heard the staccato of her feet or the labor of her breathing over the wind's buffeting whistles. But she knew he felt her there. He was waiting for her to initiate this.

"Rodrigo." Her gasp trembled against the wind's dissipation. He turned then. Cool rays deposited glimmers in the emerald of his eyes, luster on the golden bronze of his ruggedness. She stepped closer, mesmerized by his magnificence. A step away, she reached for his hand. She wanted to take it to her lips. That hand that had saved her life, that changed the lives of countless others daily, giving them back their limbs and mobility and freeing them from pain and disability. She settled for squeezing it between both of her trembling ones. "Besides everything you've done for me, your roses are the best gift I've ever been given."

His stare roiled with his discomfort at receiving gratitude. Then he simply said, “Your book beats my roses any day.”

A smile ached on her lips. “You have issues with hearing thanks, don’t you?”

“Thanks are overrated.”

“Nothing sincere can be rated highly enough.”

“I do what I want to do, what pleases me. And I certainly never do anything expecting…anything in return.”

Was he telling her that his gift wasn’t hinting at any special involvement? Warning her about getting ideas?

It wouldn’t change anything. She loved him with everything in her, would give him everything that she was if he’d only take it. But if he didn’t want it, she *would* give him her unending appreciation. “And I thank you because I want to, because it pleases me. And I certainly don’t expect you to do anything in return but accept. I accepted your thanks for the book, didn’t I?”

His lips spread in one of those slow, scorching smiles of his, as if against his will. “I don’t remember if I gave you a choice to accept it or not. I sort of overrode you.”

“Hmm, you’ve got a point.” Then, without warning, she tugged his hand. Surprise made him stumble the step that separated them, so that he ended up pressed against her from breast to calf. Her hand released his, went to his head, sifting through the silk of his mane, bringing it down to hers. How she wished she had the use of her other arm, so she could mimic his earlier embrace. She had to settle for pressing her longing against his forehead with lips that shook on his name.

They slid down his nose…and a cell phone rang.

He sundered their communion in a jerk, stared down at her, his eyes echoing the sea’s tumult. It was shuddering, disoriented moments before her brain rebooted after the shock of interruption, of separation from him. That was her cell phone's tone.

It was in her jacket. Rodrigo had given it her, and only he had called her on it so far. Who could be calling her?

"Are you expecting a call?" His rasp scraped her nerves.

"I didn't even know anyone had this number."

"It's probably a wrong number."

"Yeah, probably. Just a sec." She fumbled the phone out, hit Answer. A woman's tear-choked voice filled her head.

"Agnes? What's wrong?" Instant anxiety gripped Rodrigo, spilled into urgency that had his hand at the phone, demanding to bear bad news himself. She blurted out the question that she hoped would defuse his agitation, "Are you and Steven okay?"

"Yes, yes…it's not that."

Cybele covered the mouthpiece, rapped her urgent assurance to Rodrigo. "They're both fine. This is something else."

His alarm drained, but tension didn't. He eased a fraction away, let her take the call, watching for any sign that necessitated his intervention, his taking over the situation.

Agnes went on. "I hate to ask you this, Cybele, but if you've remembered your life with Mel, you might know how this happened."

Foreboding closed in on her. "How *what* happened?"

"M-many people have contacted us claiming that Mel owes them extensive amounts of money. And the hospital where you used to work together says the funding he offered in return for being the head of the new general surgery department was withdrawn and the projects that were under way have incurred overdrafts in the millions. Everyone is suing us—and you—as his next of kin and inheritors."

Ten

"So you don't have any memory of those debts."

Cybele shook her head, feeling crushed by doubts and fears.

It didn't sound as if Rodrigo believed her. She had a feeling Agnes hadn't, either. Did they think Mel had incurred all those debts because of her? Worse, had he? If he had, how? Why?

Was that what Agnes had almost brought up during Mel's funeral? She'd thought Mel, in his inability to express his emotions for her any other way, had showered her with extravagant stuff? Not that she could think what could be *that* extravagant.

If that hadn't been the case, she could think of only one other way. She'd made demands of him, extensive, unreasonable ones, and he'd gone to insane lengths to meet them. But what could have forced him to do so? Threats to leave him? If that were true, then she hadn't been only a heartless monster, but a manipulative, mercenary one, too.

She had to know. She couldn't take another breath if she didn't. "Do *you* know anything about them?"

Rodrigo's frown deepened as he shook his head slowly. But his eyes were thoughtful. With suspicions? Deductions? Realizations?

"You know something. Please, tell me. I have to know."

He looked down at her for a bone-shaking moment, moonlight coasting over his beauty, throwing its dominant slashes and hollows into a conflict of light and darkness, of confusion and certainty.

Then he shook his head again, as if he'd made up his mind. To her dismay, he ignored her plea. "What I want to know is what has taken those creditors so long to come forward."

"They actually did as soon as Mel's death was confirmed."

"Then what has taken Agnes and Steven so long to relate this, and why have they come to *you* with this, and not me?"

She gave him his foster mother's explanations. "They wanted to make sure of the claims first, and then they didn't want to bother you. They thought they could take care of it themselves. They called me in case I knew something only a wife would know, that would help them resolve this mess. And because I'm involved in the lawsuits."

"Well, they were wrong, on all counts." She almost cried out at the incensed edge that entered his voice and expression. The words to beg him not to take it up with them, that they had enough to deal with, had almost shot from her lips when he exhaled forcibly. "Not that they need to know that. They've been through enough, and they were as usual misguidedly trying not to impose on me. I think those two still don't believe me when I say they *are* my parents. But anyway, none of you have anything to worry about. I'll take care of everything."

She gaped at him. *Was* he real? Could she love him more? All she could say was, "Thank you."

He squeezed his eyes on a grimace. "Don't."

"I will thank you, so live with it." He glowered at her. She went on, "And since I'm on a roll, throwing my problems in your lap, I need your opinion on another one. My arm."

His eyes narrowed. "What about it?"

"My fractures have healed, but the nerve damage isn't clearing. Eight weeks ago, you said I wouldn't be able to operate for months. Were you being overly optimistic? Will I ever regain the precision I used to have and need as a surgeon?"

"It's still early, Cybele."

"Please, Rodrigo, just give it to me straight. And before you say anything conciliatory, remember that I'll see through it."

"I would never condescend to you like that."

"Even to protect me from bad news?"

"Even then."

She believed him. He would never lie to her. He would never lie, period. So she pressed on. Needing the truth. About this, if she couldn't have it about anything else.

"Then tell me. I'm a left-handed surgeon who knows nothing else but to be one, and I need to know if in a few weeks I'll be looking to start a new career path. As you pointed out before, the arm attached to my hand had extensive nerve damage…."

"*And* I performed a meticulous peripheral nerve repair."

"Still, I have numbness and weakness, tremors—"

"It's *still* too early to predict a final prognosis. We'll start your active motion physiotherapy rehabilitation program the moment we have proof of perfect bone healing."

"We have that now."

"No, we don't. You're young and healthy and your bones *look* healed now, but I need them rock solid before I remove the cast. That won't be a day before twelve weeks after the surgery. Then we'll start your physiotherapy. We'll focus first on controlling the pain and swelling that accompanies splint removal and restoration of motion. Then we'll move to exercises to strengthen and stabilize the muscles around the wrist joint then to exercises to improve fine motor control and dexterity."

"What if none of it works? What if I regain enough motor control and dexterity to be self-sufficient but not a surgeon?"

"If that happens, you still have nothing to worry about. If worse comes to worst, I'll see to it that you change direction smoothly to whatever field of medicine will provide you with as much fulfillment. But I'm not giving up on your regaining full use of your arm and hand. I'm stopping at nothing until we get you back to normal. And don't even *think* about how long it will take, or what you'll do or where you'll be until it happens. You have all the time in the world to retrain your hand, to regain every last bit of power and control. You have a home here for as long as you wish and accept to stay. You have *me,* Cybele. *I'm* here for you, anytime, all the time, whatever happens."

And she couldn't hold back anymore.

She surged into him, tried to burrow inside him, her working arm shaking with the ferociousness of her hug. And she wept. She loved him so much, was so thankful he existed, it was agony.

He stilled, let her hug him and hold onto him and drench him in her tears. Then he wrapped her in his arms, caressed her from head to back, his lips by her ear, murmuring gentle and soothing words. Her heart expanded so quickly with a flood of love, it almost ruptured. Her tears gushed faster, her quakes nearly rattling flesh from bone.

He at last growled something as though agonized, snatched her from gravity's grasp into his, lifted her until she felt she'd float out to sea if he relinquished his hold.

He didn't, crushed her in his arms, squeezed her to his flesh until he forced every shudder and tear out of her.

Long after he'd dissipated her storm, he swayed with her, as if slow dancing the Sardana again, pressing her head into his shoulder, his other arm bearing her weight effortlessly as he raggedly swore to her in a loop of English and Catalan that he was there for her, that she'd never be without him. His movements morphed from soothing to inflaming to excruciating. But it was his promises that wrenched at the tethers of her heart.

For she knew he would honor every promise. He would remain in her life and that of her baby's. As the protector, the benefactor, the dutiful, doting uncle. And every time she saw him or heard from him it would pour fresh desperation on the desolation of loving him and never being able to have him.

She had to get away. Today. Now. Her mind was disintegrating, and she couldn't risk causing herself a deeper injury. Her baby needed her healthy and whole.

"Cybele..." He shifted his grip on her, and his hardness dug into her thigh.

She groped for air, arousal thundering through her. Voices inside her yelled that this was just a male reaction to having a female writhing in his arms, that it meant nothing.

She couldn't listen. It didn't matter. He was aroused. This could be her only chance to be with him. And she had to take it. She needed the memory, the knowledge that she'd shared her body with him to see her through the barrenness of a life without him.

She rubbed her face into his neck, opened her lips on his pulse. It bounded against her tongue, as if trying to drive deeper into her mouth, mate with her. Every steel muscle she was wrapped around expanded, bunched, buzzed. She whimpered at the feel of his flesh beneath her lips, the texture, the taste, at the sheer delight of breathing him in, absorbing his potency.

"Cybele, *querida*..." He began to put her down and she clung, captured his lips before he said any more, before he could tell her no.

She couldn't take no for an answer. Not this time. She had to have this time.

She caught his groans on her tongue, licked his lips of every breath, suckled his depths dry of every sound. She arched into his arousal, confessing hers without words. Then with them.

"Rodrigo—I *want* you." That came out a torn sob. "If you want me, *please*—just take me. Don't hold back. Don't think. Don't worry. No consequences or considerations. No tomorrows."

Rodrigo surrendered to Cybele, let her take of him what she would, his response so vast it was like a hurricane building momentum before it unleashed its destruction.

But her tremulous words replayed in his mind as she rained petal softness and fragrant warmth all over his face, crooning and whimpering her pleas for his response, her offer of herself. He felt things burning inside him as he held back, the significance of her words expanding in his mind.

Carte blanche. That was what she was giving him. With her body, with herself. No strings. No promises. No expectations.

Because she didn't want any? Because her need was only sexual? Or because she couldn't handle more than that? But what if she couldn't handle *even* that? If he gave her what she thought she wanted and ended up damaging her more?

And though he was nearly mindless now, powerless against the force of her desire, he'd conditioned himself to protect her from his own. "Cybele, you're distraught—"

She sealed his lips again, stopping his objection, her tongue begging entry, her kisses growing fevered, singeing the last of his control. "With need for you. I sometimes feel it will shatter me. I know what I'm asking. Please, Rodrigo, please…just give me this time."

This time. She thought he could stop at once, that he could possess her then walk away? It wasn't carte blanche, just a one-time offer? Would all that need she talked about then be quenched? Did she not feel more for him because her emotions had been buried with Mel, even if she didn't remember?

That thought gave him the strength to put her down, step out of reach when she stumbled to embrace him again.

Her arms fell to her sides, her shoulders hunching as she suddenly looked fragile and lost.

Then her tears flowed again, so thick it seemed they shriveled up her face. "Oh, no—y-you already showed me that you don't want me, and I—I came on to you again…."

She choked up, stumbled around and disappeared from the roof.

He should let her go. Talk to her again when his body wasn't pummeling him in demand for hers. But even if he could survive his own disappointment, he couldn't survive hers. He couldn't let her think he didn't want her. He had to show her the truth, even if the price was having her only once. He would take anything he could have of her, give her anything she needed.

He tore after her, burst into her room, found her crumpled facedown on her bed, good arm thrown over one of the bouquets he'd flooded her room with. She lurched at his entry, half-twisted to watch his approach, her wet gaze wounded and wary.

He came down on his knees at the foot of the bed. Her smooth legs, which had tanned honey-colored under his agonized eyes these past weeks, were exposed as the long, traditionally Catalan red skirt he'd picked for her to wear today rode up above her knees.

He wanted to drag her to him, slam her into his flesh, overpower and invade her, brand her, devour her whole.

He wanted to cherish her, savor and pleasure her more.

She gasped as he slipped off her shoes, tried to turn to him fully. He stopped her with a gentle hand at the small of her back. She subsided with a whimpering exhalation, watched him with her lip caught in her teeth as he prowled on all fours, advancing over her, kissing and suckling his way from the soles of her feet, up her legs, her thighs, her buttocks and back, her nape. She lay beneath him, quaking and moaning at each touch until he traced the lines of her shuddering profile. The moment he reached her lips, she cried out, twisted onto her back, surged up to cling to his lips in a desperate, soul-wrenching kiss.

Without severing their meld, he scooped her up and stepped off the bed. She relinquished his lips on a gasp of surprise.

"I want you in my bed, *querida*."

She moaned, shook her head. "No, please." He jerked in alarm. She didn't want to be in his bed? He started to put her down when she buried her face and lips in his neck. "Here. Among the roses."

"Dios, si..."

He'd fantasized about having her in his bed from the day he'd first laid eyes on her. Even when she'd become a forbidden fantasy, her image, and the visualization of all the things he'd burned to do to her, with her, even when he'd hated her and himself and the whole world for it, had been what had fueled his self-pleasuring, providing the only relief he'd had.

He'd covered his bed with the royal blue of her eyes. The rest of the room echoed the mahogany of her hair and the honey of her skin. He'd needed to sleep surrounded by her.

But this was far better than his fantasies. To have her here, among the blazing-red beauty of his blatant confession that she was his most important woman. His most important person.

He hadn't meant to confess it, but couldn't stop himself. He also hadn't dreamed it would lead to this. To beyond his dreams.

He laid her back on the bed, stood back taking her in. Unique, a ravishing human rose, her beauty eclipsing that of the flowers he'd filled her room with. She must have realized their significance, encouraging her to divulge her own need.

He felt his clothes dissolve off his body under the pressure of his own, under her wide-eyed awe, her breathless encouragement.

Then he was all over her again, caressing her elastic-waist skirt from her silky legs, kneading her jacket off, then the ensemble blouse over her head. Her bra and panties followed as he traced the tide of peach flooding her from toes to cheeks, tasting each tremor strumming her every fiber.

Then he was looking down on what no fantasy had conjured. Thankfully. Or he would have lost his mind for real long ago.

He remained above her, arms surrounding her head, thighs imprisoning hers, vibrating as the sight, the scent and sounds of her surrender pulverized his intentions to be infinitely slow and gentle. Blood thundered in his head, in his loins, tearing the last tatters of control from his grasp in a riptide.

Then she took it all out of his hands, her hand trembling over his back in entreaty, its power absolute.

He surrendered, moved between her shaking thighs, pressed her shuddering breasts beneath his aching chest. Then she conquered him, irrevocably.

Her lips trembled on his forehead, his name a litany of tremulous passion and longing as she enveloped him, clasped him to her body as if her life depended on his existence, his closeness, on knowing he was there, as if she couldn't believe he was.

Tenderness swamped him, choked him. He had to show her, prove to her, that he was there, was hers. He'd already given her all he had. All he had left to give her was his passion, his body.

He rose on his knees, cupped her head in one hand, her buttocks in the other, tilted one for his kiss, the other for his penetration. He bathed the head of his erection in her welcoming wetness, absorbed her cries of pleasure at the first contact of their intimate flesh, drank her pleas to take her, fill her.

He succumbed to the mercilessness of her need and his, drew back to watch her eyes as he started to drive into her, to join them. Her flesh fluttered around his advance, hot and tight almost beyond endurance, seeming to drag him inside and trying to push him out at once, begging for his invasion while resisting it.

He tried again and again, until she was writhing beneath him, eyes streaming, her whole body shaking and stained in the flush of uncontrollable arousal and unbearable frustration.

His mind filled with confusion and colliding diagnoses.

"Please, just do it, Rodrigo, hard, just take me."

The agony in her sobs was the last straw. He had to give her what she needed, couldn't draw his next breath if he didn't.

He thrust past her resistance, buried half of his shaft inside her rigid tightness.

It was only when her shriek tore through him that he understood what was that ripping sensation he'd felt as he'd driven into her. And he no longer understood anything.

It was impossible. Incomprehensible.

She was a *virgin?*

Eleven

Rodrigo froze on top of Cybele, half-buried in her depths, paralyzed. A virgin? *How?*

He raised himself on shaking arms. Her face contorted and a hot cry burst from her lips. He froze in midmotion, his gaze pinned on hers as he watched her eyes flood with the same confusion, the same shock along with tears.

"It shouldn't hurt that much, should it?" she quavered. "I couldn't have forgotten *that*."

Dios. He'd wanted to give her nothing but pleasure and more pleasure. And all he'd done was *hurt* her.

"No" was all he could choke out.

She digested that, reaching the same seemingly impossible explanation he had. "Then you have to be…my first."

Her first. The way she said that, with such shy wonder, made him want to thrust inside her and growl, *And your only.*

Something far outside his wrecked restraint—probably

the debilitating cocktail of shock and shame at causing her pain—held him back from that mindless display of caveman possessiveness.

"I remember I wanted to wait until, y'know, I met…the one. I assumed that when I met Mel… But it—it seems I wanted to wait until we were married. But…"

He'd been trying to get himself to deflate, enough to slip out of her without causing her further pain. He expanded beyond anything he'd ever known instead. His mind's eye crowded with images of him devouring those lips that quivered out her earnest words, those breasts that swelled with her erratic breathing.

"But since there are ways for paraplegics to have sex, I still assumed we did one way or…" She choked with embarrassment. It was painfully endearing, when their bodies were joined in ultimate intimacy. "But it's clear we didn't, at least nothing invasive, and artificial insemination is essentially noninvasive…."

He shouldn't find her efforts at a logical, medically sound analysis that arousing as she lay beneath him, shaking, her impossible tightness throbbing around his shaft, her torn flesh singeing his own. But—curse him—it was arousing him to madness. He wanted to *give* her invasive.

He couldn't. He had to give her time, for the pain that gripped her body to subside. He started to withdraw. Her sob tore through him.

He froze, his own moan mingling with hers until she subsided. Then he tried to move again. But she clamped quaking legs around his hips, stopping him from exiting her body, pumping her own hips, impaling herself further on his erection.

"I'm hurting you." He barely recognized the butchered protest that cracked the panting-filled silence as his.

"Yes, oh, *yes*…" He heaved up in horror. She clung harder, her core clamping him like a fist of molten metal. "It's…

exquisite. You are. I dreamed—but could have never dreamed how you'd feel inside me. You're burning me, filling me, making me feel—feel so—so—oh, Rodrigo, take me, do everything to me."

He roared with the spike of arousal her words lashed through him. Then, helpless to do anything but her bidding, he thrust back into her, shaking with the effort to be gentle, go slow. She thrashed her head against the sheets, splashing her satin tresses, bucking her hips beneath his, engulfing more of his near-bursting erection into her heat. "*Don't.* Give me…all of you, do it…hard."

He growled his capitulation as he rose, cupped her hips in his palms, tilted her and thrust himself to the hilt inside her.

At her feverish cry, he withdrew all the way, looked down at the awesome sight of his shaft sinking slowly inside her again.

He raised his eyes to hers, found her propped up on her elbows, watching too, lips crimson, swollen, open on frantic pants, eyes stunned, wet, stormy. He drew out, plunged again, and she collapsed back, crying out a gust of passion, opening wider for each thrust, a fusion of pain and pleasure slashing across her face, rippling through her body.

He kept his pace gentle, massaging her all over with his hands, his body, his mouth, bending to suckle her breasts, drain her lips, rain wonder all over her.

"Do you know what you are? *Usted es divina, mi belleza, divina.* Do you see what you do to me? What I'm doing to you?"

She writhed beneath him with every word, her hair rippling waves of copper-streaked gloss over the crisp white sheet, her breathing fevered, her whole body straining at him, around him, forcing him to pick up speed—though he managed not to give in to his body's uproar for more force.

"I *love* what you're doing to me—your flesh in mine—give it to me—give it all to me…."

He again obeyed, strengthened his thrusts until her depths started to ripple around him and she keened, bucked up, froze, then convulsion after convulsion squeezed soft shrieks out of her, squeezed her around his erection in wrenching spasms.

The force, the sight and sound and knowledge of her release smashed the last of his restraint. He roared, let go, his body all but detonating in ecstasy. His hips convulsed into hers and he felt his essence flow into her as he fed her pleasure to the last tremor, until her arm and legs fell off him in satiation.

He collapsed beside her, shaking with the aftershocks of his life's most violent and first profound orgasm, moved her over him with extreme care, careful to remain inside her.

She spread over him, limp, trembling and cooling. He'd never known physical intimacy could be like this, channeling into his spirit, his reason. It had been merciful he hadn't imagined how sublime making love to her would be. He *would* have long ago gone mad.

He encompassed her velvet firmness in caresses, letting the sensations replay in his mind and body, letting awe overtake him.

He was her first. And she'd needed him so much that even through her pain, she'd felt so much pleasure at their joining.

Not that it had mattered to him in any way when he'd thought she'd belonged to Mel, had probably been experienced before him.

But now he knew she'd been with no one else, he almost burst with pride and elation. She *was* meant to be his alone.

And he had to tell her that he was hers, too. He had to offer her. Everything. *Now.*

"Cybele, *mi corazón,*" he murmured into her hair as he

pressed her into his body, satiation, gratitude and love swamping him. *"Cásate conmigo, querida."*

Cybele lay draped over Rodrigo, shell-shocked by the transfiguring experience.

Every nerve crackled with Rodrigo-induced soreness and satiation and a profundity of bliss, amazement and disbelief.

She'd been a virgin. Wow.

And what he'd done to her. A few million wows.

The wows in fact rivaled the number of his billions since he'd given her all that pleasure when she'd simultaneously been writhing with the pain of his possession. But the very concept of having him inside her body, of being joined to him in such intimacy, at last, had swamped the pain, turned it into pleasure so excruciating she thought she *had* died in his arms for moments there.

Love welled inside her as she recalled him looking down at her in such adorable contrition and stupefaction. The latter must have been because she'd babbled justifications for her virginal state with him buried inside her. Another breaker of heat crashed over her as she relived her mortification. Then the heat changed texture when she recalled every second of his domination.

What would he do to her when pain was no longer part of the equation? When he no longer feared hurting her? When he lost the last shred of inhibition and just plundered her?

She wondered if she'd survive such pleasure. And she couldn't wait to risk her life at the altar of his unbridled possession.

She was about to attempt to beg for more, needing to cram all she could into her one time in his arms. But she lost coherence as he caressed and crooned to her. Then his words registered.

Cásate conmigo, querida.

Marry me, darling.

Instinctive responses and emotions mushroomed, paralyzed her, muted her. Heart and mind ceased, time and existence froze.

Then everything rushed, streaked. Elation, disbelief, joy, shock, delight, doubt. The madly spinning roulette of emotions slowed down, and one flopped into the pocket. Distress.

She pushed away from the meld of their bodies, moaning at the burn of separation, rediscovering coordination from scratch. "I meant it when I said no tomorrows, Rodrigo. I don't expect anything."

He rose slowly to a sitting position, his masculinity taking on a harsher, more overwhelming edge among the dreamy softness of a background drenched in red roses. He looked like that wrathful god she'd seen in the beginning, decadent in beauty, uncaring of the effect his nakedness and the sight of his intact arousal had on flimsy mortals like her. "And you don't want it, either?"

"What I want isn't important."

He stopped her as she turned away, his grip on her arm gentleness itself, belying his intensity as he gritted, "It's *all*-important. And we've just established how much you want me."

"It still makes no difference. I—I can't marry you."

He went still. "Because of Mel? You feel guilty over him?"

She huffed a bitter laugh. "And you don't?"

"No, I don't," he shot back, adamant, final. "Mel is no longer here and this has nothing to do with him."

"Says the man whose every action for the last ten weeks had everything to do with Mel."

He rose to his knees, blocked her unsteady attempt to get off the bed. "Care to explain that?"

Air disappeared as his size dwarfed her, his heat bore down

on her, as his erection burned into her waist. She wanted to throw herself down, beg him to forget about his honor-bound offer and just ride her to oblivion again.

She swallowed fire past her hoarse-with-shrieks-of-pleasure vocal cords. "I'm Mel's widow, and I'm carrying his unborn child. Need more clues?"

"You think all I did for you was out of duty for him?"

She shrugged dejectedly. "Duty, responsibility, dependability, heroism, nobility, honor. You're full of 'em."

And he did the last thing she'd expected in this tension.

He belted out one of those laughs that turned her to boiling goo. "You make it sound like I'm full of…it."

Words squeezed past the heart bobbing in her throat. "I wish. You make it impossible to think the least negative thing of you."

He encroached on her as he again exposed her to that last thing she'd thought she'd ever see from him. Pure seduction, lazy and indulgent and annihilating. "And that's bad…why?"

Oh, *no*. She'd been in deep…it, when he'd been only lovely and friendly. Now, after he'd kick-started her sexuality software with such an explosive demonstration, had imprinted his code and password all over her cells, to all of a sudden see fit to turn on his sex appeal intentionally was cruel and unusual overkill.

She tried to put a breath between them. He wouldn't let her, backed her across the bed, a panther crowding his prey into a corner. She came up against the brass bars, grabbed them, tried to pull up from her swooning position.

"It's bad because it makes it impossible to say no to you."

His lips twitched as he prowled over her, imprisoning her in a cage of muscle and maleness. But instead of his previous solemn and tender intensity, that mind-messing predatory sexiness spiked to a whole new level. "That has always been my nefarious plan."

"Okay, Rodrigo, I'm confused here," she panted. "What's brought all…*this* about?"

His eyebrows shot up in mock-surprise and affront. "You mean you don't remember? Seems I have to try much…harder—and longer—to make a more lasting impression."

She coughed in disbelief. "You're telling me you suddenly want to marry me because of the mind-blowing pleasure?"

He tightened his knees around her thighs, winding the pounding between them into a tighter rhythm, licking his lips as his gaze melted over her captive nakedness, making her feel as if he'd licked her all over again. "So it was mind-blowing for you?"

"Are you kidding? I'm surprised my head is still screwed on. But I can't believe it was for *you*. I'm not by any stretch hot stuff, not to mention I must have cramped your style, being your first pregnant virgin and all."

"I admit, I was and am still agonizingly cramped, as you can see. And feel." He pressed his erection into her belly. Feeling the marble smooth and hard column of hot flesh against hers, the awe that she'd accommodated all that inside her, the carnality of the sharply recalled sensations as he'd occupied her, stretched her into mindlessness made her gasp, arch up involuntarily into his hardness. He ground harder into her as he drove a knee between her thighs, coaxing their rigidity to melt apart for him. "And in case you want to know my style…" His other knee joined in splaying her thighs apart as he leaned over her, teasing her aching nipples with the silk-sprinkled power of his chest. "…it's a woman who has no idea she's inferno-level stuff who happens to be a pregnant virgin. Or who was one, until I put an end to that condition."

She couldn't wrap her head around this. "So if it isn't out of duty to Mel, it isn't something more moronically honorable as doing the 'right thing' since you took my 'innocence,' is it?"

He chuckled. "*Dios,* you say the funniest things. First, I don't equate virginity with innocence. Second, *your* innocence seems to be almost intact. But don't worry. I didn't even scratch the surface of all the ways I plan to rectify that." He nipped her nipple, had her coming off the bed with a sharp slam of pleasure. He withdrew on a sigh of satisfaction. "Any more far-fetched reasons you can come up with to explain why I'm proposing to you?"

"Why don't you tell me your not-so-far-fetched ones?" she gasped. "And don't say because I'm your one and only aphrodisiac. That wasn't the case up until a few hours ago."

"Up until a few hours ago, I didn't know you wanted me."

"That's as straight-faced a lie as I've ever heard," she scoffed. "I'm as transparent as the windows Consuelo keeps spotless. I showed you I wanted you weeks ago. Hell, I showed you I wanted you two minutes after I regained consciousness."

He tasted her nipples in soft pulls as if compelled. "That you did so soon, coupled with your loss of memory, made me wonder if your mind wasn't scrambled and you didn't know what you wanted, or why. I thought I might be what you clung to, to reaffirm your life after surviving such a catastrophe, or because I was the one closest to you, or the one you seemed to perceive as your savior."

She pushed his head away before her breasts—her whole body—exploded. "You *are* my savior, but that has nothing to do with my wanting you." She devoured his beauty as he loomed over her, felt her core clench with the memory, the knowledge of what he could do to it. "I remember you had hordes of women you didn't save panting for you. I think *not* wanting you is a feminine impossibility."

The intimacy and seduction on his face turned off like a

light, plunging her world into darkness. "So it's only sexual for you? That's why you wanted it to be only once?"

"Which part of me lauding your responsibility, dependability, heroism, nobility and honor didn't you get?"

The mesmerizing heat flared back on like floodlights, making her squirm. "So you like me for my character not just my body?"

"I *love* you for your character." That made that smug, male assurance falter, crack. He stared at her, stunned, almost vulnerable. She groaned. "I didn't intend to say that, so don't go all noble pain-in-the-derriere on me and find it more reason to—"

He crashed his lips onto hers, silencing her, wrenching keens from her depths on scorching, devouring kisses. He came fully over her body, grinding into her belly, lifting her off the bed, one hand supporting her head for his ravaging, the other at her back holding her for his chest to torment her breasts into a frenzy.

She tore her lips away before she combusted and it was too late to vent her reservations. "Please, Rodrigo, don't feel you owe me anything. And I can't owe you any more than I already do."

He plastered her back to the bed, seemingly by the force of his conviction alone. "You owe me nothing, do you hear? It's been my privilege to see to your health, my joy to have you in my home, and yes, my mind-blowing pleasure to have you in my bed."

She started shaking again. It was too much. Loving him, needing to grab at him, to take him at his every magnificent word, blocking her mind to the fear that she'd be taking advantage of him, end up causing them both misery and heartache.

She trembled caresses over his beloved face. "I know you're always right, but you're totally wrong here. I owe you far more than medical care and shelter. And mind-blowing pleasure. I owe you for restoring my faith in humanity, for showing me what a family could be like, and letting me be a part of yours for a while, for stabilizing my outlook so much that I feel I will at last have a relationship with my own family, not just cynical and bitter avoidance. I owe you memories and experiences that have made me a stronger, healthier person, that will be a part of me forever. And that was before what you offered me today."

He grabbed her hand, singed it in kisses, all lightness burned away as he, too, vibrated with emotion. "Mel's debts…"

She rushed to make one thing clear. "I don't know what hand I had in them, but if I had any, I'll pay my part, I swear."

"No, you won't. I said I'd take care of them."

"You'd do anything to protect your foster parents, and me, too, won't you? And *this* is what I'm indebted to you for. The—the… carte blanche support. And you're offering it forever now. And I can't accept. I can't burden you anymore with my problems. Any more support from you would burden *me*. Whatever your reasons are for offering to marry me, I have nothing to offer you in return."

His hands convulsed in her hair, pinned her for the full impact of his vehemence. "You have everything to offer me, *querida*. You've *already* offered me everything and I want it all for the rest of my life. I want your passion, your friendship, and now that I know I have it, I want your love. I *need* your love. And I want your baby as mine. I want us to be lovers, to be a family. And the only reason I want all this is because I love you."

She lurched so hard she nearly threw him off her. He pressed down harder, holding her head tighter to imprint her with every nuance of his confession. "I love you, *mi amor,* for your character and your body, for being such a responsible, dependable, heroic, noble and honorable pregnant has-been-virgin who had no idea you started a fire in me that can never be put out."

She broke into sobs. "How can you say that? I was going to leave, and if I hadn't almost attacked you, you would have never—"

"I would have *never* let you leave. Don't you get that yet? I was going to keep shooting down your reasons and demands to leave for months to come, and when I was out of arguments, I was going to make you offers you can't refuse so you'd have to stay. I would have confessed my feelings to you when I felt secure you could make such a life-changing decision and lifelong commitment, could handle my feelings and my passion. You only freed me from the agonizing wait. Thankfully. I was suffering serious damage holding back."

Her tears slowed down with each incredible word out of that mouth that sent her to heaven no matter what it did or said. Scary joy and certainty started to banish the agony of grief and doubt.

"You hid that perfectly," she hiccupped, her face trembling, with a smile of burgeoning belief in his reciprocated emotions.

His sincerity and intensity switched to bedevilment in a flash as his hands and lips started to roam her again. "I'm a neurosurgeon. Covert turmoil is one of my middle names."

"Another one?" She spluttered on mirth and emotion, finally felt she had the right to reciprocate his caresses, delighting in the silk of his polished, muscled back and swimmer's shoulders.

But she had to voice her concerns one last time. "This is a major step. Are you sure you considered all the ramifications?"

"The only thing that stopped me from snatching you up the first time you offered yourself was that I thought *you* were nowhere near aware of the ramifications, had no idea what you'd be letting yourself in for, weren't ready for a relationship so soon after such a loss and trauma. I, on the other hand, am positive of what I want. What I *have* to have. You, the baby. *Us*."

She cried out and dragged him down to her, surging up to meet his lips, devouring with her own. She was begging when he suddenly rose, swept her up in his arms and strode into her bathroom.

He put her down on the massage table and ran a bubble bath, came back to slide her off it, locking her thighs around his hips, gliding his erection along her core's molten lips before he leaned forward, pressed it to her belly, undulated against her, filled her gasping mouth with his tongue.

She arched, tried to bring him inside her. He held her down, wouldn't let her have what she felt she was imploding for.

"You haven't said yes."

"I've been saying 'yes…but' for a while now," she moaned.

"Didn't sound like that to me."

"Is that why you're punishing me now?"

"I would be punishing you if I gave you what you think you want again tonight. But don't worry, there are so many other ways I'll go about erasing that innocence of yours."

"No, please…I want you again."

"Let me hear that *yes* without the *but* and you can have me. For the rest of our lives."

"Yes."

And for the rest of the night, she lost count of how many *yeses* she said.

Twelve

Three months and a half to the day that Cybele opened her eyes in Rodrigo's world, she was trying not to run down the aisle to him.

She rushed down the path between their guests, his family and friends and colleagues, in one of the plateau gardens overlooking his vineyards on one side and the sea on the other, feeling like she was treading air, forging deeper into heaven.

He'd insisted on scheduling the wedding two weeks after he'd removed her cast, to give time for the physiotherapy to control any lingering discomforts. But he hadn't insisted on holding the wedding in Barcelona's biggest cathedral as he'd first planned, succumbing to her desire to hold it on his estate. The land that was now theirs. Their home. And their baby's home.

That was what completed her happiness. That it wasn't only she who was being blessed by the best gift the world had to offer, but her baby, too. Only Rodrigo would love as his own the baby of the man he'd loved like a brother.

He stood there looking godlike in his tuxedo, his smile growing more intimate and delighted as she neared him. She only noticed Ramón standing beside him when she stumbled the last steps to grab Rodrigo's outstretched hand. She absently thought that they could be brothers. Not that Ramón, who was arguably as esthetically blessed as Rodrigo, was anywhere near as hard-hitting. Or perhaps it was she who had terminal one-man-one-woman syndrome.

Ramón winked at her as he kissed her and left them to the minister's ministrations. He'd come to her quarters an hour ago, where Rodrigo had insisted she remain until their wedding night, and performed the Catalan best man's duty of giving the bride her bouquet, which he'd picked for her, while reciting a poem he'd written. She'd almost had a heart attack laughing as he turned the poem that was supposed to extol her virtues and that of her groom into a hilariously wicked medical report.

Apart from that, and standing by Rodrigo's side until she reached him, Ramón's role had ended. In Catalonia there were no wedding rings for the best man to bear. Rodrigo would transfer the engagement ring from her right hand to her left one.

He was doing that now. She barely remembered the preceding ritual beyond repeating the vows, crying a river as Rodrigo made his own vows to her, lost in his eyes, singed by his love.

She watched their hands entwine as he slipped the ring onto her trembling finger, the ten-carat blue diamond part of the set she was wearing that totaled a breath-depleting fifty carats. He'd said he'd picked them for being a lighter version of her eyes.

Then he kissed her. As if they were now one. Forever.

From then on, everything blurred even more as their guests

carried them away to another extensive session of Sardana dances and many other wedding customs and festivities.

At one point she thought she'd had a brief exchange with Mel's parents. She had the impression that they were doing much better and seemed genuinely happy for her and Rodrigo. Her family was here, too, flown in by Rodrigo. His magic had encompassed them, as well, had infused them with a warmth they'd never exhibited before.

Then the dreamlike wedding was over and he carried her to his quarters. Theirs now. At last.

She'd almost lost her mind with craving these past weeks, as she hadn't slept curved into his body, or taken him inside of hers.

She was in a serious state by now. She'd die if he took her slowly and gently like he'd done that first night.

She was about to beg him not to when he set her down, pressed her against the door and crashed his lips onto hers.

She cried out her welcome and relief at his fierceness, surrendered to his surging tongue. His hands were all over her as he plundered her mouth, removing the *peineta* and pins that held her cutwork lace veil in place, shaking her hair out of the imprisonment of her Spanish chignon, undoing the string lacing of her traditional wedding gown's front.

He pushed it off her shoulders, spilling her breasts into his palms, weighing and kneading them until she felt they would burst if he didn't devour them. He was looking down at them as if he really would. Then he crushed them beneath his chest, her lips beneath his, rubbing, thrusting, maddening.

"Do you have any idea how much I've hungered for you?" he groaned against her lips. "What these past weeks were like?"

"If it's half as much as I hungered for you, and they were half as excruciating as mine, then…serves you right."

He grunted a sound so carnal and predatory yet amused,

sowed a chain of nips from her lips to her nipples in chastisement as he dragged her dress down. It snagged on her hips.

He reversed his efforts, tried to get it over her head, and she hissed, "Rip it."

His eyes widened. Then with a growl, he ripped the white satin in two. She lurched and moaned, relishing his ferocity, fueling it.

He swept her underwear down her legs, then stood to fling away his jacket, cummerbund and tie then gave her a violent strip-show shredding of his shirt. Candlelight cast a hypnotic glow to accompany his performance. Passion rose from her depths at the savage poetry of his every straining muscle. To her disappointment, he kept his pants on.

Before she could beg him to complete his show, he came down before her, buried his face in her flesh, in her core, muttered love and lust. When she was begging for him, he rose with her wrapped around him, took her to bed, laid her on her back on its edge, kneeled between her thighs, probed her with deft fingers.

He growled his satisfaction as her slick flesh gripped them. "Do you know what it does to me—to feel you like this, to have this privilege, this freedom? Do you know what it means to me, that you let me, that you want me, that you're mine?"

Sensation rocketed, more at the emotion and passion fueling his words than at his expert pleasuring. She keened, opened herself fully to him, now willing to accept pleasure any way he gave it, knowing he craved her surrender, her pleasure. She'd always give him all he wanted.

He came over her, thrust his tongue inside her mouth to the rhythm of his invading fingers, his thumb grinding her bud in escalating circles. He swallowed every whimper, every tremulous word, every tear, until she shuddered apart in his arms.

She collapsed, nerveless and sated. For about two minutes.

Then she was all over him, kissing, licking, nipping and kneading him through his pants. He rasped, "Release me."

She lowered the zipper with shaking hands. Her mouth watered as he sprang heavy and hard into her palms. He groaned in a bass voice that spilled magma from her core, "Play with me, *mi amor*. Own me. I'm yours."

"And do you know what hearing you say this means to me?" she groaned back.

He growled as her hands traveled up and down his shaft, pumping his potency in delight. She slithered down his body, tasted him down to his hot, smooth crown. His scent, taste and texture made her shudder with need for all of him. She spread her lips over him, took all she could of him inside. He grunted his ecstasy, thrust his mighty hips to her suckling rhythm.

His hand in her hair stopped her. "I need to be inside you."

She clambered over him, kissing her way to his lips, "And I need you inside me. Don't you dare go slow or gentle… *please…*"

With that last plea, she found herself on her back beneath him, impaled, filled beyond capacity, complete, the pleasure of his occupation insupportable.

"Cybele, *mi amor, mi vida,*" he breathed into her mouth, as he gave her what she'd been disintegrating for, with the exact force and pace that had her thrashing in pleasure, driving deeper and deeper into her, until he nudged her womb.

Her world imploded into a pinpoint of shearing sensation, then exploded in one detonation after another of bone-rattling pleasure. He fed her convulsions, slamming into her, pumping her to the last abrading twitches of fulfillment.

Then he surrendered to his own climax, and the sight and sound of him reaching completion inside her, the feel of his body shuddering over hers with the force of the pleasure he'd found inside her, his seed jetting into her core, filling her to overflowing, had her in the throes of another orgasm until she was weeping, the world receding as pleasure overloaded her.

She came to, to Rodrigo kissing her, worry roughening his voice. "Cybele, *mi alma, por favor,* open your eyes."

Her lids weighed tons, but she opened them to allay his anxiety. "I thought you knocked me senseless the first time because it *was* the first time. Seems it's going to be the norm. Not that you'll hear anything but cries for an encore from this end."

She felt the tension drain from his body, pour into the erection still buried inside her. His gaze probed her tear-drenched face, proprietary satisfaction replacing the agitation in eyes that gleamed with that Catalan imperiousness. "In that case, prepare to spend half of our married life knocked senseless."

She giggled as he wrapped her nerveless body around him and prowled to the bathroom. He took her into the tub, already filled, laid her between his thighs, her back to his front, supporting her as she half floated. He moved water over her satiated body, massaging her with it as he did with his legs and lips. She hummed with the bliss reverberating in her bones.

She would have taken once with him, would have lived on the memory forever. But this *was* forever. It was so unbelievable that sometimes she woke up feeling as if she were suffocating, believing that it had all been a delusion.

She had serious security issues. This perfection was making her more scared something would happen to shatter it all.

He sighed in contentment. *"Mi amor milagrosa."*

She turned her face into his chest, was about to whisper back that it was he who was the miracle lover when a ring sounded from the bedroom. The center calling.

He exhaled a rough breath. "They've *got* to be kidding."

She turned in his arms. "It has to be something major,

if they're calling you on your wedding night. You have to answer."

He harrumphed as he rose, dried himself haphazardly and went to answer. He came back frowning. "Pile up, serious injuries. Son and wife of an old friend among them." He drove his fingers in his hair. "*¡Maldita sea!* I only started making love to you."

"Hey. Surgeon here, too, remember? Nature of the beast." She left the tub, dried quickly, hugged him with both arms—an incredible sensation. "And you don't have to leave me behind. Let me come. I hear from my previous employers that I was a damn good surgeon. I can be of use to you and the casualties."

His frown dissolved, until his smile blinded her with his delight. "This isn't how I visualized spending our wedding night, *mi corazon*. But having you across a table in my OR is second on my list only to having you wrapped all around me in my bed."

After the emergency, during which their intervention was thankfully lifesaving, they had two weeks of total seclusion on his estate.

The three weeks after that, Cybele ticked off the two top items on Rodrigo's list, over and over. Daily, in fact.

They worked together during the days, discovering yet another area in which they were attuned. It became a constant joy and stimulation, to keep realizing how fully they could share their lives and careers.

Then came the nights. And if their first time and their semi-aborted wedding night had been world-shaking, she'd had no idea how true intimacy would escalate the pleasure and creativity of their encounters. Even those momentous occasions paled by comparison.

It was their five-week anniversary today.

She was in her twenty-second week of pregnancy and she'd never felt healthier or happier. Not that that convinced Rodrigo to change her prenatal checkups from weekly to biweekly.

"Ready, *mi amor?*"

She sprang to her feet, dissolved into his embrace. He kissed her until she was wrapped around him, begging him to postpone her checkup. She had an emergency only he could handle.

He bit her lip gently, put her away. "It'll take all of fifteen minutes. Then I'm all yours. As always."

She hooked her arm through his, inhaled his hormone-stimulating scent. "Do you want to find out the gender of the baby?"

He looked at her intently, as if wanting to make sure of her wish before he voiced his opinion. Seemed he didn't want to risk volunteering one that opposed hers. "Do you?"

She decided to let the delicious man off the hook. "I do."

His smile dawned. He *did* want to know, but considered it up to her to decide. Surely she couldn't love him more, could she?

"Then we find out."

"So what do you hope it is?"

He didn't hesitate, nuzzled her neck, whispered, "A girl. A tiny replica of her unique mother."

She surrendered to his cosseting, delight swirling inside her. "Would you be disappointed if it's a boy?"

His smile answered unequivocally. "I'm just being greedy. And then, you know how seriously cool it is to be female around here."

She made the goofy gesture and expression that had become their catchphrase. "Women rule."

Four hours later, they were back in their bedroom.

They'd made love for two of those, only stopped because

they had a dinner date with Ramón and other colleagues in Barcelona.

She was leaning into him, gazing in wonder at his reflection in the mirror as he towered behind her, kissing her neck, caressing her zipper up her humming body, taking extra care of her rounding belly. She sighed her bliss. "Think Steven and Agnes will be happy it's a boy?"

His indulgent smile didn't waver. But she was so attuned to his every nuance of expression now, she could tell the question disturbed him. Since it indirectly brought up Mel.

And the mention of Mel had been the only thing to make him tense since they'd gotten married, to make him even testy and irritated. He'd once even snapped at her. She'd been shocked that day. And for a moment, black thoughts had swamped her.

She'd wondered if this fierceness was different from his early moroseness concerning Mel, if now that he was her husband, Mel was no longer simply his dead foster brother, but her dead first husband and he hated her mentioning Mel, out of jealousy.

The implications of that were so insupportable, she'd nearly choked on them. But only for a moment. Then he'd apologized so incredibly and she'd remembered what he was, what Mel had been to him.

She'd come to the conclusion that the memory of Mel was still a gaping wound inside him. One that hurt more as time passed, as the loss solidified. With him busy being the tower of strength everyone clung to, he hadn't dealt with his own grief. He hadn't attained the closure he'd made possible for everyone else to have. She hoped their baby would heal the wound, provide that closure.

His hands resumed caressing her belly. "I think they'll be happy as long as the baby is healthy."

And she had to get something else out of the way. "I called

Agnes this morning and she sounded happier than I've ever heard her. She said those who filed the lawsuits weren't creditors but investors who gave Mel money to invest in the hospital, and that the money was found in an account they didn't know about."

His hands stopped their caresses. "That's right."

"But why didn't they ask for their money instead of resorting to legal action, adding insult to injury to bereaved parents? A simple request would have sent Agnes and Steven looking through Mel's documents and talking to his lawyer and accountant."

"Maybe they feared Agnes and Steven wouldn't give back the money without a strong incentive."

"Apart from finding this an incredibly irrational fear since Mel and his parents are upstanding people, there must have been legal provisos in place to assure everyone's rights."

"I don't know why they acted as they did. What's important is that the situation's over, and no harm's done to anyone."

And she saw it in his eyes. The lie.

She grabbed his hands. "You're not telling me the truth." He tried to pull his hand away. She clung. "Please, tell me."

That bleak look, which she'd almost forgotten had ever marred his beauty, was back like a swirl of ink muddying clear water.

But it was worse. He pushed away from her, glared at her in the mirror like a tiger enraged at someone pulling on a half ripped-out claw.

"You want the truth? Or do you just want me to confirm that those people acted irrationally, that Mel was an upstanding man? If so, you should do like Agnes and Steven, grab at my explanation for this mess, turn a blind eye and cling to your illusions."

She swung around to face him. "You made up this story to

comfort them. The debts were real. And you must have done more than settle them to make Mel's creditors change their story."

"What do you care about the sordid details?"

Sordid? Oh, God. "Did…did I have something to do with this? Are you still protecting me, too?"

"*No.* You had nothing to do with any of it. It was just more lies Mel fed me, poisoned me with. I lived my life cleaning up after him, covering up for him. And now he's reaching back from the grave and forcing me to keep on doing it. And you know what? I'm *sick* of it. I've been getting sicker by the day, of embellishing his image and memory to you, to Agnes and Steven, of gritting my teeth on the need to tell you what I figured out he'd done to me. To *us*."

She staggered backward under the impact of his exasperated aggression. "What did he do? And what do you mean, to 'us'?"

"How can I tell you? It would be my word against a man who can't defend himself. It would make me a monster in your eyes."

"No." She threw herself in his path. "Nothing would make you anything but the man I love with every fiber of my being."

He held her at arm's length. "Just forget it, Cybele. I shouldn't have said anything…*Dios,* I wish I could take it back."

But the damage had been done. Rodrigo's feelings about Mel seemed to be worse than she'd ever feared. And she had to know. The rest. Everything. Now. "Please, Rodrigo, I have to know."

"How can I begin to explain, when you don't even remember how *we* first met?"

She stared at him, the ferocity of his frustration pummeling her, bloodying her. She gasped, the wish to remember so violent, it smashed at the insides of her skull like giant hammers.

Suddenly, the last barricade shattered. Memories burst out of the last dark chasm in her mind, snowballing into an avalanche.

She remembered.

Thirteen

She swung away, a frantic beast needing a way out.

The world tilted, the ground rushed at her at a crazy angle.

"*Cybele.*"

Her name thundered over her, then lightning hit her, intercepted her fall, live wires snaring her in cabled strength before she reinjured her arm beneath her plummeting weight.

Memories flooded through her like water through a drowning woman's lungs. In brutal sequence.

She'd first seen Rodrigo at a fundraiser for her hospital. Across the ballroom, towering above everyone, canceling out their existence. She'd felt hit by lightning then, too.

She'd stood there, unable to tear her eyes off him as people kept swamping him in relentless waves, moths to his irresistible fire. All through, he'd somehow never taken his eyes off her. She'd been sure she'd seen the same response in his eyes, the same inability to believe its power, to resist it.

Then Ramón had joined him, turned to look at her, too, and she knew Rodrigo was telling him about her. He left Ramón's side, charted a course for her. She stood there, shaking, knowing her life would change the moment he reached her.

Then a man next to her had collapsed. Even disoriented by Rodrigo's hypnotic effect, her doctor auto-function took over, and she'd rushed to the man's rescue.

She'd kept up her resuscitation efforts until paramedics came, and then she'd swayed up to look frantically for Rodrigo. But he'd vanished.

Disappointment crushed her even when she kept telling herself she'd imagined it all, her own response, too, that if she'd talked to him she would have found out he was nothing like the man she'd created in her mind.

Within days, she'd met Mel. He came with a huge donation to her hospital and became the head of the new surgery department. He offered her a position and started pursuing her almost at once. Flattered by his attention, she'd accepted a couple of dates. Then he proposed. By then, she had suspected he was a risk-taking jerk, and turned him down. But he'd said he used that persona at work to keep everyone on their toes, and showed himself to be diametrically different, everything she'd hoped for in a man, until she accepted.

Then Mel had introduced Rodrigo as his best friend.

She was shocked—and distraught that she hadn't imagined his effect on her. But she'd certainly imagined her effect on him. He seemed to find her abhorrent. Mel, unaware of the tension between the two people he said meant the most to him, insisted on having Rodrigo with them all the time. And though Mel's bragging accounts of his friend's mile-high bedpost notches had her despising Rodrigo right back, she'd realized she couldn't marry Mel while she felt that unstoppable attraction to his best friend. So she broke off the engagement. And it was then that

Mel drove off in a violent huff and had the accident that had crippled him.

Feeling devastated by guilt when Mel accused her of being the reason he'd been crippled, Cybele took back her ring. They got married in a ceremony attended by only his parents a month after he was discharged from hospital. Rodrigo had left for Spain after he'd made sure there was nothing more he could do for his friend at that time, and to Cybele's relief, he didn't attend.

But the best of intentions didn't help her cope with the reality of living with a bitter, volatile man. They'd discussed with a specialist the ways to have a sex life, but his difficulties had agonized him even though Cybele assured him it didn't matter. She didn't feel the loss of what she'd never had, was relieved when Mel gave up trying, and poured her energy into helping him return to the OR while struggling to catch up with her job.

Then Rodrigo came back, and Mel's erratic behavior spiked. She'd confronted him, and he said he felt insecure around any able-bodied man, especially Rodrigo, but needed him more than ever. He was the world's leading miracle worker in spinal injuries, and he was working on putting Mel back on his feet.

But there was one thing Mel needed even more now. He was making progress with the sex therapy specialists, but until he could be a full husband to her, he wanted something to bind them, beyond her sense of duty and honor and a shared house. A baby.

Cybele had known he was testing her commitment. But was feeling guiltier now that she'd lived with his affliction reason enough to take such a major step at such an inappropriate time? Would a baby make him feel more of a man? Was it wise to introduce a baby into the instability of their relationship?

Guilt won, and with her mother promising she'd help out with the baby, she had the artificial insemination.

Within a week, her conception was confirmed. The news only made Mel unbearably volatile, until she'd said she was done tiptoeing around him since it only made him worse. He apologized, said he couldn't take the pressure, needed time off. And again Cybele succumbed, suspended her residency even knowing she'd lose her position, to help him and to work out their problems. Then he dropped another bombshell on her. He wanted them to spend that time off on Rodrigo's estate.

When she'd resisted, he said it would be a double benefit, as Rodrigo wanted Mel there for tests for the surgeries that would give Mel back the use of his legs. And she'd had to agree.

When they'd arrived in Barcelona, Rodrigo had sent them a limo. Mel had it drive them to the airfield where his plane was kept. When she objected, he said he didn't need legs to fly, that flying would make him feel like he was whole again.

But during the flight, in answer to some innocuous comments, he got nasty then abusive. She held her tongue and temper, knowing it wasn't the place to escalate their arguments, but she decided that once they landed, she'd face him, as she'd faced herself, and say that their relationship wasn't working, and it wasn't because of his turmoil, but because of who he was. A man of a dual nature, one side she'd loved but could no longer find, and the other she couldn't bear and seemed was all that remained.

But they hadn't landed.

Now she heaved as the collage of the crash detonated in image after shearing image, accompanied by a hurricane of deafening cacophony and suffocating terror.

Then the maelstrom exchanged its churning motion for a linear trajectory as all trivial memories of every day of the year before the accident burst like flashes of sickening light, obliterating the blessed darkness of the past months.

Everything decelerated, came to a lurching stop.

Her face was being wiped in coolness, her whole self bathed in Rodrigo's concern. She raised sore eyes to his reddened ones.

His lips feathered over them with trembling kisses. "You remember."

"My end of things," she rasped. "Tell me yours."

The heart beneath her ear felt as if it would ram out of his chest.

Then he spoke. "When I saw you at that fundraiser, it was like seeing my destiny. I told Ramón that, and he said that if anyone else had said that, he would have laughed. But coming from me, I, who always know what's right for me, he believed it, and to go get you. But as I moved to do that, all hell broke loose. You rushed to that man's aid and I was called to deal with multiple neuro-trauma cases back here. I asked Ramón to find out all he could about you, so I could seek you out the moment I came back.

"I tried for the last almost eighteen months not to reconstruct what I instinctively knew and didn't want to—*couldn't* face. But the more I knew you, the more inconsistencies I discovered since the accident, the more I couldn't pretend not to know how it all happened anymore. Mel was there, too, that initial day. He was right behind me as I turned away from Ramón. He must have overheard my intentions. And he decided to beat me to you."

She couldn't even gasp. Shock fizzled inside her like a spark in a depleted battery.

"And he did. Using money I gave him to gain his new position, he put himself where he'd have access to you. For the six weeks I stayed away performing one surgery after another, all the time burning for the moment I could come back and search you out, he was pursuing you. The moment you accepted his proposal, he called me to tell me that he was engaged. He left your name out.

"The day I rushed back to the States to find you, he insisted I go see him first, meet his fiancée. I can never describe my horror when I found out it was you.

"I kept telling myself it couldn't have been intentional, that he wouldn't be so cruel, that he couldn't be shoving down my throat the fact that he was the one who'd gotten you. But I remember his glee as he recounted how it had been love at first sight, that you couldn't get enough of him, and realized he was having a huge laugh at my expense, wallowing in his triumph over me, all the while dangling you in front of me until I was crazed with pain."

"Was that why…?" She choked off. It was too much.

"Why I behaved as if I hated you? *Sí.* I hated everything at the time. Mel, myself, you, the world, the very life I woke up to every morning in which you could never be mine."

"B-but you had so many other lovers."

"I had *nobody.* Since I laid eyes on you. Those women were smoke screens so that I wouldn't sit through our outings like a third-wheel fool, something to distract me so I wouldn't lose my mind wanting you more with each passing day. But nothing worked. Not my efforts to despise you, not your answering antipathy. So I left, and would have never come back. But he forced me back. He crippled himself, as I and his parents always warned him he one day would."

A shudder rattled her at the memory. "He said I made him lose his mind, drove him to it…."

He looked beyond horrified. "*No. Dios,* Cybele…it had *nothing* to do with you, do you hear? Mel never took responsibility for any problem he created for himself. He always found someone else to accuse, usually me or his parents. *Dios*—that he turned on you, too, accused you of this!" His face turned a burnt bronze, his lips worked, thinning with the effort to contain his aggression. She had the feeling that if Mel were alive and here, Rodrigo would have dragged him out of his wheelchair and taken him apart.

At last he rasped, "It had to do with his own gambler's behavior. He always took insane risks, in driving, in sports, in surgeries. One of those insane risks was the gambling that landed him in so much debt. I gave him the money to gamble, too. He told me it was to buy you the things you wanted. But I investigated. He never bought you anything."

So this was it. The explanation he'd withheld.

"As for the stunt that cost him his life and could have cost yours, it wasn't his first plane crash but his third. He walked away from so many disasters he caused without a scratch that even the one that cut him in half didn't convince him that his luck had run out and the next time would probably be fatal. As it was."

For a long moment, all she heard was her choppy breath, the blood swooshing in her ears, his harsh breathing.

Then he added, "Or maybe he wanted to die."

"Why would he?" she rasped. "He believed you'd put him back on his feet. He said you were very optimistic."

He looked as if he'd explode. "Then he lied to you. Again. There was nothing I could do for him. I made it absolutely clear."

She squeezed her eyes shut. "So he was really desperate."

"I think he was worse than that." His hiss felt as if it would scrape her flesh from her bone. "I think he'd gone over the edge, wanted to take you with him. So I would never have you."

She lurched as if under a flesh-gouging lash.

Rodrigo went on, bitterness pouring out of him. "Mel

always had a sickness. Me. Since the first day I set foot in the Braddocks' house, he idolized me and seethed with jealousy of me, alternated between emulating me to the point of impersonation, to doing everything to be my opposite, between loving and hating me."

It all made so much sense it was horrifying. How she'd found Mel so different at first, how he'd switched to the seamless act of emulating Rodrigo. So it *had* been Rodrigo she'd fallen in love with all along. It was unbelievable. Yet it was the truth.

And it dictated her next action. The only thing she could do.

She pushed out of his arms, rose to unsteady feet, looked down at him, the man she loved beyond life itself.

And she cut her heart out. "I want a divorce."

Cybele's demand fell on Rodrigo like a scythe.

Rage, at himself, hacked him much more viciously.

He'd been so *stupid*. He'd railed at a dead man, not just the man he'd considered his younger brother, but the man Cybele still loved, evidently more than she could ever love him.

He shot to his feet, desperation the one thing powering him. "Cybele, *no. Lo siento, mi amor.* I didn't mean…"

She shut her eyes in rejection, stopping his apology and explanation. "You meant every word. And you had every right. Because you *are* right. You at last explained my disappointment in Mel, my resentment toward him. You rid me of any guilt I ever felt toward him."

Rodrigo reeled. "You—you didn't love Mel?"

She shook her head. Then in a dead monotone, she told him her side of the story.

"Seems I always sensed his manipulations, even if I would have never guessed their reason or extent. My subconscious must have considered it a violation, so it wiped out the traumatic time until I was strong enough. I still woke up with overpowering gut feelings. But without context, they weren't enough to stop me from tormenting myself when I felt nothing but relief at his death and anger toward him, when I wanted you from the moment I woke up. Now I know. I always wanted you."

Elation and confusion tore him in two. "You did? *Dios*—then why are you asking for a divorce?"

"Because I don't matter. Only my baby does. I would never have married you if I'd realized you would be the worst father for him. Instead of loving his father, you hate Mel with a lifelong passion. And though you have every right to feel that way, I can never subject my child to the life I had. Worse than the life I had. My stepfather didn't know my father, and he also didn't consider me the bane of his life. He just cared nothing for me. But it was my mother's love for him, her love for the children she had with him, that alienated her from me. And she doesn't love him a fraction of how much I love you."

He should have realized all that. He knew her scars in detail, knew she was barely coping now, as an adult, with her alienated childhood and current bland family situation. But he got it now. The sheer magnitude of his blunder. It could cost him his life. *Her.*

"I never hated Mel," he pleaded. "It was Mel who considered me the usurper of his parents' respect and affection. I loved him, like brothers love their imperfect siblings. Mel did have a lot to him that I appreciated, and I always hoped he'd believe that, be happy playing on his own strengths and stop competing with me in mine. But I could never convince him, and it ate at him until he lashed out, injured you while trying to get to me, the source of his discontent. It was foolish, tragic, and I *do* hate his taking you away from me, but I don't hate *him*. You have to believe that."

She clearly didn't. And she had every reason to distrust his words after that moronic display of bitterness and anger.

She confirmed his worst fears, her voice as inanimate as her face. "I can't take the chance with my baby's life."

Agony bled out of him. "Do you think so little of me, Cybele? You claim to love me, and you still think I'd be so petty, so cruel, as to take whatever I felt for Mel out on an innocent child?"

She stumbled two steps back to escape his pleading hands. "You might not be able to help it. He did injure you, repeatedly, throughout his life. That he's now dead doesn't mean that you can forget. Or forgive. I wouldn't blame you if you could do neither."

"But that baby is *yours,* Cybele. He could be yours from the very devil and I'd still love and cherish him because he's yours. Because I love you. I would die for you."

The stone that seemed to be encasing her cracked, and she came apart, a mass of tremors and tears. "And I would d-die for you. I feel I *will* die without you. And that only makes me more scared, of what I'd do to please you, to keep your love, if I weaken now, and it turns out, with your best intentions, you'd never be able to love my baby as he deserves to be loved. And I—I can't risk that. Please, I beg you, don't make it impossible to leave you. *Please*…let me go."

He lunged for her, as if to grab her before she vanished. "I *can't*, Cybele."

She wrenched away, tears splashing over his hands. His arms fell to his sides, empty, pain impaling his heart, despair wrecking his sanity.

Suddenly, realization hit him like a vicious uppercut.

He couldn't *believe* it. *Dios*, he was far worse than a moron.

He *did* have the solution to everything.

He blocked her path. "*Querida*, forgive me, I'm such an idiot. I conditioned myself so hard to never let the truth slip, that even after you told me your real feelings for Mel, it took seeing you almost walking out on me to make me realize I don't have to hide it anymore. It is true I would have loved any baby of yours as mine, no matter what. But I love *this* baby, I want him and I would die for him, too. Because he *is* mine. Literally."

Fourteen

"I *am* the baby's father."

Cybele stared at Rodrigo, comprehension suspended.

"If you don't believe me, a DNA test will prove it."

And it ripped through her like a knife in her gut.

One thing was left in her mind, in the world. A question.

She croaked it. "How?"

He looked as if he'd rather she asked him to step in front of a raging bull. Then he exhaled. "A few years back, Mel had a paternity suit. During the tests to prove that he didn't father the child, he found out that he was infertile. Then he told me that you were demanding proof of his commitment to your marriage, the emotional security of a baby. He said he couldn't bear to reveal another shortcoming to you, that he couldn't lose you, that you were what kept him alive. He asked me to donate the sperm. Just imagining you blossoming with my baby, nurturing it, while I could never claim it or you, almost killed *me*.

"But I believed him when he said he'd die if you left him. And even suspecting how he'd stolen you from me, I would have done anything to save him. And I knew if I said no, he would have gotten any sperm donor sample and passed it as his. I couldn't have you bear some stranger's baby. So I agreed.

"But believing you were suffering from psychogenic amnesia so that your mind wouldn't buckle under the trauma of losing him, I couldn't let you know you'd lost what you thought remained of him. I wouldn't cause you further psychological damage. I would have settled for being my baby's father by adoption when he was mine for real."

So that was why. His change toward her after the accident, treating her like she was the most precious thing in the world, binding himself to her forever. This explained everything much more convincingly than his claim that he'd loved her all along.

It had all been for his baby.

"Te quiero tanto, Cybele, *más que la vida. Usted es mi corazón, mi alma."*

Hearing him say he loved her, more than life, that she was his heart, his soul now that she knew the truth was…unbearable.

Feeling her life had come to an end, she pushed out of his arms and ran.

Rodrigo restrained himself from charging after her and hauling her back and never letting her go ever again with an exertion of will that left him panting.

He had to let her go. She had to have time alone to come to terms with the shocks, to realize that although they'd taken a rough course to reach this point, both Mel and fate had ended up giving them their future and perfect happiness together.

He lasted an hour. Then he went after her. He found her gone.

Consuelo told him Cybele had asked Gustavo to drive her to the city, where he'd dropped her off at a hotel near the center.

He felt as if the world had vanished from around him.

She'd left him. But…why? She'd said she loved him, too.

When his head was almost bursting with confusion and dread, he found a note on their bed.

The lines swam as if under a lens of trembling liquid.

Rodrigo,

You should have told me that my baby was yours from the start. I would have accepted your care for its real reason—a man safeguarding the woman who is carrying his baby. Knowing you and your devotion to family, your need to have your flesh and blood surrounding you, I know you want this baby fiercely, want to give him the most stable family you can, the one neither of us had. Had you told me, I would have done anything to cooperate with you so the baby would have parents who dote on him and who treat each other with utmost affection and respect. I don't have to be your wife to do that. You can divorce me if you wish, and I'll still remain your friend and colleague, will live in Spain as long as you do, so you'll have constant access to your son.

Cybele.

Rodrigo read the note until he felt the words begin to burn a brand into his retinas, his brain.

After all the lies and manipulations she'd been victim to, she had every right to distrust his emotions and motives toward her. From her standpoint, he could be saying and doing whatever it took to get his son.

But he'd prove his sincerity if it was the last thing he did.

If he lost her, it just might be.

Twenty-four hours later, he stood outside her hotel room door, feeling he'd aged twenty-four years.

She opened the door, looking as miserable as he felt.

All he wanted was to take her in his arms, kiss her until she was incoherent with desire, but he knew that might only prove to her that he was manipulating her even worse than Mel had.

He never gambled. But he'd never known true desperation, either. Now a gamble, with potentially catastrophic results, was the last resort he had left.

Without a word, he handed her the divorce papers.

Cybele's heart stopped, felt it would never beat again.

She'd made a desperate gamble. And lost. She'd owed him the choice, the freedom to have his baby without remaining her husband. She'd prayed he'd choose to be with her anyway.

He hadn't. He was giving her proof, now that she'd assured him he'd always have his son, that he'd rather be free of her.

Then her eyes fell on the heading of one of the papers.

Before the dread fully formed inside her mind, it spilled from her lips. "You won't take the baby away, will you? Any court in the world would give you custody, I know, but please don't—"

He grimaced as if she'd stabbed him. "Cybele, *querida, por favor, le pido.* I beg you…stop. Do you distrust me that much?"

Mortification swallowed her whole. "No…no—oh, God. But I—I don't *know*. Anything. It's like you're three people in my mind. The one who seemed to hate me, the one who saved me, took such infinite care of me, who seemed to want me as much as I want you, and the one who always had an agenda, who's handing me divorce papers. I don't know who you are, or what to believe anymore."

"Let me explain." His hands descended on her shoulders.

"No." She staggered around before his grip could tighten. She couldn't hear that he cared, but not enough to remain married to her. She fumbled for a pen by the hotel's writing pad. The papers slid from her hands, scattered across the desk. Fat tears splashed over the blurring lines that mimicked the chaos inside her. "After I sign these papers, I want a couple of days. I'll call you when I'm thinking straight again and we can discuss how we handle things from now on."

His hands clamped the top of her arms, hauled her back against the living rock of his body. She struggled to escape, couldn't bear the agony his feel, his touch, had coursing in hers.

He pressed her harder to his length. She felt his hardness digging into her buttocks, couldn't understand.

He still wanted her? But if he was divorcing her, then all the hunger she'd thought only she could arouse in him had just been the insatiable sexual appetite of the hot-blooded male that he was. And now...what? Her struggles were arousing him?

All thought evaporated as his lips latched onto her neck, drew on her flesh, wrenching her desire, her very life force with openmouthed kisses and suckles. She tried to twist away, but he lifted her off the ground, carried her to the wall, spread her against it and pinned her there with his bulk, his knee driven between her thighs, his erection grinding against her belly.

He caught her lower lip in a growling bite, sucked and pulled on it until she cried out, opened wide for him. Then he plunged, took, gave, tongue and teeth and voracity. Wave after wave of readiness flooded her core. She squirmed against him, everything disintegrating with her need to crawl under his skin, take him into hers. His fingers found her under her panties, probed her to a screeching climax. Then she begged for him.

In a few moments and moves, he gave her more than she could take, all of him, driving inside her drenched, clenching tightness. Pleasure detonated from every inch of flesh that yielded to the invasion of the red-hot satin of his thickness and length. He powered into her, poured driven words in an inextricable mix of English and Catalan, of love and lust and unbearable pleasure into her gasping mouth as his thrusting tongue ravaged her with possession and mindlessness.

Pleasure reverberated inside her with each thrust, each word, each melding kiss, like the rushing and receding of a tide gone mad. It all gathered, towered, held at its zenith like a tidal wave before the devastating crash. Then the blows of release hit like those of a giant hammer, striking her core again and again, expanding shock waves that razed her, wrung her around his girth in contractions so violent they fractured breath and heartbeats. She clung to him in the frenzy, inside and out as if she'd assimilate him, dissolve around him. Then she felt him roar his release as he jammed his erection to her womb, jetting his pleasure to fill it, causing another wave to crash over her, shattering her with the power of the sensations, of wishing that they'd make a baby this way in the future. When they didn't have one…

She came back to awareness to find him beneath her on the bed, still hard and pulsating inside her, setting off mini quakes that kept her in a state of continuous orgasm.

A question wavered from her in a scratchy rasp. "So was that goodbye sex?"

He jerked beneath her. "You go out of your way to pick the exact words that will cut me deepest, don't you?"

And she wailed, "What else could it be?"

"It was you-turn-me-into-a-raging-beast-in-perpetual-mating-frenzy sex. It was I-can't-have-enough-of-your-pleasure-and-your-intimacy lovemaking." Every word flowed over her like a balm on a wound, drowning the doubt demons who whispered he was just over-endowed and would enjoy any sexually voracious female. "Not that that excuses what I did. I didn't come here intending to take you like that. I was resolved not to confuse issues. But I saw you about to sign those papers and almost burst an artery."

Her lips twitched in spite of her confusion. "Glad the pressure found another outlet." She relived the moments when it had, splashing against her inner walls, filling her with his scalding essence, mixing with her pleasure… But…wait a sec! "But you *want* me to sign the papers."

He rose onto his elbow, looked at her with the last trace of heavy-lidded male possession vanishing, that bleakness taking over his eyes. "I want a bullet between the eyes more." She gasped, the thought of anything happening to him paralyzing her with terror. "But since I can't prove that to you by words or lovemaking, and you have every right not to accept either as proof, after all the lies that almost cost you your mind and your very life, I'm down to action. And the proof of time."

He extricated himself from her, rose off the bed, walked to gather the papers and came back to lay them beside her.

Before she could say she didn't want any proof, just wanted to be his, if he really wanted her, he turned and gathered his clothes.

She sat up shakily as he started dressing, his movements stiff, his face clenched with that intensity she now believed betrayed his turmoil. And finally, she understood. Just as she'd given him the freedom to divorce her, the divorce papers were his proof that she was equally free. Even if he'd rather end his life than lose her, he was letting her go, if it meant her peace of mind. Oh, God…

She'd caused him so much pain, even if inadvertently. Then, when he'd told her how long and how much he'd been hurting, she'd added indelible insult to injury when she'd imposed her distrust of those who'd blighted her life with letdowns, who'd made her doubt that she was deserving of love, as pretext to condemn his motivations.

But a man who wanted only his child wouldn't have done one thousandth of the things he'd done for her. He would never have said he loved her, would rather die than lose her. And even if any other man might have lied to that extent to achieve what he considered a highest cause, the stability of his child's family life, Rodrigo wouldn't. He was too honorable.

Even when he'd kept the truth about their baby's paternity from her, he'd done it only to protect her, had been willing to never proclaim his baby as his own flesh and blood, to preserve the illusion he'd thought essential to her well-being.

She made a grab for the papers, sprang off the bed and ran to him, grabbed one of his hands as he started buttoning up his shirt, tears of humility and contrition and heart-piercing adoration pouring from her very soul to scorch down her cheeks. "Those papers are your I'm-free-to-come-back-to-you-of-my-own-free-will gesture, right?"

He seemed to struggle to stop himself. He lost the fight, reached out with his other hand, wiped away her tears, cupped her cheek, his face the embodiment of tenderness. "They're not a gesture. You *are* free. And you must not consider me in your decision. You're not responsible for how I feel." Exactly the opposite of what Mel and her family had done to her. They'd made her feel responsible for their feelings toward her, guilty of inciting Mel's pathological possessiveness or their equally unnatural negligence. "In time, if you become satisfied that I am what you need, what will make you happy, come back to me. If you don't, then sign those papers and send them back to me instead. The other documents should prove you are in no way pressured to make the best of it for anybody else's sake but yours."

And she revealed her last and biggest fear. "W-what if in time *you* decide I'm not what you need?"

He huffed a harsh laugh, as if she were asking if he might one day fly under his own power. Certainty solidified in her every cell as she grinned up at him with sudden unbridled ecstasy. Then the rest of his words registered. "The other documents…"

She looked through the papers, found those with the heading that had triggered her crazy doubt that he'd take the baby.

Custody papers. Giving away his parental rights. To her. Unconditionally. She'd choose if he was part of his baby's life.

She stared at the words, their meaning too huge to take in.

Her eyes flew dazedly up to his solemn ones. "Why?"

"Because without you, nothing is worth having, not even my child. Because I trust you not to deprive him of my love even if you decide to end our marriage. Because I want you to be totally free to make that decision if you need to, without fearing you'll lose your baby, or become embroiled in a custody case. Because I need to know that if you come back to me, you do it not out of need or gratitude or for our baby's best interests, but because it's in *your* best interests. Because you want me."

Then he turned away, looking like a man who had nothing to look forward to but waiting for an uncertain verdict.

She flew after him, joy and distress tearing at her. She wrenched him around, jumped on him, climbed him, wrapped herself around him and squeezed him as if she'd merge them. His shuddering groan quaked through her as he hugged her back, crushed her to him, his arms trembling his relief.

She covered his face and neck and anything she could reach

of him in tear-drenched kisses and wept. "I don't just *want* you! I worship you, I crave and adore and love you far more than life. And it's not out of need or gratitude. Not the way you fear. I don't need you to survive, but I need you to be alive. I'm grateful you exist, and a few light years beyond that that you love me, too. I don't deserve you or that you should feel the same for me. I—I hurt you and mistrusted you and it doesn't matter that I was reeling from the shock of the regained memories and the revelations—"

His lips crushed the rest of her outburst in savage kisses. Then she was on the bed again, on her back, filled with him as he drove into her, growled to her again and again that he believed her and in her, and she screamed and sobbed her relief and gratitude and love and pleasure.

It was hours before that storm abated and she lay over him, free of doubt or worry, of gravity and physical limitations.

She told him, "You make me feel—limitless, just like what I feel for you. But you are too much, give too much. It would have been criminal to have all this without paying in advance with some serious misery and heartache. I love the fates that tossed me around only to land me in your lap, and by some miracle make you love me, too. I just adore every bit of misfortune and unhappiness I had that now make me savor every second of what we share all the more."

Rodrigo swept Cybele with caresses, agreed to every word she said. They were the exact ones that filled his being. He did believe they wouldn't have come to share this purity and intensity without surviving so many tests and…

He shot up, his nerves going haywire.

Under his palm. He'd felt it.

"The baby…" he choked. "He moved." And for the first time

since he'd shed tears over his mother's death, his tears flowed. With too much love, pride and gratitude.

She pushed him onto his back, rained frantic kisses all over his face. "No, please—I can't bear seeing your tears, even ones of joy." That only made the tears flow thicker. After moments of panting consternation, wickedness replaced the stricken look on her face and she attacked him with tickling.

He guffawed and flopped her onto her back, imprisoning what he swore were electricity- and magic-wielding hands over her head with one of his, his other returning the sensual torment.

She squirmed under his hand, nuzzled his chest. "I can't wait to have our baby. And I can't wait to have another one. One we'll make as we lose ourselves in love and pleasure, flesh in flesh."

"This one *was* made of our love…well, my love, at least."

She nipped him. "Yeah, I have to make up for my initial lack of participation in the love department. But from now on, I'm sharing everything with you. And not only about our baby. I want to be involved in everything you do, your research, your surgeries…." The radiant animation on her face faltered. "Uh—that came out as if I'll hound your every step…."

He squeezed her, cutting short her mortification, laughter booming out of his depths. "Oh, please, do. Gives me an excuse to hound yours." Then he grew serious. "But I know exactly how you meant it. I want you involved in everything I do, too. I've never felt more stimulated, more empowered, more satisfied with my work than when you were there with me. And then there's every other instance when I see or feel or think anything, and it isn't right, isn't complete until I share it with you, knowing you're the only one who'll understand, appreciate."

She attacked him with another giggling, weeping kiss

that almost extracted his soul. Then she raised a radiant face, gestured for him to stay where he was.

He watched her bounce out of bed to rummage in her suitcase. He hardened to steel again, licking at the lingering taste of her on his lips as she walked back, ripe and tousled and a little awkward, all the effects of his love and loving, short- and long-term ones. She was holding something behind her back, impishness turning her beauty from breathtaking to heartbreaking.

"Close your eyes." He chuckled, obeyed at once. He couldn't wait to "see" what she had in store for him.

Her weight dipped the mattress. Then he almost came off it.

She was licking him. All over his chest and abdomen.

He growled, tried to hold her head closer, thrusting at her, offering all of him for her delicate devouring.

"Keep those lethal weapons of yours closed."

He did, his heart almost rattling the whole bed in anticipation. Then he felt a sting on his chest.

The tail end of the sensation was a lance of pleasure that corkscrewed to his erection. It slammed against his abdomen. Air left his lungs on a bellow of stimulation.

Another sting followed. Then another and another, on a path of fiery pain and pleasure down his body. He'd never felt anything like this sourceless manipulation of his sensations. He could swear she wasn't touching him, was pricking each individual nerve cluster mentally.

He thrust at her, incoherent with arousal, his growls becoming those of a beast in a frenzy. He at last thrust his hands into her hair, tugged until she moaned with enjoyment.

"Tell me to open my eyes," he panted the order, the plea.

Another skewer of delight. "Uh-uh."

"I don't need them open to take you until you weep with

pleasure," he threatened, almost weeping himself again with the sharpness of the sensations she'd buried him under.

"Which you routinely do." Another sting. He roared. She purred, "Okay, just because you threatened so nicely. Open 'em."

He did. And couldn't credit their evidence for moments.

Then he rasped between gasps as she continued her meticulous sensual torture, "This is—hands down—the most innovative use of a micro-grasping forceps I've ever seen."

She was tugging at his hairs using the most delicate forceps used in micro-neurosurgery. And sending him stark raving mad.

"It's also the most hands-on method I could think of to say thanks." Her eyes glittered up at him, flooding him with love.

"Not that I'm not deliriously thankful for whatever made you invent this new…procedure, but thanks for what, *mi vida?*"

"Thanks for all the patience and perseverance you put into getting my hand back to this level of fine coordination."

He dropped his gaze to her hand. It was true. There was no sign of clumsiness, weakness or pain as her precious hand performed her pioneering form of carnal torment.

He groaned, glided her over his aching body, grasped her hand gently and took it to his lips, thanked the fates for her, for letting him be the instrument of her happiness and well-being.

"Thank *you*, for existing, for letting me be forever yours."

Cybele cupped his face as he continued his homage, wondering how one being could contain all the love she felt for him.

She caressed his hewn cheek, traced the planes of his chiseled lips. "If you're satisfied with my precision, can I apprentice at your hands in neurosurgery?"

He enfolded her and she felt as if his heart gave her the answer. To everything. "Just wish for it and it's done, *mi alma*. Anything you want, the whole world is yours for the asking."

She took his lips with a whimper, then she whispered into his mouth, "I already have the whole world. You, our baby and our love."

* * * * *

HER TYCOON TO TAME

BY EMILIE ROSE

Bestselling Desire™ author and RITA® Award finalist **Emilie Rose** lives in her native North Carolina with her four sons and two adopted mutts. Writing is her third (and hopefully her last) career. She's managed a medical office and run a home day care, neither of which offers half as much satisfaction as plotting happy endings. Her hobbies include gardening and cooking (especially cheesecake). She's a rabid country music fan because she can find an entire book in almost any song. She is currently working her way through her own "bucket list," which includes learning to ride a Harley. Visit her website at www.emilierose.com or email EmilieRoseC@aol.com. Letters can be mailed to PO Box 20145, Raleigh, NC 27619, USA.

To the man upstairs for giving me more
time with my mom.
Each day is a blessing.

One

Hannah Sutherland pressed the pedal of the golf cart to the floorboard, racing the battery-powered machine up the long curving driveway toward the main house.

Guest. My office. N.O.W.

That had been her father's text, and as irritable as he'd been lately, she didn't dare keep him waiting. But who could be so important that she had to drop everything and hurry to the house?

When she reached the stairs leading to the back patio, she slammed on the brake, leaped from the vehicle and hustled into the house, straightening her hair and adjusting her hastily changed clothing as she crossed the black-and-white marbled foyer. The sound of her boots echoed off the vaulted ceiling.

At the sight of the closed office door, her step hitched. She hadn't seen that door closed since the day her mother had died. Apprehension climbed her spine like a spider.

She shook off her uneasiness and knocked on the glossy surface. A moment later, the panel opened revealing Al

Brinkley, the family's lawyer. He'd been her father's friend as well as his legal council for as long as Hannah could remember.

"Good to see you, Mr. Brinkley."

Brinkley's smile seemed forced. "Hello, Hannah. I swear you look more like your mother every day."

"So I've been told." Too bad looks were all she'd inherited from her mom. Hannah's life would have been so much easier if she'd picked up a few more traits.

His expression sobered, resurrecting Hannah's concern. "Come in."

Her father stood behind his desk, his face tense, a highball glass in his hand. It was a little early for cocktails.

Movement by the French doors overlooking the east paddock interrupted the thought. Tall and lean, the other occupant of the study smoothly pivoted in her direction.

His glossy brownish-black hair had been clipped short, but not short enough to hide a tendency to curl that did nothing to soften his uncompromisingly hard jaw and a square chin.

And while his features combined to form a tough but attractive face, nothing would soften those cool, distrusting eyes, and no amount of expensive tailoring could conceal his broad shoulders and firm, muscled body. He had the lean, mean, fighting machine look often displayed on military recruiting posters and an alert and dangerous air. She estimated his age as mid-thirties, but it was hard to say. He had old eyes.

"Come in, Hannah." The odd tension in her father's tone made her wary. "Brink, close the door."

The lawyer did as he was bid, sealing Hannah into the wainscoted room with the three men and a tense atmosphere. Private discussions were not the norm in the house. Nellie, who served as housekeeper, house manager and surrogate mother, was the only one who might overhear, and she was family in every way but blood. So why the secrecy?

"Wyatt, this is my daughter, Hannah. She's the veterinarian

overseeing Sutherland Farm's breeding operation. Hannah, Wyatt Jacobs."

Jacobs's searing scrutiny strangely repelled and yet attracted her. Duty compelled her into motion. She crossed the Aubusson carpet. Who was he and what kind of closed-door business could he have with the stable?

Judging by his expensive clothing and the platinum watch on his wrist, he had money, but then all of their visitors did. Grand Prix show jumping wasn't for paupers or even the middle class. Their clients ranged from nouveau riche to established royalty, spoiled brats to dedicated, die-hard horsemen. Where did Wyatt Jacobs fit in?

She'd bet he looked good on a horse with that erect, confident carriage. His eyes were the color of roasted coffee beans, the pupils barely discernible with the sun streaming through the French doors at his back.

"Welcome to Sutherland Farm, Mr. Jacobs," she recited by rote and extended her hand.

His long fingers closed around hers, and his firm, warm grip combined with the impact of that hard, dark gaze made it difficult to breathe. She might as well have had a girth cinched around her chest considering the sudden pressure on her lungs.

"Dr. Sutherland." His deep, slightly raspy and seriously sexy voice would be perfect for radio.

He held her hand, extending the contact and making her wish for a split second that she'd taken the time to freshen her makeup, unbraid and brush her hair and splash on some perfume to mask the scent of stables when she'd quickly changed from her soiled work clothes in her office. But she'd been rushing and done only the absolutely necessary repairs.

Stupid girl. He's a client. And you're not looking for romance, remember?

She tugged her hand and after a brief resistance he released her. She pressed her prickling palm to her thigh. She'd broken her engagement fifteen months ago and in that time she hadn't thought about sex even once. Until now. Wyatt Jacobs made her tingle in places that had been dormant for a long time.

Her father offered her a highball glass of amber liquid. “Dad, you know I can’t drink when I’m working. I still have to deal with Commander this morning.”

Her frustration with the stallion she’d left in the stables resurfaced. Commander wanted to kill everyone—especially the vet in charge of collecting his semen. In the arena he’d been a phenomenal competitor, but in the barn he was a bloodthirsty beast. His bloodline and list of championships meant she couldn’t ignore him. His ejaculate was liquid gold. But she, her team and the stubborn stud had needed a cool-down period after an unproductive hour. Her father’s interruption had actually come at a good time.

Her father set the glass on his desk beside her as if he expected her to change her mind, reactivating the warning itch on her nape. Hannah brushed aside her misgivings and returned her focus to their guest. Jacobs watched her with an unwavering, laser-like intensity that stirred a strange, volatile reaction inside her, and try as she might she couldn’t look away.

She’d met movie stars, congressmen and royalty with less charisma. For pity’s sake she’d dated and even kissed a few of them with no effect. So why did Jacobs rattle her cage?

Wait a minute. Was that anger lurking in his eyes?

There was only one way to find out.

“What brings you to our stables, Mr. Jacobs?”

“Luthor, would you care to explain why I’m here?” Jacobs deferred. Funny, she would have sworn on her mother’s earrings that he wasn’t the type to defer anything and doing so now appeared to irritate him.

When the silence stretched, she pried her eyes from Jacobs’s handsome face and discovered her usually unflappable father looking defensive and uncomfortable, his pale features set—totally unlike his usual calm demeanor. He drained his glass in one gulp and set the tumbler on the desk with a thump.

Her anxiety level spiked. "Daddy, what's going on?"

"I've sold the farm, Hannah," her father stated baldly.

She blinked. Her father had never possessed a sense of humor. Odd time for him to find one. But the idea was too ludicrous to be anything but a bad joke. "Really?"

He glanced at Brinkley's stoic expression, then back. "I have places to go and things to see—none of which I can do if I'm tied to this business every single day of the year."

She searched her father's resolute face. He wasn't joking. The floor beneath her feet seemed to shift. She clutched the edge of the desk for balance. Her knuckles bumped the cold highball glass, but the chill of the crystal couldn't compare to the ice spreading through her veins.

She could feel her mouth opening and closing, but couldn't force out a sound. She shuddered in a breath then stuttered it out again while struggling to gather her shattered thoughts.

"You couldn't have sold the farm. You *wouldn't* have. You live for the stables." As far as she knew he had no other interests, no hobbies. Nothing except horses, winning and Sutherland Farm. He didn't even have friends outside the horse biz.

"Not anymore."

Something had to be wrong. Terribly wrong. Fear splintered through her and cold sweat beaded her lip.

Her neck felt like a rusty hinge as she forced her head to turn to Jacobs. "Would you excuse us a moment, Mr. Jacobs?"

Their visitor didn't budge. He studied her—as if trying to gauge and anticipate her reaction.

"Please." She hated the desperate edge of her voice. It verged on begging. And she never begged.

After a moment he nodded, crossed the room in purposeful strides and stepped through the doors out onto the veranda. A fresh-cut grass-scented breeze drifted in the open door, but the familiar aroma failed to do its usual job of soothing her.

"Would you like for me to go?" Brinkley asked.

Her father held up a hand. "Stay, Brink. Hannah might have questions only you can answer."

"Daddy, what's wrong? Are you ill?"

He sighed. "No, Hannah. I'm not sick."

"Then how could you do this? You promised Mom you'd keep the farm forever."

The lines in her father's face seemed to deepen. "That was nineteen years ago, Hannah, and she was dying. I said what I had to say to let her pass peacefully."

"But what about me? I promised Mom, too, and *I* meant it. I'm supposed to take over Sutherland Farm. I'm supposed to keep Grandma and Papa's property in the family and pass it on to my children."

"Children you don't have."

"Well, no, not yet, but one day—" She paused as an idea pierced her like a nail. "This is because I didn't marry Robert, isn't it?"

Disapproval clamped her father's mouth into a tight line. "He was perfect for you, and yet you refused to settle down."

"No, Dad, he was perfect for *you.* Robert was the son you always wished you'd had. Instead, you got me."

"Robert knew how to run a stable."

"So do I."

"Hannah, you don't ride. You don't compete. Your heart is not in this business, and you don't have the drive to keep Sutherland Farm at the top of the Grand Prix community. Instead you waste your time and money on animals that ought to be euthanized."

No matter how many times she heard it, the old attacks still chafed. She stuffed down her emotional response and focused on the facts. "Mom believed in rescuing horses, too, and my horse rehabilitation program is a success. If you'd take the time to look at the statistics and read the success stories—"

"Your operation runs in the red every quarter. You're careless with money because you've never had to fight and scratch for a living."

"I work."

He grunted in disgust. "A few hours a day."

"My job isn't the eight-hour-a-day variety."

"When your mother and I assumed responsibility for my parents' old tobacco farm, this place was losing money hand over fist. We built Sutherland Farm into the showplace it is today by fighting and clawing our way up the ranks. Your mother had ambition. You do not. Robert might have managed to talk some sense into you and divert your attention to more suitable hobbies. But that didn't work. Did it?"

She'd ended her engagement the day she'd realized Robert had loved the horses and farm more than he had her. He'd been willing to trample people in pursuit of the almighty dollar. But her father would never listen to that. The men were like peas in a pod—identical in their drive for success despite the costs.

Robert had been her father's ideal of the perfect son-in-law—aggressive in business and a star in the show ring—but ultimately, he wasn't her ideal husband or life partner. She would have come lagging in a distant third in his heart at best. But she could hardly tell her father the only time Robert was passionate was in the riding ring.

"Robert wasn't right for me."

"You're twenty-nine, Hannah, and no man has ever held your attention for more than a few months. You're too picky."

"Daddy, I'm sorry I didn't inherit mother's grace and ability on horseback or your competitive streak. But this farm was her dream. And now it's mine. I can run it. I may not know how to ride a champion, but I know how to breed one. I have what it takes."

"No, Hannah, you don't. You've had a few successes with your stock, but you lack fire and ambition and you have absolutely no head for business. You're never going to be ready to take the reins of Sutherland Farm."

She flinched. His cruel words only confirmed what she

knew he'd been thinking for years, but they still stung like the whip of a crop. "That's not true."

"I'm doing you no favors by continuing to coddle you." He paused and glanced at his friend. "I won't always be here to support you, Hannah. It's time you learned to take care of yourself."

"What do you mean?"

"I'm cutting you off."

Shock followed by a chaser of panic sent her staggering backward. "What do you mean?" she repeated.

"I will no longer support you or your lost causes."

"Why? What did I do? How will I survive?"

"You'll have to learn to live on your salary."

Hurt, fear and betrayal ignited like a barn fire beneath her breastbone. "Couldn't we have talked about this before you made such a drastic decision?"

Her father shrugged and realigned the pen beside a thick pile of papers on his desk. "What good would that have done?"

"I would have talked you out of it. Somebody should have talked you out of it." She shot an injured and confused glance at the attorney who shrugged apologetically. "This farm, this property has been in our family for generations. There are a lot of people depending on you and me and—"

"It's too late, Hannah." Her father sighed and suddenly the starch left his spine, making him look old and tired. He refilled his drink, then sank into the leather chair.

She turned to Brinkley. "Can he do this? What about my mother's share of the business?"

"Your grandparents put the farm in your father's name before he married your mother. Her name was never added to the deed. You received the only inheritance you'll get from her estate when you turned twenty-one."

And most of that was gone. She'd spent the money on her horses, confident in the belief that her father would continue to fund her efforts.

Then realization clicked, jolting Hannah out of her

stupefaction. Wyatt Jacobs must be the one who'd bought the farm right out from under her. The sneaky, conniving, inheritance-swindling bastard.

Cold eyes, cold heart, Nellie had always said.

Hannah's pulse galloped in her eardrums like stampeding hooves. If she couldn't make her father or Brinkley see sense, she'd have to talk to the jerk who had usurped her and convince him to renege on the deal. Then she'd figure out a way to change her father's mind before he found another buyer.

She stalked through the patio door and spotted the interloper at a table, calmly eating from a plate of Nellie's cookies and drinking a glass of milk as if he hadn't just blasted the foundation right out from under her life. She marched toward him and pulled up at his elbow.

"This is my home. You can't waltz in here and steal the property. My father is having a momentary bout of senility and—"

Jacobs rose to tower above her, his face like granite. "I didn't steal Sutherland Farm, doc. I paid more than fair market value."

He calmly lifted the cookie and took another bite. His insolence stung like a slap in the face. Then as she focused on the cookie she realized she wasn't the only one who would be blindsided by today's disastrous news. She swung to her father who had followed her onto the patio.

"What about Nellie? She's lived with us since Mom died. She has no other home, no other family. Just us. You can't turn her out to pasture. She's too young to retire, and jobs are hard to find right now."

"Wyatt has promised to continue employing Nellie."

Wyatt has promised. Right. And she trusted him about as far as she could throw all six feet plus and two hundred whatever rock-solid pounds of him. She glared at him. "What about the other employees, the clients' horses and the stables? Are you going to do a clean sweep?"

Most new owners brought in their own teams, and she

hated to think of the people she'd known and loved like an extended family being scattered across the globe—that was if they were able to find jobs with so many farms downsizing.

"I'll maintain the status quo while I assess the property and the business."

"And then what?"

"My decisions will depend on what I discover about the operation."

"What's to discover? You bought a world-class stable—"

"Hannah," her father interrupted, "Brink will go over the particulars of the agreement with you. All you need to know is that Wyatt has agreed to keep the current staff for a full year unless obvious incompetence leads him to decide otherwise."

Her shoulders snapped straight at the insult. "Sutherland Farm doesn't employ any incompetents."

"Then no one need be concerned," Jacobs said.

Desperation clawed at her throat. "Daddy, please don't do this. I'm sure there's a way you can undo the paperwork. Give me a chance to prove to you that I can run the farm and—"

"Hannah, we closed the deal a week ago. Today was merely the first time Wyatt and I could meet personally to discuss the transition."

"A week ago," she parroted. Her world had crashed and she'd been oblivious. Head reeling and legs shaking, she tried to make sense of the upheaval to come.

"I've already purchased a townhome and the movers have been scheduled," her father added, sending another shockwave rippling through her.

Jacobs stiffened. "A townhome? What about the cottage?"

My cottage! Ohmigod. Where will I live?

Her father's expression turned cagey. "Hannah lives in the cottage."

Jacobs's hands fisted by his sides and anger lit his eyes.

Confused by the exchange, Hannah looked from the interloper to her father. "My home and my job are part of

Sutherland Farm. Where will I go? Where will I live and work?"

Her father sighed and turned toward the bar cart. "I'll let Wyatt explain."

"Luthor excluded the cottage and two acres inside the stone fence surrounding it from the deal. You'll get to keep your house. And, as your father has already explained, like any other employee you'll be kept on staff as long as the quality of your work meets my standards." Jacobs's voice carried about as much warmth as liquid nitrogen.

The man would be her boss.

"Your standards?" From his tone she gathered his standards would be impossible to meet.

Her cottage, the original Sutherland homestead, sat smack in the middle of Sutherland Farm. She'd be surrounded by enemy territory. But at least she'd have a roof over her head.

She swallowed her panic and fought to clear her head. "When is all this upheaval scheduled to take place?"

"I'm taking over as CEO today and moving into this house as soon as your father has vacated."

In other words, life as she'd always known it had ended.

Two

Anger licked along Wyatt's nerve endings like kindling catching fire. Luthor Sutherland had deliberately deceived him.

The man had no intention of "retiring" to the original homestead as he'd led Wyatt to believe when he'd insisted the parcel be excluded from the sale, and Sutherland's daughter was one of the employees Sutherland had been so eager to protect. If Wyatt had known, he would never have signed the employee agreement Sutherland had insisted on.

But if Luthor expected Wyatt to cut his princess any slack, he'd be disappointed. If Hannah couldn't carry her weight, she'd be fired—per the performance clause Wyatt had included.

What incensed him the most was that he knew he had no one but himself to blame for deception getting past him. He'd been neck-deep in closing an international distribution deal and because he didn't have the time, interest or knowledge in running a horse farm, he'd delegated the job of finding a self-sufficient operation—one that wouldn't require him to be on-site—to the best buyer's agent in the business.

Sutherland Farm met all his criteria. He couldn't help wondering if there were any more surprises in addition to the leggy brunette liability yet to discover. Whatever the issues, he would find and eradicate them.

He had enough problems without having to deal with a pampered heiress who had been living out of her daddy's deep pockets. The snippets of conversation he'd overheard through the patio door made it clear that description fit Hannah Sutherland from her silk shirt to her polished high-heeled boots.

He'd bet his seven-figure investment portfolio that Hannah had coasted through life on her beauty and pretty-please smiles. His gut warned him she'd be nothing but trouble. And his instincts about people were rarely wrong. He didn't need to see the two carats of diamonds in her ears or the watch on her wrist so pricey that a thief could pawn it to buy a car or her short but perfectly manicured nails to confirm her overindulged status.

"I want every employee's file before I leave today," he demanded without looking away from the smoky blue eyes shooting flames at him.

"That's confidential information," Hannah protested.

"Hannah," Sutherland's lawyer interjected, "as the new owner of Sutherland Farm, Mr. Jacobs has unrestricted access to employee records."

"But—"

Wyatt nailed her with a hard look. "I'll start with yours. I have a pretty good idea what I'll find. Private schools. Sororities. European vacations paid for by Sutherland Farm."

Hannah glared at him. Tension quivered through her slender, toned body. Her breasts rose and fell rapidly, and despite his aversion to spoiled women and his anger over his predicament, awareness simmered beneath his skin.

Something about her got to him. She had a subtle grace

and elegance about her that both attracted him and, because of his past relationships with her type, repulsed him. He'd been burned by her kind before.

"I graduated from an accredited veterinary school," she said through barely moving lips. "My credentials are valid, and since Warmbloods are a European breed, visiting the established and successful breeding farms to study their setups and evaluate their stock for potential matches is a necessary part of my job."

"I'm sure you have references from your previous employers to prove your worth as an employee."

Her chin jerked up a notch and she managed to look down her straight nose at him in the way only wealthy women could—a lesson he'd had driven into him like a railroad spike when he'd been seventeen and green and working at his stepfather's stable. Back then he hadn't been smart enough to know rich daddy's darlings didn't marry boys who cleaned stalls for their stepfathers' stables no matter how intimate the relationship might have become.

"I have worked here since graduating—almost five years. I'm good at what I do."

"I'll be the judge of that."

She folded her arms and cocked back on one of those long legs. "Tell me, Mr. Jacobs, what exactly are your credentials for determining whether or not staff members are performing well?"

"Hannah—" the attorney cautioned, but Wyatt silenced him with a look.

"I'm CEO of Triple Crown Distillery. I employ over six hundred. I recognize incompetents and slackers when I see them."

Anger stained her cheeks a fiery red, proving she'd picked up his implication that he considered her one. "As I've already stated, the Sutherland team doesn't have any weak links. We're a cohesive unit, one of the best in the industry."

"That remains to be seen." Wyatt was beginning to wish

he'd chosen one of the other dozen properties the real estate agent had presented. But as wise as that option now appeared, none of those farms had fit Sam's descriptions and all would have required Wyatt's input as a manager. Input he didn't have the time or inclination to give.

When Sam reminisced about the Kentucky thoroughbred farm he'd once owned, he sounded so lucid Wyatt could almost forget his stepfather was fading away right before his eyes. Sutherland Farm resembled Sam's old farm more than any of the other properties, and Sam deserved to be comfortable, happy and, most importantly, safe for however long he had left. He would be here. Wyatt would make damned sure of it.

And he had no intention of letting Hannah Sutherland prevent him from repaying the debt he owed to the man who'd been a better parent to him than his own flesh and blood.

"Just watch your step, doc. Your father may have indulged you, but I won't. You'll earn your keep if you want to remain employed here. Now, if you'll excuse me, I have files to review and you need to get back to work."

Exhausted, Hannah plodded down the driveway toward her cottage, a hot bubble bath and a glass of wine.

One of her rescue mares kept pace beside her on the opposite side of the white board fence. Hannah found the horse's undemanding company soothing. Unlike people, who were easily disappointed, horses never expected too much.

It had been a tough week. Since her world crashed she'd been juggling her usual duties plus the new ones thrust unexpectedly on her. The staff had turned to her for answers—answers she didn't have.

The mood in the barns grew more oppressive, like an impending summer storm, with each day that Wyatt Jacobs failed to make an appearance. Usually affable employees were on edge and snapping at each other. Even the horses had picked up on the bad vibes and been harder to handle than usual. Hannah wished Jacobs would show up just to break the tension. Not that she wanted to see him again.

The phone on her hip vibrated. The digital display read private caller. Could be a client or, if she was lucky, a wrong number. She didn't have the energy to deal with another crisis or panicking coworker.

She hit the answer button. "Hannah Sutherland."

"Wyatt Jacobs. Come to my office in the house. Now."

Click.

Her feet stuck to the pavement as if she'd stepped in fresh tar. She scowled at the now silent phone then she looked across the lawn toward the main house. A light glowed in her father's—*Wyatt Jacobs's*—study.

The usurper had arrived. And he'd hung up on her. The rude, inconsiderate jerk. Anger charged through her system, riding on the back of a burst of adrenaline. How dare he demand an appointment this late in the evening?

She considered calling back and telling him she was off the clock and she'd see him tomorrow. But according to the clause in her new contract, which Brinkley had pointed out, she couldn't refuse the boss's summons without jeopardizing her job.

She glanced at her stained clothing. If she were truly interested in making a good impression, she'd clean up first.

She wasn't.

She'd done an internet search on Jacobs and found nothing linking him to horses in any way. Why had he bought the farm?

Was he one of those new-money guys who thought owning a horse farm would be trendy and fun? If so, he wouldn't have a clue how much work, money and commitment were involved in a stable the size of Sutherland. If she had to teach him herself, he'd learn, and if she smelled like sweat and horses and other unpleasant stuff, she'd only be furthering his education.

As much as she hated going into the meeting at a messy

disadvantage, he'd have to deal with her dirt. "Welcome to the horse business, Wyatt Jacobs."

Energized by resentment and determination Hannah marched across the lawn and up to the kitchen door. A sideways glance down the patio brought her hand to a halt inches shy of the knob.

An unfamiliar rectangular teak table and chairs occupied the space once graced by elegant glass-topped wrought iron furniture and classic urns overflowing with spring flowers. The sight drove home the reality that this wasn't her father's house anymore, and she didn't have the right to casually enter through the kitchen and feast on Nellie's delicious cooking.

Ten yards away the patio door leading to the office opened, and Wyatt Jacobs's tall, broad-shouldered frame filled the gap. His dark gaze pinned her like a thumbtack stabbing into a bulletin board.

"Come in, doc." He gestured with a sharp beckoning motion of his hand—the same way he would order a dog.

Her hackles rose. Everything about him made her want to snarl and growl and that surprised her. Who was this strange woman with the bad attitude who had taken over her body? It certainly wasn't her. She preferred gracious smiles, gentle persuasion and Southern charm. Kill 'em with kindness, Nellie had always said, and the strategy had worked for Hannah thus far.

Wyatt Jacobs brought out her witchy side. Her churning stomach warned her to handle this encounter with care. Jacobs, the one man she didn't know and didn't care to know, held her future and that of her horses and the rest of the staff in his hands. Being cooperative was imperative.

She'd be damned if she'd let him know how afraid she was of losing everything.

"I'd rather talk out here." Even though she delivered the words with a civil smile, Hannah Sutherland bristled with visible animosity. She pointed to her dust-covered black low-heeled boots. "Since I wasn't expecting your call this late in the day, I've brought barn with me."

Her boots weren't all that was dirty. He noted the smudge filling the hollow beneath one high cheekbone, then a stain on her white Sutherland Farm logo polo shirt drew his eyes to the curve of her breasts. Another dirty streak on her khaki pants ran down the inside of her lean, taut thigh. Her current garb was a far cry from the designer duds she'd been wearing the day they'd met, but she still wore the pricey watch and ice-cube-size earrings.

He caught a subtle whiff of the stables on the breeze. But along with the smell of horses, wood shavings and hay another scent—something feminine and alluring like expensive French perfume—snagged his attention. His heart inexplicably and annoyingly pumped faster.

He'd studied her résumé and bio the way he would a blueprint, searching for flaws and weaknesses, and he'd found nothing to like in her privileged, worry-free upbringing. She'd apparently been given everything she'd ever wanted on a silver platter.

"Other than your years at college you've never lived away from dear old dad or his checkbook, have you?"

Her slender frame stiffened and her smile faltered. "No."

"You never held a job, before waltzing into this one."

"I didn't waltz in. I earned my degree. And I gained experience by volunteering at the university's stables. I wasn't on the payroll because I didn't need the money. I didn't think it fair to take it from someone who did."

Even with, or possibly because of, Sam's help, Wyatt had worked his ass off to get where he was today. Sam might have paid the tuition, but he'd made Wyatt prove himself every step of the way. He'd learned the business from the ground up, and Triple Crown Distillery's distribution and profit margins had increased by sixty percent since he had taken control after Sam's "retirement."

But Wyatt's bitterness and resentment over Hannah's

worry-free life didn't stop the spurt of energy racing through his veins when Hannah glared at him.

"I'm off the clock, Mr. Jacobs. Was there something you needed that couldn't wait until tomorrow?"

The setting sun highlighted the streaks of gold in her brown wavy hair—streaks probably applied by an overpriced hairdresser. Her blue eyes showed no mercy, no interest and no feminine softness. She didn't want him here, and her attempt at hiding her feelings failed miserably.

"Meet me in the stable's business office tomorrow at noon."

"Why?" Her eyes narrowed with suspicion.

"You're going to show me around the farm."

Her stiff shoulders snapped back, becoming even more rigid. She hit him with that hoity, looking-down-the-nose appraisal that reminded him of his first love, first heartache and first betrayal by a woman.

"I can't drop everything to play tour guide for you. Sir," she tacked on at the last minute.

He wasn't used to openly antagonistic females. He would have to be an idiot not to realize his looks and money made most of her gender eager to please. But from the tension and displeasure radiating from her, he would hazard a guess that she didn't give a rat's ass what he thought of her and her disheveled state. Or maybe she'd dirtied up intentionally to make it look as though she worked hard. Yeah, that was probably the case. He doubted Ms. Perfect Manicure ever got her hands dirty.

"You'll report at noon if you value your job."

"I have a full schedule tomorrow. This is the busy season."

"Why?"

She blinked, revealing long, thick lashes he hadn't noticed before. "Why what?"

"Why is this the busy season?"

A pleat formed between her eyebrows. "Not only do we have a lot of boarders showing up to ride on Saturdays, I shouldn't have to tell you we're preparing for the breeding season."

His knowledge of horse breeding was limited. Sam had always given Wyatt more menial jobs—the kind that built character as well as muscle and calluses. Or so Sam had insisted. "Noon, Dr. Sutherland."

"I'll find someone else to show you around, someone who has the time."

"Your father claims you know more about Sutherland Farm than any other employee. I don't want someone else. I want you. That's not negotiable."

"Of course I know the most about the farm. I've lived here all my life, and I've covered every inch of the property. But as much as I'd love to show you all the wonderful things about Sutherland Farm, I have a production schedule to maintain."

Something—maybe a primitive urge to knock her off the pedestal she'd put herself on—made Hannah's resistance both challenging and a turn-on.

That makes you one twisted fool, Jacobs.

A nerve at the corner of his mouth twitched as he fought to conceal his irritation with her and himself. "You're not going to make it that easy for me, are you, Hannah?"

"What do you mean?"

"Per your contract, if you fail to meet my expectations you'll be fired. Make time to show me around or pick up your final paycheck."

Her lips flattened into a thin line and anger flagged her cheeks with red. "You like the power of holding the contracts you made us sign over our heads, don't you? We're all here on a trial basis even though we've been successfully doing our jobs without your interference for years."

"I'm the boss. *Your* boss. That's the way it works."

Her irritated gaze snapped up and down his Armani suit without the admiration he usually received. She heaved an aggravated breath. "I'll be there, but leave the fancy duds behind unless you plan to stay in the golf cart."

She pivoted on her heel with military precision then marched off the patio, her firm, round bottom swishing with each long, angry stride. He couldn't peel his gaze away and his body reacted with unexpected and unwanted appreciation.

Oh, yeah, he'd called it right. Hannah Sutherland with her expensive jewelry, highlighted hair, manicured hands and entitled attitude was going to be nothing but trouble.

Until he got rid of her.

And that couldn't happen soon enough.

Three

The door to Hannah's lab opened abruptly on Saturday morning, startling her. Wyatt stalked in as if he owned the place…which he did, technically. But this was *her* domain—the only place that remained orderly and tranquil no matter what chaos reigned in other parts of her life.

Her muscles snapped taut and the hair on her nape sprang to attention. She'd never experienced such instant antagonism toward anyone before, and the strength of the emotion roiling inside her now surprised her.

"You said twelve. You're early." She tried to keep her tone polite, but judging by his scowl, she failed.

His dark eyes panned the spotless room as if inventorying each piece of equipment before returning to her and examining her as thoroughly. "The rain is predicted to worsen. I want my tour now."

Rain? Hannah blinked and listened. Sure enough, rain snare-drummed on the barn's metal roof. She'd been so engrossed in her tasks and her troubles that she hadn't even noticed the rat-a-tat-tat before now. Usually the sound relaxed her. But not today, thanks to the irritant in front of her.

She stood her ground and returned his appraisal. The hard line of his jaw gleamed from a recent shave and his hair looked damp—either from the weather or a recent shower if he were the type to waste a morning lying in bed. A picture of him on twisted sheets popped into her head.

Where had that come from? She kicked it away.

A black cashmere sweater stretched across his broad shoulders, the white of a T-shirt showing in the V-neck, and faded jeans clung to his hips and long, muscled thighs. Something—most likely aggravation—quickened her pulse. It couldn't be anything else. She didn't like him or his arrogant attitude.

"I still have orders to process before the courier service arrives. Come back at twelve. Please," she added. She wasn't going to let him disrupt her schedule and thereby give him grounds to fire her.

"Reviewing employee performance is part of any new business venture. I'll start with yours. You work. I'll observe."

Anxiety tangled with the coil of exasperation snaking through her. She couldn't throw him out. "Then at least close the door. This is a controlled environment. The room needs to remain dust-free, and the temperature as constant as possible."

"Is it that important?"

"Considering I handle thousands of dollars' worth of product every day, yes, quality control is important."

Curiosity sharpened his eyes. He strolled toward her, encroaching on her personal space, but she kept her boots planted, refusing to surrender her spot by the microscope despite an almost visceral urge to back far, far away.

"What are you working on, doc?"

An odd question from the man who owned everything in front of him. Everything except her, that is. "I'm confirming the viability of the sample before I chill and ship it."

"Sample of what?"

He was kidding. Right? But if so, he did so with a straight face. Hey, she could play along. "Sperm. Want to take a look?"

His short, thick lashes flickered, then he moved forward, calling her bluff and forcing her to yield territory to avoid contact. He bent over the microscope. "Tell me what I'm looking for."

Unsure whether he was testing her knowledge or simply being a pain in the rear, she scowled at the thick, dark strands covering the back of his head. "You're checking to see whether the sample has enough potency to get the job done."

He straightened. Their gazes collided unexpectedly and held. Her thoughts scattered like bowling pins. Tension crackled between them.

"And the answer?"

She inhaled slowly, trying to remember his question, but a trace of his cologne—something hinting of patchouli, sandalwood and cypress—distracted her. He smelled good and looked good. Too bad he was a jerk. She'd dealt with enough overinflated egos over the years to know bad attitude cancelled out any positives.

"Yes, this is a fertile stud, and a good thing, too, since Commander is Sutherland Farm's top moneymaker."

Determined to get back to business, she waved him out of the way and bent over the eye pieces, but his presence disturbed her. She could feel him dissecting and cataloging her every action as if he were waiting for her to make a mistake. When she adjusted the focus her hands weren't as steady as they'd been before his arrival, and it annoyed her that he could rattle her so easily.

"What's the purpose of all the equipment and charts?"

Another odd question from Sutherland's new owner. She lifted her head and put down the pencil she'd been using to make notes. "If I explain, will you go away and let me finish my job?"

"I'm not leaving until you've given me a satisfactory tour."

Not what she wanted to hear. “Are you completely ignorant of the business into which you’ve invested millions?”

Whoops. Not nice, Hannah. What happened to killing him with kindness and not making waves?

“You mean the business I own, the one that pays your salary?”

He had her there. And if she wanted to continue receiving that paycheck so that she could care for her horses and put food on her table, she’d better dam the resentment pouring from her mouth. “I apologize. The clock is ticking and I really need to get this order ready before the sample is ruined.”

“Answer my question, Hannah.”

“The shelves are filled with the collection equipment we use. Each stud has his own—” Her cheeks warmed and her tongue tangled. Oh, for pity’s sake. Reproduction was her job. Discussing it was routine. So why did explaining it to *him* make her uncomfortable? They weren’t discussing *her* personal sexual preferences.

Or his.

An image of him bare-chested, braced on his forearms above her and with passion instead of irritation tightening his features flashed in her mind. Her womb clenched. She inhaled sharply.

Girl, you have been too long without a man’s attention.

She cleared her throat and, trying to ignore the unwelcome warmth seeping through her, carefully chose her words. “Stallions have likes and dislikes that could interfere with or assist in production and collection. We get our most successful outcomes when the positive elements are in place, and we keep track of each stud’s preferences with the charts.”

His eyes narrowed and for a moment the air seemed to hum with tension. “Sutherland Farm has two veterinarians on staff. Your position seems redundant. Why should I continue paying your salary?”

Alarm froze any lingering awareness faster than a liquid nitrogen dip. “You’re asking me to justify my job?”

"Correct. Convince me nepotism wasn't a factor in your hiring."

She dampened her suddenly dry lips. "Our staff vet oversees general animal health. I oversee breeding."

"Something animals have managed without assistance or all this equipment since the beginning of time."

"Breeding is Sutherland Farm's bread and butter. Without the raw material, our trainers can't produce champions. We continue to make money off successful mares and studs for years, sometimes even decades, after they leave the show ring."

"And why can't the staff vet oversee that?"

"Developing a winning bloodline is far more complicated than randomly pairing animals and hoping for a pretty foal. It's an intricate mix of genealogy, genetics, biology and veterinary science aimed at producing an animal with optimal traits and minimal deficiencies. It's a science—one at which I happen to excel."

He didn't look impressed.

"Tell me, Wyatt, exactly how much do you know about horse breeding?"

"My knowledge of horses is limited to thoroughbreds."

That explained a lot. "And yet you bought a Warmblood farm. Thoroughbreds are bred naturally. Sutherland Farm does almost everything by artificial insemination."

"Why?"

"There are several reasons. Our horses are too valuable to risk one of them getting injured during the natural breeding process, and artificial insemination allows us to service mares globally and not only in our barns. It's cost-effective and less stressful for the mares than being shipped to the stallion's home stable. Shipping a horse overseas is expensive and often disturbs her cycle. Plus quarantine is a hassle. Shipping semen is less aggravating. We simply freeze or chill it and send it out."

He pointed to yet another chart. "And this?"

Hannah grimaced. She was fond of her charts and graphs. Charts were predictable. They made sense. She could weigh the pros and cons of practically any permutation on paper and erase her mistakes. Unlike life's bad choices.

"That's the stallion schedule. Regular, predictable collection encourages better production. In layman's terms, it's our way of aligning supply to demand so we know where to set our stud fees. And the chart beside it is the pending shipment list—the one I need to get back to before I can give you the tour and before this sample loses viability. So please, Mr. Jacobs, go away and let me do my job."

"Wyatt," he corrected.

She didn't want to be on a first-name basis with him. That implied friendship—something they would never have. But he was the boss and that meant she had to mind her manners.

"*Wyatt.* Sutherland Farm bloodstock has been producing champion jumping and dressage stock for years. Let me show you to the visitors' lounge in the office building. You can have a cup of coffee and look through the catalogue of our studs, mares and foals until I finish here."

His dark gaze lingered on hers until an odd sensation stirred in the pit of her stomach and her toes curled in her boots. "I can find the lounge."

The moment he left the room tension drained from her shoulders, torso and legs as if leaking through her soles. She sagged against the work table, bowing her head and taking a moment to collect her composure.

Damn the man. How was she going to work with him when she couldn't even stand to be in the same room with him? He made her uncomfortable with his long, intense examinations and he was clearly searching for a reason—*any* reason—to fire her.

She'd barely gotten back into the groove when the door opened again. She snapped upright. Her stomach sank as Wyatt strolled in carrying one of the farm's many photo albums and ending her short-lived reprieve. He parked himself on the stool directly across the table from her microscope.

No. “I thought you were going to let me work.”

“I’m not stopping you. The sooner you finish, the sooner we can get on with business.” He directed his attention to the book in front of him.

Irritation sputtered through her. If he didn’t quit distracting her, he’d never get his tour, and he acted as if the delay was her fault.

Determined to ignore him, she gritted her teeth and returned to the job at hand. Every time she looked up from the microscope her gaze slammed straight into his, and each time she felt those dark eyes on her or his body shifted her pulse skipped.

She wanted him gone. From her lab. From her farm. From her life. *Daddy, what have you done?*

Forcing herself to concentrate, she powered through her work with sheer determination. When she finally sealed the last tube in the shipping package, relief coursed through her. Dread trotted close behind. Finishing meant she’d have to spend time alone with her new boss.

Resigned to the torture, she sighed. “Where do you want to start?”

He closed the portfolio and slowly rose, unfolding one smooth muscle after the other. As much as she hated to admit it, Wyatt Jacobs had great conformation and grace in motion, like one of Sutherland’s prized dressage champions. “Anywhere.”

She swallowed her impatience. She wanted to make this as quick and painless as possible. He wasn’t helping. “Narrow that down. We have two thousand acres. Which parts of the property have you not seen?”

“Except for the house, this barn and the office building, I haven’t seen any of the farm.”

Her mouth dropped open. “You spent millions of dollars without seeing what you were getting for your money?”

"I had pictures, topography maps and the video package the real estate appraiser prepared. Sutherland Farm suits my needs."

She remembered the videographer's visit several months ago. Her father had told her the film would be used for promotional purposes and she'd had no reason not to believe him because they often had photographers on the premises. That meant not only had her father lied, but he'd been scheming to tear her world apart for months. That hurt.

But the past was over. She had to deal with the present, and the present included the testosterone-packed problem in front of her.

"And what exactly are your needs?" She winced when she heard the double entendre of her words.

As if a door slammed shut, Wyatt's face instantly turned inscrutable. "To own a horse farm. What else?"

Wyatt Jacobs was lying through his perfect white teeth. Hannah would swear to it. But she couldn't prove it. And even if she could, what could she do about it? Right now she was nothing but a puppet. And he held her strings.

Hannah didn't believe him, and frankly, Wyatt didn't care. He wasn't here to make friends. In fact, it would suit him better if she got ticked off and quit her job.

Playing chaperone to a spoiled princess had never been part of his plan. He'd bought the farm for Sam and had intended spending as little time here as possible. But Hannah would require more supervision than his planned sporadic visits.

The door to the lab burst open, shattering the standoff between him and the bothersome brunette. A lanky redheaded guy rushed in. "Doc Will's got another one."

Hannah's body language changed instantly from resentful and reluctant to alert and attentive. Wyatt found the switch quite intriguing. She didn't snap at the new guy for keeping the door open, dripping on the floor or tracking in mud. Instead, she wiggled her fingers in a give-me-more gesture.

"He got a call to euthanize, but he decided to give you a look first. He's down at the barn."

Those big blue eyes rounded. "He's *here* instead of calling for a consult?"

"Yep. It's that critical. He hightailed it off the property as soon as the authorities gave him the okay. He says this one will be a real test of your skills."

"He's assuming I'll say yes."

The redhead chuckled. "Hannah, you never say no."

Wyatt tried to make sense of their conversation and couldn't, but he seriously doubted the twentysomething guy meant the words in a sexual context—which was exactly where Wyatt's brain headed when he heard a woman couldn't say no.

He shut down that mental detour and cursed his traitorous libido. Hannah Sutherland might have a rockin' body and a damned sexy pout, but there would be nothing remotely intimate between him and his temporary employee.

"I'm Wyatt Jacobs. And you are?" His question brought both sets of eyes in his direction.

Hannah grimaced. "I'm sorry. Jeb Jones, our veterinary assistant. Wyatt is the new owner."

Wyatt shook Jeb's hand. "Who is Doc Will?"

Hannah ripped off her lab coat and hung it on the hook by the door. "Will is one of our county veterinarians. Your tour will have to wait."

"Are you willing to risk the consequences of refusing my request?" He didn't need to elaborate that she'd be fired, but her quick gasp told him she received his unspoken message loud and clear.

Her defiant gaze drilled him. "You didn't request, Mr. Jacobs. You ordered. And I'm not refusing. I'm postponing your tour until after I've handled this emergency."

Her exasperation came across loud and clear despite the pretty-please smile punctuating her sentence. No doubt that smile worked on most men. Not him.

"Let's go, Jeb." Hannah rushed from the lab.

The kid hesitated, as if trying to decide who was in charge, but then he mistakenly fell in behind his cohort. Taken aback by Hannah's insubordination and the kid's loyalty, Wyatt rocked on his heels. Then he reconsidered. This wasn't the case of a woman standing up for her convictions. Hannah was a spoiled daddy's girl who believed the rules didn't apply to her. He'd teach her and her flunky differently.

He followed the pair, intent on firing Hannah, giving her follower a warning and informing the veterinarian that Sutherland Farm was no longer a dumping ground for unwanted animals of any kind. Hannah might not be able to say no, but Wyatt had no such problem.

Ahead of him Hannah and Jeb raced down the driveway heedless of the rain. They veered off the paved surface and onto a gravel track leading to a building set behind a copse of trees several hundred yards from the main barn. Wyatt climbed into his Mercedes and drove the distance rather than get soaked.

Once he pulled off the asphalt, the uneven ground tested his car's suspension. Considering the pristine condition of the rest of the property, the neglect surprised him. He made a mental note to speak to the manager about ordering a load of gravel to fill the potholes.

A pickup truck with a horse trailer attached had backed through the barn's open doors. He parked beside it and surveyed the stone building through the rain streaming down his windshield. The smaller barn had the same architecturally attractive design as the other barns, but the structure, like the driveway hadn't been as well-maintained as the rest of the farm. Odd.

He climbed from his car, then squeezed between the trailer and doorjamb. While the outside of the building lacked sparkle, the interior was as spotless as a barn could be. The combined scents of fresh shavings, hay and oats ambushed him with memories of happier times with Sam.

The trailer's rear ramp had been lowered into the center hallway. Inside the metal enclosure a horse danced restlessly in the right compartment, its feet thumping hollowly on the rubberized mat covering the steel floor.

Hannah occupied the left half of the trailer, a rib-high divider separating her from the agitated creature. She stroked the animal's withers and back, and spoke calmly. "It's okay, girl. You have nothing to fear. We're going to take good care of you."

Her quiet, soothing tone contrasted with the impatient one she'd used with him each time he'd asked a question this morning.

The horse responded with a panicked sound that raised the fine hairs on Wyatt's body. It had been almost fifteen years since he'd been around horses, but even he recognized the animal's terror.

Firing Hannah would have to wait until she wasn't in physical danger. Distraction in the workplace was an invitation to disaster. "Get out of there."

"In a minute," she replied without raising her voice. "Okay boys, let's ease her out and see what we have."

"You're not gonna like it," an older gentleman wearing muddy jeans and a battered field jacket said as he came from behind the trailer and clapped Wyatt on the shoulder. "Best not to get behind this one, son."

Wyatt flashed back to his teens. He'd heard the same warning from Sam too many times to count when Sam had been at the top of his game and lucid all the time and not just intermittently.

Hannah scowled at Wyatt across the distance. "I'll call you when I'm done."

"I'm not leaving."

"If you stay, you'll end up getting in the way or getting hurt."

"I worked on a thoroughbred farm from the time I was

fourteen until I went to college. But don't unload that horse. It needs to go back to wherever it came from."

Her expression turned belligerent. "That's not an option—a fact the police will confirm if you pick up the phone and ask for Officer—"

"Harris," the veterinarian supplied when Hannah arched an eyebrow.

Her continued defiance rasped against Wyatt's last nerve. "I don't want that animal on this property."

Hannah descended the ramp and didn't stop until they were toe-to-toe, chest to chest—so close he could taste the mint on her breath and feel the heat steaming from her rain-dampened clothing.

He fought to keep his attention from the way her white polo shirt had turned almost transparent. Fought and failed. The wet fabric clung to her hard-nippled breasts and outlined her thin white bra. His hormones reacted the way a healthy man's would and, try as he might, he could not control the sudden increase in his pulse rate.

"Mr. Jacobs, *Wyatt,* if you feel the same way after I've examined her, we'll discuss other arrangements. But for now, please step aside, and let me do my job."

"I thought you were the breeding specialist."

"I only work a half day on Saturdays. In my off hours I wear a different hat."

"Have you forgotten who pays your salary?"

"You're not likely to let that happen. Give me an hour to examine the mare and see what we're dealing with. This could be a matter of life and death. I'm not ready to take a life without just cause. Are you?"

"Are you always so melodramatic?"

"Hardly ever," she answered deadpan.

Her determination impressed him. "Make it quick."

"Thank you." She returned to the trailer, apparently undaunted by the agitated creature's dancing.

Under her direction the trio coaxed the horse down the ramp

in fits and spurts. The mare's hesitant steps alternated with nervous hops and skips, then in a sudden backward lunge the horse launched from the trailer kicking up a spray of shavings. Once the dust settled the wild-eyed animal quivered in the hall, its terror-widened eyes taking in the scene.

Then Wyatt saw what the shadowy trailer had concealed. Open sores and scars crisscrossed the emaciated back, haunches and muzzle. Bloody rings circled the mare's back legs just above the hooves.

She'd been abused. His gut muscles seized and rage blazed within him. "Who did this?"

The vet shook his head without taking his eyes from the animal. "Mean SOB who owned her. I hope the cops give him a taste of his own medicine. A billy club upside his head would be a nice touch."

Hannah handed the lead rope to Jeb then eased around the horse without ever lifting her palm from the animal's dull, scarred hide. Wyatt recognized the trick as one Sam had employed. By never losing contact, the horse always knew where you were and wouldn't be startled.

"You know animal abusers get a slap on the wrist at best, Will." Her frustration came through loud and clear even though she kept her tone low and even. "She doesn't look good."

"Nope. Not much to work with," the vet replied. "She wouldn't have lasted another week in that hellhole."

Wyatt focused on the deep gouges and bloody fetlocks. Now that the fight had drained out of the mare her head hung low as if she were resigned to whatever came next and fighting took more energy than she possessed. She'd probably been a beauty once, but now she was nothing more than a broken shell. She looked ready to collapse. Her spirit seemed broken, her usefulness in doubt.

Like Sam.

The parallel was so strong it blindsided Wyatt. He hated to see anything or anyone turned into a victim trapped in a body that could no longer function or fight back. He turned to the vet who'd brought the animal. "You should have put her down."

"Maybe. That's Hannah's call now."

"Why prolong her misery? Ending her suffering would be more humane."

Hannah bristled, agitating the mare into a side step. "Just because the owner is worthless doesn't mean the animal is. Every life has value, including hers. Her teeth indicate she's less than ten years old. There could be a lot of good years in her yet."

"She's debilitated, terrified and in pain," Wyatt countered, his fists curling in frustration.

"If anyone can pull her through, Hannah can," the vet said.

A muscle jumped in Wyatt's jaw. The horse had been through hell, and someone had to find the compassion and make the executive decision to end her suffering. That someone was him, apparently.

"She's probably disease-ridden and could infect the other horses. And after being abused this severely, her trust in man has likely been irrevocably broken."

Hannah planted herself between Wyatt and the mare. She didn't look like a spoiled daddy's girl now. She resembled a mama grizzly passionately defending her cub. "You can't write her off without giving her a chance."

Her stormy gaze hit Wyatt with a fireball of pain, anger and frustration, the same emotions rumbling through him. The fight in her eyes would cause a lesser man to back down.

"Giving horses second chances is what I do, Wyatt. And if you'd done your research on the farm before you tossed around your money, you would realize it's what you do now, too."

Wyatt stiffened as the barb hit home. He couldn't argue with facts. He'd delegated his research. The agent's report hadn't included anything about Sutherland Farm being a dumping ground for damaged animals, or Hannah Sutherland, who was going to make damned sure he paid for delegating.

"That right rear leg could be broken."

Hannah didn't even glance at it. "It's cut deep from the hobbles. It looks like the brute bound her back legs so she couldn't defend herself when he beat her. But from the way she's bearing weight on it, it's most likely superficial. I'll run X-rays to confirm."

"You mean you'll run up expenses on a lost cause."

She glared at him. "This isn't about money. Find Your Center saves lives. It doesn't destroy them unnecessarily."

"What in the hell is Find Your Center?"

Irritation darkened her eyes to storm cloud gray and tightened the tendons running the length of her neck as she stuck out her chin, making the diamonds in her ears sparkle in the barn's overhead lighting. If she'd been a guy, she probably would have punched him.

"Illustrating once again, Mr. Jacobs, you should have done your homework before your underhanded purchase."

"There was nothing devious about my purchasing this farm. It was for sale. I bought it."

She visibly reined in her temper, taking a deep breath then relaxing her tense muscles. "Sutherland Farm specializes in birth *and* rebirth."

A bird swooped through the open barn door. The horse spooked and jumped sideways, its haunches knocking into Hannah. She stumbled. Wyatt instinctively sprang forward to catch her. His muscles bunched as he banded his arms around her and braced his thighs to keep them both from going down under the ragged, dancing hooves.

Her feet tangled with his as she scrambled for traction and shifted against him in ways that made him excruciatingly aware of the surprising firmness and strength beneath her curves.

"Are you all right?" he asked through a knotted jaw.

Her wary gaze locked with his. Her cheeks flushed and her lips parted. His pulse spiked and heat flooded him, proving he shared something he wanted no part of with the pampered princess.

Chemistry.

"I'm fine. Thank you. Release me. Please." She planted her palms on his chest and pushed, broke his hold and backed away. Keeping an equally watchful eye on him, she circled to the opposite side of the horse.

"I'm sorry, Hannah," Jeb said. "I have her now."

"It's okay, Jeb. My mistake," she offered. "I know better than to turn my back on an unfamiliar animal."

She flashed a brief look at Wyatt as if he were the animal in question, then she bent to reexamine the mare's fetlock the way she'd done everything this morning—with a methodical thoroughness and attention to detail that had frustrated him in the lab because he'd suspected her of deliberately stalling as she checked and rechecked each sample and then meticulously packaged and charted each vial. Slow and steady was very likely her modus operandi and not just a passive-aggressive ploy to get under his skin.

She finally stepped away from the mare and, ignoring Wyatt, approached the vet, who'd been watching Wyatt as much as he had the horse. "I'll keep her."

"She could jeopardize the safety of the other horses," Wyatt objected.

"She'll be quarantined until the test results come back."

The vet nodded. "Thanks, Hannah. I'll take care of the legalities. Can you send me the pictures documenting the abuse ASAP? I took some video with my cell phone and shot that off to the authorities. But detailed still shots will help our case."

"I'll get photos before and after I clean and treat her wounds, and I'll email those and the lab results to you as soon as I'm done."

Wyatt didn't like the way this was playing out. "The mare's suffering should end. Put her down. I'll cover the cost."

Hannah gripped Wyatt's forearm. Her touch burned

through his sleeve like tongues of fire. Heat licked up his limb and settled in his torso.

"If you don't care about the mare, let me put it another way. To stand any chance of making the bastard who did this pay for his heinous crimes and to keep him from hurting another animal, we'll need documentation. Not only was this mare beaten and malnourished, she was obviously living in filth. The judge has to see what a sadist her owner is or the jerk might be allowed to own and torture other animals. No creature deserves to live or die in those conditions. Please, Wyatt, let me do this for her."

When she put it like that how could he refuse? Reports of abuse and neglect had been the top reasons he'd refused to put Sam in a facility. The mare, like Sam, deserved to be treated with dignity.

Her movements slow and deliberate, Hannah approached the mare and smoothed a hand down the white blaze. The horse shied away, tossing her head and almost knocking Hannah over, but the stupid woman wouldn't quit. She kept sweet-talking and caressing until the horse tolerated her touch.

"Look at that face. She deserves a second chance, don't you, girl?" Hannah's eyes, soft and wide, beseeched him. "Give me two weeks. Unless she tests positive for something I can't cure, I'll prove to you, and to her, that she deserves a better life. When I'm done she'll be healthier so someone else might be willing to foster her. Worst-case scenario, her final days will be good ones. She'll be warm and clean and well-fed."

Wyatt couldn't care less about Hannah's bedroom-soft purr or the horse's face. He didn't believe for one minute this spoiled rich girl had what it took to bring the mare back from near-death, but her point about final days got to him. That's why he'd bought the farm for Sam.

"Two weeks. You pay for the costs, and no heroic measures."

Relief softened Hannah's expression. "Wait and see the miracles a little TLC can create."

"I don't believe in miracles."

She shrugged. “Your loss. They happen every day.”

“That’s Pollyanna garbage.”

“Beats pessimism.”

The vet’s pager buzzed. He pulled it from his pocket and frowned at the message. “Hannah, darling, I have a colic call on the other side of the county. I have to go. Can you manage without me?”

“Jeb and I can handle her.”

Hannah flicked her fingers at Wyatt in a dismissive gesture. “You can go, too. I’m going to be busy here for a while. I’ll call you when I’m done, and if there’s still enough daylight left, you’ll get your tour. If not, I’ll make time tomorrow.”

The liability of her getting hurt on the job outweighed his disgust with the situation, and he couldn’t think of a better way to keep an eye on her than to help. “I’m not leaving. You’ll be shorthanded without Doc.”

Hannah frowned. Her mouth opened, then closed as if she’d considered arguing but had changed her mind. “If you insist on staying, then go into the office and get my camera out of my desk drawer. You can take the before photographs while I get my suture kit. But stay out of my way.”

Her bossy tone reminded him that she was probably used to men jumping at her command. She’d learn quickly that he had no intention of being one of her minions.

Four

Hannah could barely concentrate on cleansing the mare's wounds. She wished she could think of a way to get rid of her new boss—one that didn't include angering him and making him renege on their bargain.

Her collision with Wyatt earlier had left her more than a little mystified. His touch had filled her with some weird, almost kinetic energy that she couldn't identify and didn't like. And since then it was almost as if she'd grown antennae that stayed tuned into the Wyatt channel. The constant awareness of him was exhausting. She wanted it and him gone.

His hawkeyed presence made her uncomfortable—something the sensitive mare picked up on and displayed with each nervous swish of her tail. Add in that he had removed his sweater ten minutes ago, revealing a newsworthy set of broad shoulders in his snug white T-shirt, and Hannah was practically salivating over a pair of deliciously defined pectorals.

Pitiful, Hannah. Just pitiful.

She glanced up and her gaze slammed into Wyatt's dark brown one over the mare's withers. Her pulse bucked.

"When will Jeb return?" he asked in that rumbly, make-her-insides-quiver voice of his.

"It'll take him a while to run all the tests. We'll probably finish before he does."

"Does the staff always dump the dirty work on you?"

She couldn't tell if his question arose from genuine curiosity or from the quest for information he could use against her coworkers. She would have to guard every word she said.

"They know I like cleanup detail. It gives me a chance to assess the damage and get to know the horse. But for what it's worth, a number of the employees volunteer their free time to FYC like Jeb is today. Weekends are hectic for most of us. Our trainers are away at horse shows, and the staff left behind is tied up with current or prospective clients."

Despite the crowded farm, *this* barn was empty except for the two of them—something her crazy hormones couldn't seem to ignore.

As much as she disliked the arrogant jerk she needed his cooperation and financial support to keep FYC going. If Wyatt fired her, who would care for her horses? They weren't ready for adoption yet and had little monetary value in their current conditions. She had to take every opportunity to sell the concept of Find Your Center to Wyatt and not only make him a believer, but a willing sponsor.

Making nice wouldn't kill her—or so Nellie always claimed. Afraid she'd choke on the necessary words, Hannah swallowed and forced a smile. "I appreciate your help and the extra set of hands today. You'll see that it's time well spent."

"Doubtful." He capped the antibiotic salve, drawing her attention to his hands—as if she hadn't been fixated on them already. He had good hands. Firm. Strong. Gentle when necessary.

The kind of hands a woman wanted in a lover.

Don't go there.

But she couldn't help it. She would never have anticipated tenderness and patience from the arrogant oaf. "You were good with the mare. I expected squeamishness from a guy wearing cashmere and Gucci, but you applied that slimy salve to her wounds with a deft touch and no gagging."

His appraisal turned suspicious, as if he suspected an ulterior motive behind her compliment. "I have some experience."

"So you've said, but you've left out the details."

He ignored her invitation to fill in the blanks. She smothered a sigh. There was only one way to find out what she wanted to know—by getting to know the boss better. *Not* something she relished, but it was a tactic she'd learned from her more competitive cousin. Megan always found out what motivated her adversaries, then used it against them to trounce them in the show ring.

"Tell me about your years on the thoroughbred farm," Hannah prompted.

Wyatt wiped his hands, slowly and deliberately on a rag, then stepped back to check his handiwork. "Not much to tell. My mother married the stable owner when I was fourteen. He gave me odd jobs to keep me out of trouble until I went to college."

She studied his tightly controlled hair and expression and his traditional attire. "You don't look like the type to find trouble."

His lips flattened. "Are we done here?"

"You avoided answering."

He gave her a level look. "You didn't ask a question, and my personal life is none of your business."

She tried to hide her frustration, but she wasn't admitting defeat so easily. "We're finished for now. We have pictures of her wounds and details on the severity of infection. I'll put her in the quarantine stall and let her rest. She should be exhausted from the travel and all this first aid. Once Jeb has the test results, there will likely be more work to do."

She dropped the irrigation syringe into the bucket, peeled off her gloves, set the pail aside and hitched a lead line to the halter. The moment she released her patient from the cross ties the mare tossed her head, almost dislocating Hannah's shoulder.

"She's going to hurt you."

"And let me guess, you're more worried about the worker's compensation claim than me." *Oops. Shut up, Hannah.*

"Triple Crown Distillery prides itself on running a safe operation. I will expect Sutherland Farm to do the same."

"We do, but this isn't a manufacturing plant. We work with live animals that have personalities instead of stationary vats and casks. The mare doesn't know whether we're friends or foes, and after what we've just put her through she probably thinks we're every bit as bad as her owner. Don't hold her skittishness against her. She'll reveal her true nature as she gets to know us." She stroked the mare's long neck. "Let's go to your new home, girl."

Wyatt blocked her path with a wall of solid muscle and his upper arm bumped Hannah's, splattering her with warmth. "I'll take the lead. I'll be able to control her better."

"That's a chauvinist statement if I ever heard one."

"I'm stronger and I outweigh you."

She surrendered the line. Any bonding he might do with the horse would work in her favor. "She goes in the last stall on the right."

Despite the hour they'd spent working as a team, she still knew next to nothing about her new boss. Intent on finding out as much as she could, she kept pace beside him as they traversed the center aisle. "Your parents are divorced?"

"Yes."

"Father still part of the picture?"

"No."

"Did you enjoy working at the stable?"

"Parts of it."

"Did you like your stepfather?"

"Yes."

"Still keep in touch?"

"Yes."

"Not exactly a conversationalist, are you, Jacobs?" She winced as soon as the words left her mouth.

Don't bite the hand that feeds you, Hannah.

He sliced a sharp glance in her direction. "Do I need to be?"

"Frankly, yes. Running an operation like Sutherland Farm requires you to be equal parts salesman, businessman, diplomat and horseman. From what I've seen, you lack most of those skills. But I can help you."

His eyebrows dipped. "And if I don't want or need your assistance?"

Stubborn jerk. "I think you do. I know a lot of people in the show jumping world. Connections count. I have them. From what little you've shared, you don't. And I speak four languages fluently, which means I can communicate with more of our global clients."

"I'll keep that in mind." He turned the mare into the stall, removed the lead and closed the door. His dark eyes pinned Hannah. "You seem like a detail-oriented person."

Something about his tone set her on guard. Why didn't that sound like a compliment? "I am."

"Then you should have comprehensive records on Find Your Center."

"I do," she offered cautiously.

"I want them."

Not good. He needed to see the good FYC did before he saw the balance sheets. "Let's go to my office. I'll show you the portfolio of the horses we've rescued and placed."

"Financials first. If the numbers aren't good, then the rest is irrelevant."

Her mouth went as dry as a drought-ridden pasture. A bottom-line mindset spelled nothing but disaster for FYC. "What about your tour?"

"It can wait."

"It'll take me a while to pull the reports together. Study the portfolio in the meantime. I'll get the books to you tomorrow."

"Tonight."

She bit the inside of her lip to hold back a grimace. She wasn't going to be able to stall him. "The files are on the computer in my cottage. It's late. I'll print them out after dinner and deliver them to your office first thing in the morning."

"I'll follow you home and get them now."

That sounded more like a threat than a promise. "If you insist."

"I do. And for future reference, Hannah, don't waste my time trying to evade the issue. I always get what I want in the end."

Rain drummed on the car's roof, almost drowning out Hannah's pounding pulse. The short, tense ride from the rescue barn to her cottage couldn't have been more miserable.

Wyatt parked. She debated inviting him inside but his scent enveloping her as surely as the expensive leather upholstery cradled her body muddled her thinking.

Her cottage was the only part of her life he hadn't managed to invade, but if she wanted to persuade him to keep funding FYC despite its dismal bottom line, then she had to endure his presence until she could find another solution. Besides, she had pictures inside that he really needed to see.

Resigned, she reached for the door handle. "Come in while I get what you need."

She shoved open the door and sprinted toward her front porch, but not even a chilly rain could banish the strange awareness of the man shadowing her like a hawk ready to swoop down on a hare. But she wasn't a defenseless bunny. She could fight for what she wanted.

She stepped into her foyer and held open the door. He

swept past her. "Make yourself comfortable. This'll take a few minutes. Can I get you a glass of wine?"

"No thank you." Most visitors paused to study the wall covered with framed photographs, but not Wyatt. He marched between her matching camelback sofas, his boots barely making a sound on her wooden floor as he headed for the stone fireplace and the portrait hanging above it.

"Who's this?" he asked without turning. "You look like her."

"My mother and her favorite horse, Gazpacho. He was a Grand Prix champion many times over and twice a world champion. Gazpacho was a rescue horse. So I guess you could say my mother laid the foundation for Find Your Center by rescuing Gazpacho before I was born."

Wyatt glanced over his shoulder from her to the oil painting and back, his skepticism clear in his expression. "You expect to find another champion in every nag you rescue?"

His sarcasm stung. Now he sounded like her father. "Of course not. I'm not stupid. Champions are rare. Most of our horses go to therapeutic riding schools after they're rehabilitated."

"What is a therapeutic riding school?"

She couldn't have asked for a more perfect opening for her sales pitch. She inhaled slowly, gathering her thoughts and words and trying to put them in perfect, persuasive order.

"Therapeutic riding is a form of physical therapy used to help individuals with disabilities or brain injuries strengthen their core muscles and improve their balance through finding their center of gravity. Hence, our name."

"Putting someone with balance issues on a horse is dangerous and foolhardy. Sounds a liability and an insurance nightmare."

Alarm raised the hairs on her nape. The close-minded were always the hardest to convince. "Our program is well-supervised. We run the classes here on Sundays. You can see for yourself tomorrow. Our instructors and volunteers are trained and our program is accredited. We take every precaution possible to ensure the safety of the participants. We have a long waiting list of applicants because we're so good."

"How profitable are the lessons?"

Ouch. Bull's-eye. He'd hit their weakest spot. She hesitated. "In terms of physical recovery, they're priceless."

His frown deepened. "In dollars and cents, Hannah."

She'd been hoping he wouldn't ask. "We don't charge for the sessions."

"How do you cover your expenses?"

She chewed the inside of her lip. He wasn't going to like the answer. "The farm subsidizes us."

"You're not profitable."

He seemed determined to focus on the negatives. That wouldn't help her cause. She gestured to the photo collection she'd wanted him to see. "This is my Wall of Winners. Each of these horses is a Find Your Center success story that has been rehabilitated and placed in a new home. But to know the whole story you really need to see the book in my office in the breeding barn, which contains the before and after photos. You'll be amazed by the progress."

He crossed the room to study the photographs. Silent seconds ticked past, stretching her nerves even tighter. "I don't see any pictures of you on a horse."

Hannah startled. She hadn't seen that one coming. "I—I don't ride."

His gaze burned her. "You grew up on a horse farm and you don't ride, and yet you're busting my chops for my lack of horse knowledge?"

She bristled. *She* hadn't spent millions on a business she knew nothing about. But being snarky would jeopardize what she wanted—his cooperation and continued financial backing. "I don't have to ride to love horses."

"Why don't you ride?"

Her nails bit into her palms. "That really isn't relevant."

In three purposeful strides he invaded her space, stopping close enough that she could feel his body heat and inhale the intoxicating blend of fresh rain and his unique aroma. That crazy current buzzed between them again, making her nipples tingle and tighten. She folded her arms to hide her involuntary response, then realized the defensive body language gave too much away and lowered her hands to her sides. It took a conscious effort to keep from fisting her fingers.

"Why don't you ride, Hannah?" he repeated, his voice as deep and rough as a rock quarry. His gaze roamed over her chest before returning to hold hers.

"To borrow your phrase, my personal life is none of your business."

"True, as long as it doesn't interfere with your work. But until you convince me Find Your Center is more than an expensive hobby, my checkbook and I are free to leave."

Her heart sank as she stared into that hard face.

"Let me give you a little incentive to talk, doc. From my position it looks like you're a bleeding heart who wastes money, time and valuable land that could be better and more profitably allocated. Your little operation is a high-risk, low-return venture. Convince me I'm wrong—if you can."

His challenge stirred her ire. She'd wipe that superior expression off his face. "My mother died as the result of a riding accident when I was ten. So you'll have to forgive me if I choose to love my horses with both feet firmly planted on the ground."

Instead of scaring him off, interest sharpened his eyes. "How?"

Her throat tightened as the hated movie reel replayed in her brain. "She was showing me how to tackle a water jump. We'd been at it for a while because I couldn't get it right. We were all tired. Her mount—*my* horse—misstepped and they went down. Neither got up."

The one time she'd been determined to win no matter what

the cost, the two loves of her life had paid the price. From that moment on, her life had changed forever.

She struggled to gather her composure. When she dared to look at Wyatt, the empathy and understanding in his eyes—two emotions she would never have expected from him—shook her. He cupped her shoulder. “I’m sorry, Hannah.”

As it had in the barn, the warmth of his hand seeped through her shirt and her skin tingled beneath his touch. She tried to shake off the unwelcome response. “It was a long time ago.”

“Sometimes the losses of our childhood are the hardest to forget.”

“That sounds like the voice of experience.”

“We all go through tough times.” His fingers squeezed her shoulder, and the air between them changed, becoming charged and thick. His pupils expanded and his lips parted on a slowly indrawn breath.

There was no denying or misnaming the tension expanding inside her until it almost crushed her lungs. Desire. For her boss. Her enemy.

This can’t be happening. Not with him.

Wyatt lowered his head. Every cell in her body screamed, *Run.*

But she couldn’t.

Mistake.

The word reverberated through Wyatt’s head even before his mouth touched Hannah’s, but the damned overwhelming compulsion that had steamed through him from the moment they’d met propelled him forward. Then the satiny warmth of her lips snagged him. Stopping wasn’t an option.

She stiffened, but before he could react her mouth opened beneath his—whether in surprise or welcome he neither knew nor cared—then she relaxed against him, her soft breasts nudging his chest. He sipped from her lips, but it wasn’t enough to satisfy his craving.

Greedy for a taste of her, he stroked his tongue across the lush, moist curve of her bottom lip. Her flavor hit him with the punch of a straight shot of single malt whiskey, making his head spin and his body temperature spike.

Why her? Why did this woman who stood for everything he despised get to him? Hadn't he been burned by her type often enough to learn his lesson? Before he could make sense of her strange magnetism or get his fill of her, she jerked back, eyes wide and wary, and slapped her fingers over her mouth.

"You can't do that. You're my boss."

Reality slammed into him like an oncoming train.

Stupid move, Jacobs.

There was no room for physical attraction in business. His life, work and home were in Asheville. He'd never intended Sutherland Farm to be anything more than a safe place for Sam to live out whatever lucid time he had remaining.

Hannah's presence had already forced Wyatt to spend more time here than he'd intended. But the haunted look in her eyes and the tragic story of her mother's death had resurrected old baggage about losing his father. The difference was his father hadn't died. He'd voluntarily walked away.

"You're right. A personal involvement would be unwise."

But even as he spoke the words he registered her heavy-lidded eyes, flushed cheeks and erect nipples—sure signs that her hormones were pumping as rampantly as his. And as impractical and ill-advised as it might be, he wanted her. He locked his muscles against the urge to reach for her again.

As if she'd read the desire in his eyes, she hitched a breath and retreated. "I won't sleep with you, Wyatt. Not even to save my horses."

Oh, hell. "The survival of your rescue operation depends solely on the balance sheet. We're mature enough to ignore any chemistry between us."

Her expression turned militant, that delicious bottom lip poking out. "There is no chemistry."

A blatant lie. The urge to prove her wrong charged through

him. It would be so easy to take her into his arms, cover that mouth and coerce her into acquiescence. Easy. But not smart.

Fisting his hands and gritting his teeth, he resisted. "Show me your records."

The color drained from her face but determination firmed her chin. "Find Your Center is about so much more than profit and loss."

"Spoken like someone trying to justify a losing proposition."

She pointed to a shelf packed with periodicals. "Our program has been written up in almost every horse magazine on the market, giving the stable free positive advertising globally. You can't put a value on that. You should read the articles."

"Hannah—" He growled her name in warning.

"People relocate entire families to North Carolina to take advantage of our services." Desperation rushed her words.

"I want to be certain you're not taking advantage of my deep pockets to fund an underperforming segment of your operation."

She took a deep breath and stared him down, looking more resolute than ever. "I'm sure you're aware Sutherland Farm makes a lot of money. The farm needs our charitable organization as a tax shelter."

Her evasion was beginning to irritate and strangely, intrigue him. She wasn't afraid to fight for what she believed in, but she didn't do so by throwing a tantrum as he would have expected a pampered princess to do. She argued with nearly logical data.

While a part of him respected and admired her tenacity because he shared the same trait, another part of him wanted the matter settled so he could walk away from her and the unwanted attraction, and from the involvement with suffering horses that reminded him too much of Sam's losing battle.

"An interesting argument, but not my concern."

"Did you know we've been the blueprint for other stables to start similar programs? We've actually trained their managers.

Unfortunately, there are not enough programs around to meet the needs of the special popul—"

"Hannah." He grabbed her shoulders. Her deltoids bunched beneath his fingers, revealing more strength than her slender build implied. His desire instantly resurfaced, simmering through him like thick, hot lava. "Stop with the sales pitch and bring out the financials or you're fired."

She paled, then shrugged off his hold. "I will if you promise to come out and see us in action tomorrow."

Her audacity shocked a laugh from him. "You're in no position to make demands."

"You asked for a tour. FYC is part of the farm. Stop by and watch us work our magic. Interview our students and their families and let them tell you how we've improved their lives. We even have doctors' testimonials—"

"I have other commitments tomorrow. And I'm out of patience *now.* Give me the damned books."

Resignation settled over her features. "I'll print the spreadsheets for you, but I'll need to explain them."

"Excuse them, you mean. I run a multimillion-dollar company. I can decipher a profit and loss statement."

"But—"

"*Hannah.* Stop. Stalling."

She radiated frustration. "You can't waltz in here and strip away everything good about Sutherland Farm. There's more to the business than assets and debits. You're not taking the people into account—the people who work here and the ones whose lives we change for the better with our services."

Give the stubborn woman kudos for being an articulate opponent. If he wanted a spokesperson selling his product, he wanted one with her conviction. Too bad they were on opposing teams. "Who owns the rescue horses?"

She bit her lip and he instantly recalled her taste and the texture of her soft flesh against his. "Once we get all the legalities taken care of, my name goes on the registration papers."

"Not Sutherland Farm?"

Silence pulsed between them and worry darkened her eyes, turning them more smoky than blue. "No."

Interesting. "Why is that?"

She shifted her weight on her feet. "My father didn't want our operation connected to the Sutherland Farm purebreds."

"I share your father's view, and if you don't give me the records now, then I'll get a court order to have your animals evicted from my property."

She sighed heavily. "Fine. But you haven't heard the last of this. Find Your Center is critical to Sutherland Farm's reputation and I intend to prove it."

A threat like that he could handle. It was this crazy desire for her and his admiration for her dedication to the worthless animals that he wanted no part of.

First and foremost, he had to come up with a plan to get rid of Hannah Sutherland and her nags before he did something stupid such as take her to bed to see if she was as passionate between the sheets as she was about her horses.

Five

"My office. Now." Wyatt's clipped command for Hannah's presence via cell phone made her heart skip a beat.

Not a promising start to her Monday.

"I'll be right there." She disconnected the call, slipped her phone into her pocket and trudged toward the house, feeling a bit like a horse traveling down the chute to the slaughterhouse. She'd been dreading this summons since handing over Find Your Center's financials Saturday night. Apparently, Wyatt had taken a look at her files.

And while his kiss might be hotter than a branding iron, she didn't doubt for one moment that the coldhearted bottom-line bastard was going to try to close Find Your Center. If her sales pitch hadn't changed his mind, then she had to come up with something else that would. Too many people depended on her. She couldn't let the students or their families down. And then there were her animals…

She wished her cousin were here. Megan was a brilliant strategist. She knew how to research her Grand Prix opponents and use their strengths and weaknesses against them. But Megan had chosen to ride the European Grand Prix circuit because she avoided anything that would cause her to cross paths with her uncle, and Hannah didn't dare call Megan to ask for help because her cousin would drop everything and race to Hannah's rescue, leaving her horses, her career and her hunky lover behind.

Megan had a chance at success and true happiness that Hannah refused to screw up. She squared her shoulders. If she wanted this situation resolved with the least collateral damage to the people and horses she cared about, she had to win over Wyatt.

The kitchen door opened the moment she set foot on the patio, revealing Nellie. "Good gracious, child, you've lost weight. Can't you feed yourself when I'm away?"

Hannah forced a smile and wrapped Nellie's substantial frame in a hug. "You know I forget to eat when I'm busy, and it is that time of year. How was your vacation?"

"I've discovered Caribbean Island cruises aren't my cup of tea, but I had to try it once especially since the boss was footing the bill."

Wyatt had paid for Nellie's trip? Why? Hannah couldn't believe he'd done so out of the goodness of his black heart.

"Come in, child. I made your favorite raspberry muffins. I'll wrap some for you to take back with you. You need a man to help you remember to eat—a handsome rich one like the boss."

"Don't play matchmaker, Nellie." She couldn't handle it—especially with the memory of that kiss cauterizing a hole in her brain.

"Why not? This is your home. You should be living here, not out in that old house filled with antiques. And it ain't like he's hard on the eyes."

Or the lips.

"Not interested," Hannah denied, averting her face from the eagle-eyed Nellie as she entered the kitchen. The shock of seeing a large Mission-style table in the breakfast nook instead of her mother's elegant dining set—the one where Hannah had spent countless hours doing her homework and eating meals—stalled her steps. She scanned the rest of the room.

The kitchen remained architecturally the same and yet appeared totally different because Wyatt's Southwestern paint scheme stood out jarringly in the once-familiar classic Wedgwood-blue environment. Even the appliances had been replaced with shiny stainless ones.

"You ended your engagement fifteen months ago."

"Doesn't matter. I don't have time for men or the complications that seem to be encoded on their DNA."

Nellie patted Hannah's hand. "The changes take some getting used to, but Wyatt went top of the line on everything while I was away. I 'bout had a stroke when I saw he'd repainted the whole house and replaced my ol' stove."

Nellie's words reminded Hannah that she wasn't the only one facing changes. "Is he being good to you?"

"He is. Doesn't make a mess. Doesn't complain. Keeps to himself for the most part and knows what he wants. He always says thank you. He claims he has no intention of entertaining like your father did, and that's a shame, because this house needs to be filled with people. But maybe that'll come once he stops all his traveling an' settles in. I miss cooking fancy dinners and seeing you all prettied up."

"You're assuming Wyatt would want me to act as his hostess."

"Why wouldn't he? I've seen no sign of a significant other."

Hannah filed that away while she searched Nellie's lined and now tanned face and strained for sounds of the boss. "You'd tell me if he gave you any trouble, wouldn't you?"

Nellie smiled. "Hannah, if you'd fight half as hard for yourself as you do for your causes, you'd be a force to be reckoned with. But I've had no problems with the new boss." She indicated a tray on the table holding coffee and a plate of muffins. "Take that with you to the office when you go, please."

The idea of eating while Wyatt dissected Find Your Center's budget made Hannah's stomach churn. Between his pending verdict and the kiss that should never have happened she had no appetite whatsoever, even though she'd skipped breakfast. That blasted kiss had haunted her for the past thirty-six hours.

She'd forgotten what a man's lips felt like, forgotten how the flesh could be soft and yet firm at the same time, commanding and yet giving. Forgotten the electrical charge—

Check that. She hadn't *forgotten* the electricity. She'd never experienced a jolt that strong before Wyatt.

"How are you and your horses making out?"

She blinked at Nellie's question. "That's what I'm here to find out. That bottom-line bastard wants to shut us down."

"I'm sure you'll find a solution. You're quite resourceful when it comes to your animals."

"Hannah." Wyatt's deep voice from behind her smashed into her. "I'm waiting."

Her skin caught fire. How much had he overheard? She turned and found his eyes focused on her in that laser-like, unwavering and unnerving way of his. His foreboding expression twisted her nerves like hay in a baler.

She tried not to look at his mouth, tried not to recall the texture and warmth of his lips against hers or the strength of his chest against her breasts. But she couldn't help herself. If Wyatt remembered the kiss, he didn't show it by so much as a flicker of his short, spiky eyelashes.

Moot point. The kiss wouldn't be repeated. She wouldn't let it. Wyatt made her want to take risks and she'd learned a long time ago that risks should be avoided at all costs.

"Boss, I made muffins and fresh coffee. Take them with you, and make this girl eat something. She's wasting away."

Wyatt's dark gaze skimmed Hannah from her braided hair to her booted feet, plowing up a wave of goose bumps. Her stomach quivered and her heart banged in her rib cage. Not fair. How could he rattle her with nothing more than one slow inspection?

Surprisingly, Wyatt reached for the tray, then turned for her father's—*his* study. Wishing she could retreat to the comfort of her lab rather than have this confrontation, Hannah followed him. His office presented yet another reminder that this wasn't her home anymore. His taste for clean, sharp lines and his obvious passion for electronic gadgets contrasted sharply with her father's traditional, Old World furnishings.

Wyatt set the refreshments on a square table between the two leather cushioned chairs facing his desk, then snatched up a muffin and circled to fold into his high-backed leather desk chair. "Sit down."

She hesitated. The vertical wooden slats of the Mission chairs reminded her of a cage, making her feel trapped, but she sank onto a chair anyway.

You catch more flies with honey, child, she could all but hear Nellie saying, and dredged her mind for something nice to say. "Nellie tells me you paid for her vacation. That was kind of you. But why would you?"

He bit into his muffin and took his time chewing, obviously not suffering from the same nerves that cramped her stomach. If his goal was to irritate her by making her wait for his answer, he succeeded, but she'd be damned if she'd let on. She folded her hands in her lap and deliberately relaxed her fisted fingers while she noted he had very few personal items on his shelves.

He leaned back in his chair. "I wanted her out of the way while I set up."

"You've made a lot of changes."

"I've only just begun."

That sounded ominous. "If you have big plans, perhaps you should clue in the rest of us."

"The only change that concerns you is that I'm shutting down Find Your Center and ending the free board for your rescue animals. Sell them. Give them away. I don't care how you get them off the premises. Just do it."

The speech hit her like a blow regardless of his words being exactly what she'd expected to hear. "You can't make that kind of decision without having seen us in action. We do too much good to—"

"You lose too much money and your liability is too high. The insurance premiums alone are exorbitant. The barn could be used more advantageously by paying customers. Right now, it's an eyesore."

"That's because my father wouldn't spend money on upkeep."

"You'll pay the standard boarding fees or move your horses."

Panic swelled within her. Her salary wouldn't cover that expense. "Give me three months to change your mind."

"I want the operation off the property by the end of the month."

Dismay raced through her, quickly followed by outrage. "I can't place thirty horses and find a new location for Find Your Center in three weeks."

"Not my problem."

She shot to her feet. Her legs wobbled weakly beneath her. "You're asking the impossible."

The arrogant jerk looked confident that his demands would be met. She had to find a way to fix this.

"I'll give you more time on one condition."

She knew a trap when she heard one, but what choice did she have except to hear him out? "Name it."

He wrote something on a slip of paper, then slid it across the desk before lacing his fingers across his flat abdomen. "Sell me the house and land your father deeded to you. My offer is quite generous. With this amount you can buy your own stable."

Shock stole her breath when she counted the number of zeros. But the amount was irrelevant. She wasn't going to let him drive her away. "My grandparents built that cottage and the wall surrounding it stone by stone from rocks they collected from their fields. This is my home, my heritage. So as generous as your offer is, no thanks."

Surprise flickered in his eyes then his jaw hardened. "Sell me the property and I'll allow you live in the cottage rent-free for twelve months, and I'll continue funding your money-pit operation for the duration. A year will give you plenty of time to find alternative accommodations for you and your animals."

The man had mastered bribery. And while his offer tempted her simply because of the fiscal logic behind it, for the first time in her life a strong competitive urge pulsed through her. She wanted to win—to best this heartless bastard. Failing meant losing everything that mattered.

Searching her mind for alternatives, she tucked her hair behind her ear. The post of her mother's earring scraped her fingertip, reminding her that Sutherland Farm and rescuing horses had been her mother's dream, too. This fight wasn't just about her. This was her mother's legacy and Hannah's way to leave her mark in the world.

"No thanks."

"That's my deal, Hannah. Take it or leave it."

She had to get him physically involved with the students. Seeing the joy and sense of accomplishment on those faces hooked everyone.

Everyone except her father, a voice in her head warned.

And if converting Wyatt to a believer failed, she had to find another way. All of that required time and money—neither of which she had a surplus.

Think, Hannah. What would Megan do?

She'd buy time and strategize.

"I'll consider your offer—" *over my dead body* "—on one condition." She threw his words back at him.

He dipped his head, indicating she continue.

"Give me ninety days to search for a comparable property close enough for our students to continue using our services…

and you have to spend time with us. Watch us in action. Talk to our clients and their families. See the miracles we accomplish."

His eyes narrowed, but not so much that she couldn't see that being backed into a corner had annoyed him. Well, too bad. She wasn't whistling a happy tune, either.

"You're in no position to make demands."

"On the contrary, Mr. Jacobs. I have something you want. That gives me leverage."

A nerve in his jaw twitched. "I could simply evict your horses and outwait you. At the end of the year my contractual obligation to employ you and the other Sutherland employees will be over."

The implied threat against the rest of the staff shocked her, but she held her ground. "You don't seem like the waiting type."

"You're mistaken. I can be very patient when I want something bad enough." Silence stretched between them. "I'll give you sixty days to find a new location. In the meantime, you'll accept no more rescue animals. And you will start covering the expenses for your operation. Is that clear?"

Jerk. She forced a conciliatory smile. "As Waterford crystal."

Before he could change his mind, she pivoted on her heel and bolted through the patio door for the safety and order of her lab. She'd won a brief reprieve of sorts. But that was only the beginning. She had a lot of work to do and very little money to do it with.

"Pretty gal. Your wife?"

Sam's question jolted Wyatt from an unexpected and unwanted attack of lust. His stepfather climbed the stairs from the south lawn to the patio. *Alone.* Where was his nurse?

"I'm not married, Sam."

Wyatt took one last glance at Hannah striding down the driveway toward the barn, her anger giving her hips an attention-getting sway. The fight in her eyes before she'd stormed off had been impossible to miss. And attractive. Damned attractive.

He had to figure out how to get his hands on her land and get rid of her before he did something stupid. Her horses were her most obvious weakness, and he'd expected his offer of free room and board for her and her nags to win him this war. Obviously the lady veterinarian had a higher price tag.

He forced himself to turn away from the tempting and taboo view. "Nellie made muffins. Come inside and have one."

Sam preceded him into the study and grabbed a muffin. "I could have sworn you bought the farm because you had marriage plans. Horse farms are a good place to raise kids. Fresh air. Hard work. Told your mama so."

Sam's confusion only reinforced Wyatt's decision to relocate. He'd hoped getting Sam back in horse territory might result in more lucid moments.

"I was dating someone but we didn't have marriage plans." And she'd bailed the moment Sam had become a significant part of Wyatt's future.

"Lana. Leggy blonde? High maintenance? Bit enamored with herself? No patience with old men?"

"That's her." How could Sam be so astute about some things and completely clueless about others? Alzheimer's didn't make sense. It cast a net, catching random memories and letting others slip through. Some days the weave of the net was tighter than others. The disease defied every rule of logic Wyatt lived by.

"Where's Carol?" Even as he asked the question Wyatt stepped to the door and scanned the hall and foyer. He saw no sign of the nurse who should be shadowing his stepfather.

"Who?"

"Carol. Your nurse."

"Brunette?"

"No. That was the last one. This one is in her early fifties with salt-and-pepper hair." He'd hoped a mature woman would be more diligent than the younger caregiver had been.

Sam's face scrunched in concentration as he ate his muffin. "Is she the one who likes soap operas?"

"I don't know. Is she?" If Carol had let Sam get away because she was watching TV, then she'd be fired on the spot.

"One of 'em did." Sam frowned as if searching his malfunctioning brain. "I think that was the little mousy girl, the one who didn't talk."

"Sam?" Carol's panicked voice echoed through the two-story foyer followed by quick footsteps descending the stairs.

"He's in here."

She hurried down the stairs wide-eyed and breathing hard. "Thank God. Sam, you scared me half to death."

"He was outside. How did he get away from you?" Wyatt demanded. He would fire her on the spot if she weren't by far the best qualified of the applicants he'd interviewed.

Dark flags of color swept Carol's cheeks. "I honestly don't know. I was using the bathroom, and—"

"The suite door wasn't locked?"

She grimaced. "I thought it was. I'm sorry, Mr. Jacobs. I'm not used to having to lock in a client. I must have forgotten to take the key from the dead bolt after Nellie brought up breakfast."

"Confining him is for his own safety. He likes to wander." Wyatt hated caging Sam like an animal, but after the near disastrous balcony incident at his penthouse… Wyatt's gut knotted. He severed the thought of how easily he could have lost Sam that day.

"I understand, sir. It won't happen again." She turned toward his stepfather. "Sam, you've already had two muffins. Are you sure you want another one?"

Sam blinked. "I have?"

"Yes, and eggs and juice, too. You ate quite a big breakfast because we're going for a walk today."

"Where are you taking him?" Wyatt asked.

"I thought it would be nice to let him visit the stables."

Alarm kicked through Wyatt's system. "No. Stay away from the barns. I don't want Sam getting hurt."

"But he stands at the window for hours watching the horses in the pasture. Didn't he used to work with horses?"

"'Course I did and quit talking 'bout me like I'm not here," Sam groused.

"I apologize, Sam." Wyatt surveyed his stepfather, trying to assess today's mental state. Some days Sam seemed as sharp as he had in the old days. Others he was a shell of the man Wyatt had once idolized. "I know you miss the horses, but we don't know these animals well enough to know which ones are safe and which aren't."

Sam puffed out his chest and shoved his hands in his pockets. "I would know. Common horse sense. Just 'cause you made me retire doesn't mean I've forgotten everything I ever knew."

Only most of it. Intermittently. "Let's get settled in first."

"I am settled. Been here a week."

Carol looped her arm through Sam's. "Why don't we walk to the pond and check out that flock of geese that flew over this morning? They passed so quickly we didn't get to count them." She led him toward the door, looking over her shoulder with what Wyatt assumed was supposed to be a reassuring expression.

"Don't let him out of your sight again."

"No, sir. I won't."

Frustration, helplessness and sadness twisted like a corkscrew deep in Wyatt's chest. Over the past two years Sam had been fading away right before his eyes, and none of the specialists Wyatt had consulted could do a damn thing about it. Neither the medications nor the supplements seemed to help much. But he'd be damned if he'd give up without a fight. He owed Sam that much.

Six

Hannah had sixty days to work a miracle.

Panic welled inside her as she studied the new mare. Would that be enough time to change Wyatt's mind?

Sipping her coffee, she sagged against the fence post at her back, stretched her legs out into the grass and watched the birds flying above the tree line.

The mare tossed her head and snorted, looking beyond Hannah's shoulder, then she galloped a few yards away and circled back, pausing with her nostrils flaring and muscles twitching, ready to flee.

"What's wrong, girl?"

"She's afraid of men," an unfamiliar male voice said from behind Hannah, startling her. She twisted abruptly, spooking the horse even more, then slowly rose to face the stranger. He wore jeans, a flannel shirt and down coat even though the sun had long since chased away the morning chill.

"Can I help you?"

"Just inspecting the pastures. My guess is a man is responsible for the bay's scars." He nodded toward the mare.

"You'd be right." Who was he? A prospective Sutherland client? Someone interested in observing FYC's morning session? Or maybe an agent verifying the abuse report she'd filed? After dusting off her hands she reached across the fence. "I'm Hannah Sutherland. And you are…?"

"Sam Reynolds. A little bacon grease will help those fetlocks heal faster."

An old-school remedy, but modern science was her thing. "I'll keep that in mind. Did someone from the office send you to find me?"

"Nope. Found you on my own. Who's in charge of the mare's wound care?"

"I am."

He grabbed the top rail and hoisted himself over the fence. He wasn't frail, but he had the shrunken look older people sometimes got when their lives became sedentary. She saw a lot of that in the newcomers who joined FYC. He wobbled a little at the top.

She moved forward in case he slipped. "Mr. Reynolds, I'd prefer you stay out of the pasture."

"Don't worry, missy. I know what I'm doing." He strode toward the horse surely, rapidly, scaring her farther away, then he stopped.

Apparently not. He was upsetting the mare. "Sir, please leave the pasture."

Hands relaxed by his side, he faced Hannah, turning his back on the animal. "Give her a chance to get to know me."

The horse quivered, attention riveted on her new visitor.

Hannah kept a wary eye on the mare who'd revealed a few bad habits once she'd gotten over the shock of being relocated. The mare's ears twitched forward instead of back like an angry animal intent on inflicting injury. Nose outstretched, she gingerly approached the interloper.

Hannah's breath caught as the mare leaned in for a sniff. "Be careful. She bites."

"You should be working her in a round pen. She has too much room to avoid you here. And sit on the top rail not on the ground. Shows her who's boss without you lifting a finger."

Still ignoring the horse, he paced several yards to the right. The mare trailed him, then he returned to Hannah's side. Again, after a brief hesitation, the horse followed.

Surprised, Hannah could only watch. "I've tried the Horse Whisperer method on her, but it hasn't worked before now."

"I've always had the touch."

"No kidding. Okay, I admit it. I'm impressed at how easily you snagged the mare's attention and cooperation."

He pivoted abruptly. When the animal didn't race off he rewarded her by offering his palm, then rubbing her forehead and scratching beneath her ears—something she hadn't allowed Hannah to do. "Good girl," he addressed his new friend, then angled his head toward Hannah. "It's all in your body language. If you're wary of her, she'll be wary of you."

"I'm aware of that, Mr. Reynolds. I have some experience with horses, but I still think getting you out of harm's way is a good idea."

He patted the mare's neck and raked his fingers through her matted mane. "I've missed this."

"Missed what?"

Before he could reply, a car crested a hill in the driveway at a high rate of speed. The idiot driver was going to get someone hurt. Hannah kicked into action mode, putting herself between Sam and the horse. The sedan's tires locked and skidded to a halt.

A woman threw open the door and sprang from the driver's seat. The mare bolted to the far side of the enclosure.

"Sam, you can*not* keep wandering off."

Who was this woman advancing on them in near hysteria?

Sam shook his head. "I wasn't wandering. I knew where I

was going. Now look what you've done. I'd just begun to win the bay's trust. Now I'll have to start over."

"Get in the car," the woman ordered, pointing at the vehicle. "Mr. Jacobs will be furious if he finds out you escaped again."

Escaped? Mr. Jacobs? This guy knew Wyatt? "I'm Hannah Sutherland. Could you please explain what's going on?"

The harassed woman parked her hands on her hips. "I'm Carol Dillard. Sam—Mr. Reynolds is not supposed to leave the house without me. Mr. Jacobs specifically ordered me to keep Sam away from the barns."

"I'm not at the barn," Sam added logically.

Hannah focused on the woman. "But Sam likes horses and he's good with them."

The older woman frowned. "Sam is under my care."

"You're a doctor?"

"No. I'm his nurse. He suffers from Alzheimer's."

Understanding dawned, but the diagnosis only led to more questions. "Sam lives with Wyatt?"

"Stop talking about me like I'm not here. Wyatt is my stepson. He worries because I'm a little forgetful sometimes."

Wyatt took care of his stepfather. Imagine that. The jerk might have a shred of decency in him after all. "Are you the one who used to own a thoroughbred farm?"

"I am."

"Wyatt's mentioned you. You should get him to bring you to the stables. If he saw how easily you worked that mare, he wouldn't keep you away. You made more progress with her in two minutes than I have in a week."

Sam smiled. "I'll do that."

Carol tsked and shook her head. "Good luck with that. Now get in the car, Sam, and let's get back to the house before Wyatt calls to check on us."

That caught Hannah's attention. She'd been dreading and anticipating a possible visit and another demand for a tour from the new boss since the first one had been postponed. "Wyatt's not home?"

"He had to fly to the distillery on business this morning."

That meant he probably wouldn't oversee today's riding classes. If she couldn't get him to observe, then how could she win him over?

Sam hoisted a foot to the bottom fence rail, pausing to look over his shoulder at Hannah. "Thank you for your company, Hannah. Meeting you was truly a pleasure."

"You, too, Sam. Bring Wyatt with you next time."

Hannah's skin tingled the way it did when she suddenly thought of a mare-stud genetic combination that couldn't help but produce a contender. She'd found Wyatt's weakness, or more precisely, Sam had found her. And like her übercompetitive cousin, Hannah would have to find a way to use the new knowledge to her advantage.

"Sam, do you ride?" she called as he approached the car.

A sad smile stretched his mouth. "I used to. Before I retired. Haven't been near a horse before today since..." He scratched his head, suddenly looking flustered. "I can't remember. I used to work with horses back in...back when I had a horse farm and a life." His shoulders drooped.

Hannah's heart tugged. "It's okay, Sam. I'll get the details later. And you still have a life. It's just a different one."

She saw a chance to benefit herself and Sam, but especially FYC. She turned her attention to the nurse. "We run a therapeutic riding school on Sundays. Our roster is full, but I'm sure I could pull some strings and get Sam a slot by next week. Why don't you bring him down for a ride?"

"I'll mention your suggestion to Mr. Jacobs, but I don't expect he'll approve. He's overly protective of Sam."

That meant Hannah would have to confront the very man she'd been trying to avoid, the man whose kisses knocked her out of the saddle. "I'll talk to Wyatt."

When she helped his stepfather, she'd not only prove her point about FYC's value, she'd win over Wyatt and at least part of her problems would be solved.

* * *

Anticipation Wyatt should not be experiencing coursed through his veins along with a strong dose of suspicion as he stood on Hannah's front porch.

Why had Hannah invited him to dinner? Had she decided to accept his offer and sell him the property or would the evening yield yet another attempt to milk something from him?

The door opened, revealing his hostess in a peach-colored sweater that clung to her breasts and a black skirt that displayed her long legs to lust-inducing advantage.

Not lust. Approval. There was no room for lust in business.

A tight smile flitted across her lips. "Wyatt, thanks for coming."

Wyatt forced his eyes to her face. She'd done something to her blue eyes that gave them a sleepy, sultry look that he couldn't help but appreciate. Her hair lay like a shiny curtain over her shoulders and breasts, the thick chocolate strands glistening in the overhead light—a far cry from her usual windblown appearance, and try as he might, he couldn't dam the rising tide of his libido.

Life had taught him time and time again that women used their beauty as weapons of coercion. Hannah had to be up to something. The question was what?

"Is there a reason we couldn't have had this conversation in my office?" Where he could have kept the desk between them.

"I thought it would be more relaxing to talk away from work."

The slightly husky timbre of her voice slid over him as smooth and thick as sourwood honey, reminding him of lazy mornings after a vigorous night of sweaty sex. "About?"

Her gaze slid away. "The farm. What else? Come in. Dinner's ready."

He followed her through the living room, his gaze involuntarily drawn to her rear in the snug skirt, then his eyes traveled down her legs to her low, open-backed heels. Nice. Seductive in a rich-girl-next-door kind of way. She hadn't gone for the blatant hard-sell look.

Then he spotted the candles flickering in the middle of the dining room table lending an intimacy to what should be a business dinner and corrected his assessment. "What's going on, Hannah?"

She followed his gaze to the candlelit trap. "I don't cook often and when I do I like to enjoy the effort. Would you pour the wine while I get the food?"

She disappeared through an archway without waiting for an answer. Whatever game she was playing, she'd reveal her hand soon enough.

He lifted the open bottle and studied the label—an award-winning Riesling that sold for hundreds of dollars at auction. After filling the crystal goblets, he scanned what he could see of the cottage. On his first visit he'd been more focused on the financials than decor and then that kiss had blown his observation skills to hell.

This time he noticed the antiques—not reproductions—filling the rooms. Translation: expensive furniture. Like the wine, the BMW Z4 in her driveway, the diamonds in her ears, the watch on her wrist and the crystal on the table. Hannah Sutherland enjoyed the finer things in life—things she shouldn't be able to afford on her salary. That meant she depended on someone else's deep pockets to keep her in the manner to which she'd become accustomed. Her father? A lover? The latter thought kinked the muscles between his shoulder blades.

She returned and set two china plates on the table. "I hope you're hungry. Please take a seat."

He automatically pulled out her chair—some habits were hard to break. Satiny strands of her hair caressed his knuckles, sending a ripple of awareness through him. Her floral perfume—minus the eau de barn additive—mingled with the roasted pork in his nostrils, stirring a hunger that had little to do with dinner. He stepped away and took his seat across from her.

"You have expensive tastes in wine. A gift from an admirer?"

"You could say that. One of our German clients owns the winery. Our association made him very happy, and he sent a few cases of his best vintages as a thank-you gift."

Something about the private smile teasing her lips irritated him like a whining mosquito. His fingers tightened around his utensils. "Was he your lover?"

"Heavens, no." Her surprise seemed too genuine to be faked, but then most women were accomplished actresses. "But we made a beautiful baby together—with his mare and Sutherland's stud. I was engaged at the time."

"*Was* engaged?"

She studied her glass then took a sip, savoring the Riesling slowly—the way she did everything, he'd learned.

Everything?

He derailed the sexual thought, but not before his groin pulsed to life.

"The relationship didn't work out."

"Why?"

She took a bite of asparagus then chewed, swallowed. "Does this fall into the none-of-your-business category or the tell-me-or-you're-fired column?"

"Do you have something to hide?"

Seconds ticked past while she toyed with her food. "My father loved Robert. I didn't. Not enough, anyway."

"Shouldn't you have realized that before you became engaged?"

"Probably. But on paper he seemed like the perfect match."

"On paper? Did you run a financial report on the guy?"

"I didn't need to. Our families had known each other forever. We shared the same background and interests."

"You mean he had money."

Her perfectly arched eyebrows dipped. "Of course he had money. That means I knew he wasn't marrying me for mine."

"Are you wealthy—in your own right?" If she had money stashed elsewhere, he might have more trouble getting rid of her than he'd expected.

"Not that it's any of your business, but no. However, at the time, everyone thought I'd eventually be the owner of Sutherland Farm, which I once believed to be priceless." She shifted in her seat. "Please eat before it gets cold. Nellie managed to teach me a few kitchen tricks. I'm not in her league, although it's safe to say I *probably* won't poison you."

Her teasing smile blindsided him, and an odd feeling invaded his stomach.

Hunger. For food. Nothing more.

But he couldn't deny that despite everything he knew about Hannah, she had somehow managed to derail his usual detachment. She cut a piece of meat, swirled it in the peach salsa and lifted it to her mouth. The sheer eroticism of her lips slowly and deliberately closing around the flatware sent another unwelcome bout of lust rolling over him like a runaway whiskey barrel.

Imagining the slide of the sterling silver tines across her tongue and lips sent his blood sluicing through his veins. He envied that fork, and, as ill-advised and illogical as it might be, the sample he'd had of her mouth had left him craving something more substantial. He wanted to know her taste and texture, and that desire had acted like a parasite gnawing away at him even when he'd been out of town working at the distillery.

What had she done to him? He'd never had a woman get between him and business before. He had to get back on track and out of dangerous territory. Her property was the only reason he'd accepted her invitation tonight.

"Have you considered my offer?"

"I won't deny I've thought about it."

"And?"

She shrugged one shoulder. “Could we save business for later? I’d prefer not to ruin a good meal. Besides, this is practice for you. Remember? I told you that you had a lot to learn about this business? We wine and dine our clients before closing the big deals. It’s a courtesy to let them eat in peace before twisting the thumbscrews during after-dinner coffee.”

“Are you skilled at twisting the screws?”

“Let’s just say my father made sure I knew my role.”

He didn’t need anyone telling him how to run his business, but he’d abide by her rules—this time—only because he wanted her guard down. He took out his frustration on a piece of pork, pulverizing the tender morsel between his molars.

Candlelight glimmered on Hannah’s hair and turned her skin luminescent. Her perfume teased his senses and raised his blood pressure. He needed a distraction.

“What’s the status on the new mare?”

“She’s coming along. You should stop by and see her. After days of getting nowhere, Sa—we made progress today. But if you’re asking whether I’m going to euthanize her, then the answer is no. All of the tests have come back negative. Other than the superficial wounds, she’s healthy.”

Her lips curved around the rim of the wineglass and he found it hard to swallow. Those secret smiles of hers were something else. He found himself wanting to probe the cause. This crazy obsession with Hannah Sutherland was an aggravation he didn’t need. A temporary aberration.

How had she managed to hijack his concentration? She wasn’t the most beautiful woman he’d ever met, wasn’t the sexiest and certainly wasn’t the most amenable. In fact, she might be the most argumentative. Regardless, something about her had snagged his attention.

Something besides a piece of property that put a doughnut hole in his land and devalued the farm. Something besides her faux Miss Goody Two-shoes attitude. He just couldn’t put his finger on what it was about her that didn’t add up. Yet. But he would.

His rampant hormones couldn't be anything more than a natural response to prolonged abstinence. He'd had a rough few months since his realization that Sam was a danger to himself. The subsequent frantic search for doctors who had provided frustratingly few answers had led to the decision to take responsibility for Sam and the breakup with Lana. Add in the preparation for launching the new ad campaign as well as the property search and Wyatt hadn't had any time for even the most casual encounters.

He was paying for that now with inappropriate thoughts about an employee. But soon she'd be out of the picture and life would return to normal. The sooner, the better.

"Have you looked at any properties?"

"It's only been a few days since you issued your ultimatum. I haven't had time."

Frustrated, he swirled his wine in his glass and inhaled, trying to appreciate the tart green-apple bouquet. Trying and failing. "Do you collect antiques?"

She followed his glance around the room. "Not intentionally. My grandparents started their marriage with what they called hand-me-downs from their families. When they could afford to add pieces they scavenged yard sales—yard sales they often took me to—for items that matched what they already had. This was all here when I moved in after vet school."

"The contents belong to you?" Tens of thousands of dollars worth of furniture—he could thank his greedy mother for his ability to assess value.

She nodded. "I guess you could say the furniture—like this farm—is my family history."

"You can't be ignorant of the value."

She frowned. "I've never thought about it other than the sentimental value."

He didn't believe that for a second. "And the BMW? Did you inherit that, too?"

She stiffened. "Where are you going with this, Wyatt?"

"You live beyond your salary."

"You're determined to think the worst of me, aren't you? The car was a gift from my father, a reward for a record-breaking year last year. It's totally impractical, but I won't deny it's fun to drive.

"It's a long commute to your distillery from here. Too far to drive every day. Why buy a place so far from work? There are beautiful properties closer to Asheville."

She'd done her research. But his reasons for his purchase were none of her business. "I've told you before. The property suited my needs."

"Your sudden burning need to own a horse farm? Neither the staff nor I are buying that since you have nothing to do with the horses. You haven't finished your tour and you never visit the barns."

"Sutherland Farm has a competent management team. Would you prefer I become more active in the day-to-day operation?"

"No. As you said, the staff knows what they're doing."

He pushed his empty plate aside and leaned back in his chair. "What is this evening really about, Hannah?"

Annoyance flashed across her face. She slid away from the table and rose. "You really fail at this setting-the-mood thing. Bring your wine to the living room. I have something to show you."

Setting the mood for what?

Leaving his wine behind because he needed a clear head around her, he followed her to the den, arriving in time to see her bend over the coffee table. The action made her shirt gape, revealing a tempting glimpse of her pale breasts and the white lacy edge of her bra. Wyatt acknowledged his appreciation even while he admitted the move was probably calculated to entice his cooperation.

She sank onto the sofa and her skirt slid up her bare thighs. No stockings concealed her smooth, creamy flesh. She pulled a thick book onto her lap then patted the cushion beside her. "Sit. Please."

The determination in her eyes didn't fit the capitulation he'd expected from her. "Are you going to sell me your land?"

Her eyebrows arched upward. "Your impatience is showing again. You're going to have to improve on that before we have international visitors. They'll be offended by your get-to-the-point methods. Try a little finesse. Ease into the discussions. But to answer your question, no, I haven't decided to sell. I'm still exploring my options."

"If you're hoping for a better deal you won't get one. The price I offered is more than generous, and you can't sell the property to anyone else without giving me an opportunity to match their bid."

"I'm not planning to sell to someone else."

"Then why am I here, Hannah?"

She gave him a patient look. "I'm getting to that."

Gritting his teeth in irritation, he decided to let her play out her hand. Opponents' strategies always revealed more than they suspected about their strengths and weaknesses. He sat. Hannah's scent filled his lungs and the warmth of her body drew him like a magnet.

"This is FYC's story." Her breath fanned his cheek as she leaned closer.

Finally, the motive for the sexy clothing, the wine and dinner became clear. Batter up. Sales pitch coming over the plate. "I don't need to know FYC's story."

"Actually, you do. We have a visitor from Dubai coming soon. He's interested in setting up a similar program."

"I'm not going to promote something I don't believe in."

"You will believe if you just open your eyes and your mind."

"And my wallet."

Flashing him an exasperated look, she spread the large photo album across their laps. Her fingertips made contact with his thigh, sending desire charging through his veins, hot and heavy and drugging.

Her breath caught and her widened gaze found his, telling

him she'd experienced the same jolt. Or she faked her response well. On second thought, she couldn't fake those flushed cheeks and dilated pupils.

Their last kiss in this very room consumed his thoughts. He instantly recalled the feel of her, taste of her, heat and softness of her and he wanted more. His eyes dropped to her mouth. She licked her lush bottom lip—a clear invitation.

He should have known. His experience had proven that women used sex to get what they wanted. Marlie had used sex to get extra care for her horse when she couldn't be at the stable. At seventeen Wyatt had been too naive to recognize the tactic. But by the time Lana had come along fifteen years later and used her wiles to convince him to buy her expensive trinkets and trips, he'd gained enough insight to know exactly what she was doing and he'd given in only when it suited him. He hadn't loved Lana any more than she'd loved him, but she would have been a good asset to his career, a capable and well-connected hostess. That was the only reason he'd allowed her to move into the penthouse.

Hannah had pulled out every element of a good seduction for tonight. Legs, cleavage, candlelight, good food and wine. The question was how far was she willing to go for her horses? And how far was he willing to step beyond his personal code of ethics? It would serve her right if he used her the way she was trying to use him, and then turfed her on her pretty little butt at the first opportunity.

"Is this what you're after, Hannah?"

He speared his fingers through her silky hair and cupped her nape, then yanked her forward and covered her mouth with his. He wasted no time with preliminary get-to-know-you pecks and instead plunged into her mouth.

Slick, hot, sweet and moist, he stroked his tongue along hers. Damn she tasted good, better than he remembered. The stiffness drained from her spine. She leaned into him and kissed him back. His heart slammed approval against his ribs, banging hard enough she could probably feel it against her breast.

Her hands lifted to clutch his forearms, as if she were going to push him away. A moment later, she caressed upward past his elbows, over his biceps and shoulders, leaving a trail of cauterized nerve endings in their wake.

She tilted her head, allowing him better access, and despite the warning bells clanging in his subconscious, he snaked an arm around her waist and pulled her closer, snugging her hot body to his. Instead of teaching her a lesson, the soft crush of her breast pressing his chest and her thigh burning the length of his taught him one.

He wanted her. Ethics be damned.

She felt good against him. Hunger consumed him, making him delve deeper, hold tighter, crave more. Her short nails lightly scored the back of his neck, and a shiver of need racked him.

A thud on the floor vaguely penetrated his subconscious, but Hannah flinched. "Ouch."

Casting a wide-eyed, wary glance at him, she bent and rubbed her foot, then picked up the photo album and clutched it to her chest like a shield. The flush of desire drained from her cheeks, leaving her pale and biting her bottom lip.

"That—that shouldn't have happened."

"Don't play innocent, Hannah. Seducing me into funding your horse operation was your game plan tonight."

Gaping, she bolted to her feet, dropped the book on the table and fisted her hands at her sides. "I didn't invite you here to seduce you, you egotistical jerk. I'd be lying if I didn't admit I need you to continue funding FYC, but the real reason I invited you here tonight was because I wanted to talk about Sam."

Every cell of Wyatt's being snapped to attention. His body went from hot and aroused to cool and on guard in an instant. "What about Sam?"

"*He's* good company, and *his* understanding of horses is impressive."

Wyatt ignored the insults and focused on the more critical issue. "I take it Nellie has been talking."

He'd have to fire the best housekeeper/cook he'd ever had—yet another reason he found himself eager to return to the farm every weekend. That woman could cook. And Sam liked her.

Hannah narrowed her eyes in disgust, and anger vibrated through her. "You should know better than that. You won't find a more loyal employee than Nellie. She keeps confidential information to herself. What happens in that house stays in that house."

"Then how do you know about Sam?"

Her gaze lowered. "I met him."

"When and where?" He'd ordered Carol to keep Sam away from the barns. If she'd defied him, she'd be gone.

"He was out walking Sunday morning. I was in the pasture, and…we met." She shrugged and reached for her wineglass. Her fingers curled around the stem, then stroked up, down, up. Nervous gesture, or intentionally seductive?

Despite his anger, his blood headed south. Did she have any idea how alluring the gesture was? Of course she did. Hannah might be stubborn, but from what he'd seen, she wasn't stupid. Except fiscally.

"Sam's exactly the kind of person who benefits most from our therapeutic riding program."

Her statement dashed ice water over his distraction. He would have to be especially careful about keeping her away from Sam. A woman with her skills could lure an unsuspecting old man down the wrong road.

"You're an animal doctor, not a people doctor. Leave Sam's care to the specialists who know what they're doing."

"Maybe you're seeing the wrong doctors," she retorted.

"I've hired the best in the business."

"Apparently not, or you'd have Sam physically involved in something he cares about greatly." She crossed to a desk in the corner, then returned with a sheaf of papers and stabbed them in his direction. "I printed these out for you. Read what the enlightened professionals have to say. Engaging in physical activity improves mental acuity and coordination. If you really care about Sam and want to help him, then you'll bring him to our riding class Sunday."

"You have the disposition of a leaky faucet. Do you plan to erode my resistance with persistent nagging? We've already covered this ground."

"We haven't even begun to scrape the surface. Read the documentation. Unless you're afraid I'm right. And you're wrong."

He yanked the papers from her hand. He might even glance through them while he was stuck on the plane tomorrow—just so he could discredit her research.

"Wyatt, when I invited you to observe the class before, it was with the abstract notion that you might have a crumb of human decency and compassion for others who are less fortunate somewhere inside your calculator heart. Now that I've met your stepfather, I know Find Your Center can touch *you* personally and change *your* life for the better by improving Sam's. This isn't about you generously helping others any more, Wyatt. This is about helping yourself. Looking out for number one—something at which I'm sure you excel. Sam and FYC will just happen to benefit in the process."

Anger and frustration volcanoed through him. He couldn't believe she'd stoop so low as to use Sam for her own self-interest and accuse *him* of being selfish. He shot to his feet. "Don't try to cloak your agenda behind a feigned desire to help Sam. Mind your own business."

"Find Your Center is my business. It's also yours."

"It's not profitable, and, like any other wasteful expense, it will be cut from the budget."

"You bottom-line thinkers are all alike. You're too blinded by numbers to see that sometimes there's a greater reward than profit."

"This from a woman who lives beyond her means?"

She rolled her eyes. "I have been very fortunate, but I work hard. I don't demand or expect any concessions because I'm the—I *was* the boss's daughter."

"I've seen no evidence of that."

"Give me a chance and you will." Concern replaced the fire in her eyes. "Forget your prejudices and the money for a minute, if you can, and tell me about Sam. He seemed very cognizant when we spoke, and in a span of two minutes he made more progress with the new mare than my trainers and I have made since she arrived."

That was the old Sam. The new one couldn't be trusted not to put himself in jeopardy—a point he'd proven with near disastrous results. Watching his decline helplessly from the sidelines these past few years had to be the most frustrating challenge Wyatt had ever faced. It was one of the reasons he hadn't intended visiting the farm often once he had Sam installed. He couldn't bear to watch.

"Sam has good days and bad. You caught him on a good one. Keep him off the horses."

"Why?"

"He might get hurt."

"I told you we take every precaution to—"

"No riding."

"Wyatt, Sam isn't a cask of whiskey that you can stash in storage and expect him to improve with age. Quality of life is important. Don't take away something he cares so much about. He has an affinity with horses that he should be allowed to pursue. He needs to feel useful. If you want to slow his decline you have to challenge him and keep him mentally and physically engaged. Let him participate in the class."

Her eyes narrowed, then she cocked her head and studied him the way she had the mare's infected wounds. "Maybe you don't want him to get better. Perhaps his decline benefits you and strengthens your role in the company."

Fury boiled inside him at her implication. "I am paying a

damned fortune to protect Sam and keep him comfortable. I am not holding him back."

His voice sounded more growl than human. Anyone who knew him would back off. Not Hannah. She threw back her shoulders. But it would take more than great breasts to distract him.

"And yet you're still losing him. How much worse can it get?"

"You have no idea what you're talking about. You haven't heard the doctors' prognoses or watched Sam fade away right before your eyes."

Compassion softened her face. "No, I haven't witnessed Sam's decline. But I've seen the magic happen for people worse off than Sam. I've seen hope restored to a lot of defeated faces—faces like yours. And Sam's. Riding may not be a cure, but it does buy time in a positive, enjoyable way. Give FYC a chance to work a miracle. For Sam. For you."

Rage against the situation and his helplessness surged through him. He wanted to punch something. He clenched his fists so hard the skin around his knuckles felt as if it would split. He didn't know how much time Sam had left, but he wasn't going to shorten it by letting his stepfather take unnecessary risks.

"I've told you before, I don't believe in miracles. Stay away from Sam."

"But—"

"He's too fragile and unsteady to get on the back of a horse."

"As I've explained, his balance and muscle tone will improve if—"

"I repeat, Sam is not riding. That is not negotiable. Find your new stable and get the hell out of my life."

He turned on his heel and left before he did something to relieve the tangle of volatile emotions she stirred in him. Something like yanking that lithe body of hers close and kissing her manipulative mouth to silence her. But if he did any of those things he wasn't sure he'd be able to stop at kisses.

Without a doubt, he'd end up doing something both of them would regret.

Seven

Jeb blasted through the lab door Monday a little before noon, jerking Hannah from her mental meanderings about a second kiss that should never have happened. And how dare Wyatt accuse her of using sex to sway him anyway.

"There's some old guy in the field with the bay mare. He says his name is Sam and he claims he has your permission to be there."

Hannah's heart jumped. She dropped the packaging tape on the work bench. If Sam got hurt by one of her horses, Wyatt would shut her down with no questions asked. "Sam is Wyatt's stepfather. He lives in the main house. I'll take care of him. Could you finish packaging this last shipment for me? The courier is due in ten minutes."

"Sure."

As soon as Jeb nodded she raced past him and sprinted toward the field. Not wanting to spook the mare she slowed as she neared the pasture and tried to catch her breath. Running wasn't her thing. She'd bet Wyatt ran if the lack of fat on his rock-hard body was any indication. There hadn't been anything soft or flabby about him Friday night.

Sam's nurse stood outside the fence frantically calling, "Sam get out of there."

Sam squatted in a traditional farrier's stance beside the mare's powerful hind quarters. He held a hoof in his hands, but this mare didn't need shoeing. A fist of dread clenched in Hannah's stomach. One sharp, well-placed kick could prove disastrous. "What are you doing, Sam?"

"I brought bacon grease for these fetlocks. Nellie was nice enough to provide it."

She groaned. "Nellie's in on this?"

Beside her Carol nodded. "She said something about letting Sam do a little 'horse healing.' What is that?"

Without taking her eyes off Sam, Hannah replied, "Horse healing is when you need the therapy of talking to somebody who'll listen without a bunch of backchat or judgment, someone who appreciates everything you do. Around here that *somebody* is usually a horse."

"That's crazy."

"It beats paying a therapist hundreds of dollars an hour when all you need is a good listener. Does Wyatt know you brought Sam down here?"

"I didn't bring Sam. He snuck out the door after breakfast. The wily ol' coot is always looking for an escape. When I ordered him to stop, he ignored me. I guess from now on I'll have to keep him locked in his room even at mealtimes."

Shocked, Hannah shot a quick glance at Sam, making sure he couldn't overhear. "Wyatt keeps Sam locked in? Why?"

"He claims Sam's a danger to himself so he installed dead bolts on the suite doors to keep Sam from wandering."

"Is Sam suicidal?"

"No. But there was a near-accident at the last residence. I'm not privy to the details. All I know is that close call got the last nurse fired, and it's one of the reasons Mr. Jacobs is a tad overvigilant."

"You call dead bolts on the bedroom door a *tad* overvigilant? What if there's a fire? Is there any health reason why Sam shouldn't get outside? Other than what looks like mild Alzheimer's."

"None. He's in decent shape for a man of seventy. I'm allowed to take him on walks but not near the barns. However, if Mr. Jacobs hears about this escapade, even that'll change."

"Sam, I'm coming in." Hannah climbed the fence and cautiously moved toward the mare and man. "You know Wyatt doesn't want you near the horses."

"Horses are my life…or they used to be back when I had a life."

She winced in sympathy. "He's worried about you getting hurt."

"I'd rather be dead than incarcerated."

The sincerity in his tone sent alarm jolting through her. She didn't know him well enough to know if he was serious. "You don't mean that."

"I do. Wyatt flies off to work—at the company I started, mind you—and leaves me at home to do puzzles like a school boy. I don't want to live like that."

She hated playing devil's advocate for the jerk, but she didn't want Sam upset. "Puzzles are supposed to exercise your brain."

"My brain isn't all that needs exercising. I need to keep the old ticker pumping. Puzzles put me to sleep."

"I could try talking to Wyatt again…"

But after Friday night's kiss, she wasn't sure she wanted to go anywhere near the man. She'd been tossing and turning each night, restless and itchy and needy and furious, reliving the kiss and cursing his effect on her, even though he thought the worst of her. Thoughts of him had invaded the sanctuary of her lab. She'd been disgustingly inefficient and clumsy.

Until recently she'd been satisfied with her celibate life. Why did Wyatt Jacobs, of all people, have to upset her contentment? She'd thought she had better taste in men, but apparently not. She got hot and bothered over a hunky package with no soul or personality.

"Sam, I'll get your nurse to talk to him, too, but—"

"Carol. Her name's Carol. Some days I don't remember. Today I do. Today I remember a lot of things." He seemed quite proud of the fact. The mare irritably twitched her tail and ears. "Let me finish here before this lady loses patience."

Hannah gripped the horse's halter while he worked and searched for a solution for Sam's predicament—one that could benefit them all.

Sam finished his task and straightened, then wiped his greasy hands on the rag he had tucked into his waistband.

"Mixed a little sulfur in there. That'll fix 'er right up." He tucked the rag through his belt loop.

"Dare I ask where you found sulfur?"

"Garden shed. Passed it the other day when Carol and I were walking."

Sam had thought this out sequentially and planned ahead, Hannah realized, so he wasn't mentally in too bad a shape. She'd seen worse cases in the FYC client roster, and she'd seen those clients improve. Sam would, too. "We'll give your remedy a try."

"Don't care how much pharmaceutical companies spend on product development, sometimes the old ways are the best. She'll be healed by the end of the week. What's her name?"

Hannah blinked in surprise. "I don't know. I haven't received the paperwork on her yet."

"Then I'll call her Phoenix. She's going to come back and be a fine horse. She has spunk and she's smart."

Hannah marveled that the usually skittish animal stayed close, as if wanting more of Sam's attention. "I agree with the spunky part. She's been a handful for us. I'm not sure about her intelligence yet—unless she's been outsmarting us to get out of exercising."

"Let's take her to the round pen and work out some of her excess energy. I'll need a lunge line."

Objections danced on Hannah's tongue.

"She needs to work out as much as I do," Sam insisted before she could protest. "Neither of us is ready to be put out to pasture."

Another band of sympathy squeezed her chest. "Wyatt—"

"Is in Asheville. Won't be back until Friday."

Torn between wanting to help Sam and not wanting to upset Wyatt, she chewed the inside of her lip. If she let Sam spend time with the horse, she'd get in trouble. But how could she send him back to a life he considered worse than death? She'd have to talk to Wyatt about that. One of her high school friends had threatened suicide and everyone had ignored Terri's cries for help—until it was too late.

Hannah knew she couldn't take the risk with Sam. But she still had reservations. Big ones. "Sam, Carol and I could get fired if we let you have your way."

"I'm not gonna tattle. Are you? Besides, the boy told me to stay away from the barn. He didn't say anything about the pens or pastures." Mischief glimmered in the faded blue eyes.

Hannah's lips twitched as she fought a smile. The mare wasn't the only one with spunk. And Sam was right. Wyatt had only forbidden her to let Sam ride. He hadn't said anything about letting Sam lunge a horse.

Semantics. You're looking for trouble, Hannah.

Against her better judgment, she ignored the warning. Maintaining that keen spark of excitement in Sam's eyes took forefront. Normally, the odds of keeping a secret on a farm like Sutherland where the employees were as close-knit as family were slim. But Wyatt never interacted with the staff.

She turned to Carol. "Is Sam this alert and happy at the house?"

The woman shook her head. "I've seen a side of him today that I've not seen before. It's a definite improvement."

That settled it. Hannah had never been a rule-breaker or one to push boundaries before. That had been her cousin's forte.

But this time Hannah had too much to lose by not taking a risk. Sam needed to have a sense of purpose and she could provide it.

"Sam, I'll let you rope me in on this escapade of yours on two conditions."

"Name 'em."

"One, you promise not to sneak out of the house and come down here by yourself anymore. That's really dangerous, Sam. If you're going to be around the horses, I want someone with you who's familiar with their behavior—that means me, not Carol." She wasn't about to let anyone else risk their job.

He rocked onto the balls of his feet with excitement. "Agreed. Next?"

"No riding."

"But—"

"Wyatt forbid me to allow you to get on a horse. I won't go against a direct order from the boss. We're already stretching things."

His shoulders sank. "If you insist."

"I do. I'll go get a line. Meet me and Phoenix at the round pen."

"Are you crazy?" Carol protested as they joined her at the fence. "Wyatt will be livid."

"Sam needs a little mental and physical stimulation. I'm going to provide it in the safest way possible. And apparently this crotchety mare has taken a liking to Sam. I'm trained to work with people with disabilities, and I'll take full responsibility if Wyatt finds out."

"It's on your head."

"Understood and accepted."

"But for what it's worth, I think you're on the right track."

Once Wyatt had irrefutable evidence in front of him of how much Find Your Center could help Sam, he wouldn't be able to deny the benefits of FYC or the funding, and maybe he'd quit trying to run her out of her home.

* * *

A black-and-gold helicopter buzzed the pasture, barely missing the treetops. Hannah ducked. The horses scattered as the craft hovered momentarily over the main barn before moving on.

Crazy pilot. What is he thinking?

"Does that happen often?" the client beside her asked in his sexy French-accented voice.

"It's a first. Our guests usually land at the airport and come over by chauffeur-driven car as you did."

She kept her eyes on the chopper. If he'd flown over the property two hours ago when Sam had been in the pen with Phoenix and the junior dressage students had been circling the outdoor riding ring, it could have proven disastrous.

"He appears to be landing on the front lawn," her client added.

"That's odd." Who would be crazy enough to—

Wyatt.

Her stomach took a nosedive and her heart kicked into overdrive. Wyatt wasn't due to arrive for two days. Why would he cut his trip short and come home early—via chopper, no less—unless he'd found out about her working with Sam behind his back?

She tried to conceal her rising anxiety and focus on business. "Franco, what do you think of these two?"

"Your cousin's faith in you is well-founded. Both the mare and gelding are good choices. Stacy and Natalie will love them. In a few years I'll come back for a mount for my son. At two Theo's too young for anything more than a docile pony."

"I'll look forward to your return." She hoped she'd still be employed here. "Please keep me posted on how this pair works out. Let me escort you to the business office where April can assist you with the paperwork and make the arrangements to transport your surprise gifts home."

They climbed into one of the luxurious golf carts and headed for the business office. A black Mercedes met her on the driveway outside the building. Wyatt's car. For a few heart pounding moments the vehicles faced off like gunslingers in the street. Bracing herself for a confrontation, Hannah exhaled shakily and pulled into the designated space before swinging from the cart on unsteady legs.

Wyatt parked beside her then exited his vehicle and stalked toward them bearing an I-own-the-world swagger and a custom-made black suit. He looked delicious. Hannah pushed her unwelcome appreciation aside and swallowed the lump rising in her throat.

The last thing she needed was a scene in front of a customer—a customer preparing to write a very big check. "Franco, I'd like you to meet Wyatt Jacobs, the new owner of Sutherland Farm. Wyatt, this is Franco Constantine, CEO of Midas Chocolates and Constantine Holdings. He's flown over from Monaco to purchase horses for his wife and daughter."

She couldn't help making comparisons while the men shook hands and exchanged pleasantries. Both were tall, dark and handsome, but while Franco's eyes were a startling blue Wyatt's were fathomless. And Franco's proximity didn't make her pulse stampede—a good thing since he was happily married. But she could see why her cousin found French men appealing.

Wyatt's gaze homed in on her, making her insides quiver. "Hannah, a moment, please."

Phrased nicely in his deep send-shivers-down-her-spine voice, but she didn't miss the steel behind the request. Her euphoria over closing a two-million-dollar deal evaporated.

"I'll meet you in my office after I introduce Franco to April."

"I'll be waiting." The statement sounded like a threat and her fight-or-flight instincts kicked in. But she wouldn't run.

All too soon she'd turned Franco over to the capable sales staff, then with dread miring every step, she forced her feet to carry her to the man whose presence spelled impending doom.

Wyatt stood by one of her charts, hands on hips, aggression in every lean line of his body. She closed her office door for privacy. If she was going to be fired, she didn't want the rest of the staff to hear or try to come to her rescue, thereby jeopardizing their jobs.

She slid behind her desk in an effort to establish a wall of professionalism between them and quickly realized her mistake. Sitting gave Wyatt the advantage. He loomed over her, making her tilt her head back to meet his diamond-hard gaze.

"If Constantine is here to buy horses, why wasn't he talking to our highly paid sales staff?"

"One, because he wanted detailed information about the bloodline and temperament bred into each horse—my specialty since both horses are bred from Sutherland stock. And two, Megan referred him to me."

"Who is Megan?"

"My cousin. She rides the European Grand Prix circuit." She gestured to the framed photo on her shelf of Megan with one of her champion horses.

It seemed ironic or maybe a cruel twist of fate that Megan had inherited Hannah's parents' grace, talent and the aggressive nature required to compete successfully on the Grand Prix circuit. Unfortunately, Megan's competitive instincts hadn't rubbed off on Hannah, even though the two of them had been as close as sisters—especially after her cousin had moved into Sutherland Farm following her parents' and brother's deaths fifteen years ago. The loss of their mothers had linked the cousins in a way no one else could comprehend.

And right now Megan would be telling me to put the enemy on the defensive by striking his weak spot. Wyatt's weakness was his lack of practical horse knowledge.

Only Hannah hadn't told Megan about Wyatt because... she didn't know what to say. The man put her emotions in a blender and churned them into an unrecognizable mush.

Hannah took a deep breath. "What were you thinking to let

your pilot fly that close to the ground? You scared the horses. If we'd had riders in the outdoor ring, as we did earlier, their mounts could have been spooked and the riders thrown."

"I was trying to locate you."

Her stomach muscles contracted. *Here we go.* "Why?"

He parked his fists on her desk and leaned forward, encroaching on her space and making her heart beat double-time and her mouth dry up. "I read the literature you gave me, and then I did more research on the studies and the doctors. Your theories might not be complete snake oil."

Surprise and relief whooshed the air out of her lungs. Wow. A man who wasn't afraid to admit he was wrong. "Really? I mean, of course they're not. I told you I've seen rehabilitation therapy work."

"I've made an appointment for Sam with the doctor leading one of the studies. You're coming with us. You've seen his theories in practice and will know if what he says about Sam has merit."

Problem. If she and Sam spent any time together in front of Wyatt, Sam was bound to let something slip about his work with Phoenix and their secret would be out. As much as Hannah ached to gloat over Sam's progress after only three days' work, it was too soon to prove her point. She had to bide her time until she had irrefutable evidence that even Wyatt couldn't ignore.

And then there was the whole spend-a-night-in-the-same-hotel-as-Wyatt issue. Not a good idea. Not with this unsettling whatever-it-was between them.

"Um…when?" she stalled while trying to think of a good excuse.

"The chopper is waiting to take us to the airport as soon as you pack. Sam's appointment is tomorrow afternoon. We'll fly to Atlanta tonight via the company jet and return Thursday evening."

Tension drained from her, chased by worry at the reason she had to stay here. "I can't go."

His expression darkened. "It wasn't a request, Hannah."

"Wyatt, I'm not refusing for the sake of being obstinate. I really can't go. Not this week…and probably not next."

"You'd better have a good reason for refusing an order."

She twisted a pencil in her fingertips, battling a sense of hopelessness. "One of the mares is about to foal any hour now. I need to be here with her."

"She can't give birth alone or under someone else's supervision?"

"She's older and carrying twins. Twins might be routine in humans, but not in horses. Sable is already showing signs this will be a difficult delivery."

"Why isn't the mare manager handling this?"

He wasn't going to like her answer. "Sable is one of my rescue horses."

The corners of his mouth turned down.

"Don't worry. If the foals survive, there will be horses to sell to recoup some expenses."

"If?"

She bit her lip and pushed up from her desk. "The odds aren't the best. In fact, I need to check the mare's status now. I don't know how you managed to get an appointment with the specialist so quickly when most people wait months, but thank you for agreeing to take Sam. You won't regret it, and I can't wait to hear what the doctor has to say."

She just hoped Sam didn't let their secret slip or she'd be out of a job and her dream—hers and her mother's—would be killed.

Using a flashlight Wyatt checked the brass stall numbers in the darkened barn. As crazy as it seemed, he needed to see Hannah. Tonight.

It wasn't because he missed butting heads with her, but simply because she deserved to know the doctor's findings supported her program. The neurologist believed involvement with horses could slow Sam's decline. The question was how to implement the practices without risking Sam's well-being. Wyatt was counting on Hannah's knowledge of the program to help him develop a safe but effective strategy.

When she hadn't answered the door at her cottage he'd made his way to the stables where he'd run into the security guard who'd told him where to find Hannah.

Wyatt located the stall. A strange energy hummed through him as he approached the chest-high solid wall. An eerie red glow lit the box, but he didn't see or hear Hannah. Two of the smallest horses he'd ever seen lay intertwined on a bed of straw on the far side of the compartment beneath the red lamps. Heat lamps?

Those had to be the twins Hannah had been expecting. But where was their mother and why had she been separated from them? Even with his limited knowledge of horse reproduction, he knew babies fed almost immediately after birth and often thereafter.

And where was Hannah? He'd seen no sign of her in the silent building. Had she taken the mare elsewhere? He swung the beam up and down the dark aisle. No Hannah.

A sigh and shuffle caught his attention. He leaned closer to peer through the vertical slats and spotted boots in the near right corner—boots connected to long, denim-clad legs. Legs he'd recognize anywhere because they'd planted themselves in the forefront of his thoughts lately.

His pulse jumped. Hannah slept slouched in the corner with her head tilted at an angle guaranteed to reward her with sore neck tomorrow.

He eased open the latch, but the click echoed through the silent barn. Hannah jerked upright, her owlish gaze shooting straight for the foals then turning to find him. She squinted at the flashlight beam and threw up an arm to shield her face.

"Jeremiah?"

Her sleep-husky voice zapped him like a shorted wire, jolting his pulse into overdrive.

"No. Wyatt." Who in the hell was Jeremiah and why would

she be expecting him in the middle of the night? He lowered the beam and pulled the door shut behind him while he willed his unacceptable reaction to her away. "What are you doing?

"Keeping an eye on the babies."

"Where's the mare?"

Hannah ducked her head. Her hair fell forward to conceal her face behind a tangled curtain. "I had to put Sable down. I knew the odds were against her, but I was hoping… She's gone." Her voice grew smaller and tighter with each word until the last was barely a whisper. She took a shuddery deep breath.

Irritation surged through him at Hannah's feigned struggle for composure. The women he'd known always used emotional routines to milk sympathy and cash from men. A part of him was disappointed that she had confirmed his initial opinion of her.

Then she leaned her head against the wall and swallowed. The dark strands slid across her pale skin, drawing his attention to the circles of exhaustion smudged like lavender thumbprints beneath her eyes and to what looked to be dried tear streaks on her cheeks. *Dried.* Not freshly generated for his benefit. Something shifted inside him. Her grief was real, not an award-worthy pretense.

She took a deep, shaky breath. "Life and death are routine aspects of living on a horse farm. Age, colic and injuries take horses all the time. When all else fails, putting them down is routine and humane."

The stilted speech sounded like one she'd chanted a hundred times. "Who are you trying to convince, doc? Me or yourself?"

She blinked. "I'm just stating the facts."

But the pain straining her voice was unmistakable, and the way she tried to deny she was upset impressed him a hell of a lot more than crocodile tears or pleas for sympathy would.

Empathy welled in his chest. "I saw you with the other mare. I'm sure you did everything you could with this one."

"I'd like to think I did, but…" Drawing her knees up to her chest and hugging them, she stared at the sleeping foals. "It's never easy to give up. I keep thinking of other things I could have tried."

No, giving up hope was never easy, and watching someone—some*thing*—suffer and fade away was hard, too. "Sometimes it's better to cut your losses and walk away."

She looked at him through spiky lashes. "I never quit when there's still a chance. I didn't know Daisy was pregnant when Doc brought her. When I discovered her condition I had a choice between terminating one of the twins or hoping for the best. The ultrasound showed that the filly was the smaller of the two. She's the one I would have had to—" Her voice cracked. "But she looked healthy and perfectly formed, and I couldn't—"

She plucked at a piece of straw clinging to her jeans. He caught her surreptitiously wiping her cheek on her sleeve and something inside him unraveled. She was trying to hide her tears rather than use them to manipulate him. How totally unlike the women of his experience.

He liked Hannah better when she was ornery and defiant and trying to con him into opening his wallet for her worthless nags. As perverted as it sounded, their arguments energized him. This vulnerable side of her made him uncomfortable. He didn't know how to handle it or like the way it made him feel.

The impulse to put an arm around her stiff shoulders appeared out of nowhere. He locked his knees against the urge to lower himself to the floor beside her. He wasn't into emotional displays and managed to restrain the impulse to hug her. Barely.

He didn't do hugs. His parents had taught him that hugs were meaningless gestures. Sam had been more likely to give him an encouraging slap on the back than get mushy or sentimental. But even without the hugs, Wyatt had known Sam cared—probably more than either of Wyatt's self-involved parents and definitely more than the women who had professed their love to Wyatt over the years.

That's why watching Sam become a shadow of the man he'd once been was so agonizing. It was as if Sam were leaving him one memory at a time, and it was why Wyatt had bought the farm with the intention of only making the occasional weekend visit. He wanted Sam safe, happy and comfortable, but mostly he wanted Sam out of sight, he admitted with a stab of unease between his shoulder blades. Hannah's presence and her rescue operation had derailed that plan.

Though she'd averted her face he could see her blinking furiously to keep the tears in her eyes from spilling over. "I played it safe. I didn't intervene other than to give Sable additional supplements and support. Turns out I made a mistake."

Blame. He understood that, too. Hadn't he repeatedly questioned himself on how and when he'd started missing signs of Sam's battle and what would have happened if he'd paid attention and sought treatment sooner? By the time he'd forced Sam into retirement there had been a few costly errors at Triple Crown.

"Look at that filly, Hannah. She's going to be a beauty. How could giving her life ever be deemed a mistake?"

Surprise and gratitude eased some of the pain from her eyes. Had he been such a bastard to her? Yes, he had. A slow smile curved her lips, and he instantly recalled the texture and taste of her mouth. Damn it.

"You're right. And Sable would want it this way. She'd want her babies to have a chance. Thanks, Wyatt."

"What are the foals' chances?"

When her smile faltered he congratulated himself on severing the feel-good tug between them. "Good if they make it through the first forty-eight hours, better if they make it seventy-two." She checked her watch. "We're approaching the twelve-hour mark."

"Nursing an orphan, let alone two, is a twenty-four hour job. Who's going to care for them?"

Her chin snapped up. She scrambled to her feet and wobbled. He caught her arm to steady her, feeling her muscles flex in his grip before she shrugged him off.

Touching her felt good. And right. But it wasn't. Her employee status made her taboo. And if she was a woman who lived on the edge of her messy emotions, the best he could do was avoid her.

"The foals are my responsibility, but not at the expense of my work, if that's what you're concerned about."

The prickly woman he knew had returned. Thank God. *Her* he could handle. "You can't do it alone. Who's going to help you?"

She raked her fingers through her tangled hair, then absently began to braid it. The action arched her back and displayed her breasts to mouth-watering advantage. What was it about her that made every move a sensual invitation? It took conscious effort to keep his eyes on her face and not her curves.

"A few staff members have volunteered for shifts when they're off the clock, and with the state vet school only an hour away I'll try to recruit students to lend a hand. Twins are unusual, so the mare's pregnancy and the foals' development are of interest. One of the professors has already asked to use my notes as a case study for his class. It helps to know that losing Sable might teach future vets how to get better outcomes in similar situations."

"Could you have gotten a better outcome?"

She shivered beneath her inadequate coat and wrapped her arms around her middle. "Probably not. Anyway, thanks for stopping by. Good night."

"You can't sleep here."

"I couldn't sleep anywhere else," she replied without hesitation.

He pointed to the camera mounted in the corner of the

stall. "If that's video surveillance you could watch them from wherever your monitors are located—somewhere warmer, I'll bet."

Half-defiant, half-exhausted, she glared at him. "I won't leave them, Wyatt. You can't make me."

Her challenge sent adrenaline pumping through him. "The hell I can't."

"Then you'll have to have security haul me out, and I doubt you can convince Jeremiah to manhandle me. He's worked here twenty years."

So Jeremiah was the security guard. Wyatt didn't doubt what Hannah said. In his two meetings with management, he'd learned one thing. The staff was extremely loyal to Hannah. "Why would you camp here when you could pay one of the grooms to do it?"

"You're the one who harps on not spending unnecessary money, remember?" The defiant color drained from her cheeks. "But even if I did have a rich benefactor to foot the bill, I wouldn't leave. I couldn't save Sable. Trying to pull her foals through is the least I can do for her."

The cynical side of him told him this cold, disheveled woman who put orphaned animals ahead of her own comfort seemed too good-hearted to be true. But when he looked into Hannah's eyes her dedication seemed genuine, and as unlikely as it might be, he wanted to believe she was as unselfish and unspoiled as she appeared at this moment.

Had he completely misjudged her? Or had the chemistry between them demolished his objectivity? Had to be the latter.

Whatever the case, it didn't change the fact that she stood between him and his plans for this farm.

He had to get rid of her. But having her die of hypothermia wasn't the way to accomplish his goal. And it would be bad for business.

Eight

Wyatt turned and stalked in the direction he'd come taking his narrow beam of light with him.

"Good riddance," Hannah mumbled under her breath. She didn't want him here anyway. The night had been difficult enough. She didn't have the energy to deal with him. He kept her on edge, and he had a gift for sucking the strength right out of her.

But it had been decent of him to check on her, and he hadn't seemed angry. Sam must not have let anything slip about their adventures during the trip or Wyatt would have been livid.

Forget Wyatt. You have more important things to deal with tonight.

Nearly numb from the cold, Hannah shuffled closer to the heat lamps, trying not to disturb the sleeping foals. Exhaustion weighted her muscles. She should have brought a heavier coat or maybe worn thermals, but the late spring days were so warm she hadn't brought a parka with her and she hadn't wanted to go home to get one. The wind kicking up outside didn't help. It siphoned heat from the barn.

She checked the foals' respiratory rates, then moved back to her corner and started doing knee bends to work some circulation into her legs.

A noise down the aisle made her pause and cock her head. Jeremiah wasn't due for another pass, but he did tend to worry about her. She looked over the stall wall and spotted someone stalking toward her in the darkness. The glare of a bright flashlight beam obscured his features, but she couldn't mistake that confident stride. Wyatt had returned. Adrenaline pumped through her veins chasing away her chill.

As he drew nearer she noticed he carried bundles under each arm. "What is all that?"

"Sleeping bags. Jeremiah told me where to find them. If you insist on bunking here, you need insulation. Open the door."

She did as he asked. "There are four of them."

"Two for beds. Two for pillows."

Her neck prickled a warning. She didn't have to be a mathematician to know—uh-uh. "That's two too many."

"If you're staying, I'm staying."

No! Her internal muscles contracted. "You don't need to—"

"There's only one way to get me out of this stall, Hannah. You leave first."

She didn't want him here, but she could hardly order him off his own land. And she had to admit a tiny part of her was impressed that Mr. Designer Duds would stoop to sleeping in a barn. "Not happening."

"Then you're stuck with me."

No sweet dreams in her future. "You're the boss."

"Don't forget it."

"As if you'd let me," she grumbled and took two of the bags from him. She unrolled one in her corner, then propped the second against the wall for a back brace. Determined to ignore him, she sank into the cushiony softness, slipped into the sack, tugged the warm covers to her chest and closed her eyes.

The air stirred. Her lids popped open as Wyatt's bag fluttered to the floor an inch from hers. *No, no, no.*

"You'll have more room to stretch out over there." She pointed to the opposite corner.

"You'll have more warmth if I'm here."

True, but— "Don't even suggest zipping our bags together. I'm not sharing body heat with you."

He shot her a lowered eyebrow look. "I wasn't offering."

Dread snagged like a fur ball in her throat and agitation skipped along her nerves. It only worsened when he stretched his long legs beside hers and his warmth radiated in her direction, beckoning her closer. She clenched her muscles and fought the urge.

He leaned against the stall wall. "This isn't like any stall I've ever been in. Why are you using rubber mats and fresh straw instead of shavings?"

"Birthing stalls require surfaces we can disinfect to keep the bacteria count down. So you *probably* won't catch anything sleeping here. But if you don't want to chance it..."

"Good try, doc."

"Would have been better if it had worked."

His lips twitched in what could have been a smile if he hadn't checked it, and for a moment Hannah was happy to have his company. Then she came to her senses. If he was staying, he must have an ulterior motive.

Wyatt shifted his attention to the babies in their straw nest. She could have sworn some of the rigidity in his jaw softened. "I've never seen horses this small."

"That's because the usual foal is around a hundred pounds. Each of these weighs roughly half that. The bay colt is slightly heavier than the black filly. She's the one in the greatest danger, but as long as she eats she has a chance."

He turned suddenly and their gazes collided. The boyish wonder on his face made her breath catch. When he shed his arrogant I'm-the-boss-of-you demeanor, she could *almost* like him. Suddenly sharing a stall seemed too intimate, too…close.

He observed her in that lingering, silent way of his, making her want to be somewhere else. Anywhere else. As long as it was away from him. Her toes curled in her boots and her nipples stiffened—unfortunately not from the cold. She tugged the sleeping bag to her chin and cursed her overactive hormones.

Hannah Faith, you are no better than the animals you work with. One whiff of a potential mate and you get all hot and bothered.

Okay, so Wyatt is sexy. Big deal.

And he knows how to kiss. So what?

She wasn't going to let anything happen between them. Because he was a coldhearted jerk and her boss, and she was *not* interested. But her hands grew clammy and her pulse raced out of control.

"Get some sleep," he commanded with his usual superiority.

Did he honestly believe she could calmly lie down and sleep with the enemy when he'd made it crystal clear that he wanted her long gone? "Just because you order it doesn't mean it'll happen."

"Does my presence disturb you, Hannah?"

"Don't be ridiculous."

His hiked eyebrow called her a liar. "Am I being ridiculous?"

She scowled at him. Her body tingled with awareness. Not awareness. Irritation. Heat invaded her limbs and torso. On the upside, she wasn't cold anymore. But on the downside… It had been a tough night. Watching Sable's struggle had brought back horrible memories, and she needed a hug.

But not from him.

His lips tipped in a half smile. "Good night, Hannah."

Cocky, autocratic bastard. "I have to feed them in a couple of hours."

"I'll help."

"Wyatt, you don't need—"

"Didn't we already establish that I'm the boss?"

She clamped her molars shut and silently fumed. She should have known the nice guy wouldn't last. At least now she had her hormones under control.

"I'm not likely to forget who's in charge since you rub it in my face every few minutes. If you want to rough it in a cold, drafty barn, I won't try to stop you."

In fact, she'd even enjoy his discomfort—even if it meant she had to suffer his company. But if he thought he could order her to sleep and she'd blindly obey, he had another thought coming. She would never, ever be able to relax with him nearby—especially now that she'd discovered Wyatt had a crumb of human decency buried somewhere under his thick ogre hide.

"Hannah."

Hannah ignored the voice, snuggled deeper into the pillow beneath her cheek and curled her fingers into the pillow case. Then several things needled her to consciousness simultaneously.

That hadn't been her father's voice trying to wake her for school. Her pillow smelled like sandalwood and cypress rather than her lilac-scented sheets, and the case didn't feel like crisp Egyptian cotton. Her down pillow was hard, warm and thumping.

Thumping?

Awareness of where she was and why and who she had her cheek pressed against thundered through her like a jumper's hooves racing the time clock. She stiffened and her eyes flew open to the dim red glow of the heat lamps. A strong band tightened around her and long, strong fingers curled into her waist, anchoring her in place.

Wyatt's arm. Wyatt's hand.

"Move slowly. Don't startle them." His chest rumbled

beneath her ear, and the vibration traveled straight down her spine, settling like a seltzer tablet in the pit of her stomach.

She shoved her hair out of her eyes and eased upright. Wyatt reclined beside her with his head and shoulders propped against the rolled up sleeping bag and his legs stretched out in front of him. His coat had fallen open to reveal his charcoal grey cashmere sweater—the softness she'd felt against her palm and cheek.

Embarrassment toasted her face. "I'm sorry. I—"

"Forget it. Look."

The softness of his voice snagged her attention, and then he smiled and she couldn't have turned away if flames had been licking at the stall door. Her stomach swooped like a barn swallow.

Wow.

That white smile slashing across his stubble-darkened face was a sight to behold. She'd never seen him smile before. And he looked good. Good enough to make her remember the kisses they'd shared and to want to curl up beside him and experiment with a few more. Her gaze fell to his tenderly curving lips.

Bad idea. Seriously bad idea, Hannah.

But the troublemaker in her head automatically registered the still-dark skylights overhead, which meant the staff hadn't arrived yet. Unless Jeremiah did a walk-by, then she and Wyatt were alone and unlikely to be interrupted.

His gaze locked with hers, and the temperature climbed a dozen degrees. The high stall walls enclosed them in a private world, wrapping them in a cocoon of intimacy. A hundred heartbeats raced past. Then his Adam's apple bobbed and a muscle in his jaw bunched.

"Hannah. *The. Foals.*"

An itty-bitty part of her brain noted his quietly rumbled order, but processing the words was a different matter when her skin steamed and her mind had apparently drowned in a hormonal hot spring.

He cupped her jaw. Desire bubbled up her throat. Her mouth watered in anticipation of his kiss, then his lips hardened. He pushed her chin toward the opposite side of the stall and withdrew his hand.

The sensual haze clouding her vision vanished like a popped bubble. The filly trembled on her haunches, extending one spindly front leg then the other. Everything in Hannah urged her to rush forward and help, but as if he'd read her mind, Wyatt's long, strong fingers closed around her wrist and held her back.

The filly's fumbling efforts rousted the colt. He wobbled and wavered and made it to his feet seconds before his sister, then he gave a triumphant little buck and promptly stumbled and fell.

Wyatt's low laugh startled them all—probably Hannah more than the four-legged occupants of the stall. She stared at him. How had she ever thought his eyes cold? The brown irises glimmered like the tiger's-eye ring she'd bought as a teenager.

Her entire body tingled at the awareness in his eyes. Awareness and restraint. *He* had control of *his* impulses. They shared another moment of silent connection—a connection she didn't want or need *with him.* She tried to shake off her unacceptable response, cleared her throat and twisted her wrist from his hold.

She peeled her gaze from his and spotted the straw clinging to his no-longer-crisply-pressed pant leg. She grimaced. "I'm sorry about your clothes."

He shrugged, bringing her attention to those broad shoulders. Specifically the one she'd slept on—the one with the tiny damp spot where her mouth had been. She'd drooled on him. A fresh wave of embarrassment swamped her.

"They're just pants, Hannah."

"Yes, I guess they are, and if you can afford to spend millions on a farm more or less sight unseen, then I guess you can afford to replace a pair of custom-made pants." She forced out the acidic words hoping to sever the intimacy of the moment. Judging by the way his expression hardened, she'd succeeded.

Strangely, annoying him didn't provide nearly as much satisfaction as she'd hoped.

Then he shook his head. "Seeing this is worth an entire wardrobe."

Her breath hitched in surprise. Who was this man and where had the arrogant bottom-line bastard who'd been her boss gone? She actually liked this version of Wyatt. And liking a man with a calculator for a heart was dangerous territory.

She could *actually* feel her body willing her to move in his direction. Instead, she swallowed and shook her head. "This chemistry between us can't go anywhere. You know that, don't you, Wyatt?"

Wyatt, like Robert, wanted her land and not her. Both were bottom-line, budget dictators like her father, who had apparently forgotten all about the farm he'd once loved.

And yet the knowledge that Wyatt shared traits with the men who'd done her wrong didn't stop her heart from bucking in her chest. A current of electricity hummed from his palm to hers, then traveled up her arm across her breasts and down her torso to settle heavily below her navel.

"At least you're admitting there is chemistry now. And yes, it is inappropriate." If she wanted to break this link—and she did—she'd have to find the strength to push him away.

"What happened with Sam and the doctor?"

Wyatt's expression went blank, but at least she'd broken the push-pull bond. He rose and towered over her. "Isn't it time to feed the foals?"

"In other words, none of my business." Maybe Sam would tell her later.

"It's not none of your business. It's just—" He shook his head and extended his hand. "We need to prepare the formula."

She didn't want to risk touching him again, but she couldn't pretend she didn't see the big, broad palm in front of her face.

Reluctantly, she put her hand in his. His fingers closed around hers and her body, apparently still in loco land, reacted with a skipping pulse and another bubbly burst of fizz.

Why did she react this way to the one man who had the power to destroy everything that mattered to her?

They stood inches apart—inches that seemed to shrink like the formerly spacious enclosure around them. His pupils expanded and his gaze dropped to her mouth, causing it to flood with moisture. The shared hours and kisses encircled them with a tightening lasso of awareness cinching tighter with each passing second.

"Should I stay with them?"

She blinked. At least one of them was thinking. "No. They'll be fine for a few minutes."

Gathering every fading thread of resistance she possessed, she yanked her hand free, and with one last glance at the babies, hurried toward the prep room. Wyatt followed like a dark shadow. His looming, hawkeyed surveillance as she measured and scooped made her clumsy and slow. She had to think through every action as if she were performing the task for the first time instead of the hundredth.

Even then, warm rivulets of formula splashed over the rim of the bottle and her fingers because her thoughts drifted into the taboo territory of what would have happened if she'd unwisely given in to the hunger they were both trying to deny.

Once both bottles were full Wyatt took them from her and headed toward the birthing stall.

"I'll take the colt," he volunteered and, grasping the container awkwardly, offered it. The colt ignored him.

Hannah set down her bottle, grabbed Wyatt's arm and hand and positioned him. "Tuck the bottle into the crook of your arm like this and brace yourself. He's going to pull hard."

Then she realized she was touching him, smelling him, and quickly stepped away. "Offer him the teat."

The colt immediately latched on—a great sign.

Hannah repeated the process with the filly, but the poor

baby seemed too tired from her earlier antics to nurse. Worry gnawed Hannah's middle. "Come on, girl. You have to eat."

But the velvety muzzle wouldn't open. Anxiety and desperation stretched her nerves. She tried again and again, then after several failed attempts the filly latched on with startling suddenness. Hannah's eyes stung, and a sob of relief built in her throat. She bit her lip hard to keep the sob there and turned her head to hide her reaction from Wyatt. The last thing she needed was for him to believe she was too much of a wimp to do her job.

"You don't give up easily, do you?" he asked.

She risked glancing his way and instead of disgust, she found compassion and maybe even a touch of admiration in his eyes. She would swear he—the man she'd deemed a soulless bastard—cared.

"Nellie says when I set my mind to something I can outstubborn a mule. Some days that trait's an asset…and some days a curse."

The colt finished his breakfast first and nudged Wyatt for more. "Now what?"

"Rub him. Pick up his feet. Get him used to being handled."

He frowned. "Why waste the time if they might not survive?"

"For the same reason you're taking care of Sam. You want whatever time he has left to be the best it can be. And if they make it we'll be ahead of the game because we didn't lose an opportunity for training them."

Wyatt's reserve was obvious as he stroked the colt's back. The little guy responded by nuzzling Wyatt's hip, then dancing away and back again. Slowly, Wyatt relaxed. His frown faded and his touch became surer. She even caught a brief smile at the colt's antics.

The filly finished her meal. Hannah raked her fingers through her fuzzy mane and smothered a sigh. Despite their lack of verbal skills, horses were so much easier to understand than people. Their needs and motives were simple. She handled the filly, gently lifting each tiny hoof under Wyatt's watch.

She finally opened the stall and headed for the prep room to clean up. "They'll be okay alone?"

"They'll probably sleep off their breakfast, and my first volunteer is due soon."

Wyatt kept pace beside her. "You were right about Sam. The doctor says he needs more physical and mental stimulation than he's getting. Your horses could be the answer."

Hope swelled tentatively in her chest. "I hear a *but*."

"The studies weren't as controlled as they should have been, and the results are open to misinterpretation. I don't want to put too much faith in this unorthodox approach until I see Sam progress."

A skeptic. Hannah sighed. "I understand your reluctance to believe without proof, but what do you have to lose, Wyatt? Let Sam join the Sunday class."

His obstinate expression returned. "He's not riding. You should understand my concerns. You lost your mother to a horseback riding accident, and I'm sure as a champion athlete she was in peak physical condition. Sam's fragile, and he no longer grasps the concept of danger. He'll take risks and make mistakes. He's getting clumsier. A fall and a broken hip could finish him off. Survival rates after a broken hip are—"

"I know the statistics." She paused by the sink. "And as I've pointed out before, we take every precaution to ensure the safety of our riders. Sam would only be walking his mount around the ring which is covered with six inches of soft sand."

"Are you saying you've never had anyone fall off or sustain an injury?"

She sighed. "No."

"Then he'll work with the horses from the ground or not at all."

"I can arrange that." She already had. But she wasn't volunteering that tidbit. Not yet. But she hated the lie between them.

"Sam will want to see these two." Then his eyes narrowed. "He'll help with the foals."

It was the open door she'd been waiting for. She liked Sam. His wealth of horse knowledge reminded her of her father, but unlike her father, Sam had a warmer and more approachable personality. "That would be great. I'll supervise him myself."

"No, I'll do it. As long as my work permits it, Sam and I will take a daily shift with the foals."

Her stomach sank. "Sam…and you? But—"

"It's a package deal, Hannah. Both of us or neither."

A blessing and a curse. She'd wanted to get Wyatt involved so he could comprehend the importance of FYC, but if she let him hang around the barns too much, he'd surely find out she'd been working with Sam behind his back and that could destroy any goodwill they had developed.

Not to mention his presence would wreak havoc on her concentration and her ability to get her job done. Wyatt Jacobs was definitely a distraction. She didn't know what to make of his less hostile side or if she could trust it. He'd stated very clearly that he wanted her land. Was he trying to lure her into acquiescence?

The only way to determine his real character was to treat him like one of her rescue animals and spend time with him. But she'd have to tread carefully—the same way she would with any unfamiliar animal.

She didn't want to think what would happen without animosity to keep them apart, but she'd find a way to ignore the attraction, keep Sam quiet and make it all work. She had no choice if she wanted to keep her home and her horses.

"You've got yourself a deal."

Exhaustion clouded Wyatt's thinking and infused his shoulders with a dull ache. His condition had little to do with last night's makeshift bed on the barn floor and everything to do with a certain leggy brunette.

It had been months since he'd slept beside a warm body, and

Hannah's soft curves curled against him combined with her silky hair teasing his chin had kept him awake. And aroused. *Very* aroused.

He needed a shower—preferably cold—and a bed, but more than anything, he needed distance from the woman whose scent clung to him.

Hannah crossed to a chart on the wall. "If you and Sam take a shift with the foals, you'll need to log in the feeding time and the amount each consumes."

"Got it."

She faced him, shifting uneasily on her feet. "The least I can do to repay you for your help is make you a cup of coffee."

Every cell in his body screamed a warning. "Are you inviting me back to your place?"

Her lips parted, then she shook her head. "There's a coffeepot in the lounge."

He should refuse and head for the safety of the house before he crossed a line he shouldn't cross—one that blurred more every minute. Hannah tempted him too much with her flushed cheeks and sexy disheveled hair. But if he wanted to find a way to convince her to sell her land, then he needed to take advantage of her guard being down to pump her for information.

"I could use a cup." The caffeine might clear his head and give him back his edge. Against his better judgment he followed her toward the office suite in the main barn.

She headed straight for the small but well-equipped kitchen provided for Sutherland clients. She didn't detour by the luxurious guest bathroom to waste time in front of the mirror as he would have expected of her. But he was beginning to see Hannah was much more complex than he'd originally surmised. She might be her daddy's pampered princess, but she also appeared to be as dedicated to her horses as she was to her expensive toys.

Unless she was giving one hell of a convincing performance.

He prowled the lounge while the fragrant brew perked. A

shelf containing multiple leather-bound volumes lured him across the room. The one with *Horses by Hannah* inscribed in gold on the spine caught his attention. Wyatt opened the cover to a glossy mare's photograph.

A chart beneath the picture listed the dam and sire as well as the animal's numerous wins to date. He flipped the pages and found more of the same on subsequent entries. As he studied each data sheet something became clear—something he wished he could deny.

He'd underestimated Hannah. She hadn't exaggerated her expertise in equine genetics. In five short years as Sutherland Farm's breeder, she'd racked up credentials. Valid, impressive credentials. She bred winners. And that complicated his situation.

"Wyatt?" Hannah stood beside him holding two tall insulated mugs bearing the Sutherland crest. She glanced past him toward the door as if she couldn't wait to be gone. "Help yourself to cream and sugar."

"I take it black. Thank you."

She rocked in her boots. "Thanks again for your help last night. I have to get going. Please tell Sam I said hello."

"I will." If this was one of Sam's more lucid days, he might even remember her. Sam's decline since Wyatt had forced him to retire had been rapid. So rapid Wyatt dreaded the first encounter with his stepfather each day because he never knew which Sam he'd see—the wise man or the shell.

Hannah hustled from the lounge. Her butt in snug jeans wasn't a sight Wyatt needed to appreciate at the moment, but the sensual sway pulled his gaze like a tugboat nonetheless. It took far more effort than it should have to concentrate on the remainder of the photos in the album while he drank his coffee.

He closed the cover, his conclusion unaltered. Unfortunately. With Hannah's talent for breeding champions, getting rid of her would be a bad business decision. Whenever Sam no longer recognized his surroundings Wyatt would move Sam to a more restricted environment and put the farm on the market. Hannah's position as the breeder on staff was undeniably an asset that would make the stable more desirable and valuable.

That meant he couldn't run her off, even though every iota of common sense he possessed urged him to cut her loose. He had to find a way to keep her on board but stay away from her, and still use her skills to help Sam. And he had to control the flow of cash into her money pit. Though the doctor's research showed the validity of such programs, FYC ran deep in the red. That had to change.

Finding a solution required a clearer head than he had at the moment. His concentration was shot. He needed food and a couple hours' sleep.

He left the building and stepped into the empty parking lot. The absolute silence of the farm at 5:00 a.m. settled over him like a heavy, dew-laden blanket.

When he'd begun working for Sam years ago, Sam had insisted Wyatt accompany him on his sunrise inspections of both the barns and later the distillery. During those early hours Sam had dispensed his wisdom and guided Wyatt on life. Back then, Sam would have been able to identify each birdsong and every animal footprint.

Wyatt missed those quiet moments now as much as he'd resented them when Sam first started dragging his ass out of bed before sunup and making him participate. After Wyatt had joined Triple Crown's team, he and Sam had made it a practice to walk the distillery floor together every morning before the machinery roared to life and shattered the silence of the night. Wyatt still prowled the concrete floors each morning, but it wasn't the same without his mentor by his side.

That reminded him he'd neglected to ask Hannah which shift she wanted him and Sam to take with the foals. He scanned the horizon and caught a smudge of movement in the Charleston-style lampposts lining the driveway. Hannah was too far away to shout for her. He dug out his cell phone and dialed. It dumped straight to her voice mail. She must have turned off her phone.

By the time he'd climbed into his car, started his engine and backed out of the parking space she'd disappeared. He steered toward her cottage, but failed to locate her in the headlight beams ahead of him.

He reached a V-shaped opening in the fence and a line through the damp grass caught his attention. He slowed. In the dim light he could barely make out a path leading toward distant trees. Hannah ought to have sense enough to know it was too cold and dark for her to wander through the woods alone. He pulled over and parked, then grabbed the flashlight from under his seat and followed.

Dew dampened his boots and the cuffs of his pants and slickened the stones underfoot. He'd yet to tour the property beyond the buildings and driveways and had only a vague idea from the topographical maps that an old rock quarry now filled with water lay in this direction.

Wishing he had on his hiking boots, he made his way carefully through the shadowy woods with the aid of the flashlight beam. He didn't see or hear Hannah ahead of him as he descended a hill and rounded a bend.

He reached a clearing and stopped. The brightening sky illuminated a pond, its surface disturbed along one side. Hannah sat on the end of a small dock in front of a white structure that resembled a boathouse. Despite the cold bite of the morning air she had her pant legs rolled up and her feet kicking in the water. She looked young and carefree—something he hadn't been in a long time.

A twig snapped beneath his foot as he closed the distance and she startled, twisting his way with her hand to her chest. "Wyatt, you scared me."

"You shouldn't be wandering through the woods alone in the dark."

"I know this property as well as I know my own skin."

Becoming familiar with Hannah's skin was not a path he

needed to travel. "It's a rough trail. If you had slipped on the wet rocks, no one would have known where to look for you."

She shrugged. "I needed a minute to clear my head."

"You could do that in the warmth and safety of your cottage."

She stared at the pinkish-orange glow emerging above the pine trees lining the sheer rock wall at the far bank of the lake and tinting the water with the same sherbet hues.

"This is…tradition. My mom and I used to come here every time we lost an animal. She always said this place reminded her that the end of anything was always the beginning of something else."

"A philosophy that makes loss a little easier to swallow, but it's not always true."

"Says you. Mom was a fierce competitor, but she had another side that only Dad and I were allowed to see. She was a pushover for any injured or orphaned critter. She rescued cats, dogs, birds, rabbits, squirrels…just about any living thing."

Hannah swirled her feet, sending fresh ripples across the surface and drawing his attention to her sexy red toenail polish. "This was the place where we set the wild ones free or said goodbye to those that didn't make it. I've kept up her practice of coming here to say goodbye to stock and students."

"Stock and *students?*"

"FYC's clients often have health issues. A few have passed away while still enrolled." Her drawn face said more than words.

"And you mourn them all."

"Of course."

He couldn't fathom lining up for dose after dose of pain. He'd learned the hard way from his father, his mother and a parade of lovers that relationships always ended. He'd found it easier to keep his emotional distance.

Hannah's connection to this land was another factor working against him. That made finding a solution to his problem more complicated. "You could save yourself a lot of heartache if you didn't get attached."

She flashed him a look of disbelief.

"I couldn't do it any other way. If I give my time to something, usually a little piece of my heart goes along for the ride. Every life, whether human or animal, teaches us something and we're richer for having experienced it. Like the cliché says, I'd rather love and lose than never feel anything."

"Do you honestly believe that nonsense?"

She shook her head. "That sounds cold and unfeeling, Wyatt, and we both know you're neither. If you were, you wouldn't go to so much trouble for Sam and you wouldn't have helped me last night. Nor would you have followed me down here to make sure I was safe."

He stiffened at the accusation. He was no damned bleeding heart. "You're mistaken. We both know I'm a bottom-line bastard."

She winced. "You heard that, huh? I'm sorry."

"Did you mean it?"

She shifted her bottom on the dock, tucking her hands beneath her thighs. "I did at the time."

"Then don't apologize. First impressions are usually the correct ones." A fact he needed to remember. "Don't try to paint me as some kind of hero, Hannah. The only reason I bought Sutherland Farm for Sam was because my mother screwed him royally when she divorced him. He was forced to sell his thoroughbred farm to pay off her part of the divorce settlement. I owe him."

"Your mom sounds lovely," Hannah replied sarcastically. "I suppose I'll get to meet her when she comes to visit."

"She won't visit unless she runs out of money or men." Why in the hell had he volunteered that information? Hannah had no need to know his personal business.

She checked her watch. "I'm sure you have a busy day ahead. Don't let me keep you."

"I'll follow you out."

"Afraid you can't find your way?"

Her sassy comeback caught him off guard. He was beginning to like her quick tongue. "I'm not leaving you here alone."

"Then you'd better pull up a chair." She picked up her coffee mug and sipped, ignoring him. "I'm here to watch the sunrise."

She was calling his bluff. He decided to take her up on it, and since there were no chairs, he'd have to join her. He had a fleeting thought as he kicked off his shoes and tugged off his socks that his time could be more valuably spent going over the new Triple Crown ad campaign. Even if he couldn't be in the office, he needed to get some work done.

He sat beside her and the cold water enclosed his feet. He whistled in a sharp breath.

"Keep your feet moving and it won't be so cold."

A fish splashed along the bank. Birds chirped all around him. A bat skimmed along the water's surface. He couldn't remember the last time he'd done anything so laid-back and… wasteful as kicking his feet in a pond. But he couldn't work up any regret. The peacefulness of the setting enveloped him, easing the ache from his shoulders.

The sun crested the trees, illuminating Hannah's face, the flush on her cheeks and the dampness of her lips. Hunger rekindled in his gut—hunger he wasn't sure he had the reserves to deny.

As if she sensed his acceptance of the inevitable, she turned her head. Their eyes met and her feet stilled. Awareness crackled in the air between them, parting her lips, widening her pupils and lifting the fine hairs on his body like the static charge of atmospheric electricity before a lightning strike. If he had any sense, he'd leave before he did something he'd regret.

He didn't get involved with employees and he'd sworn off silver-spoon women. And yet he didn't move. The longer he remained stationary, staring into those smoky blue eyes, the stronger the magnetic pull between them tugged.

"Hannah, if you don't get out of here now, I'm going to kiss you," he threatened in a Hail Mary effort.

Her lashes fluttered. She bit her lip. Then the wariness faded from her expression, replaced by resignation.

"You can't scare me off, Wyatt. Not from my home. Not from my horses. Not from you. I'm made of sterner stuff than that."

Nine

You're going to regret this.

But Hannah knew she'd regret it more if she didn't kiss Wyatt. The man had something—something that lit her up like a string of Christmas lights—and it was her duty as a scientist who studied winning genetic combinations to figure out what made the him-her connection so much more stimulating than anything she'd experienced before.

Once she figured out that secret, she'd be able to insulate herself against it…whatever *it* was.

So when Wyatt cupped her cheek in his big, warm hand to pull her closer, she leaned across the gap and met him halfway. His mouth collided with hers, hot, hard and hungry. He took control from the get-go. His tongue penetrated her lips and tangled with hers, gliding, stroking, unraveling her reservations.

She knew she was in over her head immediately and debated breaking away, because no matter how she dissected it, until a few short hours ago, she hadn't even liked Wyatt.

And one day did not a relationship make. But she couldn't pry her lips from his.

Last night she'd discovered a caring side of him—one the hard-edged tycoon fought hard to hide from the world. And today he'd come looking for her because he feared for her safety. She found Wyatt's softer side extremely attractive.

His fingers wove through her hair and curled around her nape. He sucked her bottom lip between his, lightly grazing the tender flesh with his teeth. Her senses overloaded and her head spun. Any objective analytical ability she might have possessed dove right off the dock.

How could she figure out how he did whatever he did when she could barely think? Barely breathe. In a last-ditch effort to recapture her diminishing reasoning skills she planted a hand on his chest, but the wild bump of his heart beneath her palm only exacerbated the irregular rhythm of hers.

His fingertips glided from her cheek to her neck, dusting over her sensitive nerve endings in a featherlight caress that sent ripples of pleasure across her skin like a rock skimming the lake's surface. She shivered as the sensation skipped to the pit of her stomach.

He caressed her shoulder then her upper arm, trailing his thumb along the inside of her bicep and wreaking havoc with her concentration. She tried to focus on his technique. What made his approach so much more effective? Was it the gentle tug of his lips? The inflaming slide of his tongue? The unique taste of him? The texture of his hair between her fingers? Pheromones? His…um… Mmm.

Dizzying desire made it impossible to keep a clear head. Then his arm banded around her, urging her closer. His thigh seared hers, and all she could do was revel in the soft, firmness of his lips and the strength of his arms.

She'd never been the sexually aggressive type, but the craziest urge to straddle his lap and mash herself against him from zipper to collar blindsided her. She needed to get closer. Much closer.

Just one more minute and you'll have this crazy connectivity all figured out.

She tilted her head and met him kiss for kiss, stroke for stroke and sip for sip. The muscles of his shoulders bunched and flexed beneath her palms as he smoothed the curve of her waist, rhythmically and hypnotically stroking up and down between her hip and rib cage. She mirrored the movement, feeling the leashed power beneath his clothing.

Then he covered her breast, accurately finding and buffing her nipple through her shirt and bra, and everything inside her sizzled like a hot branding iron hitting cold water. Desire curled through her like wisps of steam. It's a wonder the water lapping at her ankles didn't boil. She moaned approval into his mouth.

He broke the kiss, sucked a sharp breath and rested his cheek against hers. The mild abrasion of his morning beard rasped erotically against her skin.

"This is not smart." The movement of his lips and the whisper of his breath against her ear made her shiver.

She searched for the willpower to pull away. Searched… and didn't find it. "No. It's not."

He grasped her shoulders and held her at bay for a moment. The hunger in his eyes incinerated her. Then with a muttered curse, he yanked her in for another reservation-wrecking kiss. When he lifted his head again, she dug her nails into his thick biceps and whimpered in disappointment.

"I want you."

The gravelly words vibrated through her.

This would be the right time to come to your senses, Hannah.

Who was she kidding? Even if he hadn't anchored her with his firm grip, she was honest enough to admit she'd already lost the battle. She wanted this. *Needed* this. After last night she needed to feel alive, needed to feel sexy and desirable and not like a failure. And Wyatt, for whatever reason, seemed to be the only man up to the task. But…

Sex with him was wrong on so many levels. She gulped air, hoping to inhale a little sanity, then tilted her head back, taking in his passion-darkened eyes, *ravenous* eyes that fanned the flames of her own hunger. “I want you, too, but I don’t have protection.”

“I do.”

Her tummy fluttered. So much for reason, because there was no way she’d say no. “The boathouse, then.”

He shot a glance over his shoulder at the structure, then rose with that athletic grace of his and offered his hand. When Hannah curled her fingers around his a sense of rightness and purpose washed over her.

How could passion this strong be a mistake?

He lifted her to her feet and their chests gently collided, sending a current of sensation from her breasts to her toes, and then he lowered his head and kissed her again, this time raking his hands through her hair and unraveling her loose braid, then down her back to grip her bottom and press her hips against his. The thick column of his erection burned her. She shifted restlessly and blood pulsed to the contact site.

Hannah broke the embrace to gasp for air and led him toward her sanctuary. Their bare feet made no sound on the wooden dock, or maybe she simply couldn’t hear their steps over her thundering heart. She opened the French doors and warmth enfolded her. Solar panels on the roof kept the small space balmy year-round. She entered the room, trying to see it from a newcomer’s eyes.

Her father had left all this furniture behind in the girly summer house that her mother had decorated in whites and pastels. Twin daybeds draped with colorful quilts and lacy pillows flanked the tile-floored room with a white iron table between them.

She’d never shared this space with a man—only her mother and Megan. She could almost hear Megan cheering her on.

You go, girl. Get you some of that delicious man.

But Hannah wasn’t Megan and sexy trysts had been few

and far between in Hannah's life. She'd always been more comfortable with horses than humans. Second thoughts edged in, slowing her steps.

Wyatt closed the door behind her, then his arms encircled her. His front blanketed her back with heat. He nuzzled her hair aside. Then his warm breath on her neck preceded a hot, openmouthed kiss. His tongue danced over her wildly beating pulse point, pouring fuel on the fire burning deep in her belly. His palms slid under her shirt, scorching a trail across her abdomen. A short fingernail raked along the waistband of her jeans, making her muscles contract involuntarily, then he flattened his hands on her belly.

"Mmm." Her lungs emptied and she wallowed against him. Oh, yes, she wanted this. How could she not?

The combination of his teeth tugging on her earlobe and the ever-widening circles he drew on her torso sent her head spinning like a centrifuge, leaving her limbs weighted and her head light. She let her skull rest on his shoulder as he unfastened the button of her jeans, loosening the fabric, allowing room for a much-needed inhalation.

The rasp of her zipper gliding down vibrated through her body, and need swelled inside her with each pendulum-like sweep of his fingers slowly descending across her skin until he reached the edge of her bikini panties. Anticipation stole her breath. Then he delved beneath the lace band and her lungs filled on a gasp.

He combed through her curls, sliding lower and lower until he found moisture, moisture he used to graze over her center. The intimate stroke struck her with a lightning bolt of desire, and her knees buckled. He caught her around the waist then lifted her arms and looped them around his neck. "Hold on to me."

The position arched her spine, pushing her bottom against his hardened flesh and thrusting her breasts upward in invitation. She lifted her heavy lids and her reflection stared back at her from the large mirror hanging opposite the doors.

Passion flushed her face and parted her lips. She'd never seen herself like this. Wanton. Hungry. Sexy. And surprisingly, it added to the urgency of the moment instead of making her turn away.

Wyatt's gaze met hers. Dark color tinted his cheekbones. He captured her nipple with his left hand, rolling, plucking, flicking. He matched the motion with his right across her most sensitive spot. Arousal bore down on her like an approaching storm. Her skin turned hot, humid, damp. Her lids grew heavier. With each slide across her center he coaxed a deeper response from her, and having him watch her increased her arousal, multiplied the eroticism of the moment tenfold.

His mouth burned her neck, ears and jaw, sucking, nipping, licking, as his fingers teased her pleasure points until she quivered in his arms. Pressure built, straining her muscles, making her quiver. She tried to keep watching him, but then release exploded from her core with such shocking sudden ferocity that her lids slammed shut and her head lolled back. She curled her tingling toes against the tiles as the sublime feeling quaked through her.

When the waves of pleasure relented her body went limp. She hung on Wyatt's supporting arm, waiting for the strength to return to her legs. She'd never ever experienced an orgasm that powerful—and with her clothes still on no less. And yet as amazing as it had been, it wasn't enough. She craved more. She needed to feel the full potency of Wyatt's passion.

She forced her eyes open and found the same hunger reflected in his expression. He shoved her jeans to the floor. Cool air skimmed her thighs as she stepped out of them. Then he whipped her shirt over her head, grasped her hand and turned her around.

The eyes she'd once thought cold burned over her like a welder's torch. His nostrils flared as he took in her lacy bra and panty set. Then he bent and brushed his lips across the swell of her breast, first one, then the other. She caught her breath and let the soft caress undulate over her.

He unfastened her bra and pulled the lace away. Her nipples puckered, shamelessly begging for his attention. A low growl rumbled from him seconds before he swept her into his arms and laid her on the nearest bed. He paused to retrieve the condom from his wallet, then dropped the black packet on the pastel quilt beside her.

He reached for the hem of his sweater, spurring her into action. "Wait. Let me."

She knelt on the bed, grasped the soft cashmere and the T-shirt beneath and pulled both over his head simultaneously. She wanted him naked. The sooner, the better. She tossed his clothing aside and sat back to admire the taut flesh she'd uncovered.

Wyatt was all lean muscle from his broad shoulders and ropy arms to his washboard abs. His pants rode low on his hips, revealing a dark trail of hair from his navel to the leather belt encircling his narrow waist. A thick bulge pushed against the fabric of his trousers, sending a fresh bolt of hunger through her. She rested her hand over it momentarily, savoring his rigid length and his sharply indrawn breath.

Then impatience took over. Her hands shook as she eagerly worked leather from the brass buckle, then tackled the hook and zipper. She looped her fingers beneath the band of his boxers and pants and eased them over his erection. His size sent her pulse skipping faster with anticipation.

She pushed his pants down his thighs. Then, wanting to share the pleasure she'd received, she curled her fingers around him and stroked his hot, hard, satiny heat. His breath turned choppy and a milky drop appeared on the thick head. A shudder of pure, animalistic need racked her.

She bent to taste him, but before she could make contact his fingers plunged into her hair, cradling her skull and lifting her for another voracious kiss. Their hot torsos melded for a heart-stopping moment, then he eased her backward and whisked away her panties before following her down. The wiry hair on his thighs tickled her tender skin in the most erotic way as his knees separated hers and his chest burned her breasts.

She wound her arms around him, dragging her palms over the muscles bunching and flexing in his back. His head snapped back, ending the tangle of tongues and teeth with a hiss. He quickly donned the protection, but instead of driving inside her and filling the void the way she wanted, needed, *craved,* he bent to capture her nipple in his mouth.

White-hot heat enclosed her. He sucked, grazed, tugged, and her womb twisted tighter with each pull. She squirmed beneath him, impatient to ease the building pressure. His hands steadied her, gripping her knees before ever so slowly gliding upward with his thumbs, sweeping an electrifying path closer and closer to where she needed his touch the most. And then he bumped over her center, flicking the swollen flesh back and forth. Raw desire ripped through her, making her gasp.

His lips worked magic on first one breast then the other, pushing her closer and closer to the edge. Her back bowed off the mattress. Her leg muscles locked and trembled as the void inside her yawned wider. He lifted his head, and she whimpered in disappointment, but the press of his arousal between her legs cut short her protest. His thumb circled again and again, holding her gaze with those hot espresso-colored eyes.

"Please, Wyatt."

"Wait for it." His passionate, deep voice rasped over her.

Her lungs filled as she teetered on the verge of climax. Then Wyatt plunged deep inside her, catalyzing an orgasm so intense the first one paled by comparison. Each of his powerful lunges carried her higher. She clung to his shoulders until the last spasm faded and her vision cleared.

Wyatt's hands fisted in the quilt beside her head. Dark swatches of color stained his cheeks. Hannah caressed his chest, savoring his supple, hot skin, his bunched muscles and tiny taut nipples, then his strong arms, back and buttocks.

Unable to satisfy her need to touch him, she skimmed his thighs and lifted her hips to take him deeper. The moment she did she felt it again—the promise of impending release.

Surprised by her over-the-top response, she met him thrust for thrust. Her heart raced. Her skin dampened. Wyatt's pace increased. And then another climax rocked her and she didn't care about anything except the heat pulsing through her. His groan filled her ears, then seconds later he eased down onto her. His flesh, hot and slick, molded hers. His heart slammed so hard she could feel it through her breasts.

Wow. Wow. Wow.

She melted against the mattress, buried her face in his shoulder and gulped for air. They'd come so far from their initial animosity to the most explosive sex of her life. Wyatt definitely wasn't as cold-blooded as he liked to pretend, and a relationship this passionate had to have potential. "That was… amazing."

His body went rigid. He pushed up on his arms, and his arctic eyes chilled her to the bone. "This won't change our business relationship. Don't expect any extra concessions for you or your horses."

Anger geysered up her spine. How dare he accuse her of trading sex for favors when his body was still buried deep inside hers? She'd forgotten what a jerk he could be.

"I didn't have sex with you for my horses." She saw disbelief in his eyes and shoved on his chest. "This was a mistake. We don't even like each other."

She waited for him to contradict her. Instead, his silence spoke volumes. Regret and humiliation swamped her. She pushed harder on his shoulders. He disconnected from her, rolled off the bed and reached for his pants.

She suddenly couldn't bear the thought of being naked in front of him. One whiff of the man, and animal instinct had overridden intellect. She saw it happen with studs all the time, but she'd thought herself smarter. Apparently not.

Cursing herself for letting chemistry make her stupid, she

sprung from the bed and grabbed her panties, stepping into them quickly before snatching up her bra and stabbing her arms into it. She kept her back to him, but it didn't help—not with the mirror reflecting his every move.

His gaze met hers in the glass. "What time do you want Sam and me to help with the foals?"

She blinked in surprise at his change of subject, then fought a cringe as realization sank in. How could she avoid him now without hurting Sam and abandoning her plan to prove FYC's value? She couldn't.

She clutched her shirt to her chest. "Anytime is fine. You're the boss."

His eyes narrowed at the sarcastic bite she hadn't managed to suppress. "Sam and I will take the next feeding. Go home and get some sleep."

His implication couldn't be clearer. "In other words, don't be there."

"That would be best."

"I'll post a schedule outside my office door. After today please work around the other volunteers' times." His scrutiny remained steady, making her muscles tense and her heart rate erratic. How could he go from volcano-hot to North Pole–cold so quickly?

"Don't let me keep you, Wyatt…unless you can't find your way out."

His eyebrows dipped at the challenge, but instead of hurling another barb her way or insisting she go first, he turned on his heel and stalked out of the boathouse. She heard him pause to put on his shoes.

The moment he left the dock, her knees buckled. She fumbled her way onto a chair at the bistro table and dropped her head into her hands. For the first time in her life, she wanted to take a page from her cousin's book and run away from home. But as she'd told Megan repeatedly, running from your problems never solved them.

She had to stay and fight if she ever wanted her life to

get back to normal—or whatever normal was now that a Sutherland didn't own Sutherland Farm.

Life would be so much easier if she could avoid paying for her mistakes, Hannah decided as she entered the barn. But hiding out in her cottage until her pride quit stinging wasn't an option even if Wyatt had ordered her to stay out of his way.

She had to ensure the foals' formula was properly mixed. At this stage, mistakes could be fatal. If all went according to plan, she could prepare the formula and escape before Wyatt and Sam arrived.

Butterflies swarmed in her stomach at the memory of making love with him this morning, and even if she wanted to forget, the fatigue lingering in muscles she didn't use often wouldn't let her. But the intimacy was over. No encores on the books.

And she was okay with that.

Mostly.

She'd survived the messy endings of intimate relationships before, but this one felt different. She'd never reacted as viscerally to any man as she did to Wyatt. Ignoring a connection that powerful wasn't going to be easy. But if life had taught her anything, it was how to say goodbye.

She deliberately kicked the unpleasant thought aside. The foals needed one hundred percent of her attention to pull them through. It had been only a couple of hours since she'd left them, but so much could happen in that short time span at this critical stage. She had to be extra vigilant.

She stepped inside the barn and a voice carried down the aisle. Sam's voice. "Been a long time since I saw foals this small," he said.

Her steps slowed. If Sam was here, so was Wyatt. An hour early. So much for her plan to avoid them. The sawdust on the floor sucked at her feet like quicksand, and her stomach filled with lead-like dread as she approached the stall. Their early appearance also brought up a second sticky issue. She prayed Sam wouldn't let anything slip about their secret rendezvous.

A low chuckle—*Wyatt's*—made her heart beat unevenly.

"Likes to buck, that one," Sam said. "He's going to be a handful."

"If he makes it."

"He'll make it. He's a fighter."

"You can't be sure, Sam. There's no point in getting attached."

"Son, nothing in life is guaranteed. But you can't live life long-distance. You have to get down and dirty and sample everything—even if it might be a bitter brew. Do you know how many failed attempts Triple Crown had before we hit on the right recipe?"

"One hundred forty-seven. You've told me."

"That means one hundred forty-six failures. But the success was worth it. Henry Ford believed failure was an opportunity to begin again with more knowledge. Sometimes you get a gut feeling about whiskey or animals or people and you just have to trust it. My intuition tells me this fella will make it, and so will the filly. She's a mite timid and small, but there's an alertness in her eyes that says she's gonna try to stick around."

Hannah inched closer, positioning herself where she could see into the stall without being seen. Wyatt had shaved away his sexy beard stubble and tamed the hair she'd mussed with her fingers. And though the morning was still cool, only a snug black T-shirt and jeans hugged his supple muscles—muscles she'd mapped with her hands, tasted with her tongue.

Within the smothering confines of her jacket her body steamed from embarrassment and lingering arousal—arousal that would be denied if she had a functioning brain cell remaining in her body. Her attraction to Wyatt made no sense—the explosive sexual chemistry even less so.

Sam briskly rubbed the colt, then turned his attention to the filly. He rambled on about conformation, but Hannah barely registered Sam's words. She couldn't peel her attention from

Wyatt. He looked so different with his shoulders relaxed and the rigid control missing from his expression. He'd brought no trace of the stiff bottom-line bastard into the stall. Instead, he seemed likeable. Approachable.

Like the man who had tempted her instead of repelling her.

The easy camaraderie between the men was something she'd never had with her father who'd been more likely to order and criticize, trying to get her to be the one thing she never could be—her mother. Her father's lack of communication since he'd left the farm and her behind only confirmed the emotional gulf between them.

"Good-looking foals," Sam concluded. The filly latched on to his finger, trying to nurse.

"And hungry," Wyatt responded with a smile in his voice that made Hannah's knees weak. "We need to feed them."

Not wanting to get caught spying, she took a bracing breath, gathered her courage for the initial awkward encounter ahead and stepped into view. Wyatt's head snapped up. His shoulders went rigid, and his dark eyes speared her.

Every cell inside her jumped like a spooked herd. "Good morning, Wyatt, Sam."

She gave herself a mental pat on the back for keeping her voice level when her nerves and knees quivered like gelatin. Wyatt didn't need to know that her palms were damp or that her mouth watered from the memory of his passionate kisses. Nor did he need to know that despite the asinine way he'd acted after their encounter, her body still lit up like a Fourth of July salute for his.

Wyatt scowled. "I told you to sleep in."

"Some of us have to work for a living. Besides, I didn't show you how to prepare the formula last night."

"I can read the directions on the container."

"I'm adding additional nutrients since they're underweight."

If what had happened between them haunted him the way it did her, then his cool eyes and tone didn't reveal it. Didn't he remember each kiss, each touch, the feel of their bodies coming together? Or was she just another woman in a long line of them? That possibility bothered her more than it should.

But why? Was she actually developing feelings for a guy who slept with her then shoved her away? Surely she had better sense?

Then his gaze slowly raked over her. He looked at her differently now—in a way that said he'd seen her naked, had his mouth on her breasts and his body deep inside hers. The respective intimate parts awakened in response, and when his eyes lifted to hers again it was all she could do to avoid hyperventilating.

Apparently she wasn't smart enough not to have some lingering connection to him.

"Beautiful babies, Hannah. Sorry you lost the mare."

Sam's comment provided a much-needed and sobering distraction. She met his gaze only briefly, hoping he wouldn't let anything about their secret slip. "Me, too, Sam."

The click of the latch as she opened it sounded as loud as a rifle report, and for some silly reason her legs quivered as if she'd run a marathon as she joined them in the stall. The square seemed as cramped and stuffy as a closet with the three of them inside.

Focus. "I need to do a quick exam before we feed them."

"We'll step out," Wyatt said coolly.

"Need any help?" Sam said simultaneously, his need to feel useful impossible to miss.

"Thank you, Sam. You could hold their heads while I take their temperatures. If they have any fever, I'll need to start antibiotics."

"Will do. Wyatt will block their haunches to keep 'em from moving away."

Wyatt's reluctance to be anywhere near her couldn't be more obvious, but he moved into place. She quickly took each foal's temperature and did a cursory exam with the weight of his dark, watchful, judgmental gaze on her. Finishing was a relief and not only because neither foal had a fever.

"I'll get the formula."

"Show me how to mix it," Wyatt ordered.

"Y'all go ahead." Sam waved them on. "I'll stay with these two. Nothing like a young'un to put some life in an old body."

Wyatt hesitated, clearly debating Sam's safety. Needing to get away from him, Hannah hustled toward the prep room. He followed. The uncomfortable silence between them as she mixed the powder into warm water made her edgy, but she couldn't think of anything to say to break the tension.

When she set the spoon aside Wyatt passed her a bottle and the funnel. Their fingers brushed, sending a jolt of electricity through her that suctioned the breath from her lungs.

She scrambled for a distraction. "You said your mother did Sam dirty when they divorced. But that doesn't explain why you're taking care of him."

He positioned the funnel and held the bottle for her to fill. Was he ignoring her or choosing his words?

"I owe him," he said a full minute later.

"Because…?"

Another long silence filled the air. "He treated me like a son, paid for my education and gave me a job at Triple Crown Distillery when I graduated. Sure, he made me start at the bottom, but he mentored me. And then I stole the company from him."

Shock rippled through her, chased by disgust. Wyatt really was a heartless bastard.

Wait a minute. "If that were true, then Sam wouldn't like and trust you."

Wyatt's eyes narrowed. "What makes you think he does?"

"You're very comfortable together."

"He could be senile."

"He's forgetful sometimes but not senile. If you took the business from him you must have had a good reason—one he understands and accepts."

Wyatt's eyes narrowed with suspicion. "That's a big assumption for someone who's only met him once before."

Oops. “I have a lot of experience working with Alzheimer’s patients, and assessing their abilities is crucial to their progress.” True, but of course, not the whole truth. “What happened with Sam to make you seize control of the company? And before you tell me it’s none of my business, you made it my concern when you brought Sam in to take care of my animals.”

“At first he misplaced things. His reading glasses, his favorite pen, his car. Then he had trouble remembering names, meeting times and verbal agreements with distributors. As second-in-command I covered for him until the day he got lost on the way home from work and ended up calling for help when he ran out of gas two states away. He’d become so unreliable that I forced him into retirement and took over as CEO.”

He capped the bottles. “Sam lived for two things—his horse farm and Triple Crown Distillery. My mother took the first. I took the second. The least I can do is assume responsibility for his care.”

“Doesn’t Sam have any other family who could help?”

“No. He and his first wife never had children.”

“You have alternatives to letting him live with you.”

Anger flared in his eyes. “He deserves better than to be shoved in a facility and ignored.”

“I wasn’t suggesting you do that.”

“Others have.”

“Tell me, Wyatt, what would have happened to Triple Crown if you hadn’t taken control of the company?”

“That’s irrelevant. I didn’t allow that to happen.”

But it was relevant. It proved Wyatt was capable of seeing beyond the bottom line to the people involved. “If you were the heartless bastard I initially believed you to be, you would have institutionalized Sam and walked away without a second thought.”

“Is that what you’d do?”

“No. I’d take care of him as long as I could. And I’d keep

his dream alive the same way I'm keeping my mother's alive by continuing to rescue horses."

Their gazes held in a connection that wasn't in the least bit sexual but was satisfying nonetheless. It went deeper and filled Hannah with the hope that they could work through their awkward situation. Then he blinked, and the distrustful expression she'd come to associate with him returned.

"My mother left Sam the moment he was diagnosed. She said she wasn't wasting her life playing nursemaid to a man who was regressing to childhood. My last girlfriend ended our three-year relationship when I told her I'd be assuming responsibility for Sam. She didn't want to be saddled with his care, either."

Hannah wanted to hug him more than anything at that moment. And she knew the gesture wouldn't be welcome. "Not every woman bails when the going gets tough."

"It's not just women, Hannah, it's human nature to look out for number one. *Love* only lasts as long as it's convenient. When it no longer serves a purpose or becomes a burden, love and the people involved in it are discarded like three-day-old fish. That's why there will never be another woman in my life other than the temporary kind. If you can handle that, fine. But don't try to plant a white picket fence around me."

She flinched. And then it was as if a light bulb went off in her brain. Wyatt had a lot in common with her rescue horses. He snarled and bit because he'd been hurt before. If he pushed her away with his verbal attacks, it was only because he was afraid to trust, afraid to love. Afraid to be let down. Again.

But if anyone needed his trust restored in people, it was Wyatt. With a little TLC, he could become a decent human being.

But was she woman enough for the task? Or was this rescue beyond even her capabilities?

There was only one way to find out. She'd have to save Wyatt from himself, and doing so would be her biggest—her riskiest—rescue challenge to date.

Ten

Summonses to the house were nothing new, but today the butterflies in Hannah's stomach multiplied with each step. Given the explosive chemistry between her and Wyatt, the course she'd chosen was a risky one strewn with emotional pitfalls.

Rather than face Nellie, who could read her like a book, Hannah crossed the patio to Wyatt's office. She spotted him through the French doors sitting behind his desk, his attention focused on his laptop computer. Then he looked up and the impact of his gaze hit her, scattering the butterflies.

He looked every inch the successful millionaire in his white silk dress shirt with the neck unbuttoned and the sleeves rolled up to reveal his muscular forearms and his platinum Breitling watch. She struggled to fill her lungs without looking like a gaping guppy.

He closed the computer, rose and crossed the room to open the door. "It's about time you got here."

Textbook case of growling to warn her to keep her distance.

But she didn't scare so easily. "I was working with the studs. That's not something I can interrupt without throwing off everyone's schedule."

"Come in." He stalked away, leaving Hannah to follow.

She studied his broad back and the black trousers outlining his firm buttocks—buttocks she'd dug her nails into when she'd pulled him deeper into her body. Her heart banged faster and her mouth watered.

Wyatt stabbed a finger at the visitor chair, then sat behind his wide desk and rocked back in his seat. His gaze rolled over her in that knee-weakening way of his.

She sat. "Why the urgency?"

"Your visitor from Dubai called Nellie and informed her he'd be arriving in two days. When I told her I'd be out of town and asked that the sales staff handle him, she insisted I talk to you."

"Didn't she explain that Mr. Shakkar is too important to pawn off on the sales staff?"

"When I bought the farm I was assured the staff could handle day-to-day operations. Why not this?"

"Mr. Shakkar is a long-term customer who has spent millions on Sutherland horses in the past, and he's likely to buy more on this trip. He's very influential both stateside and on the European circuit, and he's sent a lot of business our way. My father always—"

"I'm not your father."

"I know that." Boy, did she ever. "But as I was saying, my father always gave repeat customers the VIP treatment. It encourages them to be loyal to us.

"Don't worry about it. I'll take care of Rashed. He's been interested in opening up a therapeutic riding clinic for a while. I'll walk him through FYC's practices, then cook dinner for him at my place afterward."

Wyatt's expression turned thundercloud dark. "I've experienced one of your business dinners. I wouldn't want him to get the wrong impression. Unless, of course, that is your plan."

She stiffened at the accusation, then forced her fingers to relax. *He's only snarling as a defense mechanism because he's afraid to trust.* She couldn't blame him. The attraction between them was scarily powerful.

"Just because you misunderstood my intentions doesn't mean he will."

He shot to his feet and paced to the window, hands on hips, spine stiff. "You take care of the client during the day. I'll get back in time for dinner *here.* You'll act as my hostess for the evening as Nellie tells me you did for your father. But business is as far as it goes, Hannah."

The harder he fought, the sweeter the success of winning him over would be. She bit the inside of her lip to stop an anticipatory smile. For now, she had to work on getting him to lower the drawbridge he kept closed tightly around the fortress of his heart. Only then could he heal.

"You don't need to warn me off again, Wyatt. You've done an excellent job of that already. I'm well aware you regret our…encounter. I'll talk to Nellie about the menu on my way out."

"I'll handle it. Sutherland Farm is now a Triple Crown property. From now on we do things my way."

Where in the hell was Hannah?

Wyatt checked his watch as the limo he'd hired to pick up their guest approached the house. As his hostess, she should have been beside him to greet Shakkar. But she'd failed to make an appearance, and she wasn't responding to his text messages or calls. He'd managed to make it back from Chicago on time, but she hadn't made it a half mile up the driveway punctually.

Did she believe sex with him gave her permission to be irresponsible? If so, she'd learn differently.

Triple Crown ran a first-class operation and international

visitors were common. He knew his way around entertaining, but he'd been counting on Hannah's familiarity with the guest and horse lingo to facilitate the evening. He'd obviously misplaced his trust, which only reinforced his belief that women used sex to bend the rules to suit them.

Masking his irritation, he descended the stairs to meet the limo at the end of the sidewalk. The rear door opened before he could reach it. Instead of a suit-clad middle-aged man emerging, a drop-dead sexy black do-me stiletto attached to a shapely feminine limb emerged from the dim interior. Even while he appreciated the sight, Wyatt mentally adjusted to the change in head count. Shakkar hadn't mentioned bringing a guest, but Nellie could make it work. Nellie could make anything work—as he'd discovered through her calm handling of several of Sam's crises.

Wyatt forced his gaze upward over the shiny black fabric outlining curvy hips, a narrow waist and sweet breasts, then he encountered Hannah's sexy, smoky eyes. Surprise stopped him in his tracks.

She looked beautiful with her ruby red lips and short, form-fitting strapless dress. Lust hit him like a bullet train. Her gaze ran over him in a slow visual caress and her pupils expanded. Reciprocal embers of desire ignited in his groin, despite his decision to avoid any future entanglements with her.

She turned her attention to someone in the car behind her, snapping the connection. Wyatt attributed the oddly deflated sensation sweeping him to relief that she hadn't stood him up but had been seeing to their guest.

While she was distracted, he took in the rest of her. She'd pinned up her dark hair, leaving her neck and shoulders bare. Kissably bare. Silver earrings dangled from her lobes, dancing against her neck with each movement. His mouth watered for a taste of her pale nape. He crushed the thought, but acknowledged the surplus of creamy skin on display would be a distraction tonight and a test of his control. Digging deep for composure, he took a slow, measured breath and released it.

A man with olive skin and black hair graying at the temples exited the car. The older guy eyed Hannah with a lap-her-up appreciation that set Wyatt's teeth on edge.

Hannah said something in a language Wyatt couldn't identify, but the familiarity and warmth in her tone scalded him like acid. Their guest caught her hand and carried it to his smiling lips. "Hannah, you are a true blessing. A feast for the eyes as well as the soul."

Wyatt's molars gnashed at the effusive flattery. "Good evening."

Hannah's bright smile transformed into a tense stretching of her lips as the duo faced him on the sidewalk. "Rashed, I'd like you to meet Wyatt Jacobs, Sutherland Farm's new owner. Wyatt, Rashed Shakkar."

Tamping down his instant hostility, Wyatt shook hands. "Welcome. I trust Hannah gave you a satisfactory tour this afternoon?"

One that didn't include a visit to her cottage, her bed or the boathouse. The words burned like a lit fuse through Wyatt's brain.

"Hannah is a wonderful hostess. Her knowledge of horses is outshone only by her beauty."

A ruby the exact shade of Hannah's lips twinkled on a thin chain between her breasts drawing Wyatt's gaze like a magnet. With substantial effort, he forced his attention back to his guest. "Come in. Nellie tells me she's prepared your favorites."

"Ah. Nellie. Another Sutherland treasure. Her cooking is always one of the highlights of my visit. She is as much a magician in the kitchen as Hannah is with her horses."

Wyatt tamped his irritation and led his guest inside. It was going to be a long night if he had to listen to this bombast all evening.

Ninety-two agonizing minutes later, Wyatt decided he had

to end this evening. His jaw ached from clenching his teeth. He ordered his taut muscles to relax as Nellie cleared the dessert plates.

Hannah had charmed their guest throughout the meal, playing Shakkar like a Stradivarius, drawing him into conversation and making him laugh at her stories. Wyatt's custom-tailored dinner jacket chaffed like a straitjacket, his tie squeezed like a noose, and the desire to get rid of Shakkar was quickly becoming a compulsion.

Shakkar laid his napkin beside his plate. "Wyatt, do you realize how fortunate you are that Hannah stayed on after her father's retirement? I assure you, I am not the only one who would like to lure her away."

And not only for her horse-breeding skills, Wyatt concluded. The man wanted Hannah in his bed.

"I'm well aware of Hannah's value as an employee."

And as a lover.

Wyatt set his brandy snifter aside. Perhaps he'd been too hasty in dismissing a relationship with Hannah. They had a sexual connection like no other he'd experienced. She was intelligent, worked hard and had an undeniable loyalty to the farm. She'd be a dedicated custodian of the property and would allow him to focus on Triple Crown as long as he controlled her expenditures on her rescued animals. And she treated Sam well. In fact, she might be more knowledgeable about Sam's condition than Wyatt was.

The most important selling factor of a relationship with her was that when he decided to sell, she'd insist on staying behind. There would be no emotional goodbyes or ugly scenes. She'd be nothing more than a chapter in his life—a short, passionate one—with a preset ending.

Establishing Hannah as his mistress could prove quite advantageous for each of them. He could pacify her love for material things with the gifts he could bestow upon her, and with her beauty and poise she'd be an asset to his business and an excellent hostess, not to mention sharing his bed when he came home to visit Sam. He could even use her Grand Prix connections to ink a sponsorship deal and tap into a new market.

Decision made, Wyatt pushed away from the table and stepped behind Hannah's chair to pull it back. As soon as he dispatched their guest he'd make his proposition. With all she stood to gain, how could she refuse?

Shakkar covered Hannah's hand on the table before she could rise. "Hannah, thank you for devoting your day to me, and thank you, Wyatt, for allowing her to entertain me. I regret I cannot stay longer. Hannah, my dear, before I return to my hotel I have a small gift for your horse rescue operation."

Shakkar reached into his jacket pocket and laid a check on the table. Hannah quickly covered the paper, but not before Wyatt saw the amount. Twenty-five thousand dollars.

Warning sirens screeched in his head. Had Hannah been charming the old goat to get money out of him? Would Shakkar expect favors in return for his gift? *Sexual* favors.

Wyatt's mother had made a career out of charming her "gentlemen friends" into supporting her after she'd dumped Sam. Was Hannah formed from the same mold as his mother? He'd begun to believe otherwise, but now… Hannah's flushed cheeks and sweet smile knotted the muscles along Wyatt's spine.

"Rashed, you're very generous. Thank you. And as I promised this morning, I'll keep an eye out for suitable horses for your rehabilitation program."

"You could sell him some of yours," Wyatt said to interrupt their little mutual admiration party.

Hannah stiffened, then she slowly rose and turned toward him. "I don't have qualified horses to spare at the moment."

Shakkar stood. "Just as well. Now I have a reason to keep in touch. You have my direct line should you need to contact me for any reason."

Hannah beamed and nodded. "I'll be in touch."

"Now, regretfully, I must take my leave. I would like to

stay longer, but I have monopolized your time and prevented you from breeding your future champions. I look forward to the delivery of mine. You will notify me close enough to the date for me to make arrangements for an extended stay?"

"I'll let you know. For now, pencil in late January."

By then, Wyatt intended to have her firmly entrenched as his mistress. And he would not share.

Rashed linked his arm through Hannah's, ignoring and irritating Wyatt. The duo walked through the foyer and onto the columned front porch. Humid night air clogged Wyatt's lungs and clung to his skin, making his collar feel tight and abrasive. Hannah started to descend the stairs. Wyatt grabbed her free hand and anchored her by his side where his hostess—*his woman*—should be.

Shakkar paused. His eyes dropped to Wyatt and Hannah's linked hands, then rose to Wyatt's face. His wizened expression said the old guy knew how much his attention to Hannah had annoyed his host.

"Mr. Shakkar, I hope you have an uneventful flight home," Wyatt spoke with what he hoped sounded like genuine courtesy.

Shakkar dipped his head ever so slightly to acknowledge Wyatt's claim, then released Hannah's hand. "Thank you. I wish you many years of enjoyment from Sutherland Farm, Mr. Jacobs."

Shakkar descended the stairs, then stopped by the limo door the chauffeur had opened. "Hannah, take care until next time, and please give my regards to your father. And remember what I said. If you decide you would like a change of climate, there will always be a position for someone with your considerable talents at my stable. And for Nellie, of course."

The bastard was trying to steal Hannah *and* Nellie right in front of his face. Wyatt's supply of civility vaporized. "Good night."

With a bow, their guest ducked into the car—not a moment

too soon. Wyatt waited until the limo rounded a curve in the driveway and the taillights winked out of sight.

"For what delivery is he planning to return?"

"Rashed made a one-point-eight million dollar deposit on one of Commander's yet-to-be-born foals today. You've given the staff the authority to operate as usual, so you weren't consulted." She tugged her hand from his. "It would have been polite for me to escort him back to his hotel."

"So you could thank him properly for the twenty-five grand?" Damn it. That had sounded like jealousy. And he was not.

Her cheeks reddened. "Does being obnoxious come naturally to you? You do it with such skill."

"You had him eating out of your hand."

The ruby pendant glistened in the porch light as she took an angry breath, drawing his attention to the soft swells of her breasts. Swells he yearned to touch, to taste.

"It's my job as your hostess to be charming, and that's easy to do when someone is as gracious, knowledgeable and entertaining as Rashed."

"Gracious? The man flirted with you throughout the meal. Perhaps because of your dress."

Her eyes rounded. "What's wrong with my dress?"

Besides the fact that Wyatt wanted to peel it from her? "It's provocative."

"Oh, for pity's sake. I—" She shook her head. "Never mind. Good night, Wyatt." She pivoted.

This wasn't going as planned, but Hannah, damn her, had the ability to shatter his composure. He recaptured her hand and pulled her around, knowing even as he did so that detaining her now was a mistake. He was too on edge after watching her work their guest all night. He would do better to make his pitch tomorrow—after he'd calmed down.

"You look inviting, Hannah. I wouldn't want Shakkar to get the wrong idea."

"So you've said. But I never once implied to Rashed that I was available in that way."

"Aren't you?"

She grimaced. "He's almost my father's age. And believe it or not, contrary to my recent actions, I am usually extremely selective about who shares my bed."

Once again, she jerked her hand free. Not liking the out-of-control feeling boiling through him, he let her go.

She took two steps away then faced him again with her hands curled into fists by her sides. "What is your problem, Wyatt? You don't want me so you don't think any other man should?"

He should have known Hannah wouldn't act as expected. Thus far she'd done nothing but surprise him. "I never said I didn't want you, Hannah. In fact, I do want you. Very much. I believe we could come to a mutually beneficial arrangement."

"What kind of arrangement?" she asked suspiciously.

"Our chemistry is too potent to be denied or ignored. Become my mistress and you can keep your job and your home and I'll continue funding FYC. The only difference will be that when I'm here, you'll spend your nights in my bed."

Wyatt's mistress.

Nights in his bed.

Hannah's breath shuddered from her lungs, forced out by her pounding heart. The switch from Wyatt's cool and distant demeanor during dinner to the request for her to become his mistress made her head spin.

Not his *lover,* but his *mistress.* That distinction defined their roles quite explicitly, pulling her in and keeping his distance simultaneously. Like an animal whose trust had been abused.

The air between them crackled with electricity and awareness—the way it had each time their gazes had met across the dinner table tonight. So yes, maybe she'd tried a little harder to entertain Rashed, been a bit more talkative, laughed too much and sipped a bit too much wine all in an effort to hide the effect Wyatt had on her. Her face ached from all the smiling she'd done.

"Wyatt, what do you really want? Do you even know? You claimed you wanted a horse farm, and yet you've shown no interest in running one. Then you said you wanted to help Sam, but your overprotectiveness holds him back. And now you say you want me in your bed, and yet you've insulted me at every opportunity."

"I want you. I want this." He hooked a hand behind her nape as swiftly as a striking snake. His mouth slammed over hers and he took, greedily, aggressively mashing his lips against hers and ravaging her tongue with his. But his hunger only magnified her own.

He tasted of after-dinner coffee, brandy and…Wyatt. Delicious, seductive, sexy Wyatt. Adrenaline blasted through her veins. The man knew how to kiss. But to be his mistress? She couldn't imagine going into an intimate relationship knowing it would be temporary.

With her lips tingling and her body weakened by want, she made a last-ditch attempt to reclaim rational thought by wedging her hands between them and pushing against his chest. "I don't know if I'm mistress material."

Wyatt's gaze burned with hunger. "That's all I can offer, Hannah."

Given the way his trust had been violated in the past, she couldn't blame him for being leery of relationships. But his dedication to Sam proved he had the capacity to bond deep in his wounded wary heart. All she had to do was prove it to him.

Wyatt had so much potential. The invitation to become his mistress was like the door to a perfect opportunity opening a crack. If she could earn his trust and gently break past his barriers, he would be whole again.

With each thump of his heart against her palm, heat pulsed up her arms then settled heavily in her belly. She wanted him, craved him, ached for him, yearned to relive that cataclysmic rush of desire they'd shared. But more than that, she wanted Wyatt to realize that it was okay to trust and care and open his heart to love.

A voice in her head urged her to back away and guard her heart. But what better way to teach him to trust than to open herself to him? It was risky. Very. Very. Risky. But for his sake, for Sutherland Farm's and FYC's sakes, she had to try. She would simply have to make sure to hold a bit of her heart in reserve because the time would come—as it did with every rescue—to let go.

She gulped down her doubts and took a deep breath. "I accept your terms."

His strong arms banded around her, molding her torso to his. Even before their lips met urgent desire drenched her like warm honey. As he lowered his head she rose on tiptoe to meet him and wound her arms around his waist, digging her fingers into his hard muscles. The unleashed passion in his kiss trampled her, filling her with urgency.

There were too many barriers between them. She needed to strip him down—physically, emotionally. She fumbled with the buttons of his shirt until she found hot, supple skin. While their tongues tangled, she splayed her fingers over his pectorals and impatiently shoved fabric out of her way without breaking the kiss that melted her insides. Her fingers bumped over his tiny beaded nipples once, twice.

His groan of approval vibrated through her and her womb spasmed in anticipation, then he tore his mouth away, hissing a breath between his teeth. "I want you in my bed."

"Then take me there."

He grabbed her hand and towed her through the front door. Without turning on the lights he led her up the stairs. She'd traveled this path countless times when she'd lived here so she had no trouble recalling each tread in the darkness.

He led her to the double doors that had once been the entrance to her father's suite. Uncertainties about the wisdom of this choice flickered through her. She'd come across a few animals in her time whose trust could never be regained. What if Wyatt was one of them?

But then he backed her against the door frame and kissed her again. His hands skimmed over her hips, her waist, her breasts, stealing her breath, making her dizzy with desire and vaporizing any reservations she might have had. He cupped her bottom and pulled her hips to his. The thick column of his erection against her tummy made her ache for his possession. She threaded her fingers through the springy hair at his nape, and a shudder racked him.

He swept her into his arms, kicked the door shut and crossed the inky dark room. Not even a sliver of moonlight penetrated the window coverings. She couldn't see anything, but that only magnified her other senses. A trace of his cologne lingered in the air mixed with that certain something unique to Wyatt. His breaths teased the hair at her temples, tickling her in the most erotic way.

He released her legs, easing her feet to the floor in a slow, seductive slide of her body against his. Her feet sank into deep carpet. His fingertip traced the ruffled edge of her bodice, then dipped into her cleavage. He touched her pendant, circled it, flicked it, rolled it between his fingers.

"This has been driving me crazy all night. I wanted to taste you here."

The sexual nuance in his voice rumbled over her skin like a sandpaper caress. Her nipples puckered as he bent to brush his lips across the spot his fingertip had marked.

He reached for her zipper. Then, in a frantic tangle of arms and legs, they undressed each other. She splayed her hands on his chest, mapping his muscles with her fingertips. She traced his collarbone, his broad shoulders, the veins cording his big biceps, then stroked down his sternum and circled his nipples. His breath roughened, quickened.

Her fingers bumped over the valleys between his abdominal muscles, then he caught her upper arms and snatched her forward. Bare skin slapped bare skin. Every naked scalding inch of his chest, belly and thighs branded hers. His teeth sank into the side of her neck—not hard enough to hurt, but with enough pressure to make her squeak in surprise and tremble with desire. His tongue swirled a teasing pattern across her shoulder and goose bumps lifted her flesh.

Deft fingers found her nipples, pinching and rolling with the perfect amount of pressure to make her weak in the knees. His ability to know exactly when and how and where to touch her to drive her wild couldn't be sheer luck or just skill. It had to be more—like the rare magical winning combination of a champion mare-stud combo. A meant-to-be union.

He tweaked and caressed until she squirmed impatiently. Then his fingers dug into her hair, releasing the clip. Cool strands rained down onto her shoulders, teasing like sensual feathers. She shivered and reached between them to wrap her fingers around his thick erection. Hot. Hard. Satiny. She stroked his length, up, down, up again, savoring the guttural encouragement her caresses elicited. His hands covered hers, stilling her.

"Wyatt, I can't wait to have you inside me," she whispered.

He swept her into his arms again, carried her across the room and lowered her. The cool fabric of his bed against her overheated skin shocked a gasp from her. Before she could recover, he whisked her panties away. A drawer beside her opened, then closed. The mattress dipped, then blazing heat enclosed her nipple. Wyatt sucked her, grazed her with his teeth, laved her with his tongue.

The sensations building inside her were so stupendously wonderful she didn't want him to stop. She speared her fingers into his hair and held him close. He transferred his attention to the opposite breast while his fingers outlined her waist, hips, thigh, then ever so slowly scraped along the inside of her knee before heading upward at a snail's pace.

Torn between urging him to hurry and wanting to savor each second and make it last, she tensed in anticipation as he inched near her center. And then the slightly rough pad of his finger moved over her, making her gasp and jump at the slash of desire ripping through her.

He simultaneously teased her with his mouth and his hands, until her muscles contracted and her back arched as she strained for release. She massaged his shoulders, digging her nails into his thick muscles as her climax neared.

"That feels…so good," she managed to say in a broken whisper. He lifted his head. A moan of disappointment spilled from her lips. "Please don't stop."

"One of the things I've noticed about you, Hannah, is that you take your sweet time with everything—until we're in bed. Then you rush."

"I can't help it. You make me—" She bit off the confession. He didn't need to know that she'd never felt anything even remotely as profound as she did with him.

His breath steamed the skin at the base of her breastbone, then traversed down her midline. His tongue dipped into her navel, then cruised lower. He palmed her legs apart. Then his hot tongue flicked over her. She jerked and cried out at the almost unbearable intensity of the pleasure assailing her. And then he stopped.

She fisted her hands in the sheets in frustration.

"I make you what, Hannah?"

"Want. You." *Forever.*

No. No. No. Not forever. Only until he's healed.

"The feeling's mutual." He dipped his head and set a rhythm destined to drive her insane. She focused on that rather than her crazy thoughts, and he made it easy. Each sweep of his tongue jacked up her response. Each sip of her flesh emptied her lungs. Pressure built, like an inflating balloon, then she exploded as orgasmic shock waves rocked her.

The pulsing waves receded and her tension eased, but before she could catch her breath Wyatt began his assault anew, relentlessly pleasuring her. The second orgasm hit harder, faster, before she was ready.

Decimated, weak, spent, she hooked her hands under his arms and tugged. "Wyatt, please, I need you inside me."

"Not as much as I need to be there."

She couldn't see his face in the darkness, but she could feel his heat, hear his raspy breath and the hunger in his voice and that stoked hers. He rose over her then, the thick head of his erection nudged her opening. He paused, but she couldn't wait. She lifted her hips to meet him and used her hands to guide him. He sank deep in one smooth plunge, filling her completely. His groan rolled over her, then he withdrew.

She gripped his hips and pulled him back, relishing the contractions of his buttocks as he returned. She wound her legs around him and locked her ankles behind his back. Only then did she realize she still wore her heels. The knowledge made her feel a little bit naughty, a tad kinky and very, very sexy.

Each thrust rekindled her passion, carrying her along on his journey to yet another climax. And then he rolled over, pulling her on top so that he lay on his back and her legs straddled his hips. She braced her hands on his pectorals.

"Ride me, Hannah," he ordered hoarsely. He covered her breasts, tweaking, teasing, tormenting, as she lifted and sank over him again and again until her thighs burned and her muscles strained for relief. Then his thumb found her spot. The combination of his deep penetration and deft touch, the blackness of the room and the echoes of lovemaking hurtled her over the edge. Spasms of ecstasy racked her.

Even before her body quit quaking, Wyatt's fingers dug into her bottom, holding her close as he plunged harder, deeper and faster. Then he groaned and went still beneath her.

Drained, she melted onto his bellowing chest and rested her ear over his booming heart. She'd never been so perfectly attuned to anyone. And she was very, *very* afraid she'd crossed the point of no return and let herself get too attached.

Eleven

An unfamiliar sound jolted Hannah awake from a dead sleep. She squinted at her clock, but it wasn't there. Her room was dark. Too dark. Power outage?

Then she heard steady breathing beside her and remembered where she was. *Wyatt's bed.* She'd agreed to become his mistress.

A bolus of adrenaline raced through her system, erasing all traces of sleepiness. Doubts assailed her. What did she know about being any man's mistress?

She turned her head. She couldn't see him, but she could hear Wyatt beside her, feel his heat beneath the sheets and smell the heady aroma of their passionate night.

An overwhelming urge to escape beset her. She wasn't ready to face him. Not yet. Not until she understood the rules and boundaries of her new position and charted a way to get past his guard and teach him to trust again.

She eased onto her elbow. The red digital clock on his side of the bed read 5:06. Hannah bit back a groan. Nellie would be up and about, starting coffee and tinkering with whatever recipes she'd chosen for the day. If she caught Hannah slipping out of the house, Hannah would never hear the end of it.

While Nellie might play matchmaker and push Hannah in Wyatt's direction, Nellie was too old-fashioned to accept a sex-only arrangement and Hannah didn't want to disappoint her.

She cautiously felt her way to the edge of the mattress and slid her legs over the side, all the while listening and thankfully not hearing a change in Wyatt's respiratory pattern. The sheet dragged across her bare, hypersensitive skin, stirring a hormonal response that should have been exhausted last night.

Her feet landed on something sharp. *Ouch.* Her shoes. Wyatt had removed them last night—sometime during the second round of Braille sex in the dark.

Her pulse jumped and her skin prickled at the memory of that slower and even more intense last session. She'd been so sated afterward her brain had shut down, and instead of leaving as she'd intended, she didn't have the slightest recollection of what had happened after he'd tucked her head into his shoulder.

Scooping up her shoes with one hand, she inched blindly across the thick carpet toward where she thought Wyatt had dropped her dress. She found her bra first, then the crumpled Shantung silk, and eased each on, wincing at the sound of the zipper tearing through the room. Shoes in hand, she shifted on her feet. Now what?

How was she going to make her escape? The front stairs seemed too exposed. But the back staircase passed directly by Nellie's suite. That left only one option. The hidden staircase between Hannah's old room and her parents' suite led directly to the garage. Surely she could slip out undetected from there?

She sent up a silent thank-you that her mother had been an avid devotee of historic houses and European castles with their secret passages and rooms and had insisted the architect incorporate a hidden staircase in their home.

Hannah crept toward the concealed door, hoping Wyatt hadn't blocked it with furniture. She'd loved playing in the passageway as a child, pretending she was a European princess hiding from the dark knight who'd come to kidnap her and make her his bride.

Did Wyatt know about this exit? Running her hand along the chair rail, she felt for the telltale seam in the wood. When she found it, she pushed and the spring-loaded panel clicked open. She paused, ears straining for any sound from the bed, but Wyatt's breathing remained slow and steady.

Cool, slightly stale air drifted over Hannah's bare skin. She hesitated, yearning to spend a few more moments in his arms, but knowing she must go. Then she slipped inside, gently closed the door behind her and stopped on the landing to get her bearings.

She hadn't used this passage since her senior year in high school when she and Megan had missed curfew. Hannah had been terrified that her father would find out and ground her for the rest of her life.

She was tempted to open the door on the opposite side and visit her old bedroom, but she didn't know which of the four suites Sam and his nurse were using.

Without turning on the light because she didn't want to risk the faint trace around the door to Wyatt's room alerting him of her escape, she carefully descended the stairs, counting down. Twelve, eleven, ten… She'd made it to six when she heard something below her and froze. A footstep. A human footstep.

Heart racing, she gulped and listened and heard another shuffled tread. "Who's there?"

"Hannah? Is that you?" a quiet masculine voice replied.

The familiar tone pulled the cork on her fear. It drained from her like water from a rain barrel. "Sam?"

"Yep."

The overhead light flicked on. She blinked at the sudden brightness. Sam stood at the bottom landing. He wore his usual jeans and a flannel long-sleeved shirt and heavy down coat despite the predicted high temperatures for later in the day.

"What are you doing here, Sam?"

"I live here. What are *you* doing here?" he parroted.

Her cheeks burned. "Going home."

"Sneaking out, you mean. I'm sneaking in."

"Is this how you've been getting out of the house without Carol or Nellie seeing you?"

"Shh. Whisper. Yep. Wyatt can't keep me locked up like a prisoner."

She sighed. "He believes he's protecting you. I'll talk to him again. How have you been? Phoenix and I have missed our workouts with you."

"Phoenix hasn't missed me. I can't leave during the day when Wyatt's here or Carol's hovering, so I've been seeing Phoenix every night."

Uh-oh. "Alone?"

"Yep."

That explained the horse's improved behavior. Hannah and her staff had been amazed by the mare's rapid progress now that her wounds had healed.

"How have you managed to avoid security?"

He shrugged. "I learned the guard's schedule."

A good sign cognitively, but a bad one as far as Sam's safety was concerned. "Sam, you promised not to go to the stables alone."

"I did? Oh. Yeah. Guess I did. But you promised to let me work with Phoenix. So I did."

"I promised to let you work *with me* and only with me."

He eyed her clothing. "You're all dressed up."

"I had dinner with Wyatt and a client last night."

"And you stayed. With Wyatt."

Another blush worked its way from her chest to her hairline. She stalled by descending the last few steps.

"His room and mine are the only ones at the top of this staircase," Sam pointed out.

"Yes. I stayed with Wyatt. I don't mean to be rude, but I need to get home. I have to be at work soon." She laid a hand over Sam's forearm. "Sam, as much as I appreciate what you've done with Phoenix, promise me you won't go to the barn alone anymore. It's incredibly dangerous for you to be there without anyone knowing where you are. And if Wyatt finds out I've encouraged you to work with the horses behind his back, we'll both be in trouble."

Sam tilted his head and put a finger to his lips. "Shh."

The door beside them opened unexpectedly, revealing Nellie with Wyatt right behind her. Hannah's stomach dove to her bare feet. This was not going to be good.

"Land's sake, child, I thought we had talking mice. What are you doing in here?"

"Yes, Hannah. What are you doing?" Wyatt asked, his voice and eyes ice hard and showing no signs of last night's intimacy as he took in the duo huddled in the stairwell. Jeans and a white T-Shirt outlined his lean, muscular form to mouthwatering perfection.

"I didn't want to wake anyone on my way out."

Lame, Hannah. Staying in bed with him would have been less awkward than this.

Wyatt leaned into the stairwell to examine the space, crowding her against the wall. The smell of their lovemaking still clung to his skin, and his nearness made her body flush hot from her scalp to her toes. A delicious beard stubble darkened his scowling face. Fighting the urge to test the roughness of his jaw, she tightened her fingers around her shoes until a heel dug into her palm.

Wyatt's eyes pinned Sam. "Is this how you've been getting past Carol?"

Sam shifted on his feet. “I wouldn’t have to slip out if you didn’t keep me caged like a rabid dog, son.”

“That’s for your safety. Remember the penthouse?” Wyatt’s attention shifted to her. “In my office. Now.”

A lump rose in her throat at the fury in his eyes. “Wyatt—”

“Now, Hannah. Unless you want to be fired before you’ve had a chance to make excuses for your deception.”

Her gasp echoed up the stairwell. How could he threaten to fire her after last night? She couldn’t ask, not with Nellie and Sam listening to every word.

Who was the real Wyatt Jacobs? This coldhearted bastard? Or the man who cared for his stepfather and made Hannah’s body sing?

The first she could hate. The second she could lov—

No. No!

She couldn’t love Wyatt. She didn’t know him well enough. Or did she? A sinking sensation provided her answer. She’d fallen for the man he was deep down inside—the one he tried to hide from the world.

Head and heart reeling, she stared at Sam, torn between fighting for him and self-preservation.

“Hannah,” Wyatt threatened in that low tone that rumbled over her like thunder.

Sam patted her shoulder. “Go on, child. I’ll be fine. Wyatt’s more bark than bite.”

She hoped Sam was right. She risked a glance at Nellie. Surprisingly, Nellie looked cantankerous rather than disappointed, as if she were more than willing to go to bat for Hannah, thereby risking her own job. Hannah couldn’t have that.

She headed for the office and reckoning. The once familiar room now seemed like foreign territory. Enemy territory. How could her life have changed so much in barely over a month? She’d gone from gliding along in a contented rut to life on the edge of disaster and loving a man who might never heal enough to be able to love her in return. If she couldn’t find a way to fix this, she could lose her horses, FYC, her job, her home…and her heart.

Wyatt's deliberate footsteps approached and her mouth went dry. He entered the office and slowly, precisely closed the door, his controlled movements revealing his anger more clearly than shouted words.

He stopped inches from her. His eyes weren't cold. They burned with fury. "You knew my concern for Sam's safety and you encouraged him to work with the horses anyway."

Guilty. "He didn't ride."

"Can you be sure of that, Hannah? Were you with him each time he visited the stable? From what I overheard, you weren't."

How long had he been listening? "No. I can't be certain. But he promised and I trusted—"

"You trusted him? Sam's memory is like a sieve, and his reasoning is faulty. How long have you been lying to me and working with him behind my back?"

The anger and betrayal in his eyes stung like disinfectant on a fresh wound. She swallowed, struggling to find words to make him understand. "It was only a few times. But I knew if I could show you the value of horse therapy, you'd realize FYC is an important part of Sutherland Farm."

"You lied to me and you selfishly jeopardized Sam's safety."

She cringed. "Maybe you should tell me about the incident at the penthouse so I'll understand why you're so overprotective of him."

His lips flattened in refusal and seconds ticked past. "The only reason I am explaining something that is clearly none of your business is to make you realize how stupid you've been. Sam took a bar stool from inside my apartment out onto the patio to change a lightbulb in the eaves."

She frowned, not understanding. "And that's a problem why?"

"We were forty stories above the ground. One slip and he'd

have gone over the wall and landed on the concrete below. He was inches from death on a wobbly stool."

Nausea rolled through her. "Did he not realize—?"

"No. That's the point. Sam saw a task that needed doing but not the big picture. Poor judgment, as you should know, is only one symptom of his condition. Usually his errors are as innocuous as dressing inappropriately for the weather or forgetting he's eaten, but other times he makes life-threatening miscalculations like crossing the street without checking for traffic. Some days he's the stepfather I remember. Others he's as careless as a three-year-old and needs a keeper."

She hadn't realized the range of Sam's behavior. As Wyatt had said, she'd been so worried about herself and her horses that she hadn't considered Sam might have issues she'd yet to see.

"I'm sorry. I should have asked for his medical records the way I would for any of FYC's students. But each time I've been with him he's been quite lucid—except for the clothing mix-up."

Wyatt's eyes narrowed. "Were you befriending him in hopes of finding another sugar daddy for your horses?"

Surprised, she blinked. "No. I— Why would I do that?"

"Don't play the innocent, Hannah. I saw the way you worked Shakkar. The man was practically salivating over you. And we both know you've done your research on Triple Crown Distillery. You're too smart not to know Sam's net worth."

"I didn't." But Wyatt's disbelief was clear on his face. "How can you accuse me of being mercenary? Especially after last night."

His hardening expression told her bringing up last night had not been a wise choice. "All women use sex to manipulate men into giving them what they want."

Ouch. She might have underestimated the depth of his emotional damage. "Maybe you've been associating with the wrong women."

He stalked to the French doors. "You lied to me. I can't trust you. And I can't trust Sam. I had planned to keep this place until Sam's no longer cognizant of his surroundings. That's no longer an option."

Shock flowed over her like an iceberg. "Wait a minute! You bought Sutherland Farm and flipped my world upside down with the intention of turning right around and selling the property?"

He pivoted with rigid control. "Sam spends most of his time reminiscing about his farm, and he's most coherent when he discusses horses. I wanted him to be comfortable for however long he has left. But not at an increased risk to his safety."

That he'd spent millions of dollars to make his stepfather comfortable touched her. "Because you love him."

Wyatt recoiled as if she'd slapped him. "No. Because considering what my mother and I cost him, I owe him. It's a debt to repay. Nothing more. Nothing less."

She didn't want to believe he considered Sam a duty, but the coldness in his face and eyes was irrefutable. Clues she'd ignored suddenly formed a picture so clear she couldn't miss it.

"That's why you guaranteed our jobs for a year. It wasn't altruism. It was apathy. You never had any interest in Sutherland Farm at all. You planned to dump it at the end of the year."

"It could have been longer, depending on Sam's condition. But not now."

Her stomach hollowed out and her legs folded. She plopped into a leather chair across from his desk and stabbed her fingers into her hair. This wasn't just about FYC or her world imploding anymore. This was so much bigger.

"You never tried to get to know the staff because you don't give a damn about the farm, its mission or its people. All you care about is the bottom line and making the business as profitable as possible before dumping it on the market once it's served your purpose. That's why you were so determined to shut down FYC and to buy my little piece of land—to make Sutherland Farm a more attractive package for the next buyer."

"There's nothing wrong with cutting waste and improving profitability."

How could he be so clueless? "Not if all you care about is money. But I keep telling you, Wyatt, money isn't the only measure of success. Even if you haven't bothered to attend any of FYC's classes to see how we help dozens of others, you've seen Sam's progress when he works with the horses. Every day his balance, coordination and thought processes are clearer. His plotting to work with the mare at night when he wouldn't get caught is proof of that. My gosh, he even memorized Jeremiah's schedule."

"What good is thinking more clearly if he ends up dead?" The ice in his voice sent shivers up her spine. He had a point.

"And what about us? Was I only a temporary convenience, too? One you'd shed when you sold the farm? Do you have no feelings for me at all?" She wanted the needy words back the moment she heard them. But it was too late.

His unblinking gaze drilled her. "I asked you to be my mistress, not my wife."

She flinched and cursed herself for the telling reflex. "No. Marriage wouldn't be *profitable.* Would it?"

There sometimes came a painful point during a rescue when she had to admit she couldn't save an animal and she had to let it go.

Like she had with Sable.

And now with Wyatt.

She'd been wrong about him. He was one of the few whose trust could never be regained. And in becoming his mistress she wouldn't be earning his trust. She'd only be fooling herself into believing they had a future. Wyatt would never open his heart enough to love anyone.

The pain in her chest pulsed outward. Needing to escape before he discovered how badly the discovery hurt, she forced herself to her feet.

"I have to get to work and earn my keep. I'd hate to be responsible for the slowing of the money train. But you'll have to find yourself another mistress. I'm no longer available."

"Good thing we learn from our mistakes 'cause letting that gal walk out was a doozy," Sam said from the open patio door. The rising sun illuminated the lines in his face and the droop of his once proud shoulders.

"Hannah jeopardized your safety."

"She gave me a purpose for living. Working with that mare reminded me there's something I'm still good at."

"Sam—"

"Wyatt, I know your intentions are good, son, but I'd rather be locked up in an old folks' home where all I can smell is disinfectant and dirty diapers than be incarcerated here where I can see the life I'm missing."

Consternation rooted Wyatt to the rug. "You don't mean that. You love horse farms."

"I love being part of a horse farm, not looking through the windows at one like I'm watching TV. I know I have days when I forget stuff. And sometimes I overlook important details—or so you keep telling me. But being locked up isn't living."

Guilt twisted inside Wyatt like a knife. And if anyone understood the pain of being discarded, Wyatt did. But what else could he do?

"Give it time, Sam. You'll get used to the farm and I'll visit as often as work allows."

"Time is the one thing I don't have. My life is over. Might as well be dead. Told Hannah as much. At least *she* understood."

Alarm kicked through Wyatt. "You told Hannah you'd rather be dead than here?"

"Yep. That's why she let me work with the mare. I'm the one who broke the promise I made her by sneaking out. But I forgot. Or maybe I wanted to forget."

No wonder Hannah had intervened. "She should have come to me with her concerns instead of going behind my back."

How could he trust anyone who would do that?

"Would you have listened?"

Probably not.

"Much as I love you, Wyatt, you can be one stubborn son of a bitch when you set your mind to something. That ambition is good in business, but it doesn't work so well with people."

Wyatt flinched. "I'll make sure you get more time with the foals."

"I want to do more than play with babies. I want to work with horses that try to outsmart me. Like that mare. If I can't do that, then I want to go home."

Sam's passionate words were a jarring reminder of why they were here in the first place. "You can't, Sam. You sold your house before you moved into the penthouse with me. Remember?"

Sam frowned. "I do, now that you mention it. But this ain't my home and it never will be if I can't be with the people I love and enjoy the things I love doing while I still can."

Frustrated, Wyatt watched Sam storm out. He'd done everything he could to make Sam comfortable here. And Sam would calm down as he always did after one of his emotional outbursts and things would be fine.

Hannah, on the other hand, had betrayed him. She had to go.

Hannah stood on the unfamiliar doorstep of her father's town house, wishing her first visit to his new home could be under better circumstances and hoping he'd give her the answer she sought.

Her father, wearing only his bathrobe, opened the door. His eyebrows shot up, then he glanced briefly over his shoulder. "Hannah, this is a surprise."

"We need to talk."

"It's 6:00 a.m."

"This can't wait."

"It's all right, Luthor. Let her in," a recognizable woman's voice said from inside, spurring Hannah's heart into a racing beat.

Hannah gasped. "Is that Dana?"

The door opened wider, revealing the registered nurse who had been volunteering for FYC for almost a year. She also wore a robe and her tangled hair suggested she'd just climbed from bed. Not a pleasant realization.

"Good morning, Hannah. I need to get to work, so give me five minutes, then I'll be gone and you can talk."

Flabbergasted, Hannah's gaze bounced from the forty-something blonde to her father. He had a girlfriend? She couldn't remember him ever dating anyone. "Dad?"

"Come in, Hannah. There's fresh coffee in the kitchen." He turned and headed in that direction. Dana trotted up the stairs.

Hannah entered cautiously, not sure she could handle another shock this morning. She passed a den containing the leather sofas that had once occupied her father's office. In the kitchen he indicated she take a seat at a table that hadn't been in the old house.

He filled a mug and set it in front of her. "What brings you here so early without calling first?"

"I didn't realize I'd be interrupting something."

Her father's cheeks turned ruddy. "I have a life now. One that doesn't revolve around horses."

"You could have told me you were seeing someone."

"I wasn't sure how you'd handle it."

"I won't deny it's a surprise, but Mom's been gone a long time, Dad."

A little of the tension eased from his shoulders.

Dana breezed into the room wearing pink hospital scrubs. She kissed Hannah's father square on the mouth. "Gotta go, love. I'll see you tonight. And Hannah, I'll see you Sunday." Then she was gone.

"Does she live here?"

"No."

"How long have you and Dana been seeing each other?"

"About six months."

"Is she the reason you sold the farm?"

He sighed and sat. "She's not the reason, but Dana was my wake-up call. Life was passing me by while I chased your mother's dream."

"It was your dream, too. And mine."

"It was more your mother's than mine, but I loved her and wanted to support her in any way that made her happy. I lived out her vision long after she was gone, even though my heart wasn't in it. At first I carried on because I didn't know what else to do. I missed her and working with the horses kept her memories close. But it wasn't the same without her."

Her throat tightened. He had never let his grief show before now. "You never told me that."

He shrugged. "Hannah, I don't want you to make the same mistake of forgetting to live *your* life while you're living her dream."

"I'm not."

"You were always so enamored with her diaries, her charts and her books. I should have done something sooner." He cleared his throat and fidgeted for a moment. "The accident wasn't your fault, Hannah."

She'd needed to hear that from him for so long. "If I hadn't been so determined to make that jump—"

"You inherited that persistent streak from her. She was just as determined to see you succeed."

Her chest tightened. "Her death wasn't your fault, either, Dad. I never should have accused you of murdering her when you discontinued life support. I'm sorry."

"You weren't ready to give up hope. Neither was I. Signing that form was the hardest thing I've ever done. But it was the right thing to do."

Tears stung her eyes and burned her throat. "I know that now."

"It doesn't matter how many nags you rescue, Hannah, nothing is going to bring her back. We both have to move on. I don't want you to wake up in twenty years and realize there's a list of things you never got around to doing, like having a life and a family, because you were always nursing your nags."

"They're not nags," she defended automatically, then took a breath. "So you left me to sink or swim." She couldn't keep the hurt from her voice.

"I told you I won't be around to support you forever. You have to learn to stand on your own feet."

"Couldn't you have had your relationship at Sutherland Farm?"

"This is not about my relationship with Dana. It's the all-consuming Grand Prix lifestyle. I'm tired of eating, breathing and sleeping horses. I want more and so should you. Even if that weren't the case, that was your mother's house. She designed every inch of it. I would never dishonor her memory by taking another woman there." He set down his mug. "So what brings you here this morning, Hannah?"

She blinked as reality returned. She and her father had covered more ground this morning than they had in the past nineteen years. But in light of what he'd shared, her reason for coming might not matter to him. But she had to try.

"Wyatt bought the farm you and mom devoted your lives to as a temporary investment. That's why he guaranteed the jobs. Because he has no interest in running the business. He plans to dump the property as soon as it's served its purpose."

Leaning back in his chair, he folded his arms. "What do you want me to do?"

"Buy it back!"

The corners of his mouth dipped and he shook his head. "And then we'd be right back where we started. I'm through with horses. If staying in the business is truly *your* dream, then you'll find a way to make it work."

"But Dad—"

"Believe it or not, Hannah, I'm doing this for your own good." He rose. "I love you too much to help you."

If she couldn't sleep, she might as well work.

Hannah zipped her coat to her chin and stuffed her hands into her pockets to ward off the middle-of-the-night chill as she strode through to darkness toward the barn. The weight of her day weighed heavily on her shoulders.

The confrontation with Wyatt and the dissolution of their relationship had left her feeling empty, confirming she hadn't just been rescuing Wyatt for his own good. She'd been saving him for herself. Not a good thought.

After her visit to her father she'd decided that if Wyatt insisted on selling the farm, he might as well sell it to her, and she'd spent the afternoon on the phone fruitlessly searching for financial backers. But after calling several banks and everyone in her address book, she hadn't found anyone willing to back an inexperienced stable owner in the current financial climate. She couldn't call Rashed because with hindsight she realized Wyatt might be right. Rashed did seem interested in more than a business relationship. And she wasn't going to sell herself to anyone—not even to save Sutherland Farm.

A metallic screech caught her attention. She turned and spotted the gate to the small paddock swinging in the breeze. The *open* gate. Alarm shot through her. Phoenix!

Had the mare escaped? Hannah broke into a run, stopping when she realized the pen was empty. Heart racing, she scanned the shadows between the puddles of light cast by the lampposts, but she didn't see the horse.

Sam. Had he snuck down here even after this morning's fiasco? The sinking feeling in her stomach told her Sam and Phoenix were together. She dug her cell phone out of her pocket and dialed Wyatt.

"Jacobs." Sleep graveled his voice, sending a thrill through her—one she wished she could ignore.

"Is Sam there?"

"Hannah, it's one in the morning."

"Wyatt, the bay mare is missing. Please check to see if Sam is in the house."

He cursed. Then she heard the swish of sheets and pictured them sliding over his skin. "His bed and suite are empty. Damn it. This morning Sam told me he wanted to leave the farm. I didn't take him seriously."

A chill that had nothing to do with the cool night temperatures shuddered over her. "Check the rest of the house. If he's not there, call the sheriff and get him to issue a Silver Alert. I'll get Jeremiah to help me search the grounds."

Maybe Sam had taken Phoenix to the indoor arena to work her. Hannah slid open the heavy door and flipped on the lights, but the cavernous space was empty. No Sam. No Phoenix. No indications they'd been there recently. She sprinted through each building, ending up at FYC's barn, checking to see if Sam had visited the foals. He wasn't with them, either.

A sound made her turn. Her hopes fell when she spotted the security guard. "Jeremiah, have you seen Sam or the new bay rescue mare?"

"No, Miss Hannah. It's been real quiet tonight."

Her heart bumped its way up her throat. "Get into your truck and look for either of them, please. Let me know if you see anything—anything at all—out of the ordinary."

What felt like an aeon later, Hannah's fear turned into full-blown panic when she discovered an empty saddle rack in the tack room. She heard Jeremiah's truck in the driveway and ran outside. Wyatt's Mercedes skidded to a halt right behind him.

"Did you see anything?" she asked the security guard.

"Gate's open to the back pasture," Jeremiah said. "No sign of Sam or the mare as far as my spotlight could see."

The back pasture bordered the river. "There's a saddle missing. I think Sam has taken Phoenix and run away."

Wyatt's face looked pale and drawn in the murky moonlight.

His hair was a rumpled mess. “We’ll take a truck and go after him.”

“We can’t. The terrain is too rough in that pasture, and there’s no road.” There was only one option, and it terrified her. “I’ll saddle up a horse and see if I can find him.”

“You haven’t ridden since your mother died,” Wyatt pointed out. “You don’t have the experience. Let the sheriff’s team lead the search.”

“It’ll be hours before they can assemble a team of riders and truck the horses here. It’s too cold to wait.”

“I’ll call the chopper pilot.”

“A helicopter might spook the mare. Wyatt, I know this property better than anyone. My mother and I used to ride the trails, and I still hike them. If anyone can find Sam, it’ll be me.”

Wyatt’s expression turned even more determined. “I’ll go with you.”

“Two inexperienced horsemen won’t be better than one.”

“You’re a liability out there alone in the dark. If something happened, no one would know where to look for you and we’d have two casualties instead of one. I’m going.”

The stubborn set of his jaw warned her not to waste more time arguing. “Jeremiah, round up anyone who can help.”

She turned to Wyatt. “A couple of the rescue horses are docile and trail safe. We use them with the most inexperienced FYC students. We should be okay.”

Hannah hurriedly saddled the horses. Because of her experience with helping FYC’s students, preparations went too quickly and yet far too slowly when every minute counted. She handed Wyatt a headlamp. “Put the elasticized band around your helmet.”

Dread crawled across her skin like an army of ants as she released the crossties and handed one set of reins to Wyatt.

“Wyatt, you don’t have to go with me. You can stay here and talk to the sheriff. Fill them in on Sam’s condition and show them the topographical maps.”

"To paraphrase you, I can't do anything else. Let's go."

She stuck a foot in the stirrup and swung herself into the saddle. She'd forgotten how dizzyingly high being on horseback felt. Her legs trembled wildly as she placed her feet in the irons and tried to get her bearings. Fortunately the placid gelding didn't seem to mind her agitation. "Ready?"

Wyatt sat in the saddle, his carriage every bit as perfect as she'd once suspected it might be. "Let's go."

She urged her mount out of the brightly lit barn and down the dark driveway toward the open gate. Once they entered the fence and left the lampposts behind, they had only the moonlight and the thin beams from their helmet lights to guide them.

The urge to gallop after Sam thundered through her, but the darkness, the uneven ground and her rusty riding skills kept her at a safer, albeit slower, more frustrating pace. She tried to focus on the basics and could practically hear her mother's voice. *Heels down. Back straight. Hands steady. Eyes ahead. Trust your horse, Hannah.*

"If Sam gets hurt, I hold you responsible." Wyatt's voice low and scalpel-sharp, sliced through her. "If you hadn't encouraged him to work with the mare behind my back in a selfish attempt to weasel funding out of me for your damned nags, he never would have pulled this foolish stunt."

Hannah flinched. The truth of his words stung like the lash of a bullwhip. "I was trying to help him."

"You were trying to help yourself. If we find him—"

"When," she corrected and prayed they would find Sam before it was too late.

"*When* we find him you're fired. I want you and your horses off the premises immediately. Other than cleaning out your desk, I don't want you anywhere on my property."

Hannah gasped, then gulped. Wyatt's decision was nothing less than she deserved. She'd known the risk going in and acted anyway. Nellie had always accused her of having tunnel vision where her horses were concerned.

They rode in tense silence, the cold humid air penetrating Hannah's clothing and chilling her to the bone. She tried not to think of what she'd do, where she'd go or if she could find another job breeding horses in the current economy. She had to focus on finding Sam. She'd worry about her future later.

"Look," Wyatt's voice pulled her out of her misery. "There's a trail through the dew. That's how I tracked you to the boathouse."

The boathouse. That perfect moment seemed like a lifetime ago. With hindsight she acknowledged she'd probably fallen in love with him that morning when the *heartless bottom-line bastard* had helped with the foals, then followed her to make sure she was okay.

She aimed her beam, following the trail, worry taking over. "He's headed toward the river. There's a shallow, rocky crossing upstream from here."

"And then?"

"Highway. I wish I knew how much of a head start he had on us." The idea of Sam riding along the interstate on horseback in the dark— She urged her mount into a trot and clung for dear life until her body relaxed into the motion, finding the horse's rhythm and remembering how to post with it. "I'll call Jeremiah and get him to have the sheriff patrol the highway side."

She slowed long enough to make the call. Wyatt kept pace beside her, monitoring every word. Five minutes later, he pulled his mount to a halt. Hers stopped automatically. "Is that the river I hear?"

"Yes." And she didn't like the sounds of it. The recent rains had created small runoff streams on the steeper slopes, and from the dull roar ahead, Hannah suspected the river would be swollen and flowing faster. But she didn't want to burden Wyatt with that news.

Her mount sensed her tension and took it as a cue to go faster. She rounded a bend. A downed tree blocked the trail ahead. Hannah quickly scanned the area and spotted Phoenix, the saddle on her back empty. Fear closed her throat. She pulled her gelding to a stop. The leafy top of the tree divided a small channel of water flowing fast enough to carve a path on each side of the broad trunk. A water hazard. Like the jump that had killed her mother and her horse.

Nausea rolled through her. She swallowed it. Where was Sam?

Please, please don't let him be lying on the other side of the tree.

From the saddle, Hannah did a cursory check of the horse which looked unharmed, its legs shaped as they should be, as far as her narrow beam could make out. Then she surveyed the dense bamboo forest surrounding the blocked path. The only way Sam could have continued was to go over the obstacle. Had he tried to jump and the mare refused, tossing him over her head? Sam wasn't fit enough to crash-land without injuring himself.

The image of her mother, twisted and unconscious and her horse struggling to rise with a severely fractured leg, flooded Hannah's mind, making her heart pound and her muscles freeze in terror.

"Hannah." Wyatt's tone indicated he'd called her more than once. He rode up beside her, his calf bumping hers.

She blinked away the grisly mental picture, reined in her fear and dismounted. Her legs trembled like leaves in a gale-force wind as she tried to find the courage to approach the tree.

Wyatt joined her. He scanned the scene, his light landing on the mare, and his face paled. "Sam!"

He lunged forward, but Hannah stepped into his path, planting a hand on his chest. "Stay with the horses. I'll let you know if he's there."

"Get out of my way."

"Wyatt, you don't need to see—"

Comprehension dawned on his face. "You stay here. Sam might need my help."

What if Sam was beyond help—as her mother had been? She bit her lip and tasted blood. "You're not going without me."

She jogged through the water beside him. Each step felt like a mile through mud. They leaned across the trunk simultaneously. No Sam. Air rushed from her lungs, making her dizzy with relief. She sagged against the downed trunk. "He's not here. That means he's able to walk."

"Sam," Wyatt shouted again.

Only the gurgle of water answered, then a twig snapped in the distance. Pulse-pounding seconds later, Sam entered their narrow spotlights—walking normally. "You found me. Too bad. I was hoping for a little more adventure."

Hysterical laughter bubbled up Hannah's throat, cut short by Wyatt vaulting the trunk and sprinting toward Sam. He stopped a yard short, clenching and unclenching his hands. Then he grabbed his stepfather in a bear hug. Sam patted Wyatt's back. She could see his lips moving, but couldn't hear his words. Only then did she notice Wyatt's shaking shoulders.

Everything inside Hannah turned to mush, and tears stung her eyes. She'd been right about Wyatt. He wasn't a coldhearted bastard, though he pretended to be one. And he might deny it, but he did love Sam. He just didn't, or couldn't, love her.

And who could blame him after this? She'd inadvertently put Sam's life in danger with her self-absorbed tunnel vision.

Her throat clogged. She had to stop trying to rescue people and horses, because her father was right. No matter how many she saved, she couldn't bring her mother back. And she might get someone else hurt. Or worse.

That left her with only one option. She'd have to sell her cottage to Wyatt and walk away from everyone and everything that mattered to her. Her home. Her history. Her mother's legacy.

Twelve

Too overwrought to sleep, Wyatt sat in his dark office and fought off the lingering remnants of panic.

He'd almost lost Sam. And it would have been his fault. Not Hannah's. *His.* Because he'd pushed his stepfather away when Sam had needed him most.

While listening to Sam reminisce during the horseback ride home an hour ago, Wyatt had been ambushed by memories of the good times they'd shared, and he'd realized he wasn't ready for the past to be the sum total of their relationship. He wanted to bank more memories, and the only thing preventing him from doing so was his misconceived attempt at protecting himself from the pain of eventually losing Sam. He had Hannah to thank for that uncomfortable insight.

Hannah. He'd completely misjudged her. And he owed her an apology.

A hint of pink on the horizon lured him to the French doors. He stepped onto the patio outside his office. The beginning of a new day hovered beyond the distant treetops.

The landscape looked the same and yet totally different because today he saw Sutherland Farm for the first time not as a multimillion-dollar investment he couldn't wait to unload, but through Hannah's eyes.

The rolling green pastures and stone buildings held the history of her family, a tradition of breeding champions, and imbued a sense of belonging and renewal. When he'd purchased the property, he'd robbed Hannah of all that. Despite that, she'd made room for him and Sam in her life, and last night she'd faced her fears for them.

First by climbing on a horse for the first time since her mother's death, and then, even after he'd fired her, she'd tried to save him from the pain of finding Sam's body on the other side of the tree. From her deathly pallor when she'd planted herself in front of him, he guessed she had been remembering and reliving the day she'd lost her mother and horse. But she'd wanted to spare him.

Such generosity confounded him. He always looked out for number one, whereas Hannah tried to save and protect everyone but herself. He'd encountered many women willing to hurt him. But hurt *for* him? None. Until Hannah.

Her actions last night had revealed the depth of her character in ways nothing else could. The woman he'd deemed too good to be true was the real deal, and it shamed him that he'd been so blinded by his prejudices and the superficial glitz that he'd missed the truth even though it had been right in front of his eyes all along.

Hannah's father had showered her with material possessions, but she hadn't become the spoiled, pampered princess Wyatt had assumed her to be because she dealt in a different currency—a more personal, more valuable one. She doled out chunks of her heart like coins to anyone or anything in need despite the emotional cost that inevitably followed.

Her courage humbled him. She invested herself in her

causes while he took the easy way out by paying other people to handle the messy, emotional details of life.

He'd been convinced that having Sam out of sight would equate to having him out of mind. He'd been wrong, and his emotional cowardice had not only robbed Sam of his dignity, it could cost Wyatt his relationship with the man who'd been more of a father to him than his own flesh and blood.

And it could cost him Hannah. It surprised him to discover how much that bothered him. He'd completely blown it with her. He didn't want to let her go. But he didn't deserve her. Or to put it correctly, she deserved better than a man who'd treated her badly and tried to run her off. His only excuse was that the feelings she stirred in him scared the hell out of him.

Life had taught him that emotionally investing in someone led to pain and disappointment. But when things got messy, Hannah rolled up her sleeves and waded in with her heart wide open. She took on cases that others had written off as lost causes even though she knew she could fail.

The least he could do was try to match her courage.

A flash of movement caught his attention. Hannah emerged from the crop of trees surrounding her cottage and leaned against the stone wall facing the barns a quarter mile away.

Firing her had been a mistake. She belonged here far more than he did.

She turned in the opposite direction. He considered calling her back, but with the wind rustling the leaves she might not hear him. Besides, this was a conversation best had somewhere besides the driveway. With the staff due to roll in, there would be too many interruptions.

He descended the steps and followed her. His feet sank deep into the thick emerald lawn and it brought back memories of running barefoot on Sam's farm, of lazy days fishing beside his stepfather. Even though Sam had had a stable and a distillery to run, he'd always made time for Wyatt. It was time for Wyatt to return that favor.

Hannah ducked through the fence and headed down the path to the boathouse. The secluded spot was as good a place as any for his apology. He had to slow his steps when he entered the still shadowy woods and by the time he reached the clearing, Hannah was already on the dock. But this morning she hadn't removed her shoes and she wasn't paddling her feet in the water. She stood staring at the horizon with her shoulders slumped and arms wrapped around her middle.

He knew the exact second she became aware of his approach by the tension invading her body. The platform rocked beneath his feet and the wooden boards creaked as he joined her. "Good morning, Hannah."

"Are you going to have me arrested for trespassing?" Her pallor accentuated the shadows beneath her eyes and the urge to brush the purple smudges with his thumbs almost overwhelmed him.

"No. I'm sorry I lost my temper last night. You're not fired. You're an asset to Sutherland Farm. I don't want you to go."

Her lips parted as if she were going to speak, then she turned back to the water. "How's Sam?"

Typical of the woman he'd discovered her to be, she showed concern for someone else rather than herself. "Sleeping off his exciting night. Why aren't you doing the same?"

"I couldn't sleep." She wrapped her arms tighter around her middle and stared across the water.

"Same here. I hate to think what would have happened if you hadn't helped me find Sam last night. I know it was hard for you. Thank you."

"You're welcome." She still didn't look at him.

He swallowed. Opening up wasn't easy, but if he wanted to convince Hannah to give him a second chance he had to make her understand why he'd made bad decisions. "You accused me of being a bottom-line bastard. And you were right. I was pushing Sam away because I was afraid of losing him…like I did my father."

Her head whipped in his direction. "Your father's dead?"

"No. He had an affair. When his lover became pregnant, he discarded Mom and me without a backward glance and started a new family. It was as if Mom and I had never existed."

Sympathy darkened her eyes. "How old were you?"

"Almost fourteen."

"That must have been hard. You don't keep in touch?"

"I haven't seen him since the day he walked out. I didn't mind for me, but for my mother… She became cold and distant, someone I didn't know."

"You lost both parents at the same time."

"It felt that way. And then she met Sam, and for a while she became the mom I remembered. Then Sam was diagnosed and she turned her back on him the way Dad had us."

"I'm sorry."

"I'm not asking for pity. I'm trying and not doing a good job of explaining why I fought so hard not to let myself care too much. After my father left, I promised myself I wouldn't love anyone else ever again. It wasn't worth the pain. But Sam got past my defenses. Then I started losing him one memory at a time. I bought Sutherland Farm as a place to dump him so I wouldn't have to watch his decline. I was leaving him before he left me." A lump swelled in his throat. He swallowed.

Hannah squeezed his arm. "I know how difficult it is to watch someone you love fade away. That's what happened with my mom. She held on for a week before Dad took the doctors' advice and discontinued life support."

He swore. "Hannah—"

"It's okay. In the end, her organs allowed four people to have extra time with their families. She would have wanted it that way."

"Your ability to always see the positives is mind-boggling. I envy that."

"Yeah, well, sometimes that's harder than others." She ducked her head and stubbed the toe of her sneaker on the dock. "My father is right. I have no head for business. I've never tried to learn the financial side of the operation because sticking to a budget meant cutting expenses, and cutting expenses meant making difficult decisions about which students and animals I could help and which ones I had to turn away."

She fisted her hands until her knuckles turned white. "My inability to say no put Sam in jeopardy. I'm going to dissolve the school and rescue operation and ship all my horses to Rashed for his program."

The defeat in her voice twisted something inside him. He'd done that to her—crushed her spirit and taken everything she loved away. "What about the people and horses you help here?"

"And as you've pointed out more than once, FYC is a high-risk, low-return venture and, regardless of the precautions we take, if I operate it long enough someone is going to get hurt. Last night—"

"Hannah, last night was not your fault. It was mine. Sam acted out because in my fear of him getting hurt I'd caged him like an animal. Don't let my mistakes shake your confidence and kill your dream. You do good work here."

She shook her head. "I've decided to accept your offer to buy my cottage."

Her voice broke on the last word. Desperation rose inside him. He wanted—no, needed—to find a way to make her stay. He needed Hannah in his life to show him that some battles were worth fighting.

"My purchase offer's no longer on the table."

Eyes wide, she swung toward him. "B-but this is what you wanted. You've been trying to get rid of me ever since you bought the place."

"And now I want you to stay. What would Sutherland Farm be without a Sutherland?"

"It'll be whatever the next owner calls it."

The idea of Sutherland Farm without Hannah's presence repelled him. His life without her in it appealed even less. Her damned Pollyanna attitude had gotten to him and he was addicted. "I'm not selling the farm, Hannah."

"But—"

"I have a different proposition for you."

Suspicion pleated her brow. "What is it this time?"

"I'll deed the entire property over to you if you'll allow Sam to live in your cottage and work with the horses as long as he's able. Afterward all of the property—all two thousand two acres, including the main house—will be yours."

"What's the catch?"

He took a deep breath. It was time to lay his cards on the table and risk rejection. "You've shown me that success isn't limited to numbers on a balance sheet, and the time I have left with Sam is worth far more than dollars and cents. I want to be a part of his life. And yours, Hannah.

"You've proven denying my emotions doesn't eradicate them, and you've taught me what true selflessness is and what it means to open myself up—no matter the personal costs. You dream big, Hannah, with the vault to your soul wide open. You're not afraid of hurt or disappointment and I envy that."

"Of course I'm afraid, Wyatt. I get hurt like everyone else and I fail sometimes, too. But I don't choose to let the negatives keep me from searching for the positives."

"It's that ability to see the potential in every man or beast you encounter that makes you unique and special. I like the me you see, and I want an opportunity to become that man—the one who is not afraid to admit that—" The words jammed in his chest. He cleared his throat. "I love Sam."

Her tender smile twisted something inside him. "That wasn't so hard, was it?"

"No, I'm getting to the hard part." His heart hammered like a knocking piston against his chest. He experienced the same dizzying sensation he'd felt when he'd looked over the forty-story apartment balcony and realized how close he'd come to losing Sam. But to be worthy of Hannah, he had to take the risk.

"I've fallen in love with you, Hannah. You're a woman who can't say no to lost causes. And I'm hoping you won't say no to the biggest one of all—me."

Her mouth parted in a gasp, and for several seconds she gaped at him, searching his face as if doubting his words. Tears filled her eyes, and his gut burned like hot metal. Then a weak smile twitched her lips. "I never called you a lost cause. I may have thought it, but I never said it."

"It doesn't change the fact that I was one. But I can change." He captured her cold hands in his. "Rescue me, Hannah. Help me become the man that you see—the one who has the capacity to open his heart and not just his wallet. The one who's not afraid to feel."

"You're not nearly as hard as you think you are, Wyatt. Your love for Sam proves that."

Her words filled him with hope. He moved closer and cupped her soft cheeks. "Let me love you. And learn with you. Let me hold you in my arms every night, not as my mistress, but as my wife, as the woman who keeps me grounded in what really matters."

A lone tear trailed down her cheek, spilling over his thumb. "That's a pretty tall order. But I can't think of a better place to be. You are lovable, Wyatt. Sam loves you." She rose on tiptoe and briefly pressed her lips to his. "And I love you."

He banded his arms around her, hugging her close and covering her mouth. He couldn't get enough of her taste, her scent, her warmth. When he finally lifted his head, their panting breaths mingled. "You won't regret giving me a chance."

Her swollen lips curved upward. "I know I won't."

He laced his fingers through hers and led her into the boathouse. "I'll make you a deal. I'll teach you how to run

FYC as a business and help set it up as a charitable operation. That will enable you to help more people and more horses. In exchange, you keep reminding me that life's about more than a balance sheet. But later. Much later. Right now I need your skin against mine."

Her cheeks flushed and the corners of her eyes crinkled. She held out her arm, revealing goose bumps. "I only get those when I've come across a champion combination."

* * * * *